THE IMPERISHED KINGDOM

THE IMPERISHED KINGDOM

Albert O'Hayon

To order additional copies of this book, contact:
Xlibris Corporation
1-888-795-4274
www.Xlibris.com
Orders@Xlibris.com
33501

CONTENTS

BOOK ONE: PATHS

FLIGHT 11

ONE: VALLEY 17

TWO: MARRAKECH 25

THREE: ATLAS 35

FOUR: AKKA 53

FIVE: TRAP 70

SIX: CLASH 83

SEVEN: AFFLICTION 93

EIGHT: SAVIOR 108

NINE: AIR 123

BOOK TWO: HERALD

DECISION 136

TEN: RIDDLE 138

ELEVEN: KENZA 156

TWELVE: REVELATION 167

THIRTEEN: MIRVAIS 180

FOURTEEN: AUMONT 186

FIFTEEN: CRISIS 192

BOOK THREE: BATTLE

FAITH.. 200

SIXTEEN: CITADEL... 201

SEVENTEEN: HORIZON...................................... 224

EIGHTEEN: BATTLE.. 231

NINETEEN: UNVEILED 274

TWENTY: COUNSEL 291

TWENTY-ONE: HOME... 299

RETOUR 327

GLOSSARY 339

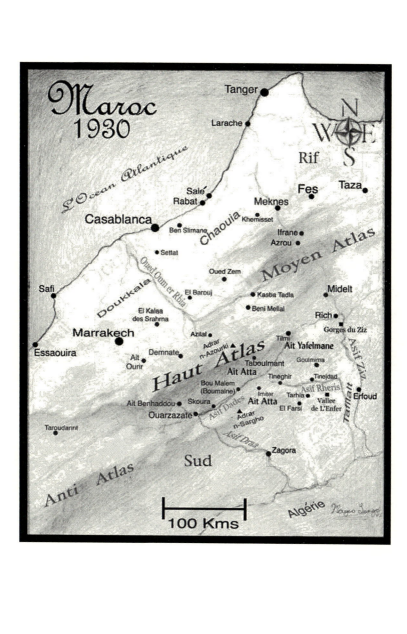

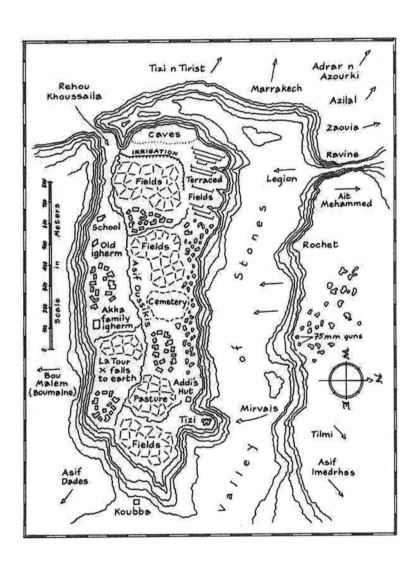

Tizi n Tirist

Rehou
Khoussaila

Marrakech

Adrar n
Azourki

Azilal

Zaouia

Ravine

Caves

IRRIGATION

Fields

Terraced
Fields

Legion

Aït
Mehammed

School

Old
igherm

Fields

Asif Oussiks

Rochet

Cemetery

Akka
family
igherm

75mm guns

La Tour
× falls
to earth

Addi's
Hut

Bou
Maïem
(Boumalne)

Pasture

Tizi

Mirvais

Tilmi

Fields

Asif
Dades

Asif
Imedrhas

Koubba

Scale in Meters

Valley of Stones

BOOK ONE: PATHS

FLIGHT

*T*he copper-hued mountains glowered beneath the high sun. His predicament, and maybe those to come, seemed aptly symbolized by their desolate beauty. Since January-just three months ago-Sergeant Jean-Michel La Tour had caromed from an ill-starred detour to Marrakech, to this forlorn Légion étrangère garrison at the enemy frontier, through minutes of battle and days of captivity, to the eruption of an ancient, horrid disease, and now to a timeworn airplane. Now he was bound for the cold calamity of exclusion. Of Exile.

Lieutenant Saint-Avold and Sergeant Dutroix led La Tour from the infirmary to the courtyard, runing a perverse spectacle before several hundred witnesses. His sullen gaze fixed on the swarthy pilot in frayed black coveralls, a scruffy leather jacket and dirty red beret, just as he concluded his chat with the Major. The peculiar fellow plodded ahead of him through the wide gate toward a dull yellow airplane on the field beyond the chevaux-de-frise.

The two escorts and their charges slouched through the gate after him. They crossed the perimeter to within speaking distance of an unshaven and scarred man, perhaps an Escadrille veteran of the Great War.

"Bags go in rear pit with you," he said gruffly in Corsican French. The airman did not want to touch them. Introductions would not be necessary. The flight was nothing but a cargo delivery, and the fellow was clearly impatient to get aloft and complete the task.

"Where am I going?" La Tour asked, with all due courtesy. The pilot let elapse several seconds of silent disregard. He somewhat resembled a beggar so coldly indignant in his submission to divine will, or skeptical that God should care.

"Take your seat. Enjoy the scenery. Flight time is about one hour." The pilot clambered into the front cockpit, primed the fitful engine to start and glared down at his wretched passenger. La Tour stilled weighed whether to run away, fight, shoot the pilot or beg for mercy. He turned to Saint-Avold, his last reliable link to home.

"Danton, please have my possessions, journals and souvenirs shipped to Grenoble. I would like for them to arrive before I do." La Tour emphasized these words wanting the day of his triumph to sound inevitable, even eminent. The plane's balky engine throbbed to potent life behind him.

"This is not over!" La Tour raged above the rising din. Anger surged through him with the heat that makes retribution certain. "Not by a long way!" I will ruin that son of a bitch! I pray that no one does it before me!"

La Tour would eagerly write any law making so in his own blood. Dutroix seemed startled by this vehemence. He turned away, neither bidding goodbye nor waiting for La Tour to take to the plane. But Saint-Avold remained. La Tour furtively slipped into his hand an envelope with the letter he had written to his brother, François, then saluted his comrade and smiled in farewell.

"Do it for me, too, Jean-Michel!" Saint-Avold replied. "And before he is reassigned from here, or out of Maroc altogether, where we can hide in plain sight!"

La Tour took heart in these wry comments, made under the gaze of the garrison and no doubt Major Mirvais. Smoke belched from the exhaust ports of a throttled-up engine. He lifted his valise and sack onto the wing, stepped up beside them, crammed the luggage on to the floor, and slid heavily into the battered alien roost.

The De Havilland jounced up the hard-packed runway La Tour had helped to construct, then departed the earth. It lofted rapidly over the rust-red hilltop garrison nestled within walls nearly two hundred meters on a side, abutted by animal corrals on two of them, all enclosed by barbed wire and obstacles at the two entry gates that formed a simple maze intended as much to trap any attackers in that field of fire as to hold them out. Nearly a kilometer forward of this outpost near the junction of desert and mountain was a short necklace of oasis and palmeries from which the fort drew its daily water; directly beyond it, Berber tribesmen who might well be lurking in the furrows of the primordial terrain.

The biplane banked northeast and at once presented an imperial panorama of the High Atlas spine. So great was their mystique and majesty, that olden cartographers had named them for the Titan mythical god Atlas, who held up the heavens with a huge stone. Only a stoic beast of infinite strength could endure such a task.

The plane cut across the Asif Dades, still enlarged from highland snowmelt and nurturing wide margins of greenery along its low rocky banks. To his right, downstream and southwest, was El Kelaa des M'Gouna, the lush valley of Persian roses. Beyond it was Skoura, a grand palm grove girdled with villages and fabled kasbahs fed by water from the Dades and Irhil M'Goun. Upstream the Gorges du Dades sliced into the Atlas flank, and in the violently carved country beside it, lay the remote villages of the fierce brethren tribes of the Ait Attta.

La Tour opened the neatly composed map he was constructing to track the route past the barren deformities of Adrar n-Sargho. The many wonders of Maroc below and behind him would take a long, peaceful lifetime to explore. Instead, he was being shuttled like rancid freight to his captivity.

Sixty kilometers to the left and northeast through Tineghir, ran the Asif Todgha, flanked by bands of palms on its cleft course out of the Atlas onto stark terrain and confluence with the Asif Rheris beyond Tinejdad. Passing Imiter, following a continuum of formidable cliffs and plateaus, the plane held course toward that meeting of the rivers to draw within sight of the palmeries.

This was La Tour's first air flight-so he briefly enjoyed a tonic of freedom from the bonds of earth, revealing an eagle-eye view that lessened his dread of the unknown destination. A sharp breeze lashed his face, raising protective tears, and then a cascade of memories of similar sensations on brisk autumn days in the hills above his home in Isére.

La Tour peered at the grand Atlas peaks. He turned away to face his fate. Lingering on where he had lived so intensely evoked a sickening fear that he may never go home again. The plane droned on, across the Todgha and nestled tracts of green, leaving them aft, into a stony red-land wastes toward Tinejdad and another cluster of loosely strewn palmeries. The earth wore like jewels on its thin necklace of water.

Minutes beyond the union of the Todgha and Rheris, the plane arced right and southeast. It glided lower over naked tabletop earth riven by huge scars. The dark-cross shadow of the plane glided lower over umber terrain, then dissipated in the buckled contours of a chasm. La Tour glimpsed sudden movement there, of animals or people, as the plane passed to set down on a broad plateau beyond. The wheels fit the grooves made by many previous arrivals and departures. This was an airport, of sorts, in the middle of nowhere.

The plane taxied about, toward the edge of the chasm and lumbered to a halt. The ornery flyer cut the engine. As if it was an irksome routine, he tossed out a stout rope ladder, rolled around a fat dowel, and hastily deplaned. The pilot shuffled to the lip of the plateau and gazed downward. La Tour was leery of this bizarre ritual and reluctant o follow.

His mind was awash in images and emotions; foremost, a panic that he was to be marooned in Bedlam. He set down his bags near the rim. With a swagger almost vile, Mr. Pilot kicked the items over the edge with his boot. He then released a ladder from two iron stakes embedded in the cliffs. The fat rod spun in his course palms as twenty or so meters of the weighted ladder plunged, then snapped taut. With a vulgar laugh, the pilot signaled La Tour's irrevocable entry.

La Tour knew, in a painful instant, what place this was. Lord have mercy, for his own people certainly had none.

"Climb down," said the pilot.

"Go to hell," La Tour replied. "You're throwing me away."

"This is hell right here, or just outside," he chafed. "I understand why you don't want to visit. But I tell you this place is not so bad, as such places are. Climb down."

The pilot waited. La Tour pondered his options. He had none but the gun in the holster beneath his djellabah.

The pilot seemed to read his thoughts; he pulled aside the left panel of his leather jacket to reveal a pistol of his own.

La Tour peered westward, to the far horizon. Contemptuous of much tradition that he had so recently respected, and of humankind in general, he kneeled on the edge, clutched the ropes, warily placed his boots on the second rung and began to descend.

"Is called Le Vallée de l'Enfer!" the brute announced with unnatural mirth. "Valley of Hell. The Valley of the Lepers!"

ONE:

VALLEY

La Tour scaled down the cliff face and reached a brow-like bulge. He eased gingerly around an outward tilt that dangled him away from the wall over the rock-strewn base. He glanced below, then with an iron grip, clung to the precarious perch as vertigo surged through him, a sensation never induced by his more dangerous climbs in Vercors. It would be nearly impossible for anyone to ascend from the floor without fixed ropes or a ladder—and this could well be the least rugged of the cliff boundaries. Had anyone tried to climb up—and lived? For that matter, had any arrival ever fallen on the way down? He was queasy at the danger and disgrace of this entry. Slothfully, he reached the next to last rung and stepped over his belongings. At once the impatient pilot shouted down to him.

"Untie your bags!"

La Tour complied at once, though it was improbable that the fool up there would want to pull out of reach and abscond with a leper's presumably infected goods. The ladder abruptly retracted. Moments later a burlap mail sack obscenely plunged to earth.

Everyone keenly eyed the arrival. And he them. Shortly, La Tour heard the plane engine sputter and growl, then recede to the take-off point. Moments later, he watched the beast climb into the gray-brown mid-afternoon sky, returning whence it came like a lone fat straggling locust chasing its vanished swarm.

La Tour felt like an exhibit in a freak show, the new sane inmate of an asylum. He grappled and trembled with fear but wiped it from his face, taking reassurance from the pistol beneath his white djellabah. *Like a lost tourist he aimlessly toted his bags to the stream. The silence howled. The peering natives gave way, perhaps in respectful welcome. La Tour studied them too; he saw apprehension in their eyes, and pity, but also enough curiosity and solace to subdue him. A man, smiling wanly, waved the stump of an arm.* This may not be hell, but it's grotesque all the same. *A shriveled old man under a filthy* kepi *sucked air into his hideous, toothless mouth. Still, silence; no one spoke. Was he among mutes? But what was there to say? What difference would small talk make except to reinforce the absurdity and cruelty of this life?*

Finally a man in Army pants, a battered and patched bush hat and a brown *djellabah* stepped forth from the flock. He pointed to a sequence of caves along the base of a broad cliff across the narrow part of the valley, more than a hundred meters off.

"Welcome to La Vallée de l'Enfer!" he said, like a circus barker at a seedy casino. Spacious single rooms, or not, if you want company. No running water, except at this convenient stream, and no room service, but our friendly staff speaks six languages among them!"

La Tour eyed the shallow, irregular cavities gouged in the foot of the limestone cliff. He scanned the valley for better quarters. In the other direction was a large cluster of makeshift huts. Latrines and blighted outhouses stood beyond them. He preferred a cave.

Vallée de l'Enfer was a somber and exhausted place, not fit to be called a hospital. La Tour detested Mirvais for describing this as a "special facility." This was nothing but a dumping ground for poor, powerless humans with little to lose and no way to gain: the wreckage of the world.

The valley cleft, more than two hundred meters across at its widest point, was enclosed west and east by the cliffs, but so long north to south that he could not see either end. The leper enclave occupied but a fraction of the valley floor, and was surrounded by dusty, rock-strewn earth for farther than La Tour would care to walk. Greenery grew only in those areas where shadows and water collected. He dully studied the cliff down which he had descended. The inward-tilted precipice rose to a rugged lip over which the terrain beyond could not be seen. This forbidding place would even make a mockery of suicide.

Perhaps the valley had an outlet. More likely, he lamented, these creatures were confined in a natural pen. And it was perhaps fifty kilometers to a village. Without enough water or food it might as well be five hundred. Escape might be a worse fate than remaining. And even after a break-out, all of them would remain trapped and condemned by their skin as surely as this *cul de sac* was their quarantine. Still, La Tour vowed to explore when his body and spirit renewed. For now, he simply walked, alone, toward the caves.

"Watch out for scorpions!" the man admonished, before moving away.

This stirred La Tour, bone-weary and in dire need of sleep. He rummaged in his sack for matches, lit an oil lamp on a hook and inspected the crude, dry hovel. He sat to ponder his lot. He was briefly addled; in the swirl of events he could not recall his whereabouts just yesterday. *Oh, yes. With Saint-Avold. Back near those goddamned palm trees. Hopeful. Hungry. Anxious to wash.*

He withdrew from sight and discreetly gnawed on figs, a strip of dried beef, and a baguette baked in the garrison that morning. The slight fare eased his pangs. Dabbing a stubby brush with dentifrice, he rubbed his teeth.

He stowed his possessions, lest someone be tempted to thievery in the night. He made a crude bed, lied upon it and quickly felt his last energy drain away. In moments, he was in a void of consciousness. Hours later, La Tour dimly awakened and, for a gladsome moment, believed he was back camping in Vercors. Light from a gibbous moon pooled in the caves, casting he and his comrades in an eerie pale lavender glow. From afar, it would look like an elaborate, ghostly theatre, a catacomb prison. He drifted back to sleep on a river of dreams.

Dawn. La Tour opened his eyes and drank in the view. The eastward cliff across the valley caught the first amber-gray wash of light, a hint of the sharp sun to follow. Its scowling facade was a remnant of a world that predated human beasts. The tilted wall seemed to bristle.

His dry throat was raw and raspy. His bladder, too, needed relief. A passersby glimpsed in at him. Most of the men—perhaps women, were in the valley, but apparently not nearby—were clad in a light *djellabah* over shirt and trousers. No one was threadbare, but most *habillement* was makeshift and cast-off. Some wore items like a leather jacket or trail-worn boots as if they felt incomplete without them. French *brodekins* were most common, but their collective condition—decrepit leather, broken laces, canvas-thin soles-forgotten, abandoned. La Tour could see such thoughts etched on their faces.

Some were washing at the stream. This was the main water supply. He hoped to discover both its source and its destination when he began a survey of Vallée de l'Enfer.

"Good morning, dear sir," the man in the bush hat offered. "We hope you slept well. Step up to the Euphrates, the Ganges, and the Dades to make yourself presentable!"

"If such a thing is truly possible for anyone here, you scabrous bastard!" a one-eyed man retorted.

Laughter followed. Wry, even ruthless in its fashion, but laughter all the same.

La Tour thought, with small satisfaction, that his human enemies were far away. The deadliest foe of all, however, was right here. Time. Escape would offer the best, or only, chance to obtain proper medical attention. If the disease progressed—he did not know the rate. It might be best to put a bullet in his head to save another the trouble. He would fate's favor no less than a good plan to get free. And so today, and maybe tomorrow, he would do little else but accommodate his new place in life with his new life in such a place.

La Tour spotted a row of flimsy canopies over tables and stools near fires and cooking pots. This was the mess hall. A breakfast line was forming. There was order in the queue, though none of the military sort. Casual rivalry, he thought. The men were restless for repast, not a flock of vultures. What would be the point of such distress? Had not leprosy and isolation inflicted enough? Fighting was for those with something to gain.

La Tour walked toward them. Fellows nodded greetings, and curiously eyed his boots and uniform pants and image of one who had been whisked to an asylum. He could read some thoughts: here is an odd one, a leper and an officer from the army of occupiers. *But he saw himself as just one more among many tribal rejects, ex-city dwellers, Europeans, world travelers, regional vagabonds and local nomads. Like himself, all had contracted this wretched infection by ugly lot or bad choice. He fell in at the end of the line.*

"How do you like your new home?" a voice said from behind. La Tour turned to the bush hat man. "Vallée de l'Enfer. A practical name, no? And biblical." He spoke from within the dim recess of the *burnoos* hood drawn over his head.

"Except no one comes to heal us with so-called Christian love and prayer," he scoffed. "Here we are, the perfect test for their theories of perfect faith. Please renew us in the light of Jesus! Alas, we are all trapped here, heathen cretins, one big family. Happy, no, but a family the same. And everyone knows you cannot pick your family."

La Tour was not in a chatting mood, but to remain silent would be rude and impolitic. He could not afford to alienate anyone. Besides, the fellow's wry philosophy made simple sense.

"And sometimes you cannot pick where you and the family will live," La Tour replied. "I thought the Légion was a second home, that good quarters, a smart order and a better officer was all I needed." His good-cheer snicker only enhanced the dull ache. "Look at the reward of my duty."

"At least you got your order, yes?" the man inquired in a sly tone.

"Yes," La Tour bridled. "Get the hell out!" He chuckled sardonically.

The man laughed, then guffawed. They attracted a variety of gazes; perhaps this valley's misery was not a good subject for humor. One fellow, pulling back his hood for a clear view of the jesters, revealed a disfigured face. His blue eyes, though, blazed with emotion, storing tears from a river of lament, anger from a desert of demons. La Tour looked away to hide his distress, sure he had nonetheless signaled horror and grief. He thought those symptoms could be a mirror image of himself in one year or three; his own future foreshadowed.

The food line drew closer to the serving tables, which were manned by three men mechanically doling out the fare. One spoke Arabic, another Spanish, and the last French.

"I am Sergeant Hector Muñoz Desaix," his new crony continued. "1ᵉʳ *etranger,* 2ⁿᵈ Battalion."

"Sergeant Jean-Michel La Tour, 2ᵉ REC."

They loosely saluted each other, comrade to comrade, sharing what they knew without uttering a word of it.

"I was near Mediouna in '25." Desaix said. "At the Battle of the Oranges. The savage bastards under Abdel Krim were virtually unbeatable. Killed half of us. Praise God that my service ended two months later, none too quickly. From Barcelona, I sailed for Cadiz. I sunk all my money into two Andalusian fish trawlers. I found Anjelena there. My sweet wife. But in September of '28, I found this, too." He pointed to his shabby boots and the feet in them. "Although at first I did not know what this shit was. It was only a tropical disease, yes? I was practically abducted here. Anjelena thought I had run off. But she learned the truth. We are divorced. And here I am, 269 days later."

"You have been here nine months?" La Tour asked, incredulous, for the moment forgetting his own plight.

"Yes. I would rather carry a camel's burden for ten years, than live with this curse one more day."

"Have you never tried to escape?"

"I cannot walk well. And there is no way out, my friend. Except the way you came in. Or . . ." He jerked his head toward a cluster of tents across the expanse. Several rudimentary coffins awaiting new occupants were piled there, next to a simple carpentry shop.

"Have you looked carefully?" La Tour replied. "I plan to go wh . . ."

"Listen, friend," Desaix said testily. "I worked reconnaissance on the rail line between Taza and Guercif. I can find a way over terrain in this country or any other. And I have poked about here, friend, when I could, since few others were willing to explore it. I saw no break in the cliffs around this hole. That is why it was chosen. To keep others out, and us in."

La Tour at once lost all desire to converse. His spirit turned to stone, with no sensation but melancholy. Almost nauseated, he was certain this dreadful feeling of helplessness would last as long as the disease.

"We are fed," Desaix continued at this reaction. "We are clothed. They bring mail from home. We are promised medical attention, which comes too seldom. We have star-lit skies, desert breezes, no one shooting at us, and plenty of time to write our memoirs. Now we eat breakfast. It has the great medicinal value of temporarily warding off boredom."

Desaix piled on to La Tour's tin plate several figs, a chunk of bread and a grain concoction. Likewise he served himself. Taking a mug of coffee, he eyed La Tour.

"Come, we have much to talk about," Desaix invited in word and gesture. "Tonight I will dream about all the money I made in Cap Tiburon, and the lovely breasts of my former wife. Now please tell me how a fine fellow like you came to be in this pit of sorrow."

La Tour trailed the affable life force of Hector Desaix to a slice of the south-facing cliff that would be in shadow for hours of daylight. They dined, such as it was, alone and mostly without conversation, taking some comfort in the other's presence, but the silence more. La Tour loathed the food but wolfed it just the same.

"Do we have any obligations here?" he asked anxiously. "To work? Should I worry about anything?"

"You will not work today," Desaix replied. "The official captain is Miege. He is the one-eyed man. With the patch. A strange man, but fair. We are soldiers. He is not. For now you have my attention and he will not bother us. Where are you from, La Tour?"

"Jean-Michel La Tour. I am from Fontaine, near Grenoble. My family once owned a small bank in Lyon. I . . ."

"How bourgeois. Were you or are you a spoiled brat? Are you proving your manliness to someone? Father, perhaps?"

"My father died in 1922. From pneumonia. He was gassed, you see, at . . ."

"How sad. So it is not father?"

"Are you a psychiatrist?" La Tour asked curtly, already tired of the interruptions.

"Of sorts. An aspiring playwright beguiled by the psyche," Desaix said mordantly. "After all, I am retired from armed service and from fishing. I must live for something."

"I will begin in Marrakech. Have you ever been there?"

"No, my friend. Of the big towns, Tanger and Taza only."

"My disease began in Marrakech, I think. Just like you, I knew nothing of it to the moment it was discovered. But the official beginning of my troubles was last year after ten months serving in the red city, the Seven Men, the Berber capital of Maroc. From a boy I remember Grandfather's description . . ."

"Ah, so it is Grandfather then. Your father's father, I will venture to guess."

" . . . and I joined the Légion. Out of desire to follow in his footsteps."

"I hope Grandfather was not a leper."

"Alive and well in an old home in Fontaine with my mother and sometimes with my brother." "How quaint . . . Please tell me about Marrakech. There are not many *maison de campagne* there. Not yet."

"I will, if you allow me to proceed."

"Oh, please do."

TWO

MARRAKECH

W e French-the Berbers call us *Iroumin*-have divided Maroc into regions like a glutton does a banquet roast. The region of Marrakech-one of seven others-is sliced into provinces-Marrakech, Ouarzazate, and Safi-that are further parceled into bureau districts. These cities and a dozen other outposts have military, Affairs Indigène, and sometimes civilian stations. Rebellious Imazighen are not far away, though their domain has shrunk to the central High Atlas and adjacent desert realms. But even now many tribes remain well-hidden and able to fight. The Army and Légion need better maps to find these resistant Berbers. Trained as a cavalier, I was sent on expeditions to survey terrain recently observed only from the air. I have been on only two missions that saw any strong combat. For almost a year, I rotated between Marrakech, Ait Ourir and Ouarzazate. But in February, my fortune changed abruptly when in Marrakech for reassignment.

On my way to the medina, I would walk down Grand Avenue to Djemaa El Fna, known in olden days as the Concourse of Sinners—"the mosque that never was." Sultans displayed the severed, salted heads of criminals and rebels. I retraced the footsteps of my Grandfather Émile, an envoy's deputy and traveler extraordinaire who came to Marrakech in 1907 when danger lurked everywhere in Maroc. I vividly recalled the photographs he showed me-the Saadian tombs, the Badi Palace, Koutoubia Mosque, every *bab*. I visited all of them after my first arrival. I felt as if I were stepping into those old photos. Truly déjà vu. I learned enough of the medina maze to assist touring Europeans guided only by their faulty

senses of direction or experiences of Continental cities. Exploring the old
city was like stepping back through nearly a thousand confusing years of
beauty and bloodshed. The Almoravid and then Almohad sultans ruled
from Marrakech for barely two centuries before it was conquered and
destroyed. The Alaouites preferred Meknes as their capital. Marrakech
fell into decay and was all but forgotten. The Saadians revived it as the
seat of their empire in the 16th century. It was doomed again in the 17th
and stayed that way until we French arrived.

*Major Mirvais, the new head of my battalion, was in Marrakech to
help devise a new strategy against Berber chief Akka n-Ali n-Brahim n-Ait
Bou Iknifen, son of Ali, grandson of Brahim of the Bou Iknifen tribe. One
man, a thousand difficulties. His nom de guerre is Ahêddây*—Guardian, *in
the Tamazight tongue. He guards quite well, leading a series of maddening
raids. His men steal from rival tribes—but only those submitting to we*
Iroumin—*or rout our supply convoys on hit-and-run forays. They have
left a trail of corpses and absconded with war booty. Ahêddây's reputation
looms large.*

*It was a Sunday. I was to meet Mirvais in Gueliz at 11:00 a.m., after
services. I expected orders for a new posting. Unmapped tracts of Adrar
n-Sargho, the "dry mountain," at desert's edge were of great interest to
Command, as were the mountains to the north and west. The Ait Atta of
Akka Ahêddây, the* ogre du jour, *straddled both regions.*

*Lately, however, I had stirred some controversy. I wondered aloud
why some mountain Berbers were now in jail for suspicion of plotting to
assassinate Makhzen officials. If the hapless, paupers I had seen arrested
were any measure, few were likely to belong to any conspiracy. I was not
shy when I reminded a Légion Capitaine that there was a higher law.
Humane conduct should be the rule, not the exception. If word became
deed, perhaps the Berbers would be less riled and less inclined to think
us devils. But I knew no one would concede that this idea was helpful to
pacification. It was easier for them to call me a trouble-maker, a dreamer
with delusions, a fool. They were certain that only a dolt would indulge
in such thoughts of justice and policy here in Maroc. They believed I
was overstepping my bounds. And complained to my commander Major
Mirvais.*

I entered a small but comfortable office promptly. On the wall, was a collection of ivory and gold 18th century pistols, French and British. Under it, a neatly organized desk of Moroccan wood and craftsmanship. A ceiling fan turned sluggishly. It was February, and unusually warm. The Major was peering at a large wall map. His shoulders blocked most of the Atlas.

"Good day, sir," I said cordially, and saluted in like manner, to his back.

Mirvais languidly turned from the map on which I saw that the Central Atlas was much less detailed than adjacent areas. I was to fix that shortfall. Mirvais halfheartedly reciprocated the salute, out of formal necessity. I sensed a slight distaste for me, but he politely gestured that I sit in a corner chair.

Mirvais began at once. I was reminded of a cranky school headmaster.

"Sergeant, your service record is good. Your reconnaissance and map-making skills are invaluable. You are a fine liaison and have good leadership potential. Discipline, attention to details, marksmanship-all well-rated. But your candor, a Sergeant to superior officers, is unbecoming."

Mirvais was befuddled, or annoyed, and glared like I was a clump of dust on a fine carpet that he would like to sweep clean. I could explain myself only by restating my position.

"Sir," I said, "I saw five Berbers arrested on conspiracy charges. A paid informer and a drunken witness allegedly testified that they had plotted to kill a Caïd in Sultan Mohammed's court during his recent visit to Marrakech. The Berbers were manacled hand and foot. Two were killed, one escaped, and two remain in custody. Still, these men have rights."

So, Mirvais said: "Our men were simply responding to the Berber reputation. They are ardent about their work."

"But Sir, they were innocent, merely pilgrims visiting a *souk*, that is all!"

Mirvais fumed. Finally he replied:

"Out of courtesy for your position, we will visit these two men. You will see they are not being abused. It is a matter of the law."

"Very well," I said. "But it is rather late, as two are already dead."

Mirvais was flabbergasted.

"And hating you, too, since you were right," Desaix observed. "The great philosophers would love this scenario. I can hardly believe you addressed your commanding officer like someone would a lackey at the Tanger docks. Please continue."

"Dare you call your officers and commanders liars?" Mirvais chided.

"Justice is a noble calling," I said coolly. But I was careful with my indignation.

Mirvais exclaimed, "We are suppressing hostile tribes! It is war! You cannot have a cause célèbre! This is no time for *manners*! You are suggesting what law and policy should be! A subordinate *follows* orders, and does not presume to give them!"

Mirvais said, "Sergeant, you've studied these people. What is there so important to know that I don't know already?" He did not expect a thorough response.

We stepped near a cell. There, in the darkness, sat two lonely dispirited creatures looking like apes in a zoo. They were fed, but that was about all. I wanted to speak to them, to ask of their tribes—but I averted my eyes and could not refrain from giving a lecture.

"Uh, oh, this will be the last straw. I predict," said Desaix gleefully and wisely.

"The Berbers call themselves Imazighen—the free men. To them, this is not a rebellion against authority but a proclamation of freedom. They will not surrender. We fight for policies based on claims or seizures, many of them a hundred years ago. They fight for their wives, children, homes, life or death. They have the spirit, the landscape to remind them, and their culture allows nothing else. They have a saying: 'Yesterday was yesterday, to-day is to-day. To-morrow is God's and who knows what it may bring?' They accept their fate, however harsh."

I paused for effect. Mirvais remained courteous, perhaps even interested.

"So now, in the Central Atlas, we face Berbers who are geniuses of deception and ambush. In mountains through which no troops, though disciplined and well-trained, can pass undetected. The tribes are allied. A mutual enemy binds them together. They lure our smart but foolish men into traps. Some are war veterans, they have fine weapons, but too many are outfoxed or shot down by fierce Ait Atta who know every inch of their terrain. We could learn from them how to make the most of few resources."

The Berber prisoners were rapt at our exchange, though they probably understood few or no words. Their wild eyes urged me on. Perhaps they saw *adjnun*—evil spirits—about.

Finally I said to Mirvais, "We demonize the Berber but ourselves kill prisoners and smash villages to rubble. But when they mutilate our dead, we are outraged."

"Sergeant, calling to question the prerogatives of officers on the scene is a form of insubordination. The truth of this matter is not for you or anyone else in the forces below the rank of General to decide."

I continued, "So now this is the Maroc we have made. In Casablanca and Rabat are black markets for ivory, gold and guns. In Tanger, are the outcast or unscrupulous entrepreneurs unable to thickly line their pockets in Europe? The economy failed as a sovereign system years ago . . . a river of commerce that dwindled to a stream of shifting alliances to the Sultan and . . ."

Mirvais finally interrupted me. He knew at last to shut me up, and how.

"Sergeant, I know you are fond of walks in this heavenly pit of an old city. Perhaps, you may think more clearly about your duty here. Return to my office tomorrow, at the same time, and we will talk further."

I tried to forget my exchange with the Major. As I passed the barracks, I saw several sections of troops assembled in drill march on a patch of dusty ground. *Droit droit, gauche gauche, demi-tour droit!* There was not the merest slip in their clockwork rhythm. I was always impressed by this, for in training I marched numerous times. The Adjutant directed them to sing, and they did so heartily:

> Au Tonkin, la Légion immortelle
> A Tuyen-Quang illustra notre drapeau,
> Héros de Camerone et frères modeles
> Dormez en paix dans vos tombeaux!

I walked towards Djemaa El Fna. The light, colors, smells, and sounds flood the senses. Just as an exotic dream. The light of the sun was a softening amber. Shadows grew long. The voices of the traders seemed to deepen with them. I entered the *souk* among the wool, textile, and sheepskin merchants. Down the long passage, near Rahba Kedima, one could hear the cries of "*Balek! Balek!*" Three over laden mules were being nudged or whacked by their owners with fat switches. The lead mule scowled at us. The pile of carpets on each of them threatened to topple off, but they passed through the hubbub like dancers.

At the edge of the *kissarias*, in the heart of the medina, the *muezzin* proclaimed *dooh*, the mid-afternoon prayer. "God is great. I testify that there is no God but God. I testify that Mohammed is his prophet. Come to prayer, come to security. God is great." All became subdued as many retired within their shops or rooms.

The *souk* shortly resumed its frenzy. I passed more stalls and shops under the canopy of rushes, called *smar*, that protects sellers and buyers from the sun. The scents of mint, cumin, olives, fresh bread, and *smen*, the butter used in *couscous*, all blended together can summon ravenous hunger. I walked on, through hazy alleys, some teeming with people, and others just nearby, eerily deserted and forlorn. Food and spice shops gave way to carpenters and leatherworkers. On one side, men carved and drilled assembling furniture from fragrant fresh cedar. On the other, craftsman turned out bags, sandals, saddles, and so forth. In front of me, the fine, glimmering tiles of the fountain offered a gift of water. I drank.

On the northern edge of the medina is the Ben Youssef mosque and its *medersa*. Both were ahead around a crumbling, strangely configured passage along an old sunken building. The street fronting the mosque leads to the alleyway where one enters the *medersa*.

I entered the alleyway, passed the wary sentinel, and emerged within. Immediately, one can feel serenity near the small rectangular pool beside the columns; six on each side, under cedar panels and stucco walls ornately hewn with Kufic passages from the Qur'an. Many hours of rapt study would be required to absorb the divine guidance of this poetry. Perhaps that is precisely the point.

I passed under a carved stone archway into a large alcove above which rose another arch dense with arabesques and above that a richly carved octagonal vault. The recess is remarkably similar to the apse of churches. I was in two worlds at once, seeing two ways of life, two Gods.

Many *medrasa* students spend years seeking through philosophy, mathematics, and strict study of the Qur'an. Some say that ancient books from Greece and Rome are buried beneath the oldest parts of the *medersa* libraries. It is not difficult to imagine that Arab scholars sought to preserve that wisdom for all.

There is a universe of difference between the commotion of the *souk* and the tranquility here. I gazed upon the inscriptions, interpreting a few words with my limited Arabic. The trickling of pool water echoed softly off the walls. Sunshine spread over the tiles. With eyes and mind open, I reveled in peacefulness.

I then left the courtyard to quickly return to my quarters to add a few more details to several maps I was compiling of the Atlas mountain region. Passing the alleyway, I noticed a rail-thin man gazing toward me. Or *at* me. People and animals moved to and fro but he paid them no heed. He just stood there. Waiting. He looked almost pathetic in his tattered clothing and scraggly beard. I grew uneasy under his unblinking stare. Now the odd fellow smiled. Beaming, like he had some heart-warming wisdom to share. I locked his gaze to my own. I could see his decades of hard life, but he was almost graceful. I was uneasy but transfixed. He drew closer.

We parted for a line of mules. "*Balek! Balek!*" But as I looked back, an intelligence agent, pistol drawn, was upon the man. My odd friend just looked to me and smiled. By now, another rushed in, the ugly *mokhazni*, with a dagger in his sash. They barked at the man, who still just smiled and said nothing, I was completely baffled. In a moment, they were shoving the old man away. I followed, yelling but the assailants ignored me. Then I saw two more manacled men being dragged away by several *mokhazni*. Two Légionnaires stood with their backs to me.

I was witnessing another round-up of suspects. But what was their crime? To my complete disbelief, the *mokhazni* drew his knife and stabbed the old man in the heart! Murder, completely unprovoked, utterly senseless. By any law, cold-blooded. I pulled my pistol. I ordered the fellow to drop his knife and be still. But I, all alone, would get little help from native or countrymen. The killer did not drop the knife. Instead, he walked toward his mates ahead. I screamed that he halt. Where were the Frenchmen?

Mind you, from first encounter to this point only about a minute had elapsed. He glanced at me and my gun with something like contempt. Now one of the others came toward us with what I thought was a pistol. Pointed at me. I fired, twice, striking him in the shoulder and chest. I paced after him, gun raised, wanting to see his fear. I did. He raised his hands with the bloody knife, still seething with contempt. Then I shot him dead. I could hardly believe I had done it. Only now did the two Légionnaires rush toward the gunfire. There I was, holding a pistol near three bloodied dead men in the street. I glanced up to see Légionnaire Sergeant Dutroix. This crude, wiry man with the buckled boxer's nose looked out of place here. I wondered the extent of his role in this travesty. He seemed rather zealous for a fellow who, just passing by, had happened to behold the dark heart of Maroc.

"Aren't you Sergeant La Tour?" he asked, as if I owed him an explanation.

"Did you see what just happened?" I received Dutroix's cold stare, waiting for my reply and acknowledgement of his authority to ask anything. I did not give it.

How could this be—an officer, in the back alleys of the medina, an active witness to a dastardly crime? He spoke to a Lieutenant at his side, who with another *mokhzani* ran to Rue de Bab Doukkala. "No, I did not see anything" he said flatly. I was dumbstruck.

He found no gun on the first man I had shot. No knife either. Just a short truncheon used to strike his prisoners. The Lieutenant and *mokhzani* were back in short order and led the way out. Dutroix shoved me into a waiting taxi and I was taken straight to Gueliz. It was all a blur. The parties departed faster than the scene had unfolded. Were the dead men quickly removed from the street, or left there in their blood as examples?

These were the most bizarre and stressful moments. I had acted on an impulse. In a rage. Two men with their own lives and stories, however ugly, were dead by my hand. Certainly I would have to account for the act. Not six hours after my visit I was back again. Mirvais shook with rage.

"I understand you have intervened in an incident."

"No, sir. I witnessed cold-blooded murder and responded."

"You are not a policeman, nor a judge nor a jury nor an executioner! You are none of the first three, and in this case all of the last."

"You understand imperfectly, sir. The agents acted reprehensibly. And there are witnesses!" Before I could explain further, he said:

"First, impertinence, questioning the orders and opinions of superior officers. Now you go on the prowl and become the sort of outlaw you have criticized! As for your witnesses, sad to say but you killed them."

He shook his head as if to clear out an ugly or unwanted thought, or simply to indicate his displeasure, like I was a frustrating, wayward child.

"Now you are in trouble," Desaix interjected. "A Captain said that to me and fined me a month's wage. All for not shining my boots. And he put me on report. Well, piss on him. He was killed the next week. You seem to have done a damned sight worse."

I would let Mirvais's question act as an invitation to honesty, not apology. I decided to speak freely as a Frenchman with my own mind.

I responded so: "I have just killed two men. They deserved it. And this, too, is clear. There is something terribly wrong here. I will bring my findings to the proper authorities. Someone willing to appreciate the law."

"My God, the balls of the righteous," Desaix said again.

Mirvais replied: "This morning I mulled your reassignment. Now you've sealed it. Your eloquence about our disservice to the natives may be one way of saying you want to be closer to them. To befriend them as they try to cut your throat. I have taken temporary post in the central Atlas, a corner of the world you greatly admire. From afar, that is. I am reassigned by Colonel Rochet to the garrison in Bou Malem. You will be my liaison. You have asked, in another way, and I readily grant your request."

I smartly saluted. My honor would hide my disappointment and fear. "Yes, sir!"

"Very good, Sergeant. Perhaps when next we meet you can tell me about the gratitude that the Berbers of Akka Ahêddây have for enlightened Frenchmen like you."

A heavy silence fell, like the pause between the tolls of a cathedral bell calling the faithful to worship. Mirvais was that schoolmaster again, having exacted punishment.

"You will leave in three days. Lieutenant Alain Aumont, who you know from Ait Ourir, will accompany you. We will evaluate our strategy with the information you have provided and will continue to provide at Bou Malem. Now take these final two days for a last look at Marrakech. I will fully investigate this sad incident and weigh your actions."

"And Sergeant, I order that you say nothing of it to anyone," Mirvais chided sharply before I cleared the door.

I turned precisely about and departed the office. It suddenly seemed open to doubt that I would live to see Marrakech again.

Desaix realized that the first chapters had been told. "This is some story La Tour. Blood and torment! It improves going forward, yes?"

"My friend, I desperately wish I did not have such a tale to tell."

THREE:

ATLAS

"So now you are well on your way to join us in this lovely hole."
Desaix said. "I must say that you are an idiot for expecting a commanding
officer to tolerate your expression of anger at hypocrisy! At injustice in
war! Ha! But your tale gets better with every word. Continue at once!"

There I was in Bou Malem. I was not assigned to study the topography
and tribal boundaries, but to kill the people I secretly respected, even

admired for their perseverance and capacity to endure. I was demoted. Hung by my own good intentions.

"Oyez, oyez," Desaix quipped. "Haven't you noticed that officers do not like to be told what to think." Desaix replied. "So now what?"

Major Mirvais arrived at the garrison that September. In October, he led two Légion companies and a Goum on reconnaissance. But the warriors of Akka n-Ali promptly spanked them home. Rochet and Command would not be pleased. Soon after, bad weather set in at the peaks. Operations halted, but the increase of garrison troops interrupted the seasonal migration of the Ait Atta. Some did not descend to the Dades and Sargho for the winter, but remained in the mountains. Mirvais schemed and dispatched scouts—called imazan—from rival tribes to spread rumors of our plans and bribe the Berbers for information. His two key liaisons, men of the Yafelman clans who loathed the Ait Atta, were the blackhearts Rehou Khoussaila and Aziz Fezzou.

Desaix added, "Using Berbers as agents is a cunning way to prepare the mission. I'm almost sorry to say that I alone am hearing this tale. Please continue. I must know how these noble Frenchmen ruin the soufflé!"

I was quickly sent from the Red City. The convoy of six trucks and three armored vehicles drove two full days on bone-rattling roads still being constructed over the peaks. The splendid land between the Skoura palms and the rose fields of El Kelaa des M'Gouna is unbaked. But Berbers and sheep abound there, in mud villages. A few koubba, the tombs of saints, can be found: chapel-sized, one-room semi-pyramids, with green tiles, small windows or other embellishments. Some are on well-traveled paths and carefully tended. Others are only of rough stonework, in lonely places and often neglected. But to Berbers they cast a spell. Within them, around them, to a distance, depending on the perceived power of the amrabt is the lhûrm, a zone to which the dead holy man casts his aura. By custom, anyone, even a criminal, can claim its protection. Many are Sufis, an ancient, mystical order. Berbers believe in four thousand hidden saints who succeed those that die in their earthly forms, and in one called the Great Helper who bears a burden of worldly sins. They say that without these igguramen rain would not fall, the land would be barren, misfortune abundant. It is believed that on occasion, these saints—their spirits, meet at koubbas or a zaouia to discuss and perhaps set the course of human events.

I received no welcome. I was just another transfer to a typical fort. Adjacent to the long red-earth walls are pens for horses, mules, and sheep, and a cemetery. Beyond, across a flat expanse enclosed in wire and cheveaux-de-frise, *are untended terraces, then long shallow slopes leading to palm trees at water diverted from the Dades. Upstream near the gorge is Bou Malem. The river rushes or trickles from it, depending on the season, and cuts the rolling plain between the Atlas and Adrar n-Sargho. In the spring, the steady sun melts the mountain snow that replenishes the Dades. Rain on the southern slopes is infrequent.*

The neatly plastered fort battlements of mud and stone are at least five meters high and a meter thick. No enemy without artillery can breach them, and the Ait Atta possess none. Nor did they dare attack. Flares turn night to day. Machine guns and over a hundred riflemen on fire platforms from within the well-protected embrasures far out-match any Berber assault. The interior—quarters for senior and junior officers, and several hundred men, the infirmary, the mess hall, store-houses, wireless communications, large water storage tanks, and other operational necessities—has little room to spare. The courtyard is barely more than a foyer, and "free space" is that not used for something else.

With Colonel Rochet's blessing, Mivais ran the garrison like a besieged castle. Sergeant Schondorff, Mivais's burly tight-lipped adjutant, led me to an anteroom near the infirmary, where I was to sit until summoned. A northwest window framed a grand view of white-shrouded Adrar-nAzourki massif. I stared at its huge sleeping form under gray clouds and wondered about the many igherman—*fortified clan villages—on and around it.*

Schondorff waved me in. I entered the command post to deliver my orders. There was Mivais—I saluted. He gazed at me from behind the desk and blinked like a lizard, saying nothing. No salute at all. He was our new commander. I did not like him and I did not trust him. I mixed this impression with the memory of him in Ait Ourir, barking orders, and my knowledge of his recent activities in Marrakech. He was now leading several units to battle one of the last fierce renegades. I was not confident that Mivais was a mighty warrior.

"'Good day, Sergeant La Tour," he smirked. "Welcome to our little paradise on the Dades. We will soon launch another campaign against Akka n-Ali, and your new maps will be key."

I grew lightheaded. Although a soldier, I specialized in surveying and topography, and not in war zones. My maps of Akka's realm were a patchwork of second-hand information, photographs taken by pilots who flew dangerous and often inexact routes over the mountains. My observations on brief treks to the edge of Ait Atta land and maps that were faulty or incomplete drawn by ill-equipped surveyors.

The Légion, Armée, Affairs Indigène and Protectorate had no complete atlas, so to speak. My righteous indignation about justice had sent me straight into an arena of bullets and blood, guiding men through an alien country crawling with the ruthless tribes of the *Guardian*.

"You are in the Légion," he said grudgingly. "I understand and appreciate that your duties have been elsewhere other than a combat post. We will guide you to become a more complete soldier. Training begins tomorrow. Corporal Schondorff will guide you to your quarters. Dismissed."

I settled in to my quarters with Sergeant Danton Saint-Avold, who led 4th Section. A taut man, his movements implied a loyal soul with a trip-wire temperament. "Don't worry, La Tour . . . or worry. Perhaps you will soon get men of your own."

Over the next hours and days I learned the names—Du Thierry, Bierbach, Autielle, Lemarche, Plau, Dinant, Buhl, Lescoux, Savesi and too many more soldiers and officers. Some were eventually assigned to my squad. Two of them, you will learn, are somewhat responsible for my presence with you right now.

Most Légionnaires are older than the average Armée regular. Many have had a harder life: manual labor, no work, fugitives, renegades. For them, the Légion is family—or simply for that lunatic who loves risk. Everyone, me included, has a story, a tale of woe. Few questions are asked for five years of adventure and hardship and killing. *Salut au drapeau! Présentez armes! Honneur et Fidelité.*

But not all is esprit de corps. Every garrison or unit has at least one scoundrel. Like Sergeant Maurice Baud. They call him Porc-épic. He does not appreciate such an epithet, but he earned it with his hairy-bear torso,

*a bristly haircut which likens him to a porcupine and a barbed personality
to go along with it. He's a prankster and a bully and a bit cruel. And he
made clear his disdain from my first minute in the fort. His contempt for
my "sympathy" for the Berbers.*

Still, rather than return to his civilization and labor in a steel mill or
a rail yard, he signed up for more duty in what he calls "this Godforsaken
bowel of the world."

On my sixth night at the garrison, I got soused with Saint-Avold and
Lieutenant Aumont. *Poireau* is a potent mix of anisette and peppermint.
When that swill ran out, Aumont bought for us, on credit, a bottle of
cognac from Christian Graves, a slovenly but jolly and vaguely respectable
soukier trader from Marrakech by way of Tanger and Marseilles. As we
drained the bottle, Graves told bawdy jokes, ridiculed both the Berber
and Légion—though clearly seeking to profit from *shleuh* and *kepi blanc*
alike. He was too nice to be criminal, too cunning for scruples. I liked
him, warily.

"I do it all—for the jingle or rustle of Mr. Franc. Wink carefully at
my last name, and ignore my first. I have nearby a truck and a plane laden
with swill and swag, balm and bags for your swollen, leaky members. I
can get swine meat in a Muslim country, if you want! Cargo, contrebande
and courteous passengers moved to all corners of Maroc! All confidences
respected. I am a man of my word.

Buying liquor from the French and Greek *soukiers* is almost easy.
That, and visits from women of the BMC—*Bordel Mobile de Campagne.*
"Don't get syphilis!" Graves quipped, raising the suspicion that the girls
had not been "inspected." Three principles for Légion happiness are: hot
food when possible, red wine—or stronger libations—and occasional
female companionship. So, the garrisons often see *soirees* with the friendly
towns rather than slaughter. Danton—named after a famed revolutionary
Frenchman—and I, and certainly Aumont, wanted little to do with the old,
or plump, or dentally deficient damsels.

As we drank, Aumont spun a reedy disc of "Bolero" on his battered
Victrola. He mused that it reminded him of horses. Aumont was a skilled
rider. We laughed, yet again, at my recollection of a pre-Légion visit to
Metz, near his hometown. After overindulging in several Moselle vintages,

I fell asleep in a field and missed the morning train. Sergeant Aumont befriended me. Last November, Alain was shot just below his right rib—he loathed the wry comparisons to Jesus when the bullet deflected off the grip of his pistol. He confessed to having vivid dreams of dying here. In a world-weary moment he said, "I dread my luck will run out." On more faithful days, Aumont vowed to fulfill God's plan for him-as long as it did not include dying before the end of his service. That would be two weeks and a day after we left the garrison. He vowed to never again be near gunfire.

I twice heard Aumont recite a passage from Luke: "When the day shall dawn upon us from on high to give light to those who sit in darkness and in the shadow of death, to guide our feet into the way of peace." His was certainly not the soul-lusty *shleuh* killer. I thought him analogous to a fine Swiss watch: ever reliable but a bit too fragile for a place such as this. His broad chipped-tooth smile in a sun-browned face showed a man much more delicate after time here, not less, as if past years of wind and summer heat had eroded his facade of duty.

Saint-Avold agreed with Aumont's suspicions of Rehou Khoussaila, Mirvais's master partisan scout. Black horse, dark eyes, cruel smile.

"I think you are right about him, Aumont. That dark-prince Yafelmane is cold as ice and twice as slippery. I would bet him to be a rogue, and that he and Mirvais have made some strange pact. Khoussaila may be up to no good, and possibly at our expense."

From this discussion of Khoussaila's unnerving presence, Aumont logically segued to Mirvais-and to rumors suggesting that he was a fraud or a rascal. Alain despised hypocrisy, and relished tales about the Major. Aumont's view of Mirvais fit with what little I had learned of him. Henri had been disinherited from his Champagne family estate. He had fallen from the privileges of a Vesle vintner. *"Mirvais is here to help tame our new nemesis. But thus far, you see, somewhat the opposite has occurred."*

Aumont told his tale well. Cynicism seeped from his voice like milk through a cheese rag. But he would smile like those painted saints and sultans he spoke of, who seemed to know what others did not. His eyes hinted of insights into vulgar secrets, though the lips beneath his moustache seldom revealed them.

Then there is Private Pietro Savesi. *Or was.* He never received the relative blessings of a court martial. Morghad warriors captured him near Tineghir on his dim-witted ride into their country. They made gruesome sport of him. The sheep slaughtered for Tafaska are granted more dignity than was he, deserting across Morghad land after foolishly heeding Baud's braggadocio about the cowardly Berbers. Savesi was on my dusk-to-dawn watch. He had failed to station a replacement when he ran to the latrine after tainted food shot right through him. Porc-épic reported Savesi for leaving his post. Mirvais exacted a pound of flesh for his contracting diarrhea without permission. Savesi had also blasphemed the Virgin Mary within earshot of the Major, who had low tolerance for such. And he was five seconds late for all-in; a deadly sin here. The handsome lad from near Lago Maggiore was reduced to pitiful distress.

"I fled home and Fascist Italy to live as a poor student in Paris. Then, bored with that," he lamented, "I fled that too. A job in a bistro, clubs . . . and women . . . I must be crazy!"

On his first action, near Tarhia, seven Berbers and two comrades were killed near him. Blood and brains spattered his uniform. Baud laughingly ordered Savesi to dig several graves. A homesick young Savesi lost his stomach for combat and wanted an early exit to evade such ignoble punishment and death. Instead, he walked into a torture few would wish upon anyone. But from a Berber point of view, that is exactly why an infidel may be subjected to castration and other horrors—to cleanse their world of demons. A horse patrol found him. The Morghad soon had hell to pay. And no one else deserted.

Training accelerated in late March. I watched the very skilled Goums and *spahis* handle their horses. A contingent of our cavalry would supplement them. We drilled from dawn to afternoon. The food was decent. Then there was road building, water supply and fort maintenance. I had ridden horses before on mapping expeditions and I knew how to cope with long days in the saddle. And how to fight from there. I was proud! We marched, with packs of twenty or more kilos, sometimes covering nearly fifty kilometers in a day. "A true Légionnaire *enjoys* his hardship!" Saint-Avold declared.

I grew reacquainted with the '09 and '14 Hotchkiss and Chatelleraut light machine guns, lugging its bulk, the tripod, the ammunition, on treks to Plateau d'Iraoun, with the Lebel or Berthier, with boots, and alternative clothing we adapted, which resembled that of the Berber. Some wrapped the *kepis* on their heads and much of their faces in a *ched* as protection from the dust and sun. I did, too, and wore a *gandourah*, a long tunic and baggy *seroual* pants. Nor was footwear closely ruled. Some men marched in sandals. We readied to fight in harsh conditions.

In April the men were galvanized by the upswing in operations—but not eager to return to the mountains. A series of convoys arrived bringing men, supplies, horse feed, munitions and such. Some trucks ferried other units of men to operations further east or southeast where Berbers still fight in alliance with Akka n-Ali.

The heavy rhythms of practice with Berthier rifle and Hotchkiss machine gun, the shouted commands of formation movement, and other activities of a garrison in the heat of preparation were certain signs that a new campaign was afoot. With all this preparation, if Mirvais expected the impending march to remain unknown to the *Imazighen* until it was about to strike, he was sorely disillusioned.

Mirvais was to lead half of the garrison on a light, fast *Groupe Mobile*. A second force would move from Tineghir, and if needed a third from Marrakech. More than a thousand Légionnaires, Goums, *spahis* and partisans were to converge on uncharted land east of Azourki, in the land of the Ait Atta alliance. Our bodies would form a pincer. Mirvais blustered about tactics—but I believe it served as much to hide his fear as to inspire us.

"The Armée and Légion have invested a half century of learning to fight in these mountains and valleys, desert and plains," he said when he unveiled the plan. "Now the Légionnaires, some of them *my* Légionnaires, will prove those lessons well-learned."

"Famous last words," Desaix added.

The mission had two basic needs: good weather and a credible sighting of Akka n-Ali. The goal was to remove him, not destroy villages or kill men. If we cut off the head, an adage says, the body dies. Mirvais was adamant that we would succeed. "Forget the frustration and casualties of previous missions, and the new, unfounded myth of this *Gardian*," he boldly asserted. But Saint-Avold and others—like me—suspected he wanted these bold words to reach Colonel Rochet and influence a transfer.

On a fair weather day in mid-Ibrir, Fezzou and Khoussaila galloped in from reconnaissance. In French-Berber babble, but coherent enough, they reported seeing Akka n-Ali and a dozen of his men near Imdiazen. Du Thierry, Saint-Avold, Aumont and I overheard these Yafelmane. Their clans, ever at war with the Ait Atta, have rejected Ahêddây's attempts to unite them.

Mirvais, unwilling to wait, and perhaps also afraid to go, ignored the absence of Lieutenant-Colonel Marcy and issued the order: three companies, three horses squadrons—a Goum, a *spahi*, and ours—and two field guns would leave the garrison in two days, taking a northward track along Asif M'Goun. Tineghir was contacted via telegraph—hopefully uncut—to commence the joint operation.

"Gentlemen," Mirvais bellowed, "this war is more than twenty years on! Now *we* may be within reach of suppressing one of the last rebellions! We have the means, the will and the right strategy. Akka n-Ali, Ahêdday, the *amghar,* the sheik, the *Guardian,* or however he is called, has the wrong enemy. So prepare. We depart in thirty-two hours."

"Here we go again," many troopers grumbled at the certain prospect of hard uphill marches. "April. Just past Easter. Time to go kill some heathen natives."

"And they us."

Saint-Avold said to me: "Mirvais seems to think the mission has only one outcome. Does he think all we have to do is march into their villages? Then they will dance to organ music until it stops with us in control?" Saint-Avold's green cat eyes flashed and his brawler's nose grew red. He has the mind-set of a gangster, but the soul of a sage. He minced no words about Mirvais. "Even a good musician does not always play precise notes, and Mirvais is no musician." *Later on, Desaix, I will tell you where we were when the music stopped.*

The men loaded ten days' provisions, weapons, and munitions— enough for several days of combat—into lorries to be driven through a desert tract to the foot of Adrar-n-Azbeg and loaded on to pack mules. Some speculated we would not be out long enough to use all the food, and would see little fighting. But they likely said the same last year, on that last foray before the snows, and as I said that confident campaign received a rude shock. These newly allied tribes, some of them perpetual enemies, are much more capable. They know this territory like their hands.

I later learned that the order for the mission went from the Major's mouth to Akka Ahêddây's ear in barely a day. So we, losing all surprise, were outfoxed from the start.

We are black sheep mercenaries, and these years after the Great War, France has too few of us. Légionnaire veterans of the mammoth trench battles now must learn the piecemeal tactics of mountain warfare. Mirvais relied on Khoussaila to advise how Akka might best be squeezed. The chieftain raids in all directions. A Berber who could write some French scrawled on sheepskin a commandment-like message signed *"Guardian"* and hung it from a dead officer tied to his horse: *"Thou shalt not trespass."*

This was to be a joint operation. We horsemen departed before the troops. The narrow road became a stony track to a junction of sheep trails between high ridges. Khoussaila, Aziz and another of their brethren were ahead with the *spahis.* The mounted Légionnaires stayed with the main column. I forgot the perils to which we marched, instead marveling at the great wonders. Atop immense Irhil M'Gouna lay a last wisp of snow. Along the Dades, fifteen kilometers behind us, were bands of palm green, and far to the east, an ocean of coarse brown hills stretching to desert. Wind gusts whipped up dust devils. Men, mules and horses climbed tracks skirting Asif M'Goun and the village of Bou Drarar terminating near a cluster of hamlets. Beyond them, were many passes where a covert path to Akka could be found. But the preferred outcome, of course, was to lure him out.

"That phantom devil," Mirvais was fond of saying. "He strikes where we are weak, retreats from strength. We will force that coward to fight on our terms."

"We will chase him," Captain Du Thierry echoed the strategy.

Du Thierry commanded sixty-five Légion horsemen and four Berbers, including Aziz and Khoussaila. The mounted soldiers, Légion and natives, were a spearhead and the Berbers scouted for the entire column. They knew all the routes and ruses. The troops continued their trek up the ridge.

"Roland, the nose of your goddam horse keeps nudging me in the ass!"

"He's just trying to read your mind."

"When can we ride?"

"Holy Christ! I think I've been walking since Jeanne d'Arc."

"Where do you think you are, on leave in Monaco?"

"Shove some foie gras up that hole, you Basque bastard! I've had enough of . . ."

I am usually patient and tolerant—but fail to suffer fools gladly. Living with this lot was like chewing glass.

"This is tiresome!" I said. "If you can't be sensible then be silent." Then I walked with deaf mutes—until the next rounds of vile exchange. This passed for camaraderie.

"Most of the men," Aumont said to me, "think that your posting here was the price of insubordination. Your assignment was an unofficial invitation to defy orders or to die for your beliefs."

I kept saying to myself, I'm a mapmaker, not a field soldier. But now I belonged to a mountain combat squad. With my knowledge of the terrain, Mirvais kept me close. Several hours into that first day, just past the gorge, a sheep path and horse road diverged. He summoned me.

"Sergeant," he said, "it is unwise to follow the river course, for that brings us past many fields and villages. I need a more desolate route."

My maps—more detailed in this lower end of the ravine—and compass suggested a turn to the west. We rose to a plateau with a steady but shallow incline. I had converted the Major, so I thought, into a believer in my prescriptions. Surely, in a few years, a road would be built along the river into the gorge.

The men were reliable. They had performed well prior to my arrival. Casualties were few, even against the Ait Atta. One may think that soldiers acquainted with dust, heat, cold, homely women, long marches, fatigue and thirst might not be enthusiastic. But most wanted to make their presence count, to drive a good fight. There is little glory in defeating an enemy long declared inferior. But these Berbers were far from beaten. *Guardian's* relatively small forces were wreaking too much havoc as a mere function of chance.

We concluded the first day on the southeastern flank of Adrar-n Aguerzouka, in land of the Mgouna, uncomfortably close to their villages. But it was a good position: a plateau about two kilometers square, beyond high ground and snipers, with an adequate stream nearby. At once, the Goums turned defensively outwards, and every Légionnaire set about erecting a *murette*, a chest-high wall of stone around the bivouac behind which the troops could take cover in an attack. Never was brute labor more impressive than these silent men moving multiple tons of stone to form a serviceable barricade—in little more than half an hour.

A platoon was dispatched to ferry water. With buckets and canteens, they set a conveyance chain. Next was the city of tents. Each man carried a tent section and a short length of pole. Assembled with his partner, the canvas becomes an open-ended A-shaped shelter barely big enough for two men to sleep side by side, with their rifles, should they be needed in a midnight hurry. This was a habit, begun the hard way years ago, when stealthy Berbers would enter camp and make off with unguarded firearms.

Our horses were well-tended. The native mounts, were clever and hardy beasts that could tolerate treks over rugged terrain on little water and just one feeding per day. They proved invaluable in country that would ruin lesser creatures.

The cool night passed uneventfully except for a chorus of yelping jackals that resounded above us or across the ravine. The *spahi* guards were unfazed by the din, perhaps even somewhat amused.

Dawn broke with an ice-gray sky that would soon turn clear blue. The air stung. Breakfast, caf noir and a large hunk of bread, was simple and good. We broke camp.

The column traversed uphill toward a trio of passes in a rough half-bowl below a ridge. Saint-Avold and I stood by, watching and waiting. The horses were restless. I thought they may want a patch of rare grass a few paces away.

Aziz Fezzou proclaimed, "That way good!" pointing to a steep pass near our line of ascent. "Akka Ahêddây will not expect Iroumin *go here!"*

Aumont was firm. "Yes, but we cannot fight as well in that terrain as on the march we agreed to this morning! The route may be shorter, Aziz, but it is steeper! And we have no good map of what is ahead! We have only your word!"

Mouha was hard-pressed to translate that much French into Tamazight.

Aziz replied, "That is more than you have without me!"

"We have come too far to alter the plan," Aumont insisted. "I see no good reason for it!"

Mouha translated, and Aziz glowered.

Mirvais trotted up on his mount and glared impatience. His pale skin looked ashen against his red epaulettes and trousers. Only his moustache seemed truly healthy.

"While you bicker precious time slips away!" he said petulantly. Aumont was my superior, but my friend too, and his appeal made sense. But Mirvais was the commander.

"Sir," I offered, "you stressed that we would not proceed unless we were sure."

"I also said we must keep moving! We cannot wait for every kilometer ahead to be well-scouted."

"Do you forget Aziz's loyalty?" Mirvais gestured to a bearded wild-eyed Aziz—who looked like a gnome or a raptor even though his easy smile was meant to assure. "I will remind you, Aziz helped me thwart an ambush last year. We destroyed them. He has never given me information that was not in some fashion useful."

Captain Du Thierry returned from his own reconnaissance on a slope to our left. He listened, and then entered the argument, pointing out that the steep trail would neutralize the cavalry horses and pack mules. And wear them out.

Mirvais replied, "They are only animals, Captain. With less sense than the dumbest man. There is no enemy here, and they do not have it much easier than us. So carry on."

Aumont sighed in submission. "We will continue there," he said, pointing above to the central route. "But I would like my squads to move ahead, on easier ground."

Mirvais just waved aloofly. "As you wish, Lieutenant. We move in five minutes.'"

We passed in silence. As the night jackals had proved, these massive rocks of ages had an eerie capacity to transmit sound, and human ears lurked among them. We prevented the clank and clatter of gear so as not to give the Imazighen warning of our approach. Best to be the hunter, not the hunted. Almost certainly, however, our presence was long noted.

On we went uphill, with the cap of Azourki in full view. According to Berber myth, a great cave—more like a large crater—near the peak had been chosen as the burial tomb of Mohammed. The camel bearing the sacred corpse had trod from Arabia to this western fringe of Islam, but the animal was frightened by loud noises made by the people of a valley chasing birds from their crops. The camel retreated all the way to Medina to bury the Prophet, and forever after pilgrims would journey there rather than to Maroc.

A stream surged beside the trail. In summer it would be a trickle. That day, the sun was melting the snow and the water rushed near a worn route on which sheep were driven to pasture. A ridge crested far above. I could not see where the stream flow might originate, but the hill resembled a crooked staircase and the water would follow its profile.

Recent Berber attacks had been successful because they cannily anticipated the place and time our vigilance would relax. We have good weapons, but of course only by luck can you kill an unseen target. Their *djellabahs* are fine camouflage. The most telltale sign of them used to be the smoke from old powder *moukhlas*.

The men were more tired than their pack mules. Mirvais would forge on. I could not imagine their strain. In these mountains, the war itself was carried by beasts of burden.

Saint-Avold's men ascended the slope. I saw Mirvais move forward, peer up in dismay and about to yell out. There was a rising crackle of gunfire, like from undisciplined or overanxious riflemen. More bullets hit the ground and rocks than men or animals. Mirvais pulled his pistol the way a pedestrian with the right-of-way might thrust a hand at an oncoming truck; a reflex of surprise and fear more than a useful action.

We swiftly returned fire to the boulders. One trooper fell with a mortal wound in the chest, but two, three Berbers tumbled from their concealments.

Saint-Avold led his men to flank the position. He chose a longer path, but one offering protection, so they could shoot along nearly every meter of the way. His men peppered the ambushers' positions as they neared an opening in the rocks. There they could gather to deliver more concentrated fire. But I saw all of them pull up in response to a chilling sight.

Now I saw it, too; to the left, perhaps thirty Berbers, lying in wait for just this moment, were rushing from a small grotto toward a wide notch in another group of boulders. Even unskilled fighters, which these Berbers were not, could inflict heavy damage with their well-protected high ground, the element of surprise, and enough guns.

I bellowed, "Eighth Platoon, third squad! Get the Hotchkiss and follow me! Move it up to the left, there!" I pointed to an open patch a brief sprint uphill where we could fire from a protected angle.

Three men jostled each other to detach the gun, mount, and ammunition from the skittish mule. Corporal Pierre Péaule, a big man, wrested it free. Aisnay and Luca followed him. We had drilled in, hastily offloading and assembling the weapon and the whip and whine and whack of bullets spurred us the faster. Aisnay, bearing the gun mount, took a bullet through his thigh and crashed face-first to rocky ground with a sickening thud. The bipod clattered beside him, and no one was nearby to retrieve it.

I howled to the little fellow dashing through rocks pinged and pocked by Berber riflemen. "Vittel, the ammunition!" He stepped to the very edge of the rocks and heaved the weighted metal box across the gap. Bullets whistled about him. He fell to earth. The box flew, bashed and burst open, spilling out shell strips. I dove belly-down the incline at the box handle, and then heaved it over me into his outstretched paw. Bullets just missed us. Péaule inserted the first strip into the breech of the light 1909. Clutching it to his hip, gritting and grinning like a death head he swung the barrel.

"Here is the soup du jour!" Péaule roared. Gallows humor. He trembled like a man with a jackhammer. The gun roar and the cracks of rifles and the clatter of striking and ricocheted rounds and the shouts and cries, together, were deafening. I fed the breech strip after strip, myself a machine, and Péaule poured it on from our position not one hundred meters below and to the left. This throttled the Berber volleys, although directly below I saw a trooper, restraining a mule, shot dead and the animal, too.

Eight or more Berbers dashed into the far side of the column. They wanted to have at the Légionnaires hand to hand with their *takummiyt,* nasty curved daggers, but four troops smartly kneeled, three stood high, and killed them with two volleys. I saw several pack mules run off. One Berber stood up to fire, but Péaule shredded him. What a mess! Three more fled, but Saint-Avold and others cut them down. I think Péaule enjoyed threshing the rocks. He had churned out a dozen strips on those fifty or so Berbers who had been undone by their poor first volley. Unmindful or careless, he edged into the open to see his handiwork. I followed him, for he needed a new strip every few moments. The surviving *shleuh* were unable to counterfire because few of them could safely stand or crouch at the rampart. They were frying on the hot pan of their own attack. Now the Goums were flowing downhill behind them. The Berbers loosed a half-hearted volley on them. They would soon vanish into the ravines, inviting us to pursue on their ground.

I scanned for snipers that might target Péaule. I saw a flash of a *djellabah* and a white turban, then for long seconds, nothing. Handing Péaule another strip, I glanced across the ravine. There, Mirvais ducked behind the small shield of a boulder. At that instant, it was hit by a round. I snapped my gaze upslope to see the white turban man, on my side of the ravine a hundred meters away, working a rifle bolt. His calm, grim look told me he had a target. He raised his face and the gun. It was Aziz!

I turned my head halfway to just glimpse that second shot hit the same spot on the rock face. Aziz deftly plied his breech bolt and took aim again at Mirvais. Then I swung my Lebel, exacting the target and I squeezed the trigger.

He moved. My shot caught the traitor in the right shoulder and punched him backwards. But he flashed more concern as the rifle fell from his grip and clattered away. He immediately tried to retrieve it. I fired again, too hastily. The bullet grazed Aziz's thigh. He fell and sprawled, still short of the gun. He rose, stumbled and lurched, but was now indecisive about the weapon.

By now at least two other soldiers had also seen Aziz. Their shots barely missed, and he immediately veered away—moving several steps closer to me and side-on. Aziz was running for the rocks, hobbled and hurting but not about to quit.

My next shot shattered his left arm. I was sickened to torture him. Aziz was crippled, his agony plain. Other rounds missed him. He seemed demonic. I was annoyed but also horrified at his determination. Doubled over, Aziz was still moving away. My next shot, to the ribs, slammed him down. Surely he could not rise from that. But the warrior did, and with his rifle, too. He would enter combat heaven bloody but unbowed. He worked the bolt and aimed with the weakened skill of a man in his last breath. I sighted again, and before Aziz fired, my bullet shattered his heart. Then as several soldiers used his teetering body for target practice, Aziz crashed in blood-soaked repose.

The enemy scattered. These endless few minutes were over. A lone Ait Atta from across the ravine peered at me like some predatory animal, as if imprinting my image. His stood defiantly, daring me to shoot. He was the last Berber to leave the battlefield.

Mirvais looked like a man who had been caught screwing in church. His long-planned mission had come close to ruin by ambush along a route he had insisted they take. And a man he trusted as a guide, and had proclaimed as loyal, was nothing but a traitor.

I had saved the Major's life. If Mirvais knew, he did not acknowledge it.

This was the first real combat for me, after fourteen months in Maroc. I started to shake and sweat and was unable to look at the aftermath of the encounter.

We had four dead, five wounded—one badly—and two dead animals. Not a disaster, but certainly a rude and ugly awakening. More crucial was the harm to our strategy and the blow to our confidence. Moreover, those Berbers not yet wise to us soon would be.

Péaule pranced like an ecstatic hyena. My new friend patted me on the back. Pistol in hand, he entered the killing field to judge the accuracy of his fire. Others joined him to collect Berber weapons. A triage was organized: lightly wounded enemy, those likely to survive, and the dying or dead. Several were shot dead as examples, or to end their agony, or simply because it was not worth the effort to prolong their lives for an hour.

But in these moments after this bitter taste of war, the memories of Grandfather's storybook adventures had been shoved aside by the racket of Péaule's gun and the gruesome image of Aziz. I recalled my outspoken disgust for the policies which had gotten me sent here. Sitting on that rock, seeing and smelling the acrid aftermath of battle, I plunged into a struggle with my love of Morocco and the sense of destiny that had lured me here. My naïveté now seemed utterly pathetic. When could I go home?

FOUR:

AKKA

Akka n-Ali n-Brahim n-Ait Bou Iknifen thought that this week would mark the beginning of his forty-second year. Mother Hejjou's delivery of her only son had fallen between *Tafaska* (Aid-el-Kebir) and the M'Gouna festival. The Arabic lunar calendar the Imazighen observed, did not flow in regular cycles. Time was further displaced during forays of Makhzen troops, and new tribal strife rooted in old vendettas to satisfy perpetual lust for land or dominance or revenge. In recent years, however, many far-flung clans—among them the Iknifen, Oussikis, Ilimshan and Yazza-had shifted their focus to the common threat of the French. The Ait Atta n-Umalu—Atta of the Shade—entered *aqbil*, or tribal federation, in the face of peril. Then it became *leff*-an alliance for defense and war.

This day summoned memories of earlier tribal rifts: thirty years ago today—this date was not forgotten—Akka's father, Ali, had been murdered on a nearby ridge by several hired rogues from a rival clan to avenge an illusory offense.

"I will honor my father there," Akka said to Addi Yacoub, his faithful mentor and surrogate father. Addi was the holy *amrabt* of the Taboulmant hamlets, the *timizar,* that had come to function as the seat this Berber alliance.

"It is wise to grow mercy and love from seeds of vengeance and hatred," said the blind Sufi graybeard. "Hatred tears us apart. We must be the people who want peace." The scars upon his face were like pages in a book that told much about malice. "Like your father and his father."

Akka's grandfather, Brahim, was a warrior chief, merchant and judge who served on many councils. On a journey to Marrakech, he toured the tombs of the Seven Saints and met with a Khalifa to discuss the trade routes. He had sent his only son, Ali n-Brahim to school in Beni-Mellal, where for two years, Ali studied the Qur'an and to read and write Arabic. But he was summoned home when Ba Brahim fell ill and died that first cold and early winter. In ensuing years, Ali formed mercantile guilds trading crops and goods. Outwitting schemers, Ali succeeded in his small enterprise by befriending rivals, or at least making few enemies—an invaluable talent in a region of chronic unrest. His income well exceeded the Atlas norm. Cedar logs were hauled from forests to the north, palms from Oued Dades in the south. With the wood and infinite local stones, and mortar of mud and gravel and straw the crumbling villages were rebuilt. Irrigation extended cultivation. The hamlets added homes, two small mosques, a school, a communal granary, and a neat stone wall around the old cemetery.

Ali wed Hejjou; two springs later Akka was born. Ali expanded the family home into a castle. He encased the walls of the two-tier structure in stone and added a third floor with a roof terrace to gain a sweeping view of the plateau-the caves, pasture, and fields to the edge of the promontory. Interlocking rhomboids and triangles and stylized hearts were painted upon the new and old doors in yellow, blue and green: patterns and colors that invited harmony. Around the entire edifice, they erected a shoulder-high stone wall, almost as a battlement. And in the middle of it, as a gated entrance, Ali set a double-wide cedar door and painted it red.

Ali lived a life of virtue. He made a fine *l'ada,* a gift to the Ihansalen *zawiya,* gaining prestige for the Bou Iknifen. Twice he was elected *amghar.* He resolved issues of water and pasture usage, and remained on good terms with the council. His main concern was peace. Under his stewardship, the clans grew stronger and the plateau became a haven. It was said that he had *baraka.*

But during the *leff* negotiations, Ali inadvertently insulted a petulant chief of the Ait Morghad. The long-festering grudge, spurred by envy, led to Ali's demise. His murder on Akka's twelfth birthday, devastated the family and dealt a cruel blow to the Ait Atta. Suddenly, Akka was *tagunt*-the sole male heir.

Akka lived with many memories. He would explore his mountain realm riding his spirited horse with his treasured saddle, a gift given to him by his father. Akka lived in the *igherm* built by Brahim, passed to Ali and then to him. His closest advisors, Lahcen n-Assu and Larbi n-Haddou, had grown up with his father, helping the Ait Atta wage peace and war. He benefited from their wisdom. And as they respected Ali, they now too, respected Akka.

One day, Akka was stunned to realize that Addi, at moments, uncannily resembled his father, both in silent contemplation and when speaking of Allah's love or human hate. Addi's hard experience showed, as did his divine grace.

Addi often wore a plain blue or black *tajjelabith*, linen or woolen es*srouel* for his spindly legs, and on his head a turban around which he pulled his hood. His noble-warrior quality seemed rooted in a wisdom deepened by many challenges. One might pity Addi's blindness—until he demonstrated his vitality by walking about just as any sighted man. Addi possessed true *baraka*, proven not only from *ihêsan*—good works, but from transcendent grace. He might announce visitors—days before their arrival. He revealed an ability to read the nature and sometimes the mind of a mere stranger. And in several witnessed scenes, he healed the sick and injured with his hands and prayers. Addi's eyes-inspired trust and devotion.

The ragged but dignified pilgrim entered Taboulmant nearly twenty springs ago. Few questioned his identity or passage, as they would other strangers. The villagers were fascinated by his refuge in the I*hûrm* shrine, noting that for the first days he fasted, he hardly stirred from the rock. He built no fires. Some remarked of the scars upon his face. Skeptics rumored he may be a fugitive, or crazy, and either way likely dangerous. Larbi n-Haddou was the first to notice the small, even scars low on Addi's forehead. These *azzmoul*, he said, were a custom of the Sufi order of Naciri to identify their believers for Allah, as the Prophet himself had done. Addi Yacoub was practicing *siyaha*—roving in poverty and through prayer seeking *ridha,* a deep trance and union with the divine. This saint in the making come among them was a gift from God.

Larbi, Lahcen, and Si Baha Youssef, the *taleb,* approached Addi. He was pacing to and fro before the *koubba*, within its shadow cast by the sun, rapidly reciting a single prayer—"God bless the Prophet . . ." over and over. At last he stopped. Silence reigned. Then, without prompting, Addi explained his quest.

"I have long seen a village—*this* village, its name and place unknown to me," he said. "The vision compelled me. After much travel, unable find the place matching my vision, I was tormented. Then I saw this *koubba*, and a black *tajjelabith*, and a large red door. Here is the *igherm* I seek. I am sure."

The three village elders gazed at each other. What to make of this fellow?

"Be patient. Be wise. Be faithful," Addi assured with gentle passion. "A brave man will come. He is near. I wish to live among you until he makes himself known."

In the soft-amber sunset, Addi ascended the rocks to survey the hamlets. A stream born in the mountains to the west flowed across its contours like a beautiful scar. This land was blessed with fertility, beauty, and isolation.

Addi knelt: "My earth and my heaven contain me not, but the heart of the faithful servant contain me. The path be hard, but I seek the face of God, to serve His will, to deliver these brethren to truth and peace through fire. My vision of the heart contains them."

Addi remained, repeating his petition. It was the purpose of his quest.

He rose and followed the lesser stream uphill to a grassy bowl formed by the hills. He entered a ravine and found its source: a thin spring issuing from a fissure in a rock wall. Such a rare feature was a favorable sign.

Addi envisioned a future of specific, perhaps inevitable, events. Some would be celebrations and others woeful. Now, for the first time, he dimly saw the Other, a lone man hidden under the hood of a white *tajjelabith*, destined to hold a pivotal fate for all. Addi caught only a glimpse which then quickly vanished.

The village prepared an official welcoming *diffa*, a feast, for Addi Yacoub. But he desired a return to isolation and did not attend. Before taking residence in the hut, he sacrificed a sheep, sprinkling blood near the door and widely around the perimeter. Then he packed his lambskin satchel, took up his cedar walking stick, and set off for the shrine.

Addi Yacoub often went unseen for weeks or months—an invisible guest—in ascetic withdrawal from this world or on mountain paths exploring it, in both ways seeking revelation. He was seer, protector, spirit guide, friend; the people were better for his presence, however inscrutable.

The villagers lived as they always had. But when the Imazighen returned from their journeys, they reported of battles between *Iroumin* and the tribes. Seldom was the information heartening: great losses, continuing encroachment, the disruption of migration, crops unattended, children without parents, families without homes, a Sultan losing power, sheiks corrupted by foreign gold, a way of life at risk.

It was an afternoon in early spring. Akka n-Ali, clad in a new black *tajjelabith* and on his best horse, was nearing home with two laden mules. He and several members of the council were at the front of the last long procession completing the ascent from the valley of Asif Dades, where clans gathered after wintering in Adrar n-Sargho. Some villages had already completed their return to the Atlas. The lean, trim-bearded fellow, born more than twenty springs ago, had high cheeks, vigilant brown eyes, and a soft demeanor in harmony with an inner fire. He had displayed both qualities on this trek, one of the worst in memory due to the new tariffs imposed by the *khalifa*, whose men had harassed the migrants along the traditional route. The work of raising crops and sheep was now for far less gain. Three dogs without such worries, drove sheep up the path along the river. Ahead, was the hilltop and above that, the imposing plateau. Home. Tomorrow, Akka would plow a fallow field and inquire about moving the flock to communal pastures.

He dismounted to climb the escarpment. Akka, a farmer and merchant, was grateful for the inheritance of his father's land and enterprise but knew that some envied him. His stepfather and former guardian, Ousaïd n-Hmad n-Burk n-Ait Bou Iknifen, had spoken up for him. Akka had obeyed all customary laws; he was simply his father's son. Akka thought himself to be a leader, but he had no grand ambitions other than to help the tribes live without war.

Ousaïd met his stepson in the field with a warm embrace. "Welcome home! You have been missed!"

"I cannot express of what joy to drink *atai* brewed on our own hearth!"

"Supper in an hour, and you shall have all you want!"

"There is much to tell. Not all of it good news, you must know."

"You are alive and well-fed." Ousaïd replied evenly. "That is always a good place to begin. The council meets this evening. You will tell us of your journey."

After the fine dinner Hejjou had prepared, Akka stood on the terrace in front of the *igherm*. Below, he saw Larbi and his brothers Haj and Amnay returning from a day of toil. Haj, the potter, struggled with a stubborn, ornery mule and by this time of day, he was short of patience. He yanked the bridle and loudly cursed the beast, to Larbi's amusement.

"I think some *djen* has infected your brain!" Haj was indignant. "What thoughts tell you that there is no need to walk home to get your feed?! That I should drag you?!"

"I think, dear friend," Akka shouted down, laughing heartily, "He wants the tender grass shoots right beside him, not the coarse grain you serve every night!"

"Akka!" Larbi exulted. "This year we returned early, to plant the crops, shear the sheep and restocked the granary, and *now* you show, in your fine new *tajjelabith!*"

Just then, Addi was descending from the stony path. He heard the warm fraternal laughter and peered at the man before the red door, at his face and black *tajjelabith*. A gasp of great excitement leapt from Addi's throat, as he ran toward Akka n-Ali to kneel on the ground before him.

Akka was baffled. Ousaïd overheard, and stepped outside towards them.

"One part of me will fail, Akka," said Addi. "But another, much more important, strengthens every moment. The merciful source of our lives commands it. This is what I want for you. A day of battle, a day of judgment is coming, and you are one key to victory."

"Your words are almost warm enough to scald." Akka replied with gentle puzzlement. "I do not seek such responsibility or burden."

"Some men are born great," Addi intoned. "Others grow into their greatness, or are chosen for it. I, Addi Yacoub n-Said n-Ait Atta du Rteb, know you. In years hence, you will be celebrated as you and your people are tested, as white fire tempers steel."

Deep silence passed like clouds over the peaks. Akka stared into the Sufi's eyes. And Ousaïd at both of them. Night descended quickly. And the mule was quiet.

A month later, Uzmir Yusef planned a journey westward from Taboulmant and was to leave his flock in the care of his cousin Amnay.

"Would you keep my animals separate from the others until I return in two days? A number of the ewes are about to yean. Keep them safe from the roaming dogs."

"Yes, I will," Amnay said, "But I have my own sheep and can not watch them alone. Akka can assist me."

Amnay turned to his friend Akka, "Uzmir has asked for my help in guarding his animals . . ."

"I still owe you for fixing my old saddle," Akka replied. "Let's consider it one less favor of the many that remain."

Akka took charge of Uzmir's flock and with the consent of the chief of pastures; he reserved a portion of *agudal* for their keep. Within it were three large stone pens, two full with animals, and the third one empty. The way in or out was accessed by a narrow ravine. Sheep could be lost on moonless or stormy nights when those out of the pen wandered away. Uzmir had entrusted to them five dozen head. Much of his livelihood.

Evening drew near, and the indigo sky filled with lowering clouds. Amnay and Akka drove Uzmir's timid beasts into the empty pen. They would be cramped, but safe within the stone walls.

That night, a rare, hard rain leaned in the wind which whistled through chinks in the hut wall. Akka giggled at the sound.

But then, he abruptly stopped laughing and grew very alert, as if he was hearing sounds before they were in the air to be heard. The persistent whistle of the wind mixed with the occasional bleat of sheep, and then the eerie, faint barks of the dogs.

Akka rose at once and donned a flaxen color sheepskin coat, wool side out.

"You stay by the fire, Amnay," he said. "I go." He took his oak walking staff and was out the door before Amnay responded. The hard patter of rain and rush of the wind muted all other sound. A minute or two elapsed. From the dark, a dog snarled distinctly but still not close by, and a second dog beside the voices of two or three men.

Moments later, the rain slowed to a halt. Akka saw that the gate of the stone pen was open. Not swung open in the wind, but untethered from the outside. Uzmir's sheep were gone. Akka was horrified. Far across the field near the ravine, he heard voices and ran at them. He heard footfalls behind him; either one of the thieves or Amnay.

In the dark, through the chill, the air cleared suddenly. Akka confronted two snarling dogs and three men on horseback who were stealing the sheep. With the mere power of his words and eyes, Akka alone forced them back. Suddenly, one of the men charged Akka. A dog sprang forward. Akka swiftly sidestepped the horse and bashed it brutally on the neck with his oaken staff. The animal brayed and stumbled and nearly threw the rider. Akka whirled on the savage dog and at once the bare-fang animal was in retreat. And to the men, in a voice like a demon, he shouted, "You parasites! Leave now and I will forget you were here. Otherwise, take my justice!"

Akka noticed that one of the men was pulling a pistol. Guns *and* dogs. He saw his life ending, snuffed in a rash moment. Still, he leapt forward at the gun, moving as water and bashed the stick down cruelly on the gun arm just as it fired. The sickening crunch of wood on bone and the crack of the shot and the howling man and the barking dogs and the two astonished companions were seen by four herders coming from the pasture below. Their rifles spoke well. The chest of the gunman exploded and the most vicious of the two dogs, was propelled dead off the ledge and a second of the rustlers was wounded by the *sasbu*, and he and the third man and the dog wheeled about, and fled two more errant gunshots into the night, much poorer than when they began.

Once again, Akka and Amnay herded the sheep into the pen, returned to the hut, and there quietly enjoyed the stew heating on the oven stones during the interruption.

"I tell you as Allah commands me," Amnay exclaimed proudly to the four men from Imizarh, "Akka has *baraka*."

Akka's patrimony and family honor eased a lineage transition that could elsewhere be tense. His quiet strength defused jealousy, and suggested leadership. Parents lobbied Ousaïd for Akka to marry their daughters. They would offer a generous dowry-a choice parcel of land, perhaps a fine herd of sheep. Horses. Guns.

Then one day at the *souk*, Akka saw Hada, daughter of Amzill n-Hammu n-Ait Ouneggui. Hada and Amzill walked by, leading two mules laden with bags of walnuts, a cedar box of jewelry handmade from amber and semi-precious stones, and other goods.

Akka smiled shyly at this ideal vision, and in the course of the day, became warm to her. Four years Akka's junior, Hada's angelic smile and melodic voice exclaimed a natural happiness. Akka returned home and spoke of her to Ousaïd. At this proper sign, a meeting was arranged. As was the custom, the stepfather broached negotiations. Gladsome gossip flitted about; few secrets could be kept in so intimate a place. The prospect of union was approved by all clans.

A spring festival joined Akka and Hada, and ten other couples. Guests from near and far erected black goatskin tents. Hada, and the other brides rode horses seven times around the *koubba* to rid themselves, their homes and marriages of lurking evil influences and to invite fertility. The extended villages enjoyed a great *diffa* and feats of horsemanship, including those of Akka himself. That night, women gathered around the great bonfires. The "Daughters of the Night" wore their best dresses and headwear, and garish paint upon their beaming faces: blue lines, black triangles, yellow circles, red cheeks. The ting-a-ling of jewelry—golden bangles, stones of amber and jade, necklaces strung with gold and silver amulets, headdress ornaments, and coins of many origins—created music of its own. Deterring evil, the spiritual power of the baubles flowed to and from the wearer. The many hues of their attire leapt forth in the flickering firelight that obscured beauty-marked faces. The flowing cloaks seemed disembodied. Eight men—"Sons of Shadow"—each in a white *tajjelabith* and turban, stood on the cusp of light and dark, beating hand-held drums. A young man sang in a steady tenor. The tempo of percussion and lyrics increased, fell and swelled again. Others joined in song. The women formed into lines and began to sway in rhythm with the drums. Flutes joined in fluttering counterpoint. This was the "Creation Dance." The gathering was shortly in thrall and the ranks moved in fluid cadence. Songs of battle victory, the wonders of nature or the tragedy of life, turned to ballads of love. The dance and the feast concluded hours later, after many songs. The next morning, re-energized by a rush of mirth, the celebrations began again for the entire day.

As a sign of faith in prosperity, Akka purchased a fine loom for Hada and six glass windows and wrought iron grids, and had them installed in his Taboulmant *igherm*. All noticed the extravagance—but the next day, Akka went to the fields like the other poor men, and labored in the hot sun with his plough and community mules.

A tiny, quiet and attentive infant was born to Akka and Hada in Ibrir of 2862. On the seventh day, after the customary sacrifice of sheep, they named her Kenza. The baby Kenza observed her parents, grandparents and visitors with gleaming emerald eyes. She delighted in cues seen and heard, seeming to absorb them directly through her light bronze skin. Come autumn, she was fascinated by the young children darting to and fro, spellbound by birds soaring over the village, and by the irrigation stream below her home. She befriended two lambs, one puppy and Addi the *amrabt*.

The *Tafaska* of 2869 drew near, and extended families gathered to celebrate. As always, the men talked of crops, weather, sheep and war while the women chatted more intimately and cooked. The villagers sang and swayed in spontaneous rhythm as the musicians played their *nnay, igembri* and *bendir.* Later, the men would walk about chanting to invite good fortune for all.

On the holy day, Arab and Berber alike commemorated Ibrahim's ancient sacrifice of the sheep, one for every family. The bleating beasts, unable to fathom their fate, were held facing toward Mecca and their throats quickly cut. In the cities, a ritual sacrifice was beheld as an omen. At the moment the throat of a chosen ram was slit, several men began a race against the creature's ebbing life. Dumping the bleeding beast into a large basket, they would drag it to a mosque. If upon arrival, the ram's vital flame still flickered, then it would be an auspicious year; if not, the coming year could bring disaster.

2876. The Ait Atta felt the ever-sharpening sting of the *Iroumin* as they edged west from the lands of the Ait Yazza and Haddidou, Ait Morghad and Aissa and north from a new post near Ouarzazat. The tribes launched raids against convoys and patrols, and met with some success. Bold *spahis* tricked Morghad and Aissa raiders to villages near Tinejdad. To prove their authority, the French captured many warriors and razed two *igherman*, and among it, a *koubba*. This announced a policy of selective destruction.

Soon, there came word of hard setbacks in Ait Atta welfare. Fifty brethren of their Ilimshan and Wahlim were lost in battle against the Yafelman clans. Among them was warrior chief Mehdi n-Rachid n-Ait Wahlim, who met his end against Rehou Khoussaila, a rogue and traitor, who was said to have leased his men to the French for payment in gold and guns.

The Ait Atta assembled a large party to counterattack. The war party passed at night over high volcanic terrain. At morning, they rode in a dry, dusty waste and soon came to a weak stream which would lead them to El Farsi. But arriving at the large *igherm* on the brink of Ait Atta and Yafelmane lands, they were aghast to find it destroyed. And not by Yafelmane raiders alone, but with the French, or at least with several of their weapons. Deserted and forlorn, its walls were the burns and blasts of explosives and the scars of machine guns. The pungent smell of death remained. Eighteen fresh graves were clustered amidst a plot of palms, now laden with ripe unpicked dates that had attracted a swarm of twittering birds. The great beauty of the place contrasted with the horror visited upon it. This made a very strong impression upon Akka. He prayed for answers and tranquility.

War was an art of peculiar cliques. The party awaited their Sargho brethren and when they arrived, a discussion ensued. An expression of fears, really. *How to confront an enemy now clearly much better armed than we, with our old sasbus rifles and moukahle?*

Akka was overcome. "Biss me Allah." He recited two Qu'ran verses shared just last week by Addi Yacoub: "Surely Allah spoke the truth, Surah 74, The One Wrapped Up, 31. 'And we have set none but angels as guardians of the Fire. Rouse the believers to the fight. If there are twenty amongst you, patient and preserving, they will vanquish two hundred: if a hundred, they will vanquish a thousand of the Unbelievers: for these are a people without understanding.' Surely Allah spoke the truth. Surah 8, Spoils of War, 65."

He fell silent and the men looked upon him. The birds interjected a joyful song.

"Have we come here for nothing?" Akka raged. "I say they do not know our strength! Our righteousness and faith are worth a thousand guns."

United and two hundred strong, that night, they swept toward Tarhia and at gray dawn, they attacked. Their swift and sudden tide caught the Morghad and Yafelmane clansmen totally by surprise. They stumbled from their tents unarmed and half-dressed.

The cache of French weapons, capable of the deeds at El Farsi, did them no good. On to enemy horses were loaded every usable piece of arsenal, as were all supplies and sandals and boots. Eighteen men-to match the deed of El Farsi-were shot and thrown into the stream, that they may be cleansed of sin before they were buried. Those spared were tied like slaves and whipped away into wastes to fend for themselves. The captured leader was defiant; inviting death, he sought no mercy. And he was given none-they kept him alive only so that he could be punished by mad Rehou Khoussaila.

"Tell Khoussaila that we will no longer tolerate his attacks," said Akka with Larbi n-Haddou at his side. "We have much wrath and are not afraid. The *Iroumin* are the enemy, not us. We take these weapons for use against them, and against you if our people are ever killed again. Say to Koussaila our rage will know no bounds!"

"And tell him," interjected a familiar voice from the far side of the stream, beneath the palm trees, "tell this madman of Aoufouss, that I wish upon him the eternal torment of wholly awakened conscience, so he bears the anguish of those he has killed without mercy."

All gazed toward the voice, to Addi Yacoub, clad in the same blue turban and plain blue *tajjelabith*, and linen *essrouel* as the day he departed Taboulmant.

No one spoke for minutes. It was the most thunderous silence in the world.

"I wish to go home now." Addi at last uttered. "We shall be at war no more for nearly a year."

The terms of the current chiefs were about to expire. The *Ait Arba'in* gathered in the old *igherm* to discuss new candidates. Addi Yacoub attended. Many of the notables, the *imuqqrann,* kept a hushed, humble distance from the *amrabt,* whose radiant energy and keen demeanor contrasted greatly with his frail appearance. In the Sufi lore, "*shaykh*" literally meant "elderly man." Addi was more than his body, and this enhanced his aura. He was a fusion of mystical teacher, religious leader and counselor.

A Sufi who could see the future, and into the intemperate ways of men. Seeing though blind, his mission was almost divine, not the impulse of a man. Solemnly, the *amghars* peered at Addi, and his eerie but calm, guided gaze fell upon each of them in turn.

The *igherm* was a large two-story tetragon with stout stone walls, precisely placed so that each of them faced a cardinal point. The *taleb* and Addi prayed and chanted to bless the gathering, chasing evil spirits and welcoming piety. Addi sat beside Ousaïd to the left of the entrance door, at which the men removed their shoes and set their weapons before entering. Drawn deep in thought, Addi seemed almost beyond this time and space. But that was hardly unusual. Somewhere nearby, someone plucked a l*eguembri.* As the music carried up the winding path, Akka n-Ali entered. He greeted no one upon his arrival, said nothing, but Addi sensed who was entering. At once, Addi stood up. With this simple gesture, he signaled Akka as his nominee for chief.

"At this time, we must be less interested in the fields, in the sheep, the irrigation, the markets and migration than in defense," Addi said. "No longer are we a mountain people tending sheep and barley. We are chattel and considered part of a collection. That is all I have to say of politics. I am a man of the heart, with you, for Allah." Addi paused, and extended a thin hand toward Akka. "But he—the son of my spirit, will guide you."

With that, the *amrabt* departed. His influence swayed Ousaïd and his colleagues to weigh the prospect. After a long consultation amongst themselves, the *Ait Arba'in* voted that Akka n-Ali n-Brahim would be the *amghar n-ufella* to rule jointly with Ousaïd, Lahcen and Larbi: the destined one, the judge, the counselor and the general. *Amghars* all.

The typical term of service as an *amghar* was one year. Eligible men would rotate around the ranks, serving in each task, advising in matters of management, maintaining fields and walls and waterways, settling disputes. In this way, the tribes remained steady in governance, and no one man was allowed to retain undue influence or power. But now tribesmen were speaking among themselves of long-term service of a man who might prove to be a true warrior leader, to whom they could pledge sacrifice and blood.

The *Iroumin* sent word that emissaries would visit the region. They were often ushered by men from tribes which had already yielded, but their presence lent a whiff of legitimacy to negotiations. These envoys would refrain from interference or aggression, but rather stress the conditions the Imazighen must accept for peace. In a rare show of unity and strength, the Ait Atta *amghars* expanded tribal alliances. Akka most wanted the Ait Atta and the Ait Yafelmane, who long had been at odds, to unite their fighting spirit in *leff*.

"The lands from Demnate to Goulmima, from the date palm to the holly oak, must remain free! We will create a warning system of scouts and spies. We can combine and coordinate our forces for defense. We have never been the subjects of other men. We will not start now! Fear and respect are no longer in the hearts of the enemy! How can we bear the disgrace of submitting to the slave of the cross? Even they do not know what it means!"

He coined a rallying cry: "If they truly want our land, the price will be high!"

After several consultations with Addi and amongst themselves, the *jmaâa* voted to make Akka n-Ali n-Brahim n-Ait Bou Iknifen the *amghar n-ufella*. In him would be trusted much of the clan's daily governance—and the formulation of effective war strategy.

Akka surveyed the hamlets, the fields, and to the mountains beyond. He reminded all that the horrors endured elsewhere in Maroc had no place within it. Families from areas of relative calm sought to live here, in a kingdom soon to be under seige. A village near Adra n-Chikra was added to the realm and the *aqbil* grew to nearly ten thousand people. All villages submitting to Akka's authority provided labor for the fields and irrigation, communal pasturage, and men for war. The "people of the good"—*l-khair*-set examples for cooperation and peace.

Akka worked quietly for months to prepare the plateau as a final line of defense. The first line was a long-range warning system to span the vast triangle from Azilal to Goulmima to M'Gouna. When the enemy moved on them, a system of couriers would race to deliver news. The second line was a good offense. The Imazighen could never match the *Iroumin* in weapons or training, but their master plan exploited the terrain they knew so thoroughly. The honeycomb of caves believed to be crypts for *adjnun* were now a bastion. This, enough brave men and the harsh lessons learned from bloody years against the enemy, could provide enough advantage to discourage and perhaps turn away the invaders.

Since his youth, Akka had roamed alone or with companions imagining that they were the first men to traverse these wild slopes. Now they would be battlegrounds. He called a conference for chiefs near and far to share details of their territories. A few chosen men in well-prepared positions could thwart invaders. In their eventual deaths, they would gain glory; but in surrender, only shame.

"We will survive if we fight well and more ruthlessly than our enemy!" Akka said to the *aggrawe*. He so seldom displayed fury that they were startled. "Every man will swear obedience to me and to you. No one else—and no fighting each other. The penalty for such failure shall be banishment. Disgrace!"

The Ait Atta men were skilled in rapid movement. Akka and Larbi devised a series of raids. They assaulted a truck convoy with kerosene bombs, stealing munitions and food. Then, warriors seized the pack mules and horses of a supply column; they let most *Iroumin* walk back to their post. Soon after valiant men repelled an Armée and Goum unit twice their number. Akka n-Ali, favorite son and new savior, became glorified on the lips of his brethren. As further proof of his *baraka*, with small effort, he reaped great victories. Soon, his name would surely begin to burn on French tongues.

"You are better a martyr than a messiah!" one hapless *Iroumin* captive uttered moments before an angry rabble of Ait Ouahlim men shot him down.

Akka felt he was neither martyr nor messiah, simply a guardian and a chief, and both required initiative and ingenuity. Determined to break with rigid tradition, he weighed all means to prevent invasion. This posed a great challenge for tribes habitually at each other's throats.

"Hundreds of men will abstain from work in their fields. They will become soldiers! Remember, the *Iroumin* have big guns and hypocrisy. But we fight with Allah and the spirits of the noble saints!"

At the approach of the *Iroumin*, these men would hasten to ambush or diversion; if that failed, they would attack. Akka had scattered about the region small caches of guns and munitions. Only two trusted men in each village knew the locations. Akka would not risk the theft of weapons, the lifeline to survival.

"Always remember," he said to Larbi, "move men at night, until dawn. Or small units only during the day. Never lure their planes. We are helpless against bombs . . ."

Akka tensely awaited retaliatory bombing, machine-gun planes or large scale invasion. Nothing happened. But it was only a matter of time. His only choice was to gamble everything, for only then would there be any chance to trade for understanding.

"It is said, Akka n-Ali," Lahcen declared, "that the French are calling you the *Guardian*-Akka Ahêddây!"

Akka did not know, could not know, that one of his stratagems was also primed to bring a personal disaster. Larbi selected two spies to infiltrate the nearest *Iroumin* garrison at Bou Malem. One of these spies, Aziz Fezzou, was the half-brother of Rehou Khoussaila.

* * * * *

Amnay and his horse were spent on this spring morning after an all-night ride. "The *Iroumin* are leaving the garrison! Three troop companies, one of horse and a Goum. Three hundred men from Bou Malem and two hundred more from Goulmima, coming this way!"

"As we expected. You and Haj observe their route. Relay messages here twice daily. Then we will send our greeting party. I trust Aziz Fezzou has been helpful."

"A cunning man," said Amnay. "What he lacks in wit, he makes up for in treachery. Perhaps we will see which is better."

Two days later, Akka rued that the ambushers were not better marksmen; there was a shortage of ammunition with which to practice firing the new rifles. These Légionnaires were very capable on defense and counter fire; even from a poor position, with superior weapons they could inflict heavy casualties, including their informant Aziz. *Ikh Tinna Rebbi.*

The French very much needed a lesson on the price of audacity. Larbi devised a plan for slaughter with camouflage and several ruses so cunning that Akka was giddy at the prospect. After considering all possible consequences, however, he decided to walk the line between teaching the *Iroumin* a hard lesson and enraging them.

"Why not kill them all?" asked Haj and Larbi. "They deserve no mercy."

"We must only balance the scales for the failed trap," Akka sagely replied. "We have not yet graduated from painful nuisance to wicked killers. If we annihilate those men, twenty times their number will come to repay us without pity. But I promise you, if Allah is willing to see them die to the last, then let it be so."

FIVE

TRAP

"Now you are at the foot of a miserable mountain." Desaix summarized while La Tour reflected on the recent scene. "The men are dazed at the treachery of gunfire in territory the Imazighen scouts had led your officers to believe was safe. You find out differently, the hard and bloody way. Now what is next?"

We had four dead and four wounded. One badly, a Corporal they tried to patch. Under proper conditions, the hole in Guillaume's chest might

THE IMPERISHED KINGDOM   71

not threaten his life. But we were two days from Bou Malem. While the doctors were skilled, there was no easy transport of the wounded. Mirvais was willing to try, but Guillaume might not survive the trip, and perhaps neither would his bearers through Berber country. Nor was M dicin Massay hopeful he would endure here. Miserable options. Either we should not get shot or, if we do, have the good sense to die. And someone always gets shot and the others suffered for our sins.

Mirvais sent Lieutenant Aumont ahead with eleven mounted men, including Rehou Khoussaila, to scout a bivouac site. They found a big level space on a ridge near a cliff. Aumont left five men and Khoussaila to secure it, and returned to the column. We resumed the climb. Guillaume and another were stretcher-borne, and a third would limp on his own. One of the runaway provisions animals was back in the line.

Mirvais summoned me to walk alongside him.

"Your map says that a Berber village is over that ridge."

"*Imi Imejdi* is a small *igherm*. It once was near a neutral zone between Mgoun and Oussikis and may be abandoned if a truce has not been reached."

"If not, tomorrow we will use it as a base for the day," Mirvais replied.

"Sir, they can surround us," I offered. "And what if people *do* live there?"

Mirvais was silent; this implied that the village would not be occupied for long.

The bivouac was almost paradise after the march and the fight. The Goums held the picket, the murette wall was built, tents erected and supper cooked. There was scant tinder for the fires, so kerosene stoves did extra duty. The night passed without incident.

Except, there was a thief among us. Some weasel had stolen a pack of Corporal Lescoux's cigarettes from his satchel which had but briefly lain on the ground. He was in a huff. A petty thief was an insult to one man, but a potential threat to the morale of all. It was rumored that *Lescoux the Lion* had strangled a Senegalese in the middle of the night for pilfering rationed sugar. Heaven help the culprit should he light a Gaulois, even on the sly.

I started waking men at five o'clock. The second cool night had taken its toll. I hadn't slept well and neither had the men. We marched off without hot coffee or warm food. Few cared. I didn't.

We reached the upper ridge two hours later in full light. Not far below, near green crop terraces, was a crumbling igherm and some drifting smoke. No longer the key to some territorial lock, it was occupied. Women skinned a sheep while several old men repaired a stone wall. I was surprised. Surely someone must have advised them to flee. But this seemed to be a sleepy realm, indifferent to the perils of war.

Mirvais chose to perceive this Berber pride or fearlessness, or even faith that they would not be harmed, as arrogance. In this view, the apparent lack of proper defense must signal hauteur, not a simple desire for peace over war.

This is what he said. "I would like them to understand us the way we had to understand them yesterday. The village knows we are here and remains unconcerned. They clearly have little respect for us. We will change that."

Saint-Avold and I puzzled at the reasoning. Were we to pound our chests?

"I would like to attack," Mirvais said from his vantage at the ridge crest. He was very explicit, but almost child-like, as if picking an item in the p tisserie window.

The village was a storybook world, not a military target. There was not a Berber warrior nor horses nor a gun in sight. Only people at work, living. Unprovoked action would surely reap the whirlwind, today, next week, soon.

I had in my dry mouth the chalky taste of disgust. Again, I was compelled to speak out of conscience. "Sir, that village is not a threat. I see women, children, the old . . . Might we send a foot patrol or a squad of horsemen? I will go . . ."

"I did not ask for volunteers! I ordered an attack!"

Saint-Avold bravely continued, "But that will send an ugly message to Akka n-Ali. It plays to his strengths. We need villages with us or neutral, but certainly not loyal to him."

Mirvais retorted, "None of them will ever be on our side. Don't you know that by now? We attack to subdue or eliminate. Not show mercy to win friends or convert enemies."

We fell silent. To some men, it was an easy attack, to others a waste of energy. And to all, illogical; the place was ripe to just walk down and take. No need to burst in guns blazing.

"Set up two Hotchkiss for a crossfire," Mirvais brusquely directed.

I was sickened by this. He wanted to set an example by taking vengeance. I wanted no part of it. Yet Mirvais's response to the Berber ambush was not so grotesque that the Légion would admonish him. Bold destruction or peaceful capture were a commander's prerogatives. Clearly, Mirvais had all the military objectivity of an arsonist in a lumber yard.

"La Tour, your squad will go into the village first! Be quick."

His shouts alerted the few villagers not already aware of us. Within moments, the women, children, and elderly there gathered to watch us, helpless before our guns.

I tried to reason, "Corporal, fire high on the first bursts. Over the buildings. Give those people time to take cover. There are no men there, no guns. This is appalling."

Lescoux was slow to acknowledge me. He neither consented nor protested. I began to repeat myself, making it sound like a request and not passing along an order.

Again Lescoux said nothing. He appeared to relent, but I think more at my seething sincerity than fear of humiliation. I moved to Corporal Bierbach to prevail similarly upon him—though he was not in my squad—but Mirvais interrupted sharply.

"La Tour, are you ready to advance? Saint-Avold, a squad to flank the place. Prepare to burn it and leave the animals for the vultures."

Lescoux fired high and wide—the people fled, most behind the walls to a depression near a hill—then he lowered the muzzle and shot up the pens and dirt. Bierbach's bullets ripped the facades of the dry mud homes, but he was not averse to living targets. An old man and a half-lame donkey could not escape, and the defiant village leader would not. All shot down.

Mirvais ordered Saint-Avold and his men to burn the village. And to take prisoners. "Why?" I glanced at Mirvais. He was raving. Coming undone. Too-bright eyes, a pallor in his voice. He waved my officer friend on with an imperious gloved hand and seemed unconcerned about the burning village. "Cease fire!" Then he rode away.

Our platoon rode with more shame than pride. We captured a group of villagers, including a lame, weather-worn old man. His only weapon was the burning, almost pitiless gaze he cast upon us.

The Major and the Berber considered each other for a moment. The villager, having taken the measure of the man before him, could only sneer.

Mirvais snapped at him. "What is the name of this village?"

"Imi Imejdi."

"Where is this leader of yours? Akka Ahêddây. The demon you adore. Tell me and I will send you food and medicine. Horses. Money."

Khoussaila translated the French. The cretin was a fixture in the garrison, a man who more than any other, wanted to help the Major seize Akka Ahêddây. But I wondered about this Berber's ulterior motive, about the price for helping us kill his brethren. Perhaps it was just loyalty to another who happens to have the only key to a hidden treasure vault. Khoussaila scowled at the old Berber, though I sensed that some of the exchange was a masquerade.

By his appearance alone, Khoussaila could inspire truth in those he interrogated. Short, bow-legged and barrel-chested, he walked with a limp. Below his protruding brow, he had a face like stale brown parchment. A creature of the sun. Perhaps fifty years old. His typical expression, around a white-flecked beard and moustache, was either blank or a scowl. When he jeered, thin lips pulled back from peculiar pegs of teeth and his skin grew tight, and he somewhat resembled a human skull. But scowling or jeering or laughing, his eyes were feral, windows to a wicked fire. His voice was beguiling and unnerving, a tenor with a texture of oily gravel. He wore upon his head a red turban, and on it a bizarre mélange: a bullet shell, a posthumous French medal, a brooch and two shriveled fingers. The trinkets announced where he had been, what he had done, and served as a warning.

"I asked him where his friends are, but he only tells me his name. Hamou Sekla."

Hamou's vacant stare conveyed his contempt for Mirvais's offer. He appeared to be half-crazy in the way that decades of harsh living wear out flesh and mind. Finally, the old fellow pointed to the western horizon, at a distant but distinct pass and spoke emphatically.

Khoussaila rendered it in short form: "Old man says *Ait Amour*. Many warriors at an old *igherm* near pasturage. Akka maybe near there."

"Tell him he lies," Mirvais told Rehou to reply. The Berber hesitated briefly, perhaps because these exact words lacked decorum, even for someone of an enemy tribe. He converted the French to Tamazight. I think Khoussaila didn't care if the old man was insulted. He just wanted to make sure the villager and Mirvais understood each other.

Mirvais's calculation was transparent, as always. He was careful to pressure someone who was neither fragile, lest he look abusive, nor too strong-willed, for he would lose face if his overtures were rebuffed.

The old man replied in a rapid, dog-like growl of words. He would spit on us if no penalty would be imposed, and almost did anyway.

Khoussaila translated into French. "More in my simple words than in your difficult philosophy. Ahêdday is not here. He fight other *Iroumin*. Go find him if you dare. It was no secret you were coming. When your men meet his, Allah decide."

The Imazighen fighters would be almost the same distance from us as we were from the garrison. Or, Akka's men could be nearby right now, watching and waiting. Either way, Akka had called our bluff. Mirvais walked off alone to ponder his options and tactics. He made a lovely target.

Corporal Lemarche seethed. "Goddamn mud dwellers. Look at those huts. Built last year, falling apart today. How can they live like nomad rats? We should kill them just to save the trouble later." His rabid bigotry was like an oozing scab. Lemarche meant what he said, and if allowed, would bring his vision of death to life.

We prepared lunch, awaiting our next move. No one spoke to the villagers. They wept over their two dead. The youngest children had never seen *Iroumin*, and were especially fearful. Mirvais stuttered when he was nervous.

"Khoussaila, r-r-ride ahead with La Tour, Pressiat and Aumont to in-in-investigate. I want to know what is out there. Take f-fast f-fresh horses. You have s-six hours. I'll decide based on your findings."

Aumont took me aside moments before we rode out. "We will watch closely for the enemy," he said, "but be wary of Khoussaila, too."

"This is Morocco. Very little is ever what it seems to be. Watch him carefully."

Our quartet rode off north and west. Rehou Khoussaila seemed to know exactly where to go, as if the landscape was a trail through his own thoughts. Any or every minute, I half-expected to be shot.

Rehou halted us at a trail juncture halfway to Ait Amour. He sniffed the air like a predator, then led us to a freshly abandoned camp. Fire embers still glowed, near the tracks of a dozen or more men with horses. Moving east and upward along the stream. We had not surprised the Ait Atta. "I can smell them watching," Rehou said. I believed he could.

Now Aumont did something unusual, for him. He dismounted, slipped a pack of Galouis cigarettes from his pocket and lit up. He offered one to Khoussaila, who accepted. Aumont knelt to light one from the Berber fire. These were Lescoux's cigarettes. He savored the admission, and slyly reveled in inducing a Moslem to accept a French gift.

The Berbers did not want to fight us, not yet. The old villager had told the truth, and he had lied, in both ways delaying our return to the Dades. The Berbers could now slip between us and the fort. If so, the only way to catch them or even find them would be to backtrack in double-time. In effect, we had chased the Ait Atta in a large, futile circle.

Koussaila said ominously, "They either fear you, or are preparing an attack. I will bet Allah knows it is not out of fear. Several hundred of Akka's fighters will strike. Soon."

On cue, Mirvais announced our hasty return to the garrison, loudly enough for all to hear. "To engage or kill that twisted Ahêddây!"

We turned homeward on a different route—straight through Ait Seddrate land. We passed only one village. The pale wilderness was lifeless, suffering. Few birds flew in the gray sky. We saw no Berbers for the remainder of that day nor throughout the next—although almost certainly they had seen *us*. Mirvais drove us across rolling ridges and down hardscrabble slopes. Alternately, we horsemen rode and walked or scouted ahead. The troops marched in dull silence with sore feet and foul moods. Their sour, sometimes obscene expressions stood for the dialogue they wanted to have. After a week in the field, we were no closer to finding Akka Ahêddây than when we first left the garrison.

Mirvais reminded the Légionnaires of pride of place and duty and proper formation. He proclaimed that they looked less like a column of soldiers than a convention of sheep. They bristled. Some whispered curses.

Aumont mumbled to me as he walked past leading his mount by the reins. "It's easy for him to urge a strong pace. He's always on horseback."

"Come now, fellows," he muttered, "We must complete our descent so we can move around the mountain flank and arrive to the garrison from the west."

Azourki loomed behind. Fat, gray clouds closed in above us. Could we touch them? A light mist turned to rain. A sharp breeze made us more irritable for the dust blew straight into our eyes. I was concerned at the low supplies and the distance to go. Mirvais should have been, too, for now we were more vulnerable to Berber stratagems.

I felt the great need for a bath. To wash away death and dirt and sweat. But also I was sore in my left arm and shoulder. This was a soldier's lot, and I paid it little mind. But the skin was very oddly taut and numb.

We passed through worlds. Barren rock fields. A thin stand of juniper. A lot of *maquis*. Broad bands of reddish earth and more boundless rock fields. Rivulets ran away, down toward rivers, oasis and desert. We were in dazzled silence broken only by hooves on stones, the thump of boots, an occasional clank of gear. We diverged around networks of veins and gullies that in eons past had been carved by water. The late afternoon sun swung behind us and began casting great shadows into the valley below.

Then I noticed Saint-Avold look behind us, uneasily peering upslope. I followed his line of sight. Fresnay was galloping his tired mount full out. Dangerously so on the broken landscape. The hoofbeats upon the loosened scree drew within earshot. Mirvais ordered a halt.

Fresnay was in a dither, his animal winded from its frenetic journey. Mirvais, Du Thierry and Fresnay had an urgent exchange beyond earshot. I heard a crop of speculation; quickly reaped from sown facts, pass from front to rear as we stood by. We were being pursued by Berbers. Fresnay had seen Ahêddây. The other garrison force had captured Akka instead of they, stealing their glory.

The banter took minds off the terrain and the heavy packs that hung from sore shoulders like ballasts of sand.

Mirvais summoned his horse and troop officers for a parley.

"'Four hours ago, Fresnay saw at least fifty Atta horsemen moving toward the valley over a far ridge to the south. Rehou is trailing them. He is sure there are others, too. Du Thierry, you Saint-Avold, and Aumont will pursue! Take extra ammunition and engage."

There was silence as everyone considered the risks of dividing a small and tired force so near the enemy. Du Thierry would take fifty French cavalry, a squad of Goums and two *spahis*, a total of about eighty men.

Mirvais asked, "Are there any questions?" But his tone implied he wanted none to answer.

Du Thierry was the wise one. "What if I don't find the enemy, but he finds me?"

Mirvais replied, "Ingenuity is the mother of victory."

"Leave now," he uttered to the gallant captain, who may have expected more guidance.

Mirvais exhorted us. "We won't stop! No rest! The faster we'll find the enemy! Or get home! And when we do, rations and wine and free time will be doubled!"

He was surely uneasy entering these extra hours. We, the hunter were now likely the prey. Or we had been all along. He impatiently waved horsemen and troops on.

The troops rose from quick step, to a trot, to a run, in good order. Nothing charges the body like the thrill of urgency. And we were heading at last to hot meals, cool wine and a warm bed. Still, this seemed like a hasty retreat. Or a headlong fool's errand.

Mirvais sent several horsemen ahead to probe the terrain with Sergeant Bierbach on Fresnay's spent mount, and Ouzzine, one of the three remaining Berbers. There was an eerie silence, and I noted apprehensively that Khoussaila turned away from us. He headed east and neither told Mirvais nor looked back, like he was just off on a casual errand. The Berber and his fine black stallion remained vigorous even after these rugged days.

We reached the valley floor a half hour later. Well ahead, we could see a wide grove of palm trees between two long gentle slopes. Beyond it was the final approach to the garrison. Mirvais ordered a regular pace. Shortly after, Sergeant Autielle raised his arm to signal a halt. Looking beyond him I saw several bareback horses just within the palms. Men would not be this far from the *tizi* at this time of day.

From the saddle, Mirvais studied the palms with his binoculars. He ordered Dinant's horsemen and Pressiat's six squads forward. He uttered casually, "Make any enemy contact," as if they were to do nothing more complicated than prepare an omelette. He ordered Sergeant Messac and ten horsemen to advance apace with him. Pressiat's fifty men fell out and formed up.

Imagine these next events. They happened in about two minute's time. The troops and horsemen advanced toward the palms. Our entire force was divided and thus reduced by over a third. Mirvais watched the men through his glasses. All of us remaining behind keenly peered on as well. Everyone was alert, but none anticipated a firefight. Not me. Perhaps we had just surprised a . . .

I sensed movement to our left, and glanced there. Others did, too, but all of us responded a flash too late. Like corpses rising from burial, a line of Berbers two deep were rising from a thick blanket of dirt over a shallow depression not fifty meters away.

"Major! Column left!" I hoped to conceal the panic in my voice.

Mirvais whirled about. He saw them aiming Lebels at us. Surprised by phantoms, we were not able to fire our guns before they. Many of us were about to be killed. But good soldiers all, the troops and horsemen responded without being ordered.

The enemy fired first, with a sickening roar. Ten of us fell dead, a near number wounded. Légion blood began to run. Some of us cried out in ungodly wrath. And terror.

Pressiat and Dinant were over one hundred meters away—closer to the trees than to us—but their men looked back to us in horror. I knew all would be inclined to return and reinforce. Together we could annihilate the Berbers. If they didn't kill most of us first.

"Men, f-f-fire!" Mirvais screamed.

Just as our guns fired, they pitched to their stomachs. We were astonished. Bullets hit eight men; the rest spattered into the earth beyond. Their return fire was ragged, but took down five more of us.

Our tactics were an open book for these fiends. Akka had precisely predicted our reactions. For just as Pressiat's and Dinant's squads peered backward, away from the palms, forty or more Berber horsemen shed a camouflage of fronds and exploded into view.

We certainly needed Pressiat's troops. But they and Dinant's horsemen now turned to face the Ait Atta—what a shock!—already coming into point-blank range and leveling their guns. But they did not fire, almost like they were daring our men to shoot first. Both sides could inflict crippling loss. We horsemen and troops near Mirvais facing the Berber rifle-men would endure another volley in the next instant. In which direction should Pressiat's men fire? The Ait Atta riders pushed a wave visible fury ahead of them. They were not to show mercy. Pressiat and his men lost the initiative and wavered. But Dinant, ahh, he led his few men into a brave charge.

"Fire! F-Fire!" Mirvais screamed at us.

I fired until my Lebel was empty. Others froze, too shocked by this lightning from a placid sky. I saw Autielle and three mates in the rank nearest the charging Berbers aim their rifles. I wondered how many of us would survive in surrender. Lescoux's men fired. His shot twisted a hard-riding Berber from the saddle. He slammed into the dust. A fine gray horse was hit by a less accurate shot, its rider flung headlong as the dead animal tumbled. Bullets whipped past me. The Ait Atta swept onward in stride. I heard Dinant's dozen fellows get off a pistol volley and the Berbers a rifle flurry, and then their lines slammed into each other. I glanced: some foe deliberately steered to collision with Dinant's horses. What sounds! Screaming animals, bodies thudding, men bellowing. Most of Dinant's men were down. The Berbers came on, less a handful, about to penetrate Pressiat's ranks. Some yielded to terror, dropping their rifles a moment before the leading attackers hurtled into them, straight towards Mirvais.

An Ait Atta rifleman shouted at my men, and at Mirvais. *"Manee drem, Tafransist tarwa n lqehab—Do you want to live Christian Bastards?"* as he gestured that we drop our weapons. It was a clear, if fantastic, implication. Casualties inflicted, victory achieved, humiliation imposed, perhaps they would let us live—or just kill us more easily if we surrendered. And break the Code-*a Légionnaire never yields.*

I drew my pistol and veered my mount toward the oncoming Berber. At that moment I blindly preferred death to dishonor. I spurred to a gallop, and the ten men with me followed. Lescoux and his comrades fired again. Three more Berbers went down. Of their horsemen, a dozen had stopped to hold rifles on Pressiat's squad. The remaining men rampaged toward Mirvais. And me. Their flaring white eyes did not blink and, surrounded by brown skin, a beard and turban and some a *tajjelabith* hood, they appeared demonic.

Lescoux and his other mates did not live two more seconds. Two riders released their reins, stood in the saddle stirrups, aimed and fired. I witnessed a bullet take off half of Lescoux's head.

Concentrating my eyes and gun on the two lead Berbers, I shot one from the saddle. At that moment, I would have killed anything. Two *shleuh* came right at me. I fired, but missed. The other one swung a sword. A French sword! I swung my head and body away but to balance myself in the saddle, I left the reins in both hands hanging out under the blade. It sliced through the leather. I was leaning too far over, and fell right from my mount. At full gallop. The bastard! My horse flew on. I hit soft dirt, just missing rocks with my backside. And my pistol tumbled away! Now unarmed, I was just about dead. I snatched up a stone in each hand and waited for the Berber to swing around on me. I focused on his head and when he was almost upon me with his upraised sword, I threw hard. Jaw shattered, teeth smashed. Now it was his turn to fall from the saddle. Now I had another horse!

I instantly saw that Mirvais was unprotected. He must escape or be captured, and so he spurred his mount across in front of me. Berbers could put rounds in his back, but quickly lost the bolt-action moment as Mirvais reached a shielding down curve in the hill. Two Ait Atta chased after him, but his horse vaulted from sight, into the safety of the palm trees.

Be they mounted or afoot, no Berber could hope to retain the respect of his fellows if he wavered in battle, no matter the odds he faced. Cowards were punished by disgrace, banishment, or worse. But it was our foot troops who lost nerve. With forty or more rifles to the right of them, and ten Berbers charging on, the crossfire would annihilate them. One choice loomed for them. Someone shouted: "Lower your weapons. Drop your weapons now!"

On this seething Berber horse, I was separated from my six remaining mates. I now faced eight *shleuh*. I had but one sane option. To bolt in the wake of Mirvais. By small miracle, the bullet meteors blazed by me. I dared not look behind. I was a *djen*, deflecting the shots. None of the Ait Atta gave chase. And soon, I would discover why.

I saw Mirvais ahead. The fort was about ten kilometers to his right. Yet he continued straight on. It occurred to me that he could not return to the fort, nor could he enter without his men. It would be the ultimate humiliation.

My Berber mount, a mottled gray steed, was magnificent. Pure raw power. I could barely control the animal. Mirvais moved at a brisk pace, but in moments, I was just yards behind him. When finally, he turned to the hoofbeats, he was thoroughly startled to see me. Guilty. Ashamed. Exposed. And he could not hide it despite the firm set to his jaw.

He said, "We will c-catch Du Thierry and help him if we can."

I did not reply.

"He is n-not far ahead." Mirvais was not riding full out. He had no choice but to continue on, with hell behind and death ahead.

In minutes we would come upon Du Thierry's contingent. And we were likely to find the Berbers that Fresnay and Rehou had seen from their lookout. It remained a question: had the Ait Atta—twice—deliberately set themselves as bait? *Far ahead I saw the blood-red uniforms of the spahis. I noticed for the first time, I was amazed at what bright targets they made-Red.* No matter the final outcome here, one reaction was already certain. The carnage we suffered on this mission would greatly stoke the rage against the Berbers, and Akka n-Ali will be no friend of anyone but the most wicked.

Mirvais hastened onward. He wanted to enter in grand style, no questions asked.

SIX:

CLASH

Akka Ahêddây, astride his horse It'ij, watched events from atop the ridge. Below to his left were Larbi's men, the front rank of whom in white *tajjelabith* were visible in a walnut grove. To his right, near the east bank of the Dades, two separate enemy horse squadrons moved across open level land. From Akka's vantage, the terrain between the river and the hills began to narrow. The French lines, three abreast and six to eight deep, flowed into the rough form of an arrow. Two more Frenchmen—an officer and a subordinate on a Berber mount—chased after them. At that moment, the cavalry crested a gentle slope.

Ahead of them in plain view were Larbi's thirty mounted Aït Atta, who by design turned away, as if roused from a nap, and receded toward a ravine at the end of the low ridge. They intended to lure the curious but cautious enemy to its mouth. Initially the *Iroumin* would only want to gauge the Berbers' direction and number. Within half a kilometer, nearing the wide funnel of the gully, the French slowed to peer after their quarry, who retreated from sight. Their prudent pause was exactly what Akka and Larbi desired.

A new swarm poured forth toward the *Iroumin*. Larbi expected that good soldiers so challenged, would not turn to flee. Exactly so. In classic fashion, the Légion horsemen broadened their lines into a rough arc and massed accurate rifle fire from the saddle. Berbers tumbled in death. A second volley ripped them. They could not sustain such losses.

Larbi expected this, too. He sent forward a third and even larger contingent of Ait Atta. Their maddened outcries were amplified by the terrain, seeming to rise up from within it. The French would not be able to fire quickly enough to assure their survival.

Akka saw the Légion falter, like a foolhardy man who reconsiders his brash entry to the lion cage. The enemy response turned bizarre, as if it had two minds. A portion of them, the *spahis* to the rear, turned away to avoid a perhaps suicidal battle. It seemed they thought their comrades would do likewise. But the commander—so intent on the enemy to the front that he did not notice the rear ranks departing—bellowed and the line of horsemen charged behind and to the side of him into an expanse several hundred meters wide.

Mirvais and I arrived at the instant the *spahis* dashed by in the opposite direction. We were confused. Then Du Thierry, oblivious to us, ordered an *advance*. The *spahis* would ride to the fort, while we collided in battle. Each side wanted to shock the other. Moments later, yelling fiendishly at the gallop, we loosed a fusillade. Twenty or so Berbers—neat punctures and jagged red holes burst upon them, it was almost beautiful—flew from their saddles as if swept by an invisible hand. Wounded or crashing horses tumbled in a frenzy of dirt and thrashing legs. The bedlam slowed and tripped the trailing ranks.

But these fellows had new tricks of their own, a gift of hard training with tactic we had not seen before. The wave of Ait Atta horsemen split left and right, to sweep around the flanks of our smaller body engulfing us on three sides. Our lines would be forced to cleave and turn away from each other, unable to safely cover any vector of the field but the one directly before us.

We hurtled through the parting Berber ranks and in that instant, they loosed a volley. Our fifty became forty. I saw Du Thierry get clipped by a bullet. Mirvais, beside him, was pale as a pearl. In that instant, he was surely thinking—*to escape from one merciless fray—only to ride directly to another that is worse.*

Our backs were briefly exposed, and as we spun about, the remainder of the first Berber wave closed from behind. Squeezed from the sides, harried from the rear, we could not fight coherently. I noticed that Mirvais remained within the core of thirty whirling and shooting horsemen, a gosling in a gaggle surrounded by foxes.

The rest of us beyond this core scattered. In an instant, like a pack selecting prey, I saw Lieutenant Aumont amidst a knot of *shleuh* bristling with French rifles, daring him to die. They did not fire, but instead swiftly separated him from the fray and drove him toward the gully. I could not imagine the purpose.

Those of us remaining had to choose instantly between fight or flight. A notch in the bottom of the hill, behind a line of boulders, offered the best position for a dismounted defense. Four men set course, the rest of us followed—and bounded towards it without orders from Mirvais or Du Thierry. The Major was swept along, a frantic swimmer on a swift tide. Most of the Ait Atta flowed after us, but only after several crucial seconds of hesitation.

Du Thierry was giving the orders. "Volley fire! Volley fire!" Mirvais was almost ashen. I looked for blood from a wound but saw none. From the boulders, we immediately unleashed two vicious barrages, further wasting the Berber ranks, which lurched and recoiled from the shock wave.

And this slight advantage presented one last, brief possibility of escape.

The Captain bellowed, "Remount! Let's get the hell out of here!"

And so we did, forty of the sixty Frenchmen and Goums who rode into this battle not five minutes ago. On horses more frightened than their riders, some among us wounded, we ran full out in headlong retreat between the confused Berbers. Mirvais was not so dazed that he could not be in the front ranks, a long horse stride closer to safety than most of the men. Du Thierry, just behind him, opened his mouth to scream, and at that instant, a Berber bullet struck him through the neck. He died right there, in the saddle, blood pumping from an artery.

Still, we kept some order. In fine fashion, several men took up the reins of horses bearing the wounded, and a five-man rear guard remained to scatter cover fire with their pistols. I was one of them. I knew the wet boundary of the Dades was ahead. By chance, we were approaching at a good ford. This time I glanced behind. A few Berbers were giving chase, but not so many that would overwhelm us. By the time the Berbers recovered from our decimating fire and hasty surprise escape, most of us were halfway to the river.

Several last shots rang out. To my horror, my magnificent animal mount sprawled to earth. I flew from saddle to dirt, from the clarity of action to black terror. In a moment, reality flooded in, and with it, visions of torture, decapitation and the like. The Berbers could be brutal, and three times in combat with them over as many days was more than proof.

My cohorts were gone. A haze of red dust hung in the air as a cluster of *shleuh* closed in around me. I stood up to die, proudly I suppose, although I felt like an unlucky fool. I did not look at them, but at the far heights of Azourki, gray and fading in the evening light. I wanted it to be my last sight in this life. But the Berbers only chattered. I was a specimen. They seemed as curious about me as they were angry.

Many of them did not fit the cliché of murderous beasts. There was no hysteria, no blood-rage, no madness. Instead, they were in subdued but odd good humor, as if we all had only been playing a childhood game.

They drove toward the gully, a herd of one. I saw some of their comrades quickly, roughly stripping our dead of weapons, ammunition, clothing. It seemed deliberate, systematic; no doubt a task undertaken many times before. At one moment or another, they prayed for their own dead. Grieving fellows draped the bloody bodies over spare mounts. In a dreadful dirge of gunshots, shattered, helpless horses and men—French and Berber—were dispatched. The dazed rider of a dying horse ended its agony with a bullet, and uttered a faster, less fervent prayer, perhaps for the animal's spirit and good service. Across the field, a writhing Légionnaire died unattended and alone. I dared not go to him or two others wounded nearby. I turned eyes to the living, to those ahead of me. I saw Aumont. Like me, he was utterly bewildered to be alive. He turned pale as he pondered the prospect of being saved for some gruesome entertainment.

A Berber boy came to bind our wrists. Aumont was almost oblivious as he watched the Ait Atta gather their dead and wounded. Both of us were stunned to see two Berbers kill one of their hopeless comrades. Then they turned their attention to the two fatally wounded Frenchmen. All their Légion horses were dead or scattered. We were appalled to see the men shot outright. As with their own comrade, maybe this was an act of Berber mercy. But I could tell Aumont chose not to see this.

Three Berbers approached, dickering rapidly amongst themselves as if haggling over sheep. From a few deciphered words, I caught their satisfaction in our valuable capture. Just then, a bearded elder fellow with a noble air, one of the leaders, signaled for imminent departure. Night was falling. The warriors would need to rapidly withdraw far into the mountains from certain French pursuit.

The *amghar* might have been proud of his men. I was proud of ours. We horsemen had fought well against high odds, avoiding utter catastrophe, inflicting heavy casualties on a larger force, and many escaped to tell the tale. The survivors would be exhilarated to reach the garrison. I hoped that some there would thoroughly repay the *spahis* for their desertion. With their courage, we may have defeated these Berbers. Or perhaps at least we would not be prisoners.

The noble old Berber rode toward a younger man in a pale blue *tajjelabith,* astride a fabulous gray horse. They were mutually respectful. I could not tell who was subordinate. They conferred half visible in deep shadow beyond my earshot. I sensed we were the subject.

It was a windfall.

"The exchange must be two-for-one," Akka said to Larbi. "We have some new advantage with the *Ifranssewen,* I think to regain most of our captured men."

Larbi also suspected another angle.

"It is possible, Ahêddây," he said, "that they know of the Légion's plans.

"Yes, that, too. But they are stubborn and loyal. You must convince them to yield what they know. Find the key as you can."

"Now we must go. Divide the men. Half will leave with me tonight for the village. The rest remain with you, for after today the *Iroumin* will thirst for revenge."

The sun set that evening with a ravishing beauty. The Berbers were preparing to move and they were taking us with them. I knew Aumont feared he would meet a terrible end. Although by his faith and intelligence he was a stronger spirit than most of us, he also somehow seemed less of a survivor. But he seemed to take heart in that he would die alongside me, his friend and countryman.

"Some sad battle, eh?" Aumont sputtered.

We discovered that Berber permission to continue breathing did not mean license to enjoy it. Suddenly, a Berber reeking of sweat and animal, leaped from his horse before Aumont and flashed a knife very close to his neck. He punctuated the display with a glare for silence. Aumont was so silent he did not breathe. If this was the moment of death—it passed like a faint shadow.

The Berbers turned toward the peaks, and we prisoners moved with them. A beautiful, final blue-gray light fell on the Azourki peak. I did not know whether to feel calm or terrified, a prisoner glad to be alive or dreading a slow death. I looked back at Aumont. A living ghost. Catching my glance, he faithfully gathered himself.

We were shoved onward by gunpoint. Again we trod uphill. Soon, darkness closed off most of the world around us. We were walking mid-column with only a few meters of visibility. In the dead of night, our slow parade of a hundred or more entered a narrow gorge where a narrow stream flowed. We plodded on beside it through a wash of starlight, with breath frosty and legs straining. I estimated the route was at least twelve kilometers across gullies and ridges. So glad to be alive, but given only warm water, I grew weary, then exhausted. I tried to focus only on the canopy of stars.

Before dawn, we arrived at an encampment beside an old *igherm*. Perhaps two hundred people, half of them warriors, were waiting to jeer us. The taunts, a raucous swelling chorus of *taghwrirt* from the women and howls from the men, were meant to humiliate and terrify. They accomplished both as they emerged from the murk, messages of glee and hatred and mourning in the general clamor for French blood.

Nor was that all. The initial Berber ambush at the palm grove had claimed its share of captives as well. We saw five, then six of our fellows: Dutroix, Lemarche, Messac, Buhl, Plau, and Pressiat. They looked half-dead from fear and fatigue, probably having been driven even farther than Aumont and I. At least eight of us, then, including two officers, had been culled, by design or at random. Mirvais had escaped enemy clutches, but barely. Perhaps he owed his life to Captain Du Thierry, who was now food for jackals upon the field. I cringed at the thought of the annihilation. And if any witnesses to the Major's flight remained alive—besides we few with the uncertain future—his career was doomed.

I knew the minds of my mates were filled with hope and dread. But I was sure that if the Berbers intended to kill us they would have done so by now. We prisoners had value as barter for their captured tribesmen. Exchanges were sometimes made for one good reason. Our men might be killed if we refused. And Command did not want it widely known that prisoners of ours were sometimes tortured or killed while the Berbers would refrain if omens indicated they show mercy. *Ddiya,* the customary payment in some acceptable form by an offending Berber to the clan of another who had been murdered, could not be claimed in war. Justice had to be accomplished by other means.

The Berbers did not chain us together but led us past bitter, sorrowful faces to a line of rooms within the *igherm.* Jail cells. In a forlorn facade, full of ghosts and death. Aumont, in the space beside mine, expressed a different kind of fear. He was a devout Catholic and we plainly heard him invoke faith in the fervent hope it would gain him reprieve.

"Dear God, I wish to atone for the killing I have helped to cause. There must be an end to this torment, a path from this world of death, Lord. Show me and I will take it . . . Blessed are the peacemakers, for they shall be called the children of God. What doth the Lord require of these, but to do justly, and to love mercy, and to walk humbly with God?"

He repeated these last two phrases over and over. A speaking meditation. Even as sleep overtook him he continued to mumble, desperately wanting some union with the Almighty. I think for all of us. I was very moved.

Several brief hours later, two captors booted me awake. I was immediately awash with harsh thirst and hunger. But no water or food was offered. My anger rose to fever pitch at the suffering imposed upon me and my fellows.

Then I thought of those wretches in the Marrakech dungeon.

The Imazighen gestured for me to stand. They abruptly led me outside. Aumont was already there, I fell in behind him. The others were pulled in after me. I could sense their misery. But also their relief; still alive, their throats not cut, they blinked like hungover dullards.

Most villagers gathered again. The two men led us toward a tent. I could not believe what befell my eyes. There, the old Berber prince, resembling an etching of Charlemagne, sat on a stool. Posing for a photograph! The photographer, wearing a motley of Berber and European garb, spoke to him in French. They were collaborating on the *amghar's* pose! Seeing us the *amghar* waved the photographer aside. He pointed to Aumont, then each of us in turn. But said nothing.

"You will remove your jackets," said one of the Berbers in dreadful French.

This must surely be that moment of truth. I began shaking almost uncontrollably, convinced that my next experience would be death, and that they did not want blood on the uniforms they wished to acquire. I began to do as ordered. What would be the point of refusal? As I released the buttons and opened the panels for the first time in several days, the foul, unconfined odor of my body swept out. My woolen undershirt, partly unbuttoned, so white and untainted when I donned it several mornings ago, was no longer much of a garment at all. Still, my skin felt comfortable this close to the cool morning air.

Then the two Berber men took a long step back from me. I reasoned that it must have been the sorry state of my hygiene. A long moment passed. They remained stupefied. Eyes fell upon me. I grew terribly self-conscious. I looked to my mates, who were as puzzled as I. Then they, too, reacted as if there was something wrong with me that I didn't know.

The old man on the stool spoke a brief command to his Berber seconds. One of them ushered me into the tent. Now I was very concerned. Except for great thirst and fatigue and hunger and a leaden heart—nothing minor, but not fatal—I felt normal, unaware of any unusual or worrisome condition. In a strange time suspension, the Berber and I just gazed at each other. Then I looked down at myself. Nothing. My hand crept up to my face. Nothing. Then down the left side of my neck to the shoulder . . .

A small monkish fellow entered the tent with the second Berber. He wore a turban and was further and fully hidden beneath a hood. It appeared big in proportion to the body, which was draped to the ankles in a black *djellabah*. The only feature to be plainly seen was his eyes, with a freakish sheen, like someone ever on the verge of weeping or mirth.

"Sh'nnu ismak?" I asked nervously in Arabic. What is your name? There was no reply.

"Comment vous appelez-vous?"

The fellow did not want to talk. Or he was deaf. Or comprehended neither Arabic nor French. He just looked at me. *"Ikh tinna rebbi,"* was all he said. He touched my face, held his fingertips to my cheek, and then snatched his hand away, as if those fingers had touched a hot stove. He turned to leave and mumbled a phrase to his cohort.

They led me out. My fellows were waiting, also stripped of their jackets. A Berber woman distributed *tijjloubah* to them. The jackets had likely been searched and were to be put to some other use. As decoys, perhaps. Then Dutroix, Lemarche, Messac, Buhl, Plau, and Pressiat—all but Aumont—were led back toward the *igherm.* Then an old man handed each of them a loaf of bread.

Aumont and I remained before the seated man. He directed his first words to Alain.

"I Ahmed Larbi. You listen my bad French. You sick of war. But not so much as we. Here are choices. Maybe one answer your prayers. But you must answer *me*, for your God will not. I can set you free, without horse. If by miracle you travel distance of a day-long ride and reach your fort while chased by men who want to kill you slowly, then you free. Soon after your brave escape, you be back killing Ait Atta to live. But . . . if you travel with us to a village and say more about your garrisons and your God, then maybe we offer another, better freedom. We consider turning you westward with a horse, safe passage and our blessing. From these valleys of death. How say you?"

I could see that Aumont was unnerved. "Valley of Death" chilled him. God worked in mysterious ways, and this was one mystery he did not want to solve with a *takummiyt* slicing his throat. At once I saw the scope of possibilities. Aumont would soon reach the long-awaited end of his service. Like all of us, he was surely already presumed dead. Emerging from a wilderness of war after his term had expired, with no questions to answer, would be true blessing. But I was leery. Helping the Berbers understand what? Aumont was being coerced to treason. Nonetheless, I would err on the side of life. Aumont felt the same.

He resolutely said, "I will take your offer. In my Lord's world two more days of life could lead to eternal happiness."

"And what of my friend here? He helped to save me."

Said Larbi, "He wise as you. Or at least not so in love with his army or nation that he, too, would not negotiate to live."

I did not know what Larbi meant. But I clearly understood what he said next.

The old man spoke directly to me. "My friend, you have ancient sick. We don't want you here. But your own afraid people won't want you anywhere. So you must stay with us until we can return you."

He gazed intensely at my left neck and shoulder.

I touched the scabrous skin there, a large patch of rough ulcerating flesh. Oddly, my left ear hurt. Still disbelieving and shocked, I glanced down at the stigma, not able to see most of it, nor truly wanting to. I did not know what to make of the ailment.

He continued ominously. "This disease almost as old as men. You may feel it a curse. Allah the Merciful gives it you as a gift. Terrible though it be, make of it what you will."

The word *leprosy* rattled through me mind, body and soul. I was sickened. Imagine receiving a death sentence in such a way.

"Aumont, you be guided by these men. Ride a horse. Eat our food. Here is object for passage. On your behalf, through Ait Morrhad and Seddrate to Akka n-Ali."

The photographer stepped up to Larbi, unbidden, and snapped the transfer of an inscribed tablet from the warrior chief to the humble captor's outstretched hand.

Larbi chafed, "Pierre, step back."

Aumont accepted the odd item. The man who few Frenchmen had seen but thousands like himself had been directed to destroy. Larbi continued.

"Akka Ahêddây leads our fight for this land and our place on it. Given by Allah. We won't be told how to live. But we are merciful people, Lieutenant. And peacemakers."

SEVEN:

AFFLICTION

The photographer Pierre was "on assignment." We seven prisoners in new *djellabahs* sat chained to stakes watching life around the *igherm*. As Pierre seized it on film. Scouts, couriers, and pack mules converged from all points. I could not guess our position, except that it was well eastward of yester morning's camp. In the land of Ait Wahlim. Everyone was wary, even tense, a flock ready to bolt at any sign of a threat. Pierre, too, but he focused on the crackling energy and used his twin-lens camera, a tool of diplomacy. After all, a Frenchman was asking Berbers for permission to photograph them. They often granted it, after a token payment of a *goursh* and with questions about his strange device and assurances from Larbi or his aides. Still, suspicion fell on Pierre like rain. He established rapport with only a few. Not with Aumont, who smiled at Pierre, nervously, and would not allow his face in the picture. A future traitor should not be identified. Nor did Pierre seem interested in photographing us. That or for some reason the Berbers would not let him.

We could not talk to Pierre, or to each other. The Berbers demanded silence. Twice we began to chat or whisper. Our captors cast intimidating glances. It was clear: shut up if we wanted to live. And several Atta spoke or at least understood a little French, so we could keep few verbal secrets. The dominant language among us became silence.

Not that I wanted to talk to my mates anyway. Lemarche, for example. Soon after my arrival at the fort, I had an encounter with him. The profane, ranting Corporal claimed with bogus *hauteur* that Maréchal Ney was five generations up the family tree. Five eons from the jungle vine is more likely. I almost wished he would burst into a tirade and commit de facto suicide. Dutroix and Messac. Both born farmers in Auvergne, both black market in Marseilles. Messac had been cooperative when he wanted something—"extra time with that brown girl" or "to be excused from the work detail"—but at other times, he was antisocial or a boor. And he displayed much fondness for cognac. If cosmic justice was in session, Dutroix might soon pay for his storied sniper practice on that M'Gouna village. Buhl was a young trooper from Schnee Eifel with a choir boy's face and soft voice. I could see he was screaming inside but bottled it tightly for fear of dishonor. Plau, a veteran of combat missions and an *aspirant* with two years of service, was our superior. A forthright fellow, he was a gambler and a pipe smoker with a talent for bawdy jokes. The sixth fellow, a rifle Sergeant, was a cipher to me. His drawn face read like a map of distrust, or maybe just exhaustion. I think he was a last minute replacement for an injured man of 2nd Section. This was his first combat mission, and perhaps his last stop. Very little inner lives, however, were on display in this day-long muteness.

Late in the afternoon, three Ait Atta—two warriors with Lebels accompanying an *anahcham* of the Bou Iknifen, garbed in a fine black robe—escorted Aumont and Pierre from the *igherm*. Aumont, again in his uniform, looked almost happy to be on his way and that God had answered some of his prayers. Because of my "terrible gift," I was privileged to know the secret he denied the others. He would lie—to his captors, to himself and his countrymen should he escape Maroc—in order to live. That was not necessarily the Christian he wanted to be. The Berbers would not know the difference—though God would.

In my exhaustion, I dozed under a coarse blanket foul with horse sweat that had been provided. I felt a strange peace, an acceptance of what awaited me. Life was so much more . . . elemental. But fear was ever-present, and this second night, it surged. Booted awake again, we were shoved with urgency toward a line of pack animals and people.

"You scum march well enough on villages of old people and children," a wolfish fellow sneered in awkward French. "Now you'll move like Imazighen warriors!"

We were kicked into a brisk pace before choosing who would have the first horse privileges. We moved cross-country under starry skies of intermittent clouds. I had no sense of direction. But most Ait Atta could travel these trails blindfolded. Three horses were provided for us to share. At intervals, three of us rode and three walked. Or stumbled.

These people seemed tireless, able to function on little fuel and much inspiration. Weary fighters anywhere were always renewed by victory. The direction went uphill, steeply for grueling minutes, gently over hours. We reached a stream and crossed it without pause. Wet boots did not help our mood. Now the retinue split up. More than half of the people and mounted men rode away, eastward I think. We and the remaining parade entered a dry gorge which was barely wide enough for two horses or four men to walk abreast. It was a natural redoubt, a splendid choke point for any force attempting to pass through. The slopes became walls, the walls became thirty-meter cliffs and the sky narrowed to a slot. The terrain was like what you read about in the Bible—arid, desolate, forbidding—and also like that of the Book, indifferent to human slaughter and divine poetry.

At dawn, the trek stopped to rest and likely to remain hidden from planes or small horse patrols that had eluded the Atta. At once, I became aware of more discomfort in my condition. The disease, dormant for so long, was making its presence known. My skin itched and throbbed. I thought it was crawling in several directions. It was more sensitive to touch or movement; a hard stroke of my finger or a sudden turn of the head or body made the flesh numb and the nerves ache. Something was dreadfully wrong.

I listened closely to the Berbers to learn more Tamizight. By now most of my mates were crawling into the cave of their own heads. All but Buhl were too arrogant to be frightened and too ignorant to learn much by watching and listening. Know thy enemy as thyself, I always say. But this maxim was lost on these fellows. Nor could I explain it to them, lest I be overheard. I was powerless to advise anyone and I was not keen to protect subordinate and surly men although Plau and I were obligated. Let him fight that battle if he chose to. The essential truth was that all of us were equally at the Berbers' mercy. Above all, I was too horrified at my own plight to give a damn. Given that, and the way they ignored me, I doubted they would listen to me anyway. I was unclean. And unworthy.

The men did not realize they had an advantage here. That they were at least as safe among the enemy as their own people. Perhaps we were being hunted by Légion men who wanted to rescue us from presumably brutal treatment. But except to be sure that no one escaped, the Berbers did not harm us, and mostly ignored us, like a food commodity that had yet to ripen and become suitable for sale.

We began to move again at dusk. In an hour or two we reached a tent village. The women and children and a few armed boys greeted their clansmen with smiles and a peculiar chorus of happiness, and we six prisoners with hard silence. No five spread fingers to ward off evil for us.

I could not refrain from asking in the absence of a forbidding Berber, "Are you happy, Lemarche and Dutroix, to be on such an adventure with the people you hate?"

Dutroix knew I was alluding to his vicious marksmanship. He sneered dismissively. "I was doing my duty under the orders of Mirvais."

"No Berber will see the distinction if we meet the people you shot up!"

"Go to hell with this endless moralizing. I know about you. You think we are here for some mission of mercy. But we are soldiers!"

"And you are an animal."

Dutroix moved to strike me, but then thought better of the contact.

A horseman tossed at us a heavy goatskin full of water and a pouch of food. The others grabbed the goatskin from me, ignoring Plau, who was a senior officer, should quench his thirst first. My contempt for these buffoons reduced my little remaining concern for them as comrades. Then I saw they would not drink after me from the same container. A diseased person. Continuing captivity among the so-called enemy would not be intolerable—unless I were to spend it chained to these pigs.

The rest of the night was frigid and boring. At dawn, the others wanted to continue sleeping, dull as reptiles. Instead we were handed spades to open a drying spring. It seemed that for now the trek was over. Our hands remained tied. Two young Imazighen with rifles, one of them, the boy who bound Aumont and I after the horse battle, wandered around nearby while we dug in the dirt to renew the water.

Lemarche spat a question at him in French. The youngster's frown and half-hearted command to be quiet was clear in any language. Lemarche, assumed that his tongue was not understood. So he began to talk softly. "I estimate it is about fifty kilometers to the garrison. I have watched the sun, and am certain we can reach it west by southwest."

The idiot was openly, foolishly suggesting escape. Of course, with his notable military pedigree he was far more eager to prove his courage than a man with good tactical sense.

Messac and Pressiat resisted the idea. Messac sensibly replied to Lemarche, "I don't care if it's right over that mountain. You are hungry and on foot. They are well-fed and have horses. Do you think a superior sense of direction will overcome that? Idiot!"

"You are trussed up like a goose! Where is your pride?"

"Stowed away until I am home again to flaunt it."

"I tell you, we can slip away. Don't you recall our night training maneuvers?'"

"How could I forget freezing my ass off next to you?"

"And we were the first to reach the objective, yes?!"

Messac was mocking. "You have me there, Claude. It's why you were promoted."

"So shut up and think about it."

I finally interjected. "You will never escape. If you are lucky, they will do nothing but chase you until you collapse half-dead from exhaustion. And have you idiots forgotten that many Berbers understand French? If you're going to babble about this like gossipers at the village fountain, why not instead just tell them what you plan to do?"

Lemarche scoffed. "Shut up, Jean-Michel. We are not in the garrison."

I suddenly no longer cared what they did. "If you morons act on this, I will never get the chance to see you shot for disobeying an order. But the result will be the same."

Lemarche hissed at me. "You can wear the same underwear for the next three days or three months. Eat this fucking barbarian food. Dig in their dirt. And let that disease eat your flesh. I'm going, and Messac will go with me. Won't you Messac?"

Buhl sighed at their feeble wits. Lemarche was clearly seduced by foolish impulse. Still, he had roused Messac's weak mind. By nightfall, I sensed that the fools had somehow fixed a plan. Neither Plau nor I would order them to refrain. Having broken with logic and reality, I knew they were simply waiting for the right moment.

That night Lemarche and Messac rolled over from the pretense of sleep. They crept toward the pack mules sixty or seventy meters away. I watched them go and said nothing, lest my voice in the dead of night ruin their plan and cause me ill fortune in the bargain.

When I awoke at dawn, Lemarche and Messac were nowhere in sight. I rose to go to the crude latrine hole. Then I saw the would-be heroes, spread on the ground like trophy game, throats and bare bellies sliced open and confusion frozen on their ash-blue faces.

The Berbers watched me more closely. I acted nonchalant. My conscience was clear. I had advised them not to go; they ignored me and paid the price. It did not seem monstrous for the Berbers to kill men so ignorant they were not fit to shovel sheep manure. In the moment of death, maybe they realized that their words had been well enough understood. Even by the boy sentry. And guards were always posted. No movement around camp went unseen. And if by some miracle they had returned to the garrison, or simply survived, Plau or I would have charged them with insubordination and imperiling our lives, assuming Plau had corroborated my charge. I was strangely at ease with the absence of Lemarche and Messac, and saw no signs that Plau felt any differently.

My affliction seemed to become more evident to everyone. I grew more conscious of it, and so it seemed to worsen. People kept a greater distance. Food was left for me nearby, but not at my tent. The Berbers averted their eyes, as if I were a living *djen* in the first stage of decay. *Amrabti* were said to have cured leprosy. As I gazed at the constellations above the Berbers at their fires, I wondered if they would provide a holy man.

That night the camp was to be moved. Perhaps it was a precaution to leave a place too easily seen by scout planes or horsemen. More likely there was word of *Iroumin* not far away. They gave me a mule to ride. I and my four fellows, all resentfully walking, were led away. The Berbers looked at me oddly. I was no longer valuable to them, just debris to be unloaded. I had not behaved like some accursed spirit, but they treated me as one. In their view, Allah had judged by inflicting a problem He did not wish to solve.

We skirted familiar rock fields and scrub grass for hours. We were back near the route taken soon after the cavalry clash. Closer to the garrison. What if I could escape? But I was realistic; thirty kilometers was a long walk when eluding horsemen. And these fellows were not hospitable, so I would run instead because death would be all the closer. I treated such notions only as fantasy. It was diverting to imagine myself on foot racing an Ait Atta horseman, and winning. Because only in my mind did I have any power or control.

We halted at daybreak beneath some low cliffs. To the west, was the Dades. Here Larbi and his men departed. We were met by a new group of *shleuh*, less kind, who grudgingly gave food and water. A stern fellow called Zin Mennou would not touch me but rebound the hands of the others more tightly, even though it was clear we had no intention of trying to escape or fight.

Dutroix observed bitterly, to Zin's agitation, "Friendly fellow, eh what?"

He then received the butt of a whip for his trouble.

Buhl protested. "Hey, no need for that, you . . . !"

"Me what? You bastard," Zin Mennou hissed in passable French.

He slapped Buhl and Dutroix in turn and equally. Then he smiled, more hyena than human. "I should trust you? For *Iroumin*, everything changes when you think you can get away with it."

We turned down a path we had come up several days before. By the middle of the day, I recognized the terrain. We were near the garrison. Far off stood the palm trees of the ambush that now seemed so long ago. Several hours later we neared the trees, the water, the rolling hill leading up to the fort plateau. I had come full circle. It was late afternoon in the grove, the same time of day as the ambush, making for an eerie déjà vu. Despite the chill, I wanted to strip off my clothes and plunge into the water. To rejoin the human race and scrape this filth from my body and soul. It would be my only pleasure since before the mission departure. But the three-day trek had been hard and direct, with little food for us and I was ravenously hungry, so cleanliness was less important. After so long under duress, Mirvais would surely grant me personal time. I could seek hygiene and medical care and report on my captivity.

Ten Légion horsemen led six empty mounts forward from the trees. Ahead of them, walked a dozen loosely linked, rather brazen Berbers. This would be a two-for-one exchange. The enemy seemed about to get the better bargain. When the two parties were less than one hundred meters apart, the prisoners from each were liberated. A Berber gruffly shoved me off the mule. I fell in behind my comrades. The hearty Ait Atta and we desultory Légion passed over the former battleground with hardly a glance. After a round of brotherly greetings, the Berber band turned about and matter-of-factly went on its way. The hard tasks ahead outweighed the pleasantries of reunion.

Dutroix led the others away from me. They peeked anxiously behind, as if I was an ogre, or a carrier of plague. They hastened to the spare horses for the return to the fort.

St. Avold, one of the riders, cantered to me with a horse and with some sadness held out the reins. Before I mounted, before anyone asked my condition or offered a gesture of respect, the others were away. Only Danton remained to ride with me. I told him that Lemarche and Messac were dead. Killed trying to escape. He had no response.

"I think that the garrison will be less than ecstatic to see me."

He replied, "It is not your fault. But it is for another reason entirely."

There was something weary in his voice, like foreknowledge of a crisis. He confessed a desire to speak to me in confidence. Heart to heart.

I reminded him he needn't be so damned formal.

St. Avold replied, "Mirvais is trying to paint himself in colors for the action. I suspect it is his way of getting out of the fight."

"No wonder," I said. "Mirvais clearly is not much of a fighter. He doesn't have the stomach for hunting Akka n-Ali, and certainly not for outsmarting him. He commanded poorly, we got mauled, and he is desperate for absolution."

St. Avold was grim and glib at the same time. "That absolution drove in two days ago. A day after the remaining men lurched back in utter disbelief they were alive. Lieutenant Colonel Marcy has been badly wounded. Colonel Rochet is at the fort, trying to establish responsibility-rather, blame. Word is that the Major is saying unkind things about you. Where you both went after galloping off the field. Rochet laments that Du Thierry is dead. I suspect he wanted him to share command. And Aumont is missing. We have no body and no word from the *shleuh*. That helps Mirvais. One less officer to report his behavior during the mission and the fight. Few others are speaking. Not the *spahis*. Mirvais insists that the Berbers were so cunning; no commander could have done more than he.

In the end, perhaps it will be your witness against his."

The sum of these words sent a chill through me. I wondered if St. Avold reasoned the implication. To my suspicious mind, Mirvais would not want me around.

"Casualties," Danton mumbled with a heavy pause, then said, "Thirty three dead. Fourteen horsemen and fifteen soldiers in the fights, four later. Twenty-four wounded."

"And seven prisoners," I added. "And Lemarche and Messac killed trying to escape. Goddamn stir-crazy idiots! I told them not to try it! I ordered them." All told, one man in five of the men Mirvais led out were casualties. And little to show for it.

"I expect Mirvais will try to hold others, including you, accountable. The commander needs a scapegoat."

I passed under the garrison portal. A dozen men milled about with false attachment. I saw Rochet the instant I entered the plaza. He stood on the *pisé porch*, peering ahead, resembling a statue fixed to the side of a cathedral, dead in nature, alive within the observer. I followed his line of sight to Mirvais and two adjutants awaiting me. I dismounted and saluted my grim-faced commander. I knew at once that I was moving from one form of captivity to another.

"Bon jour, Sergeant," Mirvais said in a condescending tone. "I see you are not entirely the worse for the wear. You are alive, and that is something, given the customs of those ruthless bastards."

I said nothing. The Major was himself a ruthless bastard. How could I best criticize his poor mission tactics? Especially at the end, in the hasty move homeward and the failure to exercise due caution? At the least, it was an outrage for the men to have marched all that distance and then be assaulted within sight of home.

Mirvais studied me, awaiting a reply, some rationale he could examine and try to use against any argument I should make. When I offered none, he took this, too, as a rebuke and appeared to grimace, like after a mouthful of rancid wine.

He invited me to accompany him to meet Rochet. And the doctor. The same doctor who had grimly tended to the casualties served up by the fight. I saw a set of dire and inescapable facts. Officers, including Mirvais, and soldiers, including myself, would bear witness about their occurrence. They would not want me to be frank. They wished to ensure my silence on the matter.

Mirvais hastened ahead to the infirmary. I followed like the exhausted *chasseur* I was, annoyed at the lack of delicacy or discretion. I was a soldier, not an animal, and surely not a pawn. At that moment I was trying to figure the angle Mirvais meant to play. If the Colonel, the Major, and the doctor had negotiated a pact.

Mirvais remained cool and wary, like one asked to disclose a painful intimacy. He held open the door of the infirmary room and bid me to enter. I caught my reflection in the mirror. What disturbed me was my worn, somewhat aged appearance. I turned away from the man in the mirror. I gazed at Mirvais, who peered and frowned like a troubled dog sizing up his quarry. Then he grew timid. Skittish. I could see he wanted to evade. And so he did.

"Let me give you some time to evaluate everything, Sergeant. I will be back with the doctor in a few m-m-moments." He left hastily, without ceremony.

I returned to my reflection. I removed my *tajjelabith* and filthy shirt. I was bewildered by the craggy, ulcerated skin down my left arm, shoulder to hand. By my newly, oddly painful earlobes. My body was speaking a language impossible for me to comprehend. Leprosy. Exploding upon me.

I churned in quiet terror. Had God cast a hard-hearted sentence upon my guiltless soul? I stared into my eyes, seeing there, the last ember of my feeble dreams. Maroc has been a part of me since Grandfather's colorful tales about the awesome mountains and desert already rich with history long before Islam. But at that moment it seemed that instead of elevating my life, Morocco could eventually take it.

I heard the doctor enter his office next door. Boot steps quietly followed. They were there for some time, discussing me—but I was not asked to attend. I heard soft speech and sibilant whispers, but grasped only an occasional murmured word. "Marrakech." "Exposure." "Discipline." "Papers." This had all the signs of a tacit conspiracy. I could sense their decision like a rainstorm.

The boots exited Brentano's office. Two sets of them. Mirvais and Rochet. They walked away, ignoring me. Or dreading my contagion. Long minutes elapsed before he stepped alone through the door from his study to the examining room.

"Please disrobe." Brentano's request was gentle but hinted impatience; reassuring demeanor was largely absent. I needed an honest diagnosis more than sympathy, but both together would have value. The doctor made a show of the examination. He peered over the top of his bifocal glasses. His moustache rippled under puffing nostrils. But he hardly touched me, mostly looked, as if at a vaguely distasteful sculpture. He clinically said, "I will give you some antiseptic soap and several towels," and stepped across the room to a cabinet. "Bathe thoroughly in the lavatory. It is an infection. You must keep it clean."

He handed the items to me, eyes downcast. A somewhat anxious assistant stood on the threshold between the office and room. Brentano shifted his attention, I thought gratefully, to the fellow, mumbled to excuse himself, and disappeared.

The cold water, any water, felt good. I scoured away the defilements, struggling to reconcile my scrubbed skin with a tainted heart. When I returned, a fresh uniform was on one of the three beds. This implied that I was to remain here. Atop the linen lay an envelopes. contained a slab of back pay. I slipped into the fresh uniform, oh my, and began to write my brother François.

Mirvais returned. I stood to salute. I could see the Major wanted to forego formality, but he reciprocated. He displayed no more concern than if he was reminding a valet about his poorly shined boots. Then Rochet entered behind him. I snapped another salute, but the emotional effort to do so far outweighed the physical one. Rochet began to speak with odd dispassion. He was like a man struggling inside rusty armor.

He intoned, with an aversion to kindly decorum, "As you know, Sergeant, you have leprosy. A serious affliction. As a soldier, you have a right to medical attention. But this ailment is a risk to others. We have no remedy. We can do nothing. It is safe to say you are wounded by fate. There is no choice. You must leave here. I will issue an immediate medical discharge and promotion to *aspirant*. Congratulations. It will be duly noted. You will be quickly notified of developments, on my word."

I could scarcely believe my ears. I said nothing, couldn't speak, as his strange Rochet soliloquy continued.

"We will arrange, for you to be flown from here to a special facility. Of course, we will give you all appropriate assistance and supplies. The authorities will be notified. Soon they will retrieve you for thorough treatment. And please, until tomorrow morning, keep away from the men. In fact, you should not leave this room."

At that pronouncement, Mirvais cavalierly bowed and clicked his heels. He could bear to hear Rochet no more. Or look at my ghastly shock. He was courtly—in other circumstances he might be considered dashing. Before I could speak, he and Rochet turned to the infirmary exit. It was a gesture, as deliberate as a slap in the face, to kill any moment for self-expression or questions. Especially about the hidden, more complex reasons for my abrupt disposal. I was confident that the greater the wrongs, the more I would be restored. In the end, I know, God willing, they will also get "thorough treatment."

Desaix groaned. "Now I have heard how low men can stoop. I once thought I knew, but this was a new form of violation, covering the full range of indecency."

I sat to write a letter home. Several weeks had elapsed since my last. But I expected that my billet-doux, sent the usual way, would be intercepted, censored or destroyed before it left Maroc. For that matter, the garrison. My own rights clearly carried little weight, so concern for my family would hardly register. I had experienced more fraternité as a Berber prisoner. I knew there would be much time to examine that conundrum.

I sensed that some of the men, Saint-Avold among them, probably wanted to visit. But by order I was quarantined, and no one had the courage to defy it. Nor the chance. Dutroix balefully stood guard. Keeping them out. And me in. Hence, no one could call to me or slip a note under the door lest they would be reported. I was virtually a condemned man, and by simply acknowledging my presence, they accepted a bit of the shame. Absent a cure, I would go to my grave in a corrupted body, maybe sooner than later. Several times during my sleepless night, I heard dull footsteps and whispers in the eerie quiet, as if a dignitary lay dying in my room. I could feel the apprehension. In their service, some men had witnessed typhus, cholera and other contagions. I knew the best of them would have compassion for my misfortune, worse than a combat wound. Peering out, I saw shadow men just beyond lantern glow. But I spent the night alone. Not even the Chaplain came to me. Ignorance, self-interest, and orders denied mercy to my soul.

That morning at about ten o'clock, I heard an airplane fly in. My private sky chariot. As all planes here, it would land on the flat road nearby and taxi to the gate. The road I had helped to build. I received no communication but silence. My fear matched my heartache. I was petrified to confront Rochet and Mirvais to demand an explanation. I dreaded what either might say. And even more what my response would be.

Brentano's aide, a pink Parisian nicknamed Corporal Claude, toted in a satchel to place upon a bed. Within it, several days' rations, a full uniform with spare pants, socks, underwear and other clothing—including this new *tajjelabith*—toiletries, matches, medicines, a wad of francs, two towels, a Bible, cigarettes—although I don't smoke—a flask of cognac, and a .32 Beretta with several clips of ammunition.

"With the Colonel's compliments," he said. "Dr. Brentano has written a report on your condition. It is there. Give it to your attendant at hospital."

I packed other items in my rucksack: my map of Morocco, a compass, my old bird guide, an ivory comb and brush. Into my jacket I slipped photos of my family, a second map, and Father's musical pocketwatch with the engraving—*May each day find you living your dreams. Grandfather*

Beyond the far wall of the fort, the plane's engine fell silent. I opened the door to stand beneath the portico. I wanted to force the Colonel's hand. A Corporal stood guard nearby. More than a half hour passed. But the commanders did not appear. I imagined them frozen with guilt or indifference, or under the spell of what they thought to be a necessary evil. I gazed from the mountains so near and so far, to the thirty or so cheerless men who gathered near the gate. I saw my friend Sergeant St. Avold and surly, disobedient Sergeant Dutroix across the yard. Danton smiled, but Dutroix was a pitiless mule.

"Good afternoon, gentlemen," I said wryly. "Your table is waiting." Both of them seemed surprised that I wore this *tajjelabith* over my uniform. St. Avold wanted to defuse the certain sadness with his endearing wit.

"Jean-Michel, that is certainly not standard issue," he said. "White, no less."

I feel he wanted to express some contrition, and great discomfort, too, but chose not to be overt. They were there to escort me away from home. I would not make it easy.

"I'm being buried alive. These men are freaks. Goddamn cowards. Damn monsters! What the hell are regulations to me in the face of that? I'll dress like a Berber if I please. A naked Gaul with a bloody sword if I could summon the courage and contempt!"

They did not reply. We churned in silence. My accusations had sufficient merit, more than enough to force a higher inquiry. We all knew that was exactly the main reason I had been confined to this room with no more rights than a street thug, and why I was to be shipped off with little immediate recourse. To a slow, convenient demise. To move me along, forgetting my malady. Dutroix lifted my bags.

We emerged single file to cross the courtyard. Apparently they were under instructions to guide me straight to the plane, no need to prolong the scene. I walked a gantlet of silence. My comrades were somber. Some were choking back words of encouragement. Of course, the commanders spied from their offices, daring anyone to support me. And defy them. Yet, the men were not dispersed. My plight demonstrated their power. Dutroix and St. Avold escorted me like wardens beyond the wall to the plane.

* * * * *

"And so here you are," Desaix said.

"Yes. Here I am."

"Looking not to be. A man too rotten cannot avenge his carcass."

"I have no choice."

"A few have escaped," Desaix said cryptically, softly.

At that very moment, the plane's engine was heard droning away to takeoff from the makeshift runway. Desaix looked up the cliff, bedimmed in the waning sunlight, as if wordlessly inviting La Tour to do the same.

EIGHT:

SAVIOR

The Ait Atta were briefly jubilant after the clashes with the *Iroumin*. But their delight waned at thoughts of the greater, inevitable frays to come. And mourned their dead, though they knew well it was one of the ways Allah charged for the principle of freedom.

Late on the second day, two saddle-weary couriers entered Taboulmant from different directions. Akka and councilmen Lahcen n-Assu and Ousaïd n-Hmad received them.

"An emissary of the Makhzen in Azilal sends this message through an *Aroumi*," the horseman relayed upon handing Akka an official looking document. "Declaring a wish to discuss a truce."

Lahcen was skeptical. "Just as the last, it will be only talk to distract us as plans are made to attack in ever greater force."

"He is already en route," Akka said as he read the message written in Arabic. "No matter. Though the Pasha and his deputy may be little more than servants of the French, courtesy obliges us to receive him. But we'll have no strangers here; we shall conference with them at the *igherm* near Tizi el Hajj."

The fort there blended into a maze of gullies. A weapons cache and assembly point for warriors, it could not be seen by from the air and was difficult to find on the ground.

The second courier, sent by Larbi, related that the amghar had yesterday departed Tizi n' Tamalout to the south with several warriors, a Légion captive and a Frenchman touring the mountains under a dubious writ of passage from the Pasha and the *Iroumin* foe.

It was expected that today, the separate parties of Larbi and the emissary, traveling from opposite points, would be equidistant in their routes.

"I do not like that one of our chiefs is traveling with so few," Akka said to Lahcen. "But the wise old strategist knows how to move around. He was doing so twenty years before I was born." To the couriers he said: "Instruct Larbi that we will meet his small flock in the ravine near Tizi el Hajj. You will direct the emissary there to meet tomorrow morning. Leave now."

"It was predictable that the *Iroumin* would seek a truce," Ousaïd observed. "I suspect that it will be their last offer. They will assemble a bigger force. To capture you," he concluded, looking directly at Akka Ahêddây. He said it not with a tone of concern, but of pride.

Akka arose well before dawn and was soon joined by Amnay. They were preparing to leave when, to their surprise, Addi Yacoub arrived to greet them, leading his horse by the reins. It was the first time in weeks either had seen him in Taboulmant. Somehow, he seemed eager. Or anxious.

"I should accompany you," he said to Akka.

"For several hours we ride," Akka imparted in a weak attempt to dissuade. But Addi likely knew this, perhaps by the usual arcane sources as no council member had seen the Sufi to mention the imminent journey. "Guide my horse. I go with you," the *Amrabt* repeated. Akka would not refuse. For years, he had known Addi's words were not always his.

The trio departed at first, cloud-burdened light. Akka tied Addi's gentle old mare to the cherished saddle upon his It'ij. The plan was to greet the party near Tizi el Hajj, then send the Légion prisoner and the Frenchman on to the fortress while Akka, Addi and Amnay met the emissary. They descended the terrace fields to move across the valley of stones below the promontory. A wide plateau split two long ridges along the rugged tracks of Azourki, where one could find the strategic passes of Tizi Laz and Tizi n'Tirist, which led to Ait Mehammed and beyond to Azilal.

In the reverse, easterly direction, a trek along the ridge extended almost to the horizon, and would soon offer Akka an excellent long-range vantage of any approaching parties. They ascended its spine riding through peaceful, solitary terrain. Several large birds spiraled lazily on warm currents in the wide sky. Then, against the immense backdrop, far down the bluff, Akka spotted the figures of a few moving horsemen, and more men lurking on foot nearby.

"Amnay, ride ahead and meet that group," he exhorted, pointing there. "They may be the scouts Lahcen sent yesterday to bring weapons."

"I should stay with you both. You will have no escort."

"We will be fine," Akka replied confidently. He smiled; not the smile of a man burdened by war. "I have the eyes, and the *Amrabt* all else. We will follow you."

Addi remained silent, drawn inward, like he was waiting in a sacred place.

Amnay cantered onward. He crested a slight rise near a jumble of boulders. He immediately saw, to his dismay, an ambush unfolding barely one hundred meters in front of him.

Two Berber bandits, brandishing pistols, had emerged from behind a knoll and loomed above five mounted men: two warriors from Larbi's group, a fellow in a white cloak, a Légion Lieutenant, and a civilian-one of the expected entourages.

His Lebel raised, Amnay crept his horse nearer the bandits' blind side. Now he heard a rustle of stones to his right. A Berber with a dog-like face and his own Lebel edged his horse from behind the large boulders. The grunting man directed Amnay to ease forward and yield his weapon. His brimstone eyes signaled that any sudden move would be suicidal. The fellow took the proffered gun and swung his mount in behind Amnay. By now Akka, still far behind Amnay, could detect the trouble but he was powerless.

The bandits wanted their horses, guns and all valuables. The blue cloaked man gestured that the two Frenchmen dismount and his yellow-capped cohort mimed for the Berber escort to drop their rifles. Instead, the defiant and noble warriors, the butts of the rifles propped on their hips, hastily fired. The bandits were ready.

"No!" screamed the Lieutenant. Too late. The bullets could not be recalled.

The yellow cap rogue was torn through the right thigh, but between the two of them, they disintegrated the head of the near Berber, pierced the heart of the second, and the neck of the third.

The Légionnaire yanked open his jacket to retrieve the potent symbol of aqbil protection. Aumont was unarmed and his hands were loosely bound. Still, this action spurred the man's angry reflex. He spun and fired.

At that very moment, a shaft of sunlight broke through the morning clouds and swept directly across the tableau. The Frenchman tottered, and then fell from the saddle, backside down with an awful thump. His countryman and one surviving Berber escort looked on in horror. The *shleuh* were indifferent. The Lieutenant's open jacket framed a gushing belly. He writhed in confusion and anguish. The wound was likely lethal. His quickly dulling eyes gazed up at the fat amber clouds and patches of sky as if fully and sadly aware this would be the last image they would ever capture. He moved his lips weakly, in silent prayer.

Ignoring the risk, the other Frenchman howled and dismounted. "Why did you shoot him?! You bastard!" He sputtered a fracture of Berber and Arabic. "He has no gun! Only a stone from the *amghar!*" He pulled wider both coat panels as proof. *"From Ahmed Larbi to Akka!* You piece of filth! Be cursed!"

The condemnation had struck a nerve in the wicked shooter. With grave shame, he tucked away his gun. The impulse to harm had gotten the better of him. In assuring swift, sure tribal justice, he had sealed the trio's doom. *"Ikha"* Amnay seethed. Bad. The two rogues gazed at him. Amnay was attired in a bright, fine *tajjelabith*. The prized *moukhala* in his saddle sheath complemented the Lebel no longer in his hand. Amnay's evident Ait Atta status might shield him from harm. But these bandits were now fully committed to their course. The robbery or murder of a chief could not increase the penalty for their crime—death—should they be caught.

Amnay again peered back toward Akka, now at a gallop but restrained by the tether to Addi's horse. The blue cloaked rogue followed Amnay's line of sight. He and the maimed, hemorrhaging yellow cap rogue quickly realized their quandary and leapt from the knoll. Seizing the horses, the trio, origin unknown, rushed east up toward the distant, looming cliffs. Unable to ride, the yellow cap shortly pitched headfirst from the Lieutenant's mount and was still. His two compatriots hastened on heartlessly.

Amnay dismounted beside the three dead Berbers. He honored and rebuked their bravery in the same silent prayer. The Frenchman wailed over his compatriot. "Far away on this godforsaken hill, you have come to this miserable end! As you feared!"

Akka and Addi were within earshot. Ahêddây deftly bounded from It'ij in motion and said in French to the victim and his attendant as he knelt beside them, "God does not forsake. Fear not. Addi, this man has been shot! Help him."

Addi displayed a deft dismount well-practiced in younger years. He reached for Akka's outstretched guiding hand, and then knelt beside the Légionnaire. Addi gently rolled the fellow onto his left side to find the exit wound. Akka grasped the knife sheath from beneath the sash around his *tajjelabith*, untied the loose knot and shrugged out of the garment. With the sharp blade he sliced the hood from the fabric. He pressed the wadded cloth into Addi's palm, who pressed it against the bullet entrance. The Frenchman gazed on in astonishment. Berbers acting to save the life of an *Aroumi*?

Addi held the fabric against the hole. Akka slid the bisected *tajjelabith* under the man, who relaxed from his throes cushioned against the rocky earth. Addi then replaced his hand on the compress with that of Akka.

"Do you know what you are doing?" the Frenchman asked. He was inclined to doubt. But his unstrung first words were at once modulated by a growing awe.

"*No, monsieur,*" Addi said. "*Oui, monsieur.*" The Frenchman locked gazes with Akka, then back to the *ambrat,* and was further startled by his unseeing cat-like eyes.

"Good Lord," the man uttered softly.

Akka let serene Addi become the key caregiver, simply easing aside the weak French hand as Addi pressed the thick swatch of dark wool against the entrance. Then he firmly held a hand on both front and back, literally taking body, and life, between them.

What dry, loving warmth, like sunlight, flowed from those palms? From Addi. Or elsewhere. He closed his eyes in prayer. There was a sense that time was lost to him.

Akka glanced across the ground and saw the metal pellet that had passed through the man. He had suffered what should be fatal harm. All eyes were fixed on Addi, not the victim. Akka was witness to a scene not easily explained: Death was being chased from the dying. Amnay had read the Qur'an and benefited from brother Lahcen's pious wisdom. For the moment, an evil deed was being corrected by something like love. When the tale of this was told, it would inspire wonderment as another revelation of *baraka.*

Addi pulled his bloody left hand from beneath the Frenchman's back. "The *zaouiat* certainly cannot ride a horse," Addi said. "We must transport him to the village."

Why on earth did he say the French fellow was a student of the holy?

Amnay kept tied on his horse a blanket of stoutly stitched sheep hides for nights in the field. The shroud easily fit over him, with extra area to tuck about his body. It was the perfect stretcher. Amnay and the Frenchman gently slid the limp, crimson form onto the stretch of sheepskin, grasped two corners each, and began to bear the load down the rock-strewn hill. They had at least six kilometers to go.

"I will hasten for help," Akka said. "The *Amrabt* will stay with you . . ."

Lieutenant Aumont's blood-soaked clothing made his condition appear worse than it was. The flow from the wound was now but a trickle. For the moment, it appeared that the patient would survive.

Akka n-Ali raced past his *igherm*. The villagers seldom saw the *amghar* in such a frenzy. He came upon three men tending unsaddled ponies near the old *agadir*. "You men! Ride there," he pointed afar to the east, "and help Amnay and the *Amrabt* hasten here. A man could die!"

The fellows immediately did as directed.

"Lahcen! Ousaïd! Come at once!" His call was unusually urgent. Both men bounded from the plot where Hejjou was tending a patch of barley.

"The Legion man sent by Larbi was shot by brigands," Akka informed them, indicating the distant ridge, "near Irhourdane. Mount six riders in pursuit. I want those men caught before they reach protection with the Morghad!"

Lahcen could see that Akka was in a rare state of distress.

"Those *iqettaân* ride stolen horses-east toward Amouguir! Straight at Larbi!"

Akka described them. And briefly, the episode itself. He ordered more men after the bandits.

In a short while, the group-Amnay, the photographer, Akka's men and the *anahcham*, whose white cloak was now red-stained-bore the injured man into the village directly to the *igherm*. Hejjou and Hada slipped inside. Other women stood ready to assist. Villagers gathered and chattered while the mystery unfolded within.

"You see he is badly hurt," Amnay effused to Lahcen. "Addi stopped the bleeding and . . ." He did not need to continue.

Lahcen, however, could see that the specter of death still hovered near this man.

"Addi saved his life," Amnay said. "He knew what to do." Akka watched from near the door, a witness to great handiwork, dazed by the marvel of such clairvoyance and the miracle worked by hands. With Hada's help, Lahcen gently removed the man's uniform jacket and pulled up the tails of the blood-drenched shirt to reveal the grisly wound.

"He healed him," Amnay whispered to Lahcen. "You see that the bullet should kill. And he believes this man is a pious Nazarene. I believe if you look . . ."

Addi gently trod across the dirt floor from the shadows of the corner. Amnay fell silent. Lahcen unbuttoned the shirt. In the light of the oil lamp and the sun streaming through the door, everyone saw a silver crucifix on a neck chain, glinting against the pale skin above the blood-slick flesh. Ousaïd and Amnay sighed at this further complication of customary law. Lahcen partly blocked Akka's gaze, then at last, the glimmering crucifix came into view, reflecting in Akka's eyes. Coincidence? Miracle? Such a feat was unknown in all Addi's years here.

The French photographer pulled an artifact from the man's inside pocket and with a shaking hand offered it to Akka Ahêddây, who instantly recognized, it was Larbi's token of passage.

"His name is Alain Aumont. This is what he was taking from his coat as he was shot."

"*Comment vous appelez-vous?*" asked Amnay.

Amany proudly revealed a welcome talent; he spoke some French.

"Pierre Duplessy, a photographer for Havas and Lefigaro," he replied. "Your two dead fellows were guiding us from Larbi n-Haddou. The Lieutenant was most important. But the escorts enforced our silence. So I barely know this man, except for his name."

"Boil more water," Addi instructed Hada. "You must clean him. He will live. But all those unnecessary must leave."

Berber treatments for grave wounds seldom exceeded poultices, crude incisions and healing by prayer and hands. The alien soldiers who marched about Maroc, perpetuating carnage, had sorely tested tribal medicine. And the more the *Iroumin* were attacked, the more soldiers they sent to wreak havoc. In earlier years, tribes rallied like hornets but were seldom victorious as the *Iroumin* grimly reaped them. Even an *Amrabt* with great *baraka* could do little to remedy the effects of their weapons on poorly armed men whose methods of warfare had scarcely changed in centuries. It was Allah's will that the brave and cowardly alike be shot or killed; no one could defy divine decision. But now, a Frenchman in Berber custody was near death in their land. *AddiAl-hámdu li-lláh,* an *Amrabt* was there to save him.

Lahcen did not request Addi to demonstrate his power again, though he hoped to soon witness it. Just as well, since Addi felt drained. He had few words to describe the transcendent connection, and feared they would not serve him well.

The village was electrified. An officer of the French Légion was being tended by Addi, Lahcen, Hajjou and Hada who all worked as a team to save a stranger, and an enemy, on the word of their leader, with no less devotion than for one of their own people. The near-murder of this man who was both an *Aroumi* of holy ways, and the bearer of information useful to the Imazighen proved that Satan was loose on this land.

Ousaïd n-Hmad waited just inside the doorway. He whispered for a moment to the Bou Iknifen *anakham*, Akli n-Moussa, and then turned to stepson Akka and their guest Pierre.

"Please. Let us all walk," said Ousaïd "Akka, tell what happened. What Addi did to that man. Where the brigands went."

Pierre trembled to stand beside his nation's enemy. But his fear was neutralized by the elation to be alive, to be witness to history. He silently stood by as Akka spent more minutes in recounting the occurrence than had elapsed in the event itself. Ousaïd thought the tale and its telling extraordinary. He and Akli were charged with revealing the facts of crimes and the application of justice mandated by customary law. Simply put, the ambushed party had been traveling under the protection of Larbi and Akka. This was a sacred pact. The bandits, attacking at random impulse, could hardly have made a graver mistake. And they were cold-blooded murderers in the bargain.

"They will be found and executed according to the laws of *ait l- 'ar*," Akka rasped. He faced Pierre and began to speak passionately. Now Akli n-Moussa revealed a surprise and welcome talent. He translated the Tamazight to French.

"Now that you see me, am I the scourge of the Christian God?" Akka asked. "A madman? An animal to be hunted and killed? I am just a man, and I want my wife, and daughter, and people to live as they were made, here, without our submission to foreign laws. If a righteous man has the power to defend himself, he must do so, praise God."

Pierre could say nothing in response. Any words would have to yield in the face of Akka's apparent ethics and logic, as a shadow disappears beneath the rays of the sun.

"So tell us what you want here, and then go tell your people what I have said."

"I want to take your picture," Pierre said slowly and mimed the function of a camera. "And your *igherm*. And your *aqbil*. So that the world knows well that you are man and not animal. My instrument will capture that."

Pierre ran to his horse upon which a travel satchel held his Rollei. In a few moments he unpacked the device, to the great curiosity of Akka, Ousaïd and others nearby.

"Yes, I have seen something like that before," Akka said. "Two years ago in Bou Malem, a Frenchman pointed such at me. It did not cause me harm. What does it do?"

Pierre indicated the end result by showing photographs of other Berbers he took. Akka and Ousaïd were baffled by the form and significance of the images, the stoicism or fear or fascination seen on the faces captured. There began a dance of uncertainty, cajoling and diplomacy before any of them would pose.

The three dead Imazighen were borne from the ambush site to the village. The men had devoutly delivered themselves to their people and to Allah. The bodies were properly washed and stored until their agnates could retrieve them. Death was too common to be much mourned. The fight for life was always more fascinating.

During the following days, Pierre spent much of his time witnessing the treatment of Aumont, who lingered in a sweaty stupor. Pierre was at first uneasy over Addi Yacoub's strange prayers and the application of herbs; it was more sorcery than surgery. But Aumont did not die; by the first evening, he had improved. The women boiled onions in a dirty pot. He saw the *Amrabt* once pack several of them directly into the wound, and the women many times rub a paste of mashed onions and a yellowish herb on the skin around it. The practice surely had antiseptic properties.

In fitful half-sleep, Aumont was reciting prayers. Amnay translated, as best he could.

"... but they who wait for the Lord shall renew their strength ... they shall mount with wings like eagles ... they shall run and not be weary ... they shall walk and not faint," he mumbled in week bursts.

Akka often kept vigil with Addi. Pierre marveled at his own poise as an interloper here in the Ait Atta war capital, but more at how much the chieftain's fiendish reputation failed to match the man kneeling in meditation on the dirt floor of his home.

Pierre set up his camera to take photographs, often near the red door of Akka's igherm or in the nearby garden. He thrilled to the glares, grins, and stern curiosity of his subjects. Most had little patience for sitting, and none had a good idea why they were asked to pose but they were proud to be the subject of attention. The young man with his handsome gray horse. His father, the talkative potter. The weary man returning home from a long day dragging boulders to improve the bastion against *Iroumin* attack.

Aumont was awake on the third day. Pierre believed that they had worked a miracle. The crisis appeared to have passed and he did not want to wait for the trap of a massive French attack or a change of Berber heart. Pierre asked if there was a wagon with which he could transport Aumont to a French garrison hospital.

"Only two carts," Akli said. "Imazighen transport is mule, horse or human back. And the garrisons to the east and west are three or four days away. And Addi says that in five or six days, Aumont may travel slowly by horse." And Akka added, with a sharp edge and a clear meaning: "By that time, the least he will give me for his life is the information he came here to exchange."

"Pierre," Aumont confessed, "I want to leave Maroc. My tour of duty is up in little more than month. I want to go home. Or at least far from death."

"Can they accuse you of desertion?" Pierre asked

"Let them. By the time they find me, my service will be done."

A weak Aumont stood and wobbled as he attempted to walk. Akka came to his aid, supporting the Frenchman as he stumbled to the garden beside the house, willing himself forward. An unspoken camaraderie developed.

"What of the brigands? Is there a search for them?" the Lieutenant inquired. With no one there to translate, Aumont resorted to a crude pantomime of gunplay, the yellow bangles on Hada's headdress, and the hole in his side.

Pointing to Hada's shroud and using hand signs, Akka indicated immediate justice for that yellow cap. Atta men were in hot pursuit of his two accomplices.

Addi Yacoub emerged from his hut to trek to the village. No matter how often they had seen it, the inhabitants he passed marveled that a blind man could safely traverse this land. The *Amrabt*, never to be imprisoned by doubt or fear, summoned his inner eye. Without guidance, he found Akka, also by a sense no one could comprehend.

"The two fugitives have been found," he pronounced in an oracular tone. "They will return soon."

Several hours later, four Berber warriors led two mounted, manacled prisoners up from Asif Imedrhas, past the *koubba* and on to Akka's *igherm*. Though the ruffians were about to topple from exhaustion, they were pulled down to stand before the villagers.

The trial would be neither formal nor protracted. What were their names? Alla n-Khuya n-Ait Yafelmane, Lyazzidw-n-Ouzzine n-Oultana. Where were they born? Tizga and Azilal. They were disowned rogues. Akka and Ousaïd weighed the damning evidence: Amnay's rifle; two French revolvers; a wad of francs and the two stolen horses.

Ousaïd n-Hmad pointed at Alla, once wearer of the blue cloak, now in the blue *tajjelabith* of a *mokhazni*. "These are the charges," he proclaimed. "Alla n-Khuya bears the weight of at least one murderous sin in his life. By testimony he has shown little remorse. He faces death for his crime. This is a just and fitting end after his long countenance with the devil. Is justice best served if the world is without him?"

"And he is Lyazzid n-Ouzzine," Ousaïd continued and indicated the other. "Brave when he points a gun at Amnay. Now we seem him as ignoble and a coward. Is justice served if the world is without him?"

"Alla murdered one of our warriors sworn to the duty of council and tribe, his third cohort, now dead, the other. And with this third man he is also guilty before God of the attempted murder of a guest under the protection of Ahmed Larbi and Akka n-Ali."

The words "attempted murder" piqued the prisoners' ears.

On cue, Aumont stepped out into the sun. The defendants gaped at the apparition of a dead man, shambling and weak, but strong-willed. Lyazzid dropped all pretense of bravery. Clasping his hands, he fell to his knees, weeping for the forgiveness of judge and victim. Allah was in this man, clearly raised from the dead.

"I have many hateful errors," he pleaded. "Harming and killing for money. And almost enjoying it. Allah will punish me, but I beg mercy before that time."

Aumont, clutching a leather sack to his breast, lay upon a crude cot set up beside the *igherm* door. His pale face yielded no sign what he thought of Lyazzid's entreaty.

When Ousaïd n-Hmad prompted them, Amnay, Akli n-Moussa, and Lieutenant Aumont each identified Alla as an assailant. He had fired a stolen French pistol with no regard for life. Akka swore an oath as witness to the aftermath, as the wicked fled.

The law allowed the possibility of mercy if an immediate male relative of a victim was present to negotiate a *ddiya* with the killer on behalf of the family. But no agnate was on hand to seek terms, which in any event would likely have been too high for the brigand to meet. Alla was doomed; only his life could satisfy the blood wealth.

"The guilt of Alla is clear," Ousaïd intoned. "Subject to laws, he will be put to merciful death. He best beseech Allah's forgiveness."

Ousaïd righteously turned to Akka, Amnay and Akli n-Moussa. They then conferred out of earshot for several long moments. At consensus, they faced Aumont beside them, and Amnay spoke.

"Alain, parler plus fort."

The Lieutenant was taken by surprise. But with very measured movements he reached into the leather bag and extracted two books. He held one out for all to see: the Qur'an. The raptness of the villagers was palpable. Together, they bowed their heads. Aumont slowly, deliberately thumbed to a page and began to read in soft, halting French—with intervals for Amnay's translation—a passage that seemed for the benefit of both the village and baffled Alla: "And We have set on the earth mountains standing firm, lest it should shake with them, and We have made therein broad highways between mountains for them to pass through; that they may receive guidance." He let the last phrase roll from his tongue with honeyed but firm eloquence. **"The Qur'an. The Prophets. Surah 21:31,"** Aumont added.

A murmur, as if in response to a revelation coursed through the assembly. Then Aumont raised the Bible, which Amnay identified as the book of the Nazarenes. Aumont, then, possessed two words of God. The attendees looked upon this moment as a form of divine grace indeed.

Aumont read again, and Amnay interpreted. "For the mountains may depart and the hills be removed, but my steadfast love shall not depart from you, and my covenant of peace shall not be removed, says the Lord, who has compassion on you. **Isaish, 54, verse 10.**"

Everyone, including Akka Ahêddây, struggled to comprehend. Aumont feebly tried to rise from the cot. The Lieutenant, bag in hand, hobbled toward Lyazzid. From the satchel he pulled an unsheathed knife. A current surged through the gathering. Surely, after reading two sacred passages the Frenchman would not take revenge? Aumont pointed to tightly bound hands, and then thrust his own wrists apart. It was a signal that he intended to cut Lyazzid's leather manacles.

The surprise of the villagers swelled to disbelief. Such mercy was uncommon, almost unknown. No one could have imagined it would be shown for a perpetrator by the surviving victim. All thought this holy soldier to surely be very wise, or very witless.

Aumont sliced through the leather cords. Lyazzid could scarcely understand his great fortune. He remained kneeling, wide-eyed, and fearful.

Ousaïd n-Hmad was moved, for he understood the compassion. Akka decreed that Lyazzid be flogged ten times, by Amnay, and then taken far from the village by the two agents who had captured him. Never was a man more happy to be beaten.

Two days later, Akka held a small *sadaka*, a banquet, to herald Alain's recovery and imminent departure. He struggled to express himself.

"Aumont and Duplessy, you are almost other members of our village. It is a great pity all *Iroumin* are not like you!"

Aumont was drunk with happiness when this was explained to him. Akka proved he had keenly absorbed some French when—over the course of a minute—he haltingly repeated: " . . . but they who wait for the Lord shall renew their strength . . . they shall mount with wings like eagles, they shall run and not be weary, and they shall walk . . . and not faint."

With that, Akka presented to Aumont a silver amulet, in the shape of an eight-pointed star, with the wings of a bird.

"Akka, it is I who owe *you* a gift. So great I can never repay."

"I foresee that some day there may come a time to do so," Akka said. Amnay fluidly bridged the language barrier.

Akka and Addi both sensed a vital link to this man Alain Aumont-that through him, somehow, they could break the chains that bound them.

NINE:

AIR

At Desaix's prompting, La Tour turned his gaze to the parapet, a long leap and a huge obstacle. Pondering the challenge replenished his determination. Beyond this pit was the world where he belonged, no matter his condition. The sooner he reached it the better.

A limping, one-eyed man wearing a black patch approached them, shuffled up and stood there. He eyed La Tour, squinting with his one eye, as if could intuit his thoughts. "My name is Miege." He shrugged. "They call me the warden."

A filthy shirt covered the affable fellow's leprous arms, but La Tour could sense the heart of a tyrant.

"I was a trooper in Algérie. Chasing those blue-people Tuaregs to and fro between the *hammada* and Merzouga. Tiresome work. Filthy stupid goddamn camels."

He shrugged again. "Bring me your papers later. We talk. I live there," he said, indicating a roughhewn shack below the caves and huts near the stream. Miege hobbled away toward home.

"Watch out you don't offend him. The rules of worldly graces," said Desaix, sweeping his hand at the sky, "don't apply in here. In the valley of the lepers the one-eyed man is king."

The next day, early morning and late afternoon, two planes brought food, a large sack of books, basic medicine, a small store of miscellaneous replacement clothing and tools. Between their arrivals, Miege sent several people, La Tour among them, to the thin juniper trees and laurel bushes and other kindling at a far section of the valley. The brief niceties accorded to new arrivals had elapsed as of last night. Now the Frenchman would work.

"We want fire in this hell!" Miege hollered. "Fire to see, to cook, to hold back the ghosts. Cut some brush! And be quick!" He was a self-appointed slave driver.

La Tour was grateful for an excuse to explore. It was impossible to see the value in any rush. He and four other inmates walked forward, among them Esterhazy, a kind but utterly failed baron turned arms merchant by way of Tanger; and Borbon, a former soldier and *kif* smuggler. The group shuffled to the outlying vegetation. Over the morning, they chopped enough kindling for a week of twice-daily cooking fires. La Tour eyed the ravaged valley and doubted that it would sustain this yield much longer. There was not enough greenery, certainly little that grew for very long. The dense groves that were once near the stream had been culled in an ever-widening zone. The terrain was starkly beautiful, simultaneously dead and alive, amber-red and strewn with boulders.

Dellafleur made his home across the way, between two flat-top boulders overlaid with a neat construction of reeds and brush. From afar, he bore a vague resemblance to the image conjured by Hugo's Hunchback. In exile from his exile, his head bound loosely in bandages, the crazy Frenchman was having an incoherent conversation with no one.

"From his roost," Borbon observed, "he often talks to birds. Like now. They probably understand him better than we do. And they are immune to his disease."

A bird had landed on the lowest branch of the juniper tree to seize a morsel of bait. As a show for their benefit, Dellafleur sprang a crude twig cage trap. The snare closed around the flailing form. The imbecile reached in, snatched the frantic bird and to La Tour's horror, casually snapped its neck.

"Hey! Hey! Why did you do that?" he screamed.

Dellafleur paid him no mind—it was vacant.

"We know why," said Esterhazy in the remnant of a noble accent.

"They can fly away."

"I should think he already has," La Tour replied sadly.

The six of them amassed the wood into a fleet of crude piles, then bundled them with rope. With effort, each dragged two loads across the bumpy ground toward camp.

La Tour considered the rope. No piece was longer than ten feet, but with enough swiped lengths he could weave a ladder. Then, of course, the basic dilemma of an escape route would solve itself in scaling the cliff to suspend it. The tilted sandstone wall, however, had few reliable handholds. He would need to drive pitons or spikes into the rock. These could be anchors for the rope, or steps in themselves. And by the hour he grew willing to die trying.

Over the next few days several new inmates were delivered as castaway baggage. One of them, a Spaniard, was a walking shell of dispirited flesh. Desaix offered kind counsel. All had been struck by an uncommon torment for which no medical enterprise was eager or able to devise a cure. They would remain here, buried alive by indifference. They were one step short of a wasteland, or the moon, for all the attention they received.

La Tour was grudgingly grateful that leprosy made slow progress. He hoped that his eventual escape would not be in vain, too late. Perhaps it was in his imagination, but the discomfort of his skin seemed to increase. He complained to Ahmad Didier, the French-Berber medical adjutant, and was issued aspirin, ointment and bandages. A truly effective remedy could well be available somewhere in the world, except he no longer lived there.

* * * * *

Late on La Tour's third day, a plane came again. The pilot who gazed on to the assemblage was a different fellow than the first armed and irritable chap. This one, a more primitive specimen, was a piggish, wobbling oaf who babbled like a crackbrain drunkard. The fool flew for charity, but in this or any condition, he may well cause more mischief or misery than he alleviated on his "good will" missions.

"Excuse me, Major, do you know that this Arab bastard is about to SHOOT you?" he slurred. "Our Lady, full of GRACE. Full of *grace* is she? . . . Pull up the NOSE, you idiot! Are you trying to get us KILLED? . . . See my satin shoes? I'm DANCING!"

His blather echoed downward like the musing of some stentorian baboon. The standard rope ladder, without sacks tied to its end, tumbled from the cliff top but snarled half-way down and would not unfurl. The new visitor hauled it up and set the coil right. On the second try, the bottom section twisted hard against the rock. In moments of wrangling, he straightened out the rope-and-wood device—barely sufficient to lower arrivals into the pit, but priceless as a stairway to freedom—and its full length played out.

A trembling young Moroccan, in a tattered black *tajjelabith,* began to descend, a personal bag slung on his left shoulder and a mail sack on his right. His leprous right arm was half-useless for grasping each rung, and his mind was equally enfeebled at the prospect of this new home. He barely made it to ground without plunging from the wall. Setting down near them, he let the mail sack slide down his ruined arm, and ran away to wretch, trailed by two compassionate fellows of the welcoming committee.

"Meet Abdel Courchavon!" the pilot shouted. "The new mailman. And your latest fresh meat!" The pilot lurched back out of sight, into silence, to commune with his demons.

Courchavon was a former railroad official and engineer who had lived in Paris prior to his gang-boss days on track maintenance between Rabat and Marrakech.

"We think," said Desaix as if conferring over the body of a friend in a coffin, "that he fled prosecution for a murder in Dijon. If so, some leper among the dirt-cheap slave labor crews meted poetic justice to him."

Courchavon blearily opened the sack and removed several bundles of letters which he untied and sorted in a cursory fashion. He began to call names.

"Esterhazy . . . Levroux . . . Ahmed . . . Porch . . . Desaix . . . Borbon . . . . We have a regular goddamn Foreign Legion of men here, you lonesome fuckers!"

"Bassoun . . . Navarre . . . Blobec . . . **La Tour** . . ."

La Tour was surprised to hear his name. What could have come so quickly? Would they offer a drowning man a drink of water? La Tour shambled forward and took the posting from Courchavon It was a worn and grimy envelope, etched with François's neat angular script, postmarked Lyon. It was so odd that their letters had crossed paths. His mild cheer turned to foreboding one second after he slit the seal and unfolded the stationery.

> *Dear Jean-Michel,*
>
> *Too many weeks have passed since your last communication. We are worried. We take heart that in the absence of word from the Légion, we can assume you are well, or at least, crude be to say it, alive in some condition in Maroc.*
>
> *I do not wish to be sad, but I write you with bad tidings. Mother is very ill. The doctors diagnosed a stroke. The doctor is not optimistic, as the ailment has damaged both her body and spirit. Lord knows what is worse. She speaks of you often, especially when we wheel her into the garden, which has fallen into some disrepair. We are not often there—I must help with the bank business, which is plagued by great difficulties. We miss your expertise. When Mother is not sad, she is sleeping, and if awake, trying to talk herself into life with a slow weak voice.*
>
> *We beg you to request leave and return home as best you can, and soon. I curse the day you went to that place. Please write of your plans at the earliest chance.*
>
> *Earnestly yours, in love and brotherhood,*
>
> *François.*

Jean-Michel's composure cracked like an egg shell. He had not cried in two years. He withdrew to his notch in the eastern wall and there, he privately poured out his grief, which soon evolved to anger, and then to fierce resolve. No matter the risk or consequences or the need for minor miracles, La Tour vowed to escape this hole, this barren stretch around it and find his way home to France.

People drifted to their hovels of caves and tents. Soft early evening conversations tossed words like "Follies Bergere" and "*merde*" and "*salaam*" into the mix like signals from separate worlds. Boot steps crunched the earth. Small cooking fires glowed. The fellows attended to personal hygiene or camp maintenance. Someone nearby poured water into a large basin. Two men giggled with vulgar mischief. La Tour wondered what might have inspired their craven mirth. He squinted at the now-obscure cliff face and in a moment of clarity he realized that this might be the perfect opportunity. If . . .

"Jean-Michel," Desaix's distinctive voice said from the dark. "I saw you were unhappy with your mail." Desaix's condolence tried to reflect their reality. "In such a situation, I don't think one can ever feel more imprisoned."

"Would you like Blobec to help you? He was a priest, too. He can help you pray . . ."

"Pray?" La Tour scoffed. "To ask mercy and guidance of the same force that put me—us—here?"

Desaix frowned at this phrase. But he seemed to deduce its meaning.

"Oddly, that is what I have come to talk about. Remember the other day I said that there were two ways out of here? In a coffin or . . . ?"

"Yes, I'm listening. Would you like a cigarette?" He offered Desaix the blue pack.

"Oh, my yes! Is it a Gaulois? Yes, yes it is. Bless you!"

Desaix sparked the tobacco and inhaled like a man taste-testing a flute of his own fine Champagne. He was momentarily lost in a man-made nirvana.

"Well?" said La Tour, suddenly impatient.

Desaix emerged from his brief nicotine trance glassy eyed and content.

"You have noticed that the pilot has not retracted that ladder? I had an inkling he would not, and I just walked by to confirm it. I wonder if anyone else has noticed . . ."

A commotion broke the night silence out in mid-valley. Two men snarled at each other, another spurred them on, shortly followed by shouts of panic as the men apparently came to blows. Men quickly gathered. Courchavon, nearby, shouted for order.

"Hey, you crazy bastards! And I mean you, the audience, goading men to fight!"

La Tour continued, "And if the ladder is still lowered, then what?"

"Climb it and take your chances. The odds are that no ladder will remain extended down that cliff face for months to come. If ever. Perhaps you . . ."

La Tour suddenly saw the great risk and the slim possibilities. In his present state of mind, he was more inclined to seize on the latter. He sprang to standing.

"Come with me."

"Pack your bags as if you're going on a trip, my friend," Desaix reminded him.

"A little conspicuous to walk around with luggage, no?"

"Put the necessities under your *djellabah.*"

"You're almost too damn smart for my own good," La Tour replied warmly. He set about doing as suggested: money, photos, the gun and bullets, a little food, socks and underwear, matches, his compass and Grandfather's watch. All of which he jammed into a small satchel and slung it over his shoulder beneath his garment. La Tour was in a daze. So much change, so quickly. His impulse was so rash as to be irrational, even suicidal. And entirely necessary. "Let's go."

They walked past the scene of conflict, as Miege gravitated to it. Esterhazy, the self-proclaimed stepson (or bastard) of a bankrupt Alsace landowner, confronted strange Dellafleur, who talked to birds, then killed them. Esterhazy feared humiliation more than he did Dellafleur, but in the real world the grotesque birdman's eyes would give one pause.

"What the hell is this, Pierre, trying to steal another man's food?" Courchavon rasped at the crazy man. He received no reply.

"So you pull a knife!" he screamed at Esterhazy in turn. "On an idiot stealing two eggs! You know that weapons are forbidden here!"

"A man can't be too careful!"

La Tour glanced at the far cliff, now shrouded in darkness.

"Can he be too dead?!" Courchavon appealed. He paused. "Dellafleur! Go home!"

"Don't tell me what to do!" the bird killer protested.

La Tour edged away from the restive scene, into the valley. What was that up top, the flicker of a fire, a silhouette?

"Do you want to spend more time in the brig?" Miege asked both.

La Tour stepped more nimbly as firelight and prying eyes fell behind and he was swallowed by the night. He hoped that the pilot was indeed touched, inept, or drunk, or for any reason had failed to retract that ladder. Only then could he depart this asylum.

La Tour neared the ebony cliff, but he did not see the ladder. His heart pounded. Where was this crude means to his crucial end? . . . There, in the recess; the ladder was still suspended. It led to a world above this valley, a form of heaven—because that would be nearly anyplace but here. He would climb soon, when the camp was asleep. He now heeded Desiax's advice to pray—that the pilot was soused and asleep, completely oblivious to the oversight.

It was past nine o'clock. The camp began to settle. In daytime there was little to do, but many inmates filled the hours with a heroic fight against boredom and despair. At night, from an hour or two after sunset and on to dawn, most surrendered to sleep. Someone broke into song, almost a lullaby. He squatted at the cliff base and listened. La Tour wondered if his absence had been noted. Here and there lanterns illuminated tent interiors and some of the far caves. His inner focus was fixed on the giant steps toward home. The first ones, up this cliff, were tiny in distance but long in risk. So he concentrated, meditated and passionately willed his success.

La Tour wondered if another inmate lurked nearby for the same purpose as he. A duel for the ladder would draw disastrous attention. He listened extra keenly for movement. His thighs, strengthened by the mountain terrain, burned from his crouching at the base of the cliff. He felt invisible, a predator patiently waiting to stalk a thing without form. No sound, not even a breeze, passed his ears.

"Vio con Dios, my friend," Desaix's crackling voice emitted from the dark, urging him on. "Tell those who matter, tell them that we have been abandoned here."

La Tour could wait no longer. He reached up, unconcerned that his *tajjelabith* may be visible in the light of stars or the rising quarter moon.

"I will."

He banished any images of failure. Animal now, fearless, placing a boot on a rung he raised hand over hand, foot over foot. No downtrodden leper he; he would be in action for the rest of his life, even if it should only last another few hours. Or minutes.

He halted halfway to gaze down and behind, listening for excited voices about an escape in progress. He only heard silence, below and above, and resumed the ascent. He fought as the ladder precariously canted out and down from the crag's jutting brow. He struggled as his wide unblinking eyes drew to the lip of the cliff. Fifty meters away, almost parallel to the cliff, the plane glinted in weak moonlight. Beyond its tail was a dwindling fire and a man, on his back and seemingly asleep. La Tour saw no one else. He paused an extra interim to be sure, then crawled atop the parapet on his belly in a cat-like alert. An object glimmered in the firelight. Glass. A bottle. From which it appeared that the pilot had indeed put himself in a stupor.

La Tour crept in a slow crouch to the right wheel and the far side of the fuselage, this being the minimum safe distance to the snoring pilot. Now he worried that someone else would climb the ladder, too. Should he raise it? But if the pilot knew he had forgotten to do so, it would surely invite suspicion if the task was already complete. Calculating the odds, La Tour thought it best to not underestimate the intelligence of someone whose ignorance was critical.

He squinted on to the nearly featureless terrain. The only cover, a low clump of rocks and brush, was a stone's throw out. If he should fall asleep there, he would have scant chance to reach the plane unseen before takeoff. If he slept here, the pilot might awaken at any time. He determined to stay awake all night and hide if necessary. The alternatives were the horns of a dilemma. His escape must remain unknown beyond the valley until the plane next arrived here, or he would never leave Morocco. In the morning, the pilot would retrieve and stow the ladder, start the engine and fly on. La Tour's one good option was stealth: perch on the struts beneath the fuselage before the plane became airborne. If he failed, the valley below and distant France would both be beyond his feeble grasp.

La Tour fixed his mind on tomorrow's best outcome. The hours ticked by. Never more alive, he was determined to remain awake. No other eyes peered over the top of the cliff. All was silent and still, like a dead planet. He watched the fractional moon arc across a clear sky and the stars dance in celestial precision. He was elated at the spectacle, but felt insignificant, too. The moon vanished, clouds came to block the stars and it was pitch dark. Night was deepest at the approach of dawn. La Tour decided that now was the time to take cover behind the rocks.

A half hour late, the still-hidden sun began to bleed thin gray light. The pilot, who had barely moved all night, soon stirred at the weak cue of daybreak like the dull fool he was. La Tour watched him groggily sit up and gaze about, most intently across the valley at the eastern rim, and then torpidly renew a small fire. He eyed the coffee pot and set it on a grid over the flame, then rose to standing like a punch-dizzy boxer. As if unwilling for the plane to bear witness, he lurched a discreet distance and, his back to the flying belle, commenced a comically long urination. He returned to squat at the fire as it licked the pot. He gnawed a crusty baguette, and shakily poured last night's brew into a dirty cup. La Tour heard the creature slurp the bleak liquid. The aviator rummaged in his sack and found nothing more for his ill-supplied breakfast. Stowing the pot and matches within, he trudged to the ladder.

At once, in the calculated risk La Tour was compelled to take, knowing the pilot would take moments to retrieve and roll the ladder, he dashed toward the near-side wheel strut. He inserted himself there and hugged the belly, merging man and metal so that the fat low fuselage would hide him from view.

The flyboy fool paused at the ladder anchor, perhaps in bovine wonder that no one had exploited his blunder. Shrugging off the notion, he rolled the ladder and tottered with it to the plane, casting his bleary eyes down to diffuse the weak, but growing sunlight. Ignoring the empty bottle near his boots, wobbling onto the wing, he dumped the ladder and his sack in the rear seat, and himself into the cockpit. Pushing the starter button, he waited for the engine to respond or refuse. If the latter, he would climb down and hand-crank the propeller to turn the starter. La Tour, then, would be plainly visible. But the engine blessedly coughed and sputtered, not unlike the pilot himself and reliably if somewhat grumpily, engaged its cylinders.

La Tour clutched the right front strut with his arms and legs. The crown of his head pointed toward the engine and his face at the worn gray skin of the beast. The plane veered rightward from the Valley. La Tour uneasily transferred to the center, where both struts joined the fuselage, so that his weight would be evenly distributed and less detectable once the plane was aloft. The Piper accelerated over the bumpy earth. To La Tour's dismay, the growing volume of discharge as the plane neared take off was not only somewhat noxious, but hot. The flyboy may already have noticed that his plane handled somewhat more sluggishly, as if bearing extra weight. But La Tour doubted that in the pilot's besotted fog, any logic would connect this oddity to the night-long suspension of the ladder. *Please, God. Please don't let this dullard even think to consider such an idea until it is too late to turn back.*

Now La Tour was improvising. He had taken his first two, huge steps to freedom. The next one required some innovation, but much more pure, naked luck. He dearly hoped the pilot would land on a base runway far from any fort or hangar. On the approach, he would shift to one of the struts. As the wheels touched earth and the machine slowed, he would drop off, away from the low-slung fuselage and oncoming rear wheel. At twenty or so knots he would sustain a bad thrashing, but he would be alive and liberated. La Tour was almost glad at this chance, faithful that the righteousness of his journey would leap all obstacles. But right now, airborne, La Tour had no way to know if the pilot was flying to his post in the vicinity, or to some other, perhaps more far-flung destination. If that was so, La Tour grew certain that his tenure aloft could not last the required time. The simple act of regaining earth alive, anywhere, would require a minor miracle.

The engine vibrations were shaking his body as if he was patched to an electric current. He inhaled both pure cool air at this 500-meter elevation and noxious warm emissions an arm's length away. The mixture was barely adequate, and only in small doses lest he foul his lungs, so he was ever short of breath.

BOOK TWO: HERALD

DECISION

*T*o gauge the direction of the shuddering plane above him, La Tour peered over his body to gaze behind, toward the crude compass of the tail. The sun, rising above the horizon, was to the right of it. He dropped his head to gaze upside down through the blur of the rotating propeller just in front of his face to view the landscape below and beyond, to the volcanic wastes of Adrar n-Sargho. Slightly left of the plane's bearing, was the crown of Adrar n-Azourki. Due west, the thin crystal snake of the Asif Dades, easing through a gullet of green. He estimated the air speed and flying time to calculate the approximate distance from the river to Bou Malem.

La Tour did not expect the drunken aviator to vault the 3,500 meter peaks in the grip of the unpredictable morning thermals. The plane began to gain altitude, rising above a seared plain toward the cliffs. Increasing engine vibrations progressively numbed and weakened La Tour's limbs. He inverted his head and peered down upon desolation on a steady northwest course over escalating ridges and plateaus towards the tremendous peaks. The singular Dades gorge carved through the terrain ahead. Beyond it, he recognized several notches in the serrated profile: passes that penetrated the Atlas wall through which the Armée and Légion moved through to Azilal and other towns in Ait Atta territory.

The plane crossed the wide cut of the Dades gorge, and turned to parallel its run. Rising now, but not enough. Relative to the prodigious terrain, the plane was losing altitude. La Tour was mystified. The engine discharged fat

*fingers of smoke, and in a gradually rising protest, the vibrations grew greater.
The heat also increased from pleasantly warm to slow roast.*

*Far below, was the blessed river, giving life this minute as always to the
grain fields, the pastures, the sheep and the Berbers. Ait Atta Berbers.
The engine took a slightly different tone of labored stress. The plane
turned leftward, northwest, toward a ridge. La Tour quickly calculated the
angle of the nose. A moment later, he reckoned again, to his distress, the
plane was closer to the earth by at least one hundred meters. If the pilot
did not pull back on the stick to gain elevation, he would barely clear the
plateau. Then it occurred to La Tour, that this might be the lout's intent.*

TEN:

RIDDLE

Addi Yacoub, holy man, healer and teacher, sat before a rapt audience of boys and young men. Their attention was no less than if he were gazing at them with perfect vision.

"I have told you that Sidi Jilani was lost in the wilderness for many years. He had only his white *tajjelabith*, made by his mother with special, blessed cotton. A small sack of figs and several handfuls of grain. Scarcely enough food for three days. How would he survive? Jilani feared death, but his greater fear was being punished for weak faith that Allah would provide sustenance. With gentle words and stalwart spirit he prayed for strength. Insh'Allah, he came upon a large oasis, one so pure it may never have been touched by man, with bounteous figs, shady palm trees and cool, clear water. A camel waited to carry Jilani anywhere he wished to travel. God had answered his prayers. He became a joyous seeker. Jilani remained truly faithful, and Allah provided for him wherever he went, gathering tribes to his benevolence, building an empire of wisdom, not war. Years later he returned home, wearing the same *tajjelabith*. Its pure, strong, sacred cloth was yet white and whole, like Sidi Jilani, long tested in the wilderness. The Sultan sought his advice on all matters. He was a godsend to his people and nation which grew mighty and prosperous. Someday soon, God willing, Jilani will return to us in our time of greatest need. He may come in an unknown way, or not be recognizable when he does. He may arrive in the old way, upon a camel or a mule, or the new, like the French. He may walk from the desert. Or fall from the sky. Or await our passage at a river. He may identify himself, or say nothing until we are wise enough and faithful enough to recognize him on our own. But I assure you he will test us, test our faith, and he will enable us to know much more about ourselves than we ever could without him."

* * * * *

The nearly sheer cliff drew closer and more ominous by the second. La Tour felt engulfed by a storm of terror. He was about to choose between identical deaths: plunging from a considerable height and speed, or making a mad attempt to climb into the cockpit behind the pilot, who would then shoot him, or heave his helpless, desperate passenger into the air with wild gyrations of the plane, like trying to shake a fat fly off a bucking horse.

Now vulnerable to swirling updrafts, the plane did not raise its flight line. La Tour detected no malfunction; a crash was not imminent. Oddly, this increased the dilemma. He imagined his maneuver the instant the plane were to touch a runway, but added a critical distinction: he would not fall to earth from one meter, but from well over twenty. At an air speed of at least fifty knots.

La Tour carefully suspended himself from the angled wheel struts and was immediately slammed face-on by a hammer-strike of rising air. The plane pitched upward. La Tour's heart followed when he saw that his last, best chance was about to vanish just as he reached for it. Then the plane veered downward, again bringing it into line with the top of the plateau. The pilot could have once more lifted sharply to clear the wall, but instead merely returned to his original glide path. This was the best La Tour could hope for.

He silently, simultaneously invoked the Christian God and Islam's Allah. But despite conviction that was this was the only option, the urgent need to open his hands was checked by its suicidal folly; rigid instincts refused to let him drop into appalling consequences. The rocks loomed, and he crudely calculated the air speed against their scale. He would not get a rehearsal or a better view of the target area. It was now or never to fall and fly: one chance in a thousand was better than none at all. Still, it took two deliberate efforts, over precious seconds, to detach himself. The plummet began.

* * * * *

Two women at a stream saw the plane from two thousand meters off, emerging from the center of the morning sun. The older woman had seen one such *djen* two winters ago—the last migration these Ait Atta clans had taken—near Taghzout. It had flown twice over their camp and with spitting guns killed three horses, two men and a child. Akka swore vengeance. Terrified, Hada felt it was about to happen again; like that demonic machine, this whining devil came in low, menacing, growling. It rose just before crossing the lip of the precipice.

Suddenly, from the flying demon, a very strange image was born. Both women witnessed cargo, a bundle of rags—no, a man—hang from the belly of the rumbling serpent. Then he fell, bird-like, face down and forward. Disbelieving their eyes, they shrieked and ran pell-mell in fear for their lives.

Gravity grabbed La Tour and sucked him downward feet first. Air pushed, inflating his *tajjelabith* which billowed like a tent in the wind. La Tour again quarter-rotated his body from vertical to horizontal, and instinctively extended his arms into stabilizing wings. This seemed to slow the descent from what would have been grave injury or death. The plane flew on, away, as if a vulture had released a white dove from its talons. Then he heard an odd sound. Like a steam whistle. Or women screaming.

The flaps of his *tajjelabith* caught a strong updraft. He felt oddly buoyant and liberated; although it was impossible, for an instant he seemed almost imperceptibly liberated from gravity, from what would be a descent to grave injury or death. Then he fell again, forward, obeying an essential natural law. Another gust punched him to vertical by its arbitrary rule. His *tajjelabith* bulged and splayed out anew. The broader surface of cloth worked to slightly slow his speed as the earth was more leisurely rising to greet him.

More eyes rose to see an angel materialize in mid-air.

La Tour glided down a chute of air toward a knoll of grass and gravel. His mind surged to gauge the speed of descent, the spot he was most likely to hit, and the best position to be in when he did. It overloaded on anticipation of impact and the agony to follow. This was likely a death sentence, unless by God's grace, he fell within walking or crawling distance of a village, which might at least gain him access to food or water. That is, if by some greater miracle they did not discover he was a Frenchman and a leper.

Time passed in tiny bursts. Rust-red stone dazzled and glowered in the sun. Wind whipped his hair and face and blew fine dust into his eyes, but he dared not close them. A blur of faces upturned from among rough squat buildings and scattered tents beside an array of green fields. The utter terror and giddy freedom of unnatural flight crystallized in each fraction of a four-second fall; in sequence they were more than the sum of their parts.

He aimed his buttock, hip and lower back, hitting in that order, sliding and half-rolling across a zone of small rocks and soft dirt that mercifully cushioned the impact.

A hard knob of dirt shattered this briefest of reveries. It bounced him forward, a meter high, off a low gravel-strewn ledge. The world briefly went black. He felt pebbles like a hundred spikes seeking to gouge the flesh in his lower back and rump beneath the *tajjelabith* and uniform. La

Tour again lifted above the stones as if he were aboard a flying carpet. This curious moment abruptly ended when he slammed down again, as gracefully as a well-stuffed potato sack that has been tossed from a speeding truck. Air blasted from him and he feared he would be unable to draw it again. He quaked, body, brain and soul. Momentum careened him across steel-hard dirt. Nearing a field, he made one final bounce, and then came to rest.

In these seconds of fall and impact, the plane had flown not even one hundred meters. La Tour had no presence of mind to peer after it, much less notice if the pilot had so quickly detected the loss of weight, or was gazing back at what he may have somehow deduced was a stowaway.

A stone's throw away the young men around Addi Yacoub, and all others viewing the spectacle, were frozen in awe, then a shudder went through them, and they collectively gasped. Just then, Akka Ahêddây stepped from his red door. The coincidence of this vision, after Addi's words of devotion, must surely signify a reply to their entreaties from Allah, even if they did not fully know all that they had asked. All kneeled at this spirit and legend before them. Nearly two hundred men, women and children waited for the holy vision to speak. Akka hastened across the plaza between his *igherm* and the school.

La Tour lay like a mannequin. Stunned, he did not move or twitch. At last, he slowly connected his brain with his body and awaited an injury report. To his surprise, his legs, arms and head all registered relative integrity. He sat up expecting agony, then very slowly rose to his full six feet. Pain radiated across his back, down his legs and up his shoulders. What else to expect after falling from a 100-knot plane? A mass of bruises would result. But he was not a victim of crippling broken bones. He had secured liberty.

He was as astonished at his profound luck as the people before him. No one was likely to ever believe this tale, should he live to recount its breathless absurdity. This scene would very difficult to ascribe to luck alone. It was nearly enough to make he, an avowed, evolving agnostic, believe in an exalted Almighty instrument.

"Wullah! Wullah! Di l-haqq n-Ullah!" By God! By God! By God's truth!

The weird chorus fully unnerved La Tour, for it seemed to be directed at him. Perhaps he had arrived in the midst of war preparations, or a religious ceremony forbidden to infidel eyes. He did not know which might be worse. He peered at the abyss behind him, then to the edge of the village, fifty meters away, he had glimpsed from above. He could hardly be more lost. He drew the *tajjelabith* hood tight about his head and the *achttan* around his chin and mouth.

La Tour and his rapt beholders were in a kind of mutual trance. Bowing, kneeling, they peeked at him, then at the dirt, as if too long a look was irreverent. Whatever this gathering, he was the center of attention and on full display. Minutes passed. No one moved. Hearts beat heavily. Breezes fluttered clothing and maize stalks. A small dust devil whirled about, but no human walked, talked, did anything but breathe. Statues all.

At last, a lean man in a white *rezzeth* and a threadbare black *tajjelabith* gently prodded a young woman holding a water jug beside him. He pointed to La Tour. But the girl in the red caftan did not budge. He took her by the shoulders, spoke words of assurance, and pushed her toward the guest.

"O, Shrif, so grateful are we for this kindness!" the man intoned. Although La Tour knew some Tamazight, the Imazighen dialect spoken across the Central Atlas, he understood only a fraction of the words. "I beg you to please accept a humble drink of welcome from our village. The bearer of the water is my daughter. Will your holiness accept her gracious offering?"

La Tour was stunned by what little he comprehended. Shrif? Holiness? How must he look to them, plunging from a strange sky machine into mid-air suspension, descending directly into their presence, without injury? Now it occurred to him that this impromptu congregation thought him a sign of divine favor. A supernatural being. A deity. At that thought, he was unable to respond, in any language. Behold the silent emissary of Allah.

The barefoot young woman, anxious but joyful, edged forward lithely, as if in a garden of jewels. She drew near and he beheld glistening jade-hued eyes. Ebony hair set in a lush, anointed coil from which several smooth strands fell across silken auburn skin. A supple, wistful set to her mouth that could not hide delight. Eyelids dusted with black kohl. Golden bracelets on both sleeves of her red *dfinth*. The back of her hands bore a simple pattern drawn in henna, and her chin a simple tattoo of two blue vertical lines. Most striking was her dignified self-regard. The elemental beauty of Maroc seemed to abound in her veins.

"Great holiness, please accept this gift from your servants," she said in a melodious voice. She peeked at him with exhilaration and fear, and as quickly averted her gaze. The people bowed and prayed more zealously as she held forth the jar and set it down within his reach. La Tour saw in her a flame of serenity but strength, and he was overcome, by what he could not explain, as charmed by her as she was faithful to him, or what she believed him to be. His muteness could well have been taken as holy tranquility, as austere appreciation. But he was only clamping tight his whirling emotions, though most of his face was concealed.

Without forethought, he raised his right hand, similar to the blessed greeting symbolizing the Five Pillars of Faith. The Berbers at once took this as his favor and praise. He had meant only to signal a greeting, or to offer deference to better hide the leprosy behind his mask. Instead the gesture further inspired their adoration.

She reversed course to the village assembly with the same feline grace. La Tour heard himself blurt to her, in poor Tamazight, "Is there an *amrabt*?" She turned to him.

This was a strange request for a purported and oddly transported god to ask a human. A deity would have little need for spiritual advice or medical attention.

"Yes, we have an *amrabt*. And whatever my lord wishes," the girl replied softly.

"Please have him come to me," La Tour replied.

She glanced at Addi Yacoub the Sufi and said, "As you wish, my *shrif*."

The young lady—woman—appeared to swell with pride. The incarnation had immediately recruited her as his messenger, to bridge her unassuming world and his supernal wisdom. She dared not speculate on his reasons for wanting an *amrabt*.

La Tour watched her struggle with her thoughts and feelings. Self-possessed, in her late teens, she was of prime bridal age in her culture. Still, even at this moment the vague desire for intimacy was oddly comforting.

"*Ashnnu smitak? Comment vouz appelez-vous?*" he whispered in Moroccan Arabic and French.

"Kenza," she replied with puzzlement. Kenza turned away, as if from an icon or a person she adored but dared not look upon despite irresistible curiosity. She rejoined her proud, waiting father. They spoke together. With some urgency the man then guided the alert old fellow next to the clutch of young men and boys.

La Tour peered out from his hillock studded with clumps of grass, marveling that he hadn't been smashed or concussed into oblivion. His gaze swept to a thin stream, an array of fields and villages and a cemetery, on both sides of a larger stream, and all a realm on a table of land tightly bound in the near distance by rugged hills west, east and north, leading to the high peaks, and beyond them to Azilal and Demnate. The dwellings, a terra cotta hue closely matching the terrain, were constructed of stone or *pisé* or a combination. Some homes, in clusters, were built into slopes, rooted in and rising from the earth; other, separate above-ground units were made of or sheathed in rock walls carefully built to repel weather and assure durability. La Tour noted rough decorative designs etched in clay facades or sandstone. Across the stream, a typical tenement rose up a far slope, an inelegant nest of weary, oblong boxes, a cousin to any European mountain hamlet of medieval birth. Narrow alleys passed low doorways. Paths were worn in the few vacant parcels. The tight jumbles maximized protection. He saw anew why these inaccessible and defensible Atlas *igherman* so bedeviled the Armée and Légion. Absent here was a design feature common to other villages: walls painted in pastel. which were more easily seen from afar or spotted from the air.

La Tour scanned the horizons for familiar features. He saw none. Great unknown peaks loomed in all directions but southerly, where the heights fell toward the westbound Dades—and the garrison from which he had been banished days ago—to meet the scorched plains near Adrar n-Sargho and beyond it, the Sahara. One northeastern patch of snow, protected in shadow, still crowned a high niche.

The villagers began to reluctantly depart. He saw the notable man, clearly a leader, pace one step ahead of the blind fellow toward a large, separate *igherm* across a section of field and a rivulet. La Tour somehow sensed that their relationship was not filial, but deeper, rooted in great friendship and trust.

Minutes later, a young man in a red turban and a white *tajjelabith* came from that *igherm* bearing a cup and a simple pot on a tray. Kenza followed with a small basket. They set their offerings down beside him. The youngster dashed away. Kenza retired politely, smiling warmly. The pot contained *atai benaanaa*, the sweet, strong mint tea that Berbers and all Moroccans imbibed in quantity on all occasions. As spirits were forbidden, *atai* was the social lubricant always proffered to guests. The basket contained a hunk of barley bread and a dozen dates. Unfed since yesterday's late afternoon meal, La Tour wolfed the morsels. He gave no thought to the incongruity of a god eating like a beggar.

An hour passed. La Tour sipped the tea. The sun rose to mid-morning height, the breeze relented, and then it was summer. He sweated beneath his double layer of clothing, but dared not shed anything. Shortly, La Tour watched as the young man escorted the blind *amrabt* from the *igherm* up the slope toward him. Anticipating a great moment, a cluster of villagers discreetly trailed them. The holy man gestured, almost imperceptibly, and his guide stepped away. For every witness this was high drama: their revered spirit guide and healer was about to interact with a deity. La Tour, a soldier of an infidel tribe and a leper fleeing forcible exile, now regretted requesting the attention of the *amrabt*.

The *amrabt* stopped a short distance away. Perhaps, La Tour thought, the old man waited for him to approach. But he sensed this was not so; for now at least the holy man maintained a careful distance. The space was filled not by words but silence. The fellow entered a standing meditation, almost a trance. La Tour could not match this power. He was intimidated. Afraid. Cultures millennia old had secrets unknown and unfathomable to modern, ignorant souls. But the *amrabt* himself was unnerving. He was old in body, but his face reflected a strange, swirling vibrancy, like fire in a bottle. Rosy skin complemented a gray-black beard. A jagged scar above his left brow was testament to a violent past. The two blind eyes captured La Tour's attention, even as they repelled it. The turbid pupils and retinas, damaged by disease or defect, were the color of speckled pearl, or a bird's egg. Seldom blinking, they glared at the world, seeing nothing, or perhaps everything. The two-way mirrors between the *amrabt* and the world had been shattered. But the old man, La Tour reasoned, had long ago mastered another way to see.

His attention was divided between the regathered villagers, the *amrabt* five meters away, and the precipice a short distance behind him. Discovery and demise could be mere moments away. But he was not afraid. Not even when the striking man in the bright *tajjelabith* crossed the stream on a fine gray stallion. He cast a tell-tale aura—everyone watching the *amrabt* in near-unison turned their attention behind—but, by remaining mounted and silent, he did not disturb the scene. The respect these two men elicited from everyone, and clearly had for each other, was evident. The *amrabt* was much more than a mendicant, a ragged seer spewing prophesies for a meal. And the other was clearly prosperous and certainly a leader.

Akka Ahêddây! La Tour's realization was almost traumatic. He felt light-headed. Disembodied. A reeling, rapid plunge to despair soared back to the summit of wonder. His mind raced through an index of images: the villagers under machine guns, dead horses and Du Thierry in his death throes and Aziz refusing to die, charging horseback Imazighen, fleeing Mirvais, the stupendous view of the Atlas from the plane . . . and the photo of the Berber Mirvais had pored over as La Tour stood before the desk, just glimpsing the inverted face.

Akka dismounted against the backdrop of mountains. La Tour refocused on the old man, on his sightless yet vibrant eyes. He could not hide, dared not speak, and was determined to yield no telling clues. Silent minutes elapsed. Finally, the *amrabt* turned away; perhaps he could wait no longer for the visitor to speak. The young man came to escort the *amrabt*, and they wearily entered Akka's *igherm*. La Tour figured that they were baffled.

The sun reached its peak. From afar, the robust tenor of the *taleb* called the faithful to *dooher*. The arrival of a little god would not inhibit worship of the Most High. *"Allah ou akbar, Allah ou akbar. Haya aala elfalah, haya aala salat. Allah ou akbar, Allah ou akbar. Kad kamat a salate, kad kamat a salate. Allah ou akbar, Allah ou akbar."*

La Tour did not know what to do. He sat cross-legged, inert on his table-sized rock, watching and being watched. Activity slowed, stopped, then recommenced at half pace. Timid or humbly reverent, people ambled by at a prudent distance and cast inquisitive glances. At a prophesy. Not a prophet. Some pretended to chat with each other, but their interest was in him. Perhaps they were waiting. For him to speak. For a cue to rejoice. If the *amghar* and the *amrabt* believed he was the reincarnation of a deity, chosen for some task, then so it must be. Better, for now, to live as a fraud. A successful deceiver is a barren moon of conscience in close orbit about a fertile planet. He had no choice.

Seeing that he was a distraction, La Tour withdrew as much as possible from sight behind a boulder and pondered his bizarre state. A new, harder breeze caressed him. The dust-laden *chergui*—in Arabic *ash-sharqi*—can occur at any time of the year, but was most common in the summer. It heralds a renewal of blessed cycles that signals the nomadic Atlas Berbers and their cousins in much of the Maghreb to soon begin their migrations.

Despite war the Imazighen went about business—up and down the mountains—that was closely regulated by complex customs and simple seasons. They knew no other way. But Akka's Ait Atta had likely been here through the winter. Hiding. Waiting.

There were other reasons; too, that Akka remained in this remote citadel. The Ait Atta reviled the Glaoua tentacles that reached from the High Atlas to Marrakech and from there to the French. The Ait Atta refused to be ruled by either of them. Once within this realm, the Glaoui envoys would become agents of espionage and acquisition for the Second Sultan in Telouet, a glutton for power, gold, and young women.

La Tour sat, and sat. The sun sank behind the western peaks, turning a thousand ridges to a dreamscape of amber. He had never seen greater beauty. And his own peculiar prelude that morning might have never been experienced before by anyone at all. Now, after his nearly fatal descent—more like a marvelous rebirth—he was apparently touted as a god by people his own countrymen were trying to conquer or kill. He tried to search his soul to determine if the gods, should there be any, were amused by the ironies of his odyssey.

Whatever his present location, his 20° century world was now on medieval time. Even an open-minded French-speaking Berber might not fully grasp this complicated tale.

La Tour felt transported to another time. Here, fact and faith were one. Berber religion blended pre-Islamic beliefs with the theology of their 8th-century conquerors to create a unique branch of Islam. They trusted much of what had been taught over the centuries by Arab imams, but clung to their own traditions: sprinkling animal blood to consecrate new buildings, sown fields and fresh wells; magical formulas; invisible saints; sacred rocks; night spirits; the living power of myth. La Tour knew he was a devil of deception. But his turn homeward would be doomed by disclosing that he was more *djnun* than deity: imposter, infidel, leper.

He saw the blind *amrabt* walking alone through a field in a peculiarly steady gait. The fellow deftly tapped his stick before him, an extension of arm and eye, and turned up the path. People peered from doorways and tents. Some edged nearer to earshot. Reaching a rock opposite La Tour, the holy man sat down. Now began a ritual; to this Légionnaire *poseur*, it was devout, uncannily sincere, and frightening. The *amrabt* alternately chanted or mumbled prayers or fell quiet, and held his palms outward to La Tour, as if to receive radiant energy. His expressions changed from a suggestion of pain to evident elation; his unseeing eyes gleamed with unnerving knowledge. La Tour felt utterly alone, more than he could ever have dreamed, with nothing more than a cocoon of illusion to protect him.

"*Whach kathadare al Fransawiya?*" La Tour at last asked in Moroccan Arabic. Do you speak French?

La Tour immediately thought this a remarkably stupid and dangerous question. They would certainly expect a Berber deity to converse in their own Tamazight.

Yes, the *amrabt* indicated with humble nod of his head. "*Imik.*" A little.

"*Mis manach?*" La Tour asked in Tamazight. What is your name?

"Addi Yacoub," the old man replied in a raspy whisper. As if he dared not raise his voice to a normal volume.

Silence reigned for a moment. Then the holy man began to tap his cane to a strange slow natural rhythm, as a dance of molecules or the pulse of a harmonious Being. On occasion Addi Yacoub ceased all movement and seemed to withdraw inside, to a deep, secret soul-place, and then set his

damaged eyes directly on La Tour, as if he was seeing much more blind
than do most humans with perfect vision. The Légionnaire grew uneasy
at the thought that by some bizarre power the old man had discerned the
truth and was prepared to wait patiently and wisely for La Tour to reveal
it himself.

The holy man rose and with gentle authority indicated that Jilani
should follow him. The Frenchmen was reluctant; attention would be
magnified and he risked the discovery of his face, uniform, affliction.
Unable to refuse, he stepped behind the blind *amrabt*, who moved as
simply as he would a path he had trod thousands of times.

All the world was hushed. Fires and oil lanterns glowed from doorways
and cast soft shadows. The rich, elemental smells of earth and animal mixed
in the air. La Tour peered through the dappled dusk to a far field where a
cluster of loosely hobbled horses grazed. All were the sturdy mounts of
Berber warriors. Though exhausted by lack of sleep and the great stress
of escape, he wanted to take the next step on a journey in a very uncertain
direction. *A horse is my only fast way out. If their riders go I must stay.*

Villagers stepped to the side with eyes averted. La Tour felt like he
was on a gauntlet. He wished to turn invisible, or to become a chameleon,
perfectly matched to the landscape, like the Ait Atta warriors and their
homes. But the mighty two-man pageant bore the power of some Holy
Word. His new identity was the finest camouflage. No questions would
be asked of him—hardly a word would be spoken at all. No doubts would
be entertained; to them his mere presence was a blessing almost without
measure.

They passed a few houses, then climbed an easy hill to a path beside a
sparse sheep meadow and a thin stream that emitted from a shallow ravine
ahead. In the twilight, the cleft seemed a likely locale for ghosts. Nestled
there, was a simple, isolated hut of stone, not within sight of the main
village but affording a splendid vista of Adrar n-Azourki and points north.
Beyond the precipice was a stony valley that extended northward by nearly
half a kilometer to the base of a ridge, like a tide meeting a sea wall.

At the far end of the ravine they came to the door. Addi Yacoub
gestured that La Tour step through. He complied—but the *amrabt* did
not follow. The door swung shut behind him. He fought paranoia and

claustrophobia edging toward panic. It eased when he saw food, a water jug and a teapot on a table, and humble furnishings: several items of furniture, copper and earthenware pots, a lantern, a bundle of clothing and two blankets, one of sheepskin and the other of bright, patterned wool. A small stone hearth had a neat supply of wood. The hut was otherwise empty, somewhat cozy, and evidently his.

La Tour peeked to see if he was being watched from outside any window. No. The *amrabt* was gone. He devoured the simple classic fare of mutton *tagine* and a hunk of fresh, over-warm *aghrum*. This was proof that his hosts revered who he seemed to be. Besides relieving the gnawing tightness of his empty belly, it was the most sensory pleasure La Tour had enjoyed in weeks. Even a man facing death may enjoy a good meal.

Soon after, he had another primal urge. Within, he found no Berber equivalent of a chamber pot. Edging the door open, he stepped outside, into the shroud of darkness, crept to boulders on the edge of precipice and relieved himself.

The night was a dry cool, like a wine cellar. He could see nothing but emerging stars and the outline of massive mountains, the nearest at least ten kilometers away.

Returning inside, he lay upon the sheepskin and beneath the woolen blanket, confident that his new position of presumed sanctity would protect him more than the entire French arsenal. Neither his disease nor the travails ahead seemed a bother at this moment; if he were to die now, it would be with a smile on his face.

In his sleep he was falling again. Down, toward the dark unseen, finally into the soft, silken, crystalline and rose-scented Dades that flowed into the rapid Isère, near his boyhood home, where he awoke in cool bed sheets to cafe au lait and warm, fresh bread.

After what seemed like long moments of fluid time, La Tour opened his eyes to dawn. In the twelve hours since nightfall, he had slept deeply for ten. He was renewed, but quickly aware of sharp hunger. During his captivity the Berbers had often provided *tahrirte*, for breakfast or dinner, a soup of maize, barley flour, salt and pepper, and a hunk of an *aghrum* dome baked in ovens made of stone or clay and using animal dung or twigs as fuel. But now he would eat any food at all. Atlas villages cultivated potatoes, barley, maize, onions, walnuts, almonds and cherries, to feed themselves or for sale in the *souk*. And, of course, sheep. Some of those treasures would be here, to fill his dull cavity.

La Tour gazed out the bare window casement. From this angle in the faint light he could see westward across a cemetery to tilled fields, and beyond the farthest one the hulking lower flank of a great ridge. After hasty ablutions, and an uneasy reflection that this could be the last day of his life, he opened the door. Near the entrance was a basket and within it, a breakfast of almonds, barley bread and *atai*. He brightened at the thoughtfulness and at this certain sign that no one had grown wise to his identity.

La Tour ate while walking past the *agudal* to a vantage point. With dismay he saw that the horses tethered in the field last evening were gone. He was again without a reliable means of escape. He could only wait; fleeing into this terrain would flirt with suicide. But he could not remain for long, no matter the reprieve bestowed by or because of his mistaken identity. *I must go, though that may be more dangerous than remaining.* Someone would surely realize his trickery. *Even if tales of Berber vengeance are half lies, it would be better to die slowly in the wilderness than face their wrath.*

La Tour crept halfway down slope and perched on a flat rock above the fields across from a village, close enough to see others but not invite scrutiny. Women passed with eyes lowered beneath colorful head coverings, or *achttan*; their long, lightweight dresses called *dfinth* wrapped with a belt called *aassam*, and adorned in hand-crafted bracelets and necklaces called *louise*. Two young women carried babies in loose pouches slung across their backs. One infant slept; the other, eyes wide, soaked up new life. Several women had facial tattoos—*ahejjam*—of plain vertical lines from the lower lip and down the chin, and others a semblance of several Tifinagh symbols. Two older women wore elaborate monochrome patterns on their hands as signs of their status. One gazed toward him catlike for a few unguarded seconds.

The sun rose on high. Across the fields, the *taleb* or *moudden* chanted the call to prayer. Weary La Tour basked like a Côte d'Azur yachtsman and fell into a nap. He awakened about an hour later to find more food beside him: bread, couscous, a few palm dates called *thini*, and tea. Evidently no one questioned the veracity of the claims made for him. Not vocally, not yet. He expected to be put to a test: perform a miracle, cut his skin, speak in Tamazight, recite the Qur'an. Instead, they merely and mercifully concluded that even a god needs nourishment. The food enhanced his peace of mind. To Berbers, hospitality was a noble virtue, and honored guests were accorded full protection.

For the next hours La Tour overlooked a strange but wondrous landscape, ever more aware that the purpose and nature of time had little meaning here. In his European world it was a measure of where one has been, needs to be, intends to go; but here there was only the everlasting moment. He peered to a small pasture. Grazing sheep stared, almost inert, as two dogs circled slowly, kneading the animals like fuzzy dough. People worked to live, and lived only to work. He wondered about Akka and the *amrabt* while sitting stoically for several more hours without expression, unwilling to reveal a whit of his truth. He knew that this must heighten the aura of mystery, perversely increasing the need for him to appear more godly.

Afternoon drew into evening. La Tour remained alone, visible to but apart from these new neighbors. He retreated to the doorway of the hut, preparing for a strange and indefinite isolation. Soon, to his alarm, he heard the footsteps of a procession moving up the ravine. He hoped they were pious, but he braced for peril.

The amrabt *came into view, the walking stick in his right hand, Akka n-Ali at his left arm. Behind them walked Kenza, and behind her three bearded and almost bashful men in black* tijjloubah. *La Tour was relieved; six representatives had come to pay him honor. And to observe him more closely. His focus flew from Addi to Akka to his daughter, where it lingered. The* amrabt *smiled as if with second sight, and wise to human nature.*

Kenza held a wooden bowl in an upturned palm. In it was a golden dome of aghrum. *She moved forward as she had with the water jar, and placed the bowl roughly distant between everyone on a low flat rock. The savory bread aroma wafted to La Tour, sparking an image of a Rue La Fontaine* boulangerie *he had frequented as a boy.*

The welcoming committee formed a loose circle as the three men—likely the taleb *and two* imuqqarann—*key members of Akka's council—moved forward. They, Akka, Addi and Kenza placed their right hands over their hearts, then extended them. To Sidi Jilani.*

Addi Yacoub began to speak in Arabic.

"Biss me Allah," he intoned. He was about to quote The Qur'an. 'But verily over you are appointed angels to protect you. Kind and honorable, writing down your deeds. They know and understand all that you do.' Surely Allah spoke the truth. Surah 82, The Cleaving Asunder, 10 to 12."

The group glanced at Jilani, then at the ground. The amber bread that lay upon the rock seemed to symbolize the life and the world they devoutly hoped Jilani would help them save.

"Biss me Allah. 'O mankind! Verily there has come to you a convincing proof from your Lord: for We have sent to you a light that is manifest.' Surely Allah spoke the truth. Surah 4, The Women, 174."

La Tour knew that they had come to bless the hut for the sky god who was to lead the Ait Atta to salvation, to make it fit for a deity to dwell in and thus consecrate their relationship with him. He stood in raptly, every moment feeling more deceitful. May it please whatever God that I not be asked or expected to recite anything from the Qur'an. *La Tour sensed that they could mistake his demeanor for serene satisfaction with their piety. But he could only want them to see his repose as that of a god casting an approving and a loving eye upon them. He gradually, oddly, felt keen and clear, more than he had in weeks; the holy man, the prayers, this place was somehow bringing relief. Even joy.* It is from outside me. I am too frightened, too guilty to summon such a state of mind and spirit.

But he lamented that in three days he had traded one prison for another, and despite his escape from that leper hellhole he was no nearer to France. *I have no guide and no means of travel. If I ask, it could raise suspicion or alarm.* He could not simply walk away. Where? How? By trying to do so he would violate a sacred trust he had, by his silence and presence, encouraged these people to place in him. *They believe me to be a god, so I must act the part.*

Addi Yacoub remained silent, waiting. Now the *taleb* began to sing solo, with a wondrous crooning cadence. In a moment he was joined by the two *imuqqarann*. An ancient synergy came from their intertwined words, chords and notes in themselves, that proceeded on an alternating scale expressing both piety and passion. Addi added his voice, a reedy but resonant tenor, and the quartet set out a rhythmic serenade that at times was almost exalted. They were blessing Jilani's house with sung passages from the Qur'an.

"Those who believed, and adopted exile, and fought for the Faith, with their property and their persons, in the cause of Allah, as well as those who gave them asylum and aid, these are all friends and protectors, of one another."

His hosts—or his charges—fell silent. They formed a line, in the order of their first appearance, and came forward. With Akka's guidance, Addi Yacoub reached down for Jilani's hand. He kissed it, as did the others in turn. Addi tapped his stick, turned away, and gestured that the others follow.

In the ravine, two men spoke in a whisper. La Tour heard but one word clearly—*baraka*. Holiness. Divine protection. It seemed to be meant as an affirmation, not the name of what was absent.

By lying to save his life—or simply just withholding the truth—La Tour would elude one fate, but meet another. This path was uncertain, and could easily end quite differently than the *amrabt* believed. No angels. No light. No *baraka*.

ELEVEN:

KENZA

J ean-Michel La Tour had entered the Légion at age twenty-five, in late 1927. France had not yet passed from the trauma of the Great War. The killing fields were green again, but the relics of mayhem-shell casings and unexploded munitions and lost weapons-rang against plows tilling ghostly trench-scarred earth. The conflict in Maroc was paltry by comparison. In the whole of the Protectorate there were fewer soldiers and Légionnaires than had struggled over key ten-kilometer spans on an Argonne battlefront.

La Tour had arrived in Tanger less than eager to kill Moroccans. He simply, naively wanted to see this land and its people. Any commander, however, would disdain a private agenda—he was a soldier, not an explorer—so he concealed it by posing as someone to help compile the better maps needed to subdue the Atlas tribes. Nearly fifteen months later, a god trapped in an imperiled kingdom, he knew far more about the fractured heart of Maroc than if he had remained home to bury a failed family enterprise, reading deficient travelogues of a dream destination. But he had little confidence he would ever see home again.

La Tour awoke before dawn to behold the domain. His body was bruised and mind tense. No matter; he would venture daily on a quest for exit from this certain battlefield. The covert Légionnaire would see how clever or how foolish Akka n-Ali's endgame position was. And he would learn how free he was to wander. More pressing and personal business awaited him than saving the Ait Atta from conquest, and to save himself it must appear that he had abandoned them. Their culture was centuries old; a few more weeks might not matter in the scheme of creation or destruction. Nor was La Tour troubled about his chances. This chain of recent events in his life, like gems on a thread of miracles, would not break just yet.

He groped the patch of infected skin to assess his condition. Unchanged. For once in these weeks, any lack of progress was a profound benefit. He held his movement and his breath at this moment, hearing the faint, far drone of a plane engine. The pilot and navigator, methodically traversing the terrain, were out seeking early-day enemy movements. Ait Atta horsemen, the Légion knew, often traveled at night or dawn to foil daytime reconnaissance. The dim echo faded like a candle.

La Tour turned right from the doorway of the hut and proceeded to the edge of the long promontory. A nearly continuous battlement of boulders lined the lip of it—a natural *murette* and a splendid defensive position—partitioned the crest from the plateau. His gaze traveled up a huge hill behind, spanning nearly the entire width of plateau, to a striking feature: the mouths of caves. Near ground level were two yawning portals.

Overall, this place was a bastion, and with proper vigilance perhaps impregnable.

To his right, down a shallow slope around an outward curve of the plateau, were the ruins of a tizi. *The eroded facade resembled giant russet bones growing from the earth. Men had once kept watch on the crenellated walls; very possibly, many had died there.*

He turned to each direction, memorizing every detail of the terrain.

The hutch offered few diversions to occupy his hours: among them, a sharp knife and a small hoard of rough cedar blocks. Yesterday, bored, La Tour had taken one and began to carve its fragrant grain. Spontaneous as a musician or a sculptor, his subconscious took over; he whittled out a rudimentary top. It did not match the well-crafted geegaw Grandfather had brought back from Paris. The toy of brass and pinewood had done more than yield hours of amusement. It conferred lessons in natural laws like gravity and angular momentum, and that self-sustaining energy could stretch boundaries. The top would whirl on a smooth area of floor when Jean-Michel imparted good spin to it with a snap between his right thumb and two fingers. Twenty or more seconds—an eternity for the toy—might elapse before it lost rotation and tottered. His memory drifted back two decades as he diligently tried to recreate the squat, balanced cylinder with a tiny knob at the top. *We are all like tops, turning until our energy is gone.* La Tour made numerous adjustments, notching here, scraping there, investing hours in the duplication of a cherished item.

He did not like to be confined, but also had little desire to stand *gazing at the far horizon he already ought to be well beyond. And at this minute, La Tour was awaiting Kenza.*

Noontime prayers had ended. Three times that day—each day—Kenza and Addi walked from her *igherm* to Jilani's hut more than a kilometer away. He was likely eating better than anyone else. In the morning, her basket might hold a pot of *atai,* hearth-warm flat bread, and a cup of sweet red *habelmlouk*; in mid-day, more *atai* and bread, generous portions of *askkif* and *llouze,* and a clutch of *thini*; and the evening some of what she had prepared for her father and mother, such as lamb seared in a paste of rancid butter, barley flour and spices. It was considered an honor and perhaps a duty to serve Jilani. Akka gave his daughter this task, accompanied by Addi Yacoub, although yesterday she visited with Ousaïd n-Hmad. She was innocent and gracious, and would surely recount to Father her visits. He would add to his stature by being a perfect host to the living saint and savior.

La Tour had met Akka n-Ali but once since his arrival. He had taken position on the large flat rock beside the sheep pasture, above the stream and village across the plateau.

"*At yage rebi d'ass akhatar*," Jilani said. A holy day to you. The *amghar* came forward with a hand over his heart, and knelt to kiss the back of his hand.

La Tour was stunned, then spellbound to intimidation by Akka's shimmering jade eyes that bespoke devotion, but also cunning and reserves of rage. His burning passion could easily be mistaken for a glare, though La Tour thought it hinted at more complex passions: fearsome anger balanced by tranquility, a lion living with the shepherd. Akka bowed his head. His salient features—expressive eyes, light copper complexion, a chiseled, stalwart visage that was accentuated by a trim black beard—evinced a noble bearing. Several moments of silence passed. They struggled to find a common reference point until, in large part through awkward gestures, and settled on the cluster of sheep in the *agudal*.

"Your garment was woven from the pure white wool of a sacred tup," Akka said. "It is blessed and almost indestructible. And it is how we know you."

The subject was weighted with symbolism of and for Jilani. La Tour listened but did not reply lest he reveal profound and fatal ignorance. Akka fell silent, not for lack of words but for fear he would offend. Mundane, obvious dialogue related little of value. Villagers looked on as the *amghar* and the holy guest stood mum. La Tour's sole concern was his behavior. Should he talk more, or not at all? Listen humbly, or lecture wisely? Praise God they accepted his near-mute presence on its own terms. They would not, did not look at their *shrif* with a critical eye. Not yet. At last, Akka bowed slowly and earnestly to Jilani, then departed. If he had any questions or suspicions, he betrayed nothing.

Cloistered in the hut, La Tour had only the visits of Kenza and Addi Yacoub. The *amrabt* never initiated conversation. Addi's silence was broken only by the need to translate Tamazight and French, as he could. The old man surely relayed his perceptions of Jilani to Akka; and thus far his demigod guise continued to entice. These people possessed a surplus of stoic devotion; in the rivers of human time, a few days or many years was not too long to learn of Allah's intentions for his children, if they would be revealed at all.

La Tour was endeared by Kenza's dignity and poise in his presence. At first, as frightened as she was friendly, the young woman said nothing, just fixed a nervous smile upon her satiny lips.

He expressed his gratitude. "*Shoukrane.*"

Kenza made a brief ceremony of pouring the *atai* and of carefully placing the food on the table. La Tour was evermore enchanted by her brown face, smiling or about to, the mirror of a tender, wistful spirit. He was fascinated by her simple but vivid dress, the bangled red or yellow headwraps tight over her coiled locks, and by the slender but strong hands and wrists that darted from the sleeves of her *dfinth*. He wondered if she was as adept with her family, and if other villagers, particularly men, were so charmed. Even if Kenza was as taciturn or less angelic in daily affairs, she would still surely have admirers. But he would see little evidence of this. The population was reduced by half. Men were away, on the raid or awaiting the enemy, and some families were at far pastures with their sheep. Nonetheless, Kenza's easy smile, flashing emerald eyes and lithe bearing would attract most men. Her eventual marriage would be arranged by her mother and given high priority for a great fête because her father was Akka n-Ali n-Brahim n-Ait Bou Iknifen.

La Tour found himself daydreaming of a completely honest conversation with her that would remove the many barriers between them. Perhaps in his isolation and peril this fantasy took on the lure of reality. Foolishly or not, it seemed to him that such an exchange could occur, and then that it should, and soon was a question of when. He imagined the scene: he would lower his *tajjelabith* hood, remove the *achttan*, and pour out his heart in an odd mélange of perfect French and crude Tamazight. La Tour appreciated that Kenza had natural compassion and sound judgment. Her people were embattled, and the blood of their noble guardian ran in her veins. She would empathize with how he had likely contracted the scourge. Then he could explain his wider dilemma. He would alleviate Kenza's distrust and perhaps repulsion by appealing to her inherited good sense. Like water, the truth seeks its own level. This terrible secret would no longer be locked within him. La Tour had learned that women highly value sincerity. Kenza could not help but accept his impassioned words. Then he would imply his new affection for her. He could turn the kind of prim but lyrical phrases that no longer interested many *femmes Francaise.*

La Tour sat on one of the two rickety chairs at the low cedar table, squarely facing the door, ready to rise in case of trouble. Back straight, hands on his knees, he stared out the square casement at the shadows of fast clouds flowing over the vista. Even they, the silhouettes of mere vapor, were going somewhere.

Afternoon passed to evening. The soft knock came again. A moment later, the door creaked open. Kenza entered first and Addi, a step behind her.

"I stopped to help Mother make extra bread," she said on entering. "For a feast tonight. That is why we are late."

"You are not late, Kenza," he slurred in Tamazight. And he concluded in French, slowly but eloquently so that she could understand: "I am not impatient for the kindness you give of your own will." And he could not refrain from his best smile.

Addi and Kenza were silent. As always, the *amrabt* sat near the door and, as always, his expression was perfectly neutral. But Kenza could not hide her fascination with the form and tenor of Jilani's reply. She was obligated to tend to him, and did so with solemn reliability, but happiness always radiated from within. Kenza half-turned away, reluctant to let such sincere pleasantries affect their relationship.

Kenza set the basket on the table and removed the familiar pot and earthenware plates. One at a time, she placed them on the surface with the delicacy of a Parisian *serveur.* She set before him a *kass* she had earlier overturned on a tray, and bent slightly from the waist over the table, firmly grasping the brown ceramic pot in her right hand. Silver and copper bracelets jangled on her arm. She tilted the spout and deftly poured from several inches above the center of the *kass.* When it was three-quarters full she set down the pot. So exacting were her movements, there was no sound of contact with the table top.

Kenza knelt next to the table on the mat of woven reeds. As if it would be insolent to take the second chair.

"*Akmyajj rebi, Kenza.*"

He gestured at the chair, inviting a guest. With a furtive glance he noted that Addi remained expressionless. Kenza was startled. His voice, he realized, conveyed sociability, a desire to repay her generosity with whatever his words could impart, and also a hint of loneliness. It was perhaps this last quality she most responded to; only that, he thought, could have caused the little jolt.

The hostess and guest graciously sat as directed, hands in lap, eyes lowered, bottom lip quivering softly. A silence hung in the air like just after an ebullient songbird has flown away. Kenza was obliged to be here, but La Tour could tell she also was glad for the honor. He felt slightly uneasy that the girl was always reverential.

La Tour sipped his tea and nibbled the bread. He was hungry, but right now would rather talk than eat.

"Have you been schooled, Kenza?"

"Father and Si Baha Youssef taught me a few words of Arabic," she said in Tamazight. "And of French. *Comment allez-vous? D'ou êtes-vous?*" Switching back to Tamazight, she concluded, "Also Arabic letters, to write a few words." She paused for effect. "Father required this of me. But not much. There is always work to be done."

"Does he ask you for more?"

"Addi teaches me." She turned toward him. He nodded humbly.

The *amrabt* spoke in passable French. "Of these studies she must walk her own path. There are many tasks. Life is long. And short. But always time to learn."

"You are right," La Tour replied in French for the *amrabt* to interpret. "Although there is never as much time as we think. And your mother, Kenza? Have I seen her?"

Addi translated slowly, lingering like the words were sweet morsels. The three were beguiled by the interchange of Tamazight and French. Kenza absorbed it as if Jilani's phrases were oracular code. La Tour keenly felt their reverence, and their excitement about his concern for them. Humans and a god, talking.

"Your mother and father have brought into the world a thoughtful child who has grown into such a . . ." La Tour became self-conscious, or prudent, and chose not to utter "beautiful woman," as he truly desired, suspecting it might be too suggestive. Addi turned the French into Berber. He, too, hung on the last unspoken word.

". . . princess," La Tour finally offered. He did not know if it fully made sense.

At Addi's last interpreted word—or its rough equivalent—Kenza cast La Tour a cheery but puzzled look, then gazed at her folded hands, which several times she unclasped and separated, opened her mouth to speak, but interwove her fingers again and remained mum.

"You wish to say something?" La Tour inquired in Tamazight.

Kenza sat, slightly hunched; head bowed, eyes down, and meekly shook her head.

"You may say anything," he remarked. "I will tell no one if you wish it to remain between us."

Kenza looked toward him. Her eyes did not directly fix upon his; such was considered indiscreet and, possibly in this exchange, unforgivable. Averting one's gaze was a sign of deference or respect. But she was plainly in the grip of colliding emotions—hope, fear, elation, anxiety. Sunshine streaming in through the window behind Kenza slid behind a cloud, and she was cast from bright backlight into soft shadow.

La Tour grasped the hand-carved top upon the table. He adroitly snapped his right thumb and forefinger, setting it to glide around and across the coarse and slightly tilted surface. Kenza was fascinated, as much by Jilani's purpose for creating the toy as by the thing itself. Sideways it went, straight and diagonally, in tiny erratic circles until its momentum was lost and it tipped off the edge to the roughhewn floor.

"Do you see?" La Tour said in French. "People are like this. We cannot stand still, but if we don't watch where we walk, run or turn, we will fall from sight and into trouble."

Kenza picked up on a clue in his phrasing. She needed no translation and replied slackly. *"Vous avez dit nous autre. Esque nous some vous?"* You said *we*. Are we *you*?

La Tour was silent for a moment while he considered that he should not trifle with her fine intuition. Then he replied, "Perhaps the reverse is equally true."

She did not fully understand, and turned to Addi.

"What did he say, please?"

Kenza carefully considered Addi's translation. Her light brown hands fluttered again, like falling leaves or fluttering birds against the green cloth of her *dfinth*.

"I think maybe that I hear most unusual words," she carefully uttered. "From one sent to help his people."

"What do you think would be usual words from me? I say that *Allah* can help you. *I* will help you. But *we* together will most help those who help themselves."

Their eyes met. Kenza briefly ignored this taboo, and they peered across forbidden zones trying to link hearts and minds. La Tour thought he felt tiny tremors pass between them. He imagined her thoughts forming. The moment was analogous to the marvel that surged through him on clear nights when he had peered at the stars. He would gaze at the luminous heaven, accepting messages of its inscrutable nature over a circuit unique to him. Kenza was like those stars, and La Tour fully realized he was no longer afraid for her to know the truth. But he was still far from blurting it out. His dilemma would sound deranged when spoken by a presumed god to the earth angel who may have just glimpsed his human soul.

"Father is uneasy," she said warily. "He says you are an omen. But he does not know of what. Have you come to save us, or to witness our destruction?"

Addi translated. His expression changed from neutral to somewhat befuddled, reflecting less mastery than mystery at this exchange.

"In complete truth, Kenza, not one or the other," La Tour intoned. "But I can save or destroy, in equal parts, even at the same time."

"I don't think anyone here would understand that," she replied. "I do not."

"No. You cannot. But in the days to come perhaps it will be clear."

Silence gathered again, and grew heavy. Their enlightenment might be costly, his own freedom exorbitant. With tight jaw, clasped hands and slumped shoulders, Kenza again looked down. Perhaps thinking that Jilani did not speak entirely like a divine being.

Addi rose from his knees, suggesting that enough had been said. The visit was over.

"If all is well, we will go," Kenza said, implying it was more in obedience to Addi than her own decision or desire. Then, without clear purpose, she stepped forward, closing the space between them as if testing a boundary. She peered down at him, almost boldly, as if suggesting that Jilani's identity did not fully add up in the light of his words and her intuition. There had been, however, nothing concrete in their exchange; Kenza could hardly proclaim him a false prophet.

She retreated several steps, to near the window. The sun had emerged again; a soft transient beam poured through the opening at such an angle to highlight her head, almost as if in halo. She turned into the light at the moment it vanished and gazed to the far ridge, just then burnished by rays that pierced the gaps between scudding clouds.

When Kenza returned home, Her mother Hada was across the way in the old, high-ceilinged *igherm* where Mimoun, Kessou and several others were grinding *com*munal barley for bread.

"You were at the hut a long time today," Mother said. "Was Addi in discussion with Jilani?"

"No. I was. Addi interpreted, when necessary."

"Too much conversation with him is not proper."

"He engaged me. He thinks I am his eyes and ears."

"He has more than enough senses of his own."

"I believe that is so, Mother, but when he talks it is only polite to respond."

They fell silent to watch Akka pace into view around the wall of their *igherm*, where he stood gazing from his hilltop toward the *agudal*.

"What are we to make of this?" Mother asked. "There are secrets within secrets. That is certain, though I am sure of little else. I believe Jilani can do no harm, although it is not yet clear he will do any good, either."

"He is wise, Mother," said Kenza. "And most interesting."

"Certainly. What did you expect?" said Hada.

"Yes. But he speaks . . . like a man. With his own fears and insights."

"It is not for us to measure him. Or weigh his words."

"I mean no disrespect to him. And if I did, I am sure he would tell me."

"What exactly, then, did he say?"

Kenza did not want to recount their exchange. Nor could she precisely explain all else that had passed between her and the visitor.

"We spoke of my learning. We touched on his general . . . purpose . . . here. He encouraged me to talk to him as I would to anyone. To ask anything of him. But I did not question him. Instead he offered words of advice to me."

Hada considered this. "And what have you concluded?" she asked.

"I have not. He is what he is. I cannot judge. But there is more to him than we assume. Or know. We hold great trust in him. But also, he in us. He kept saying *we*. 'We cannot stand in place, but if we fail to watch where we walk, run or spin, we will fall out of sight and into trouble.' He advised that there was a great secret to discover. And that only through us together would it be revealed."

Kenza paused. She searched her mother's eyes for a glimmer of insight.

She could see that in her Mother's mind a stream of thought was forming, but that there were not enough conclusions to form a pool of action.

"Did Addi Yacoub respond to him, or Jilani to he?"

"No. He just listened. And when we left the *amrabt* remained silent, thoughtful, all the way to his hut. But he is often that way."

"Tomorrow or soon Addi and Father will discuss this. But continue to do as the *amrabt* instructs. The saint is important to him, Addi is important to us, and the good blessing we deserve and need is the secret our visitor holds within."

TWELVE:

REVELATION

La Tour lay down to sleep beside the hearth's ebbing fire, strangely elated: these faithful, enduring people were more worth fighting for than against. Their unconditional reverence for Sidi Jilani proved that piety was a foundation of their lives. He could not deliberately betray that—though in his quandary betrayal was nearly inevitable.

La Tour rose before dawn and again inspected his malady. The fingers of his left hand tingled, and his earlobes ached. Still, he was more distressed at his helplessness to ease the condition than the condition itself. He rinsed the clothing he wore beneath the tajjelabith. *It was truly a good thing to have heeded Desaix and stuffed the spares before leaving Vallée de l'Enfer, but his meager wardrobe would too soon be rags.*

In the far field now, four horses grazed. He discerned a fire near the field below the caves. He edged down the crest, hoping to remain unseen among the boulders until he could draw near its flames and the sentries there. Reaching the last suitable cover a hundred or so meters away, he heard voices and for some time peeked around the contours of stone to men at the fire, sipping *atai* and gnawing bread. Though not highly alert, they appeared more than capable of their task, and of fighting to be done. The rifles beside them were not old *mokahle* but new Lebels. Smuggled, stolen in raids, stripped from the dead.

Dawn flickered. La Tour carefully crept back to the hut and passed it to the edge of the gentle slope and the path to the tizi. *From afar it looked small. Now, as he approached, its solemn dimensions grew. Slightly below and perhaps fifty meters in front of the promontory, it extended like a crooked little finger from a large right fist.*

He glanced at the crest behind him so as to gauge the distance. At that moment a naked head peered above the rocks, and hastily withdrew. It was the young man who guided the amrabt, *who had brought the tea to La Tour on his temporary throne. The spy was harmless, but now La Tour knew he would not to go unobserved. The watcher was either innocent and acting on his own, or at the behest of more suspicious minds. If the latter, he was not offended that someone had been assigned to follow him; even a god might need a guide. But alternatively the spy's master might reasonably have concluded that Jilani would need solitude to ponder his flock, and that letting him alone was a sign of good will. The lurker, then, might mean that Akka and others were unsure of him.*

La Tour did some counter-skulking. In an unobserved moment he maneuvered to a steep nearby ledge behind which he could see but not easily be seen. The young fellow with the close-cropped hair and top knot raised his head to peer after Jilani, saw his mark gazing straight at him, and realized his error. The boy was reluctant to boldly display himself, so he chose to sit discreetly and almost casually in view. La Tour returned to his stroll. But now he knew that if in this or another time an escape opportunity presented itself—a ready horse and a clear, open route—that he would be under watchful eyes.

It was clear that he must flee soon. Every passing day, hour, minute forced a choice between his distant family in crisis and the very basic need to live. The Berbers would choose for him if he abandoned the guise of a god he had accepted by simply not refusing it. Once again time was jointly a dear friend and his cruel enemy.

La Tour made his way back to the ravine via the hardest path, least visible path. Returning to the hut he found an ample supply of provisions packed in a basket left at the door: bread, almonds, dried cherries, sweet pastries. The courier, then, must know of his absence. La Tour stepped inside to sample the offerings. While gorging, he sketched a rough but detailed map of all he had seen on the back of his brother's letter. Set in graphic form, La Tour could see that the citadel of Akka Ahêddây had many strategic advantages. In fact, a shrewd and spirited defense could cost an attacking force dearly.

The boy had surely reported Jilani's secretive pre-dawn strolls. Credibility was crucial; without it he would become a corpse. La Tour expected Akka to have him monitored more closely by day, and so he let that torturous day and evening pass before going afield again, during a moonless, blustery and overcast night. The black was a tight glove; he moved by memory and by sight. He carefully traversed the edge of the plateau, toward the rocks above the field and caves. Several dogs barked, as they did day and night, to confirm territory or respond to strange scents, perhaps even his own passed on the breeze.

La Tour reached the last sizable boulders and would not go beyond them nearer to the men. The horses were gone, but three men remained a hundred meters distant, below the caves. La Tour studied the broad brow of hill above. If villagers did not already inhabit the caves there, they soon would, as a precaution against bombs. Garbled, breeze-borne talk flew to him. "*Ighazwa*," "*takat*," "Ait Mehammed," and "Akka" were among many other words he did not grasp. He deduced that they were planning to attack a Légion post. Perhaps some of what was in the caves would aid them.

Akka was at once his warden, host, protector, worshipper, and enemy. He was overhearing his warriors casually discuss the successes of their insurrection where many other *imgharin* had failed. Akka was engaging superior forces on his own terms and, to now, winning. His people thought him nearly invincible. From such a cauldron, disaster can be served hot.

Eventually the guards drifted to sleep. La Tour slinked as carefully as if they were awake; any disturbing noise would magnify the attention he attracted. Prudent not to tarry in the open, La Tour reversed course and skulked back along the boulders at cliff crest. He descended to the slope of the crumbling *tizi*, sat at an embrasure and stared westward to the caves. He imagined an impressionist painting of his view; the bountiful stars between the clouds were slowly being erased by the still-distant rays of the sun.

Emerging in this first light was a sizable encampment beside the terraced fields. La Tour saw horses and fresh cooking fires and animated figurine-men. He wondered if anyone had seen his wandering, ghostly form. Feeling bolder in the daylight, La Tour retraced his steps along the promontory, passed into a terraced field, down a short ravine and into a valley of stones. He approached the camp unseen.

The troop there was striking tents and fitting pack animals. Horses were cinched with saddles, several of which were a wooden frame with a pommel and cantle six inches high front and back—an Arab design of medieval vintage—that would be quite uncomfortable for the uninitiated to ride over distance. Others were European in origin, probably recent acquisitions, perhaps from the mounts of *spahis Marocaines*. While the men tended to the animals their dialogue shifted in and out of agitation, like a hive of bees. It was as much exhortation as expression. The trek would be difficult and the outcome uncertain.

Field goods and weapons of French origin—a World War I-vintage Maxim gun, Lebel and Berthier rifles and ammunition boxes—were loaded onto mules. The men knew that these arms were worth their weight in the gold of independence. *Iroumin* strength would meet Berber resolve. Let more European women weep for a change.

La Tour could make out only a handful of words. But these men were heading to battle. Like Légionnaires, they advised and admonished their fellows in the face of peril.

"Kessou, you led us into cross-fire before we learned the position of their guns."

"I am impatient to fight, Brka. If we had all waited to draw their fire some of us would not have made it. Instead, many of *them* didn't."

"Yes, but they killed my best horse."

"We will all become well-acquainted with our new mounts as we journey a day out of our way so as not be seen on the last five. All-night rides for a one hour raid at . . ."

The exchange froze when Jilani appeared among the horses. He was known by the great reputation preceding him. Before he spoke, the men sank to their knees, heads bowed. La Tour gazed at the one called Brka—and his knees nearly buckled at his recognition of the last Berber, glaring like a lion, he had seen across the great divide of the ambush. Now it must be he who departed the scene. How to do so without undue attention?

These Berber mounts, as others, were magnificent. The hardy animals were hybrids of chargers and mountain horses, leaner than their European kin, and typically gray. All were alert to La Tour. He slowly raised his hand toward the muzzle of a robust pearl gray mare. This was Brka's horse. Head lowered, she stared raptly at him, as did the men. Perhaps this beast was ornery, averse to strangers. But suspicions melted shortly as she nuzzled La Tour's palm, tail whisking, and eyes calm. The men glanced amongst each other in tacit agreement that this was a favorable omen.

In any case, La Tour could not bring himself to invoke Allah. He felt it would be blasphemous to Christianity and Islam alike were he, a lapsed Catholic, to use the Almighty to inspire others to war or to camouflage his dishonesty. Some of these men might not return. He did not want them to be living an outrageous lie, believing they had been touched by a deity, at the moment of death. So he opted to communicate with smiles and silence.

As La Tour was appraising the horse's sinewy contours, Kenza and a companion walked onto the forward section of the cultivated slope above them. Brka's gaze shifted between Jilani nearby and the young women a stone's throw distance. His manner subtly changed, from humble venerator to a prudent peacock. Attentions divided, Brka and his comrades watched Kenza study the tilled field, but not so as to offend their divine guest.

La Tour grew more uneasy; discretion got the better part of his scheme. In the absence of Brka or Kenza, he would have risked his rude disguise for advice about a safe route to Azilal or Demnate; from either he could reach Marrakech. But he couldn't play with the fire of confusion by asking where these men were going, or how to get a horse. *Leave now or accomplish exactly what I don't want.* He had no more tricks to hide the hoax beneath his *tajjelabith*. Escape would need more patience for a better opportunity. He began to edge away with a forced bonhomie that would help preserve his mystique.

La Tour passed Kenza and the terrace walls to the rim. He felt all eyes on him. Word of his strange visit would circulate quickly. Reaching the plateau, he spotted a Berber in a brown *tajjelabith* leading an older mare by the reins. Drawing near, he saw it was his young watcher and tea server. Perhaps moved by the scenery the fellow began to sing—the horse perked its ears—and reached into a leather bag on the pommel of the saddle. Out came binoculars: booty from a battle or a raid. La Tour watched in amusement as the puzzled young man tried to deduce their function; he peered, twice, into the wrong, fat end of the lenses. Worse, he had not removed the lens caps. Unseen, La Tour sidled up to him.

"An item of the modern world has caught your attention," he said in French.

Quivering, wide-eyed, caught unaware, the young man seemed uncertain whether to run away or to kneel. With soft gestures, La Tour tried to indicate he should do neither, certainly not before he demonstrated this instrument of wonder.

"But then," La Tour continued, though he would not be understood, "in principle they are not so modern. Here, learn how to bring a far place closer to your eyes."

With a magician's blithe showmanship, he removed the lens caps, gazed into the eyepieces and plied the focusing rings for the sheepish but attentive student. La Tour was amazed to peer two horseback days into the distance. Jubilation; here was one key to the lock of his jail. He held out the glasses so the fellow could see for himself. Affixing his eyes, the lad responded to this optical marvel from the infidel world with not much less amazement than if had been introduced to fire. He swept the glasses to the far horizons, fascinated by the intimately familiar terrain in new, almost godly perspective. Oohs and aahs and burblings of genuine wonder tumbled from his lips.

Villagers in the nearby field noticed this genial exchange. Thus far, they had not seen the saintly guest interact with anyone but Kenza, Addi or Akka himself. Perhaps Jilani was emerging from his cocoon of silence, and would speak to all of them soon.

"*Mis manach?*" La Tour asked the youth.

"Mimoun n-Haj," was all he humbly replied. The young man would speak only when spoken to; any more might be considered impertinent. But he seemed put at ease by the revelation of the lenses. Aspects of his world became less remote or hidden by a power he had never known, and could not explain except by *adjnun* magic or divine grace, either in the device itself or what Jilani could make it do. In comfortable thrall, Mimoun tittered at La Tour's next comment, uttered in inept Tamazight, though the boy could not possibly understand its purely French sensibility.

"*Maytenite meshteghite attanayeth timgharin ela Côte d'Azur souya . . .* " Imagine how you could watch the young women on Côte d'Azur with this, La Tour quipped with a wink. When Mimoun quizzically peered up at him he thought better of the allusion and dryly added, "*Ourtighhit.*" Of course you can't.

Mimoun was polite and perceptive and this delighted La Tour.

Then, to La Tour's surprise, Mimoun impulsively but graciously grasped Jilani's hands and thrust the trophy into them, making a gift of the spoils he or someone else had taken from a Frenchman. La Tour hesitated in good etiquette before politely accepting. The binoculars were vital to his plans.

"*Shoukrane,*" was all La Tour could muster, but he said it with utmost sincerity.

Mimoun bowed, proudly mounted his horse and trotted on it down toward the field. La Tour slid the reassuring binoculars under his garment, but felt a pang of guilt that he had, in effect, swindled what was likely Mimoun's most prized possession.

La Tour approached the hut. Then Kenza hastened past on an adjacent course between the boulders and reached it before he did. There, at the door, was his previously delivered breakfast. He beamed, although not for the food. She responded in kind. Her eyes suggested more than wonder; perhaps an uncanny curiosity she could not articulate. La Tour was afraid that he would grow transparent, revealed no less by Kenza's beauty and intuition then if he stripped his *tajjelabith* and sang "La Marseillaise." Her eagerness might simply express a desire to be the perfect envoy of her people, and a girlish uncertainty about what Jilani expected of her. If so, he knew less about those expectations than she did. And they could complicate matters—and the fewer complications for him the better.

La Tour knew that he must check any distraction. Still, he could not ignore Kenza's precocious, captivating spirit, remarkable in this hard life. A sensual blossom in a deadly garden. He had seldom encountered such a disposition among the fickle or benignly scheming Mademoiselles at home. Her natural wisdom might redefine how others valued their rubies.

La Tour entered the hut. He wished that he could invite Kenza in. The binoculars swayed on his chest. He could feel his heart thump against them. With each hour the risk of discovery grew greater. But, having made such an entry here, there was no exit but through one or another of equally unacceptable risks.

With more delicate flair than a ballerina, Kenza turned away and descended the slight incline of the ravine.

La Tour anticipated, no, dreaded an invitation from Akka, Addi, or the council. Perhaps they were in awe of him, or afraid he would not approve were he to walk among them. Perhaps this was why; on this fourth day, no other visitors had come to him. Or—La Tour was terrified—the *tamazirt* awaited his appearance or decree. This seemed likely, so he was eager to remain sequestered, in exile. He craved the company of people—but did not want to be spoken to. He could not answer in their language with any fluency, and did not know what words were most appropriate. So he enjoyed the scenery. The food left for him. The ebb and flow of the people below. Again, for most of that day he was excluded from life, a life turned upside down in the capital of people at war.

The next morning, Kenza and the *amrabt* arrived, up from the Oussikis and the pasture, along the stream to the hut. Kenza held his hand. They proceeded to Jilani's door.

"As-salám alákyum. Maytaanit idlabass ghourch?" *Peace be with you. How are you?*

"Wa âaláykum as-salám. Labas Al-hámdu-li-llá." *And to you peace. I am fine.*

After this exchange, a typical one, Kenza offered to take his only tajjelabith *to the village and wash it.*

"Yes. But first I must have a fresh tajjelabith." *Kenza departed to fulfill the request, leaving Addi to sit opposite La Tour in the sunshine. They waited silently. Addi smiled—faintly but often—in serenity, and La Tour was pleased. Kenza returned with a plain white garment. He stepped inside to remove the one he'd been under almost continuously since Vallée de l'Enfer, slipped on the replacement, and re-concealed himself beneath his* achttan *and hood. Kenza frowned at his reappearance, likely mystified that he was always covered, head to boot, even on this warm day. She might*

have hoped to see his entire face, now surrounded by a thatch of beard and moustache. La Tour was a mystery, even increasingly to himself.

Kenza was at or near the age of marriage. Wars could be fought or avoided, alliances broken or made on a marriage and the prospect of unified power and heirs. This had been the customary practice of many tribal leaders. But Akka was not necessarily willing to comply. Berbers were an odd branch of the Moslem tree. Many Imazighen creeds and customs far pre-dated Islam, were independent of its doctrines, and nearly impossible to dissolve. The tribes revered saints, living and dead, whose *visions were thought to channel a divine guidance. Akka and his* amrabt *Addi were a team.*

Kenza prepared tea for the simple repast of Addi and Jilani. Addi began to softly hum and chant. La Tour sensed that Addi would not initiate conversation; the amrabt *was waiting for Jilani to speak, or felt that words were unnecessary. He sensed a benevolent tension, a crucial connection not yet made, an undefined chasm not yet crossed. Nature had many storms and countless secrets. Addi's genius was to interpret or convey that energy. To pry out the revelation, not in its own time, but in his.*

La Tour felt a new, canny brotherhood with Addi. To his warm surprise, he could almost observe a kindred spirit reaching into his soul with fingers of gentle energy. If anyone could learn his secrets, be they his real or adopted identity, or where and how they had become blurred, it was Addi Yacoub.

Late that day Jean-Michel sat at a boulder near the terraced fields, admiring the efficient and cooperative system devised ages ago for tillage and irrigation. Many were aware of his presence. Women in the fields, children bearing baskets of rocks for use in the walls, men leading donkeys, all glanced his way. They saw a god in repose. Within, he churned like a devil. He turned his eyes westward. And waited. In February, Mirvais, Rochet, Khoussaila and Aziz had spoken of infiltrating these back doors to Ait Atta strongholds. It was now April.

In the valley of stones a sizable cohort of horse warriors prepared to depart. The binoculars lay at La Tour's boots. By now everyone knew the tale of Mimoun's gift. They would not be surprised as Jilani raised the glasses to his eyes to study the men below and the world above them. Gathering weapons and loading provisions, they conducted rituals of men going on adventure, or to Allah. Overhead, two impressive silhouettes passed his view. Birds with enormous wingspans. Lammergeir vultures. They soared against the Azourki backdrop, but between their size and the power of the glasses La Tour saw them as if they were but a few yards away. Their lazy semi-circular route, on sun-warmed updrafts, indicated the presence of some dead or dying creature beyond.

With wonder at such splendors his gloom could not conquer, La Tour trained the lenses on the notches of Tizi n'Igrourane and Tizi n'Tirist, then swung north. Where would the inevitable Armée or Légionnaire strike come from? The sunset light was perfect; the soft blue-gray and sepia tones and crystal air intensified the deep-focus, low-contrast magic of the panorama. La Tour focused the lenses on the farthest reaches.

His steady stare and peripheral gaze detected an irregular string of lights, like glimmers of static fireflies or candles reflecting off a pond. Neither; sixty or so kilometers afar—a two-day march with pack animals—La Tour perceived a random pattern of flickers below a dim ridge. This was no twilight covey of fairy-tale sprites. But campfires. Perhaps soldiers. The feeble shimmers upon the broad black silhouette flew through the cool air to dance in the lenses—but just then, as he was counting, they were gradually extinguished, swallowed by the new night. Almost as if someone knew he was observing. Légion moving in this direction. I must warn Akka.

This thought shocked La Tour to his core. In a swirl of unreliable options, often the first coherent notion may reflect the truest desire. There were many variables—only chaos was certain—but without a moment of deliberation he had tossed himself to the winds of treason. I must warn Akka. *A tribunal would unanimously impose execution.*

If his instinct was correct, he would have two choices: fight or flight. He dazedly mulled the means and consequences of both on the return to the hut. Glancing there and down the ravine he dimly perceived Kenza's white *dfinth*—somehow bringing flashbacks to his mind of the waving curtains of a Paris hotel. La Tour followed, but she was unaware of him. He reached the pasture and the flat rock from which he had watched the villagers, and they him. He sat down, reluctant to follow further.

"I was once a soldier, killing and deceiving men," said Aumont, "but I wanted to reveal my God to your people. Equally so, at least, you have revealed your God to me."

"Alain," Akka n-Ali said softly to his guest, "since you came and recovered more has been revealed to us. Sidi Jilani is in the *amrabt's* hut on the far hill. He fell from the sky. To save us from the *Iroumin* . . ."

Aumont was at great pains to understand what he meant. Who was Jilani? How did he fall from the sky? He stood there before the fierce but kindly *amghar*, unable to acknowledge or even imagine the purpose of these bizarre declarations.

Music struck up near Akka's *igherm*. Voices, hand-held drums and flutes began raggedly, then melded into ensemble, all set to the rhythmic clapping of hands. The song and the spirit of it would give any men heart. The lyrics would be simple: give men bravery, victory, honor, a safe return to home and family. The harmonies rose high to accompany or urge exultant dancing, to wish warriors courage and *bonne chance*. The music grew to a rapid *sustinato*, and ended when the singers, musicians and dancers were surely breathless. A wistful ballad, with one singer, began at once. Its moods alternated—revelry to yearning, burning to pensive, wistful to elated. All this music could be reduced to one theme: these Berbers wanted, more than life itself, to be the masters of their own destiny, to be free from the dictates of others, to live in the mountains of myth and deserts of fable.

La Tour knew better. Berber *ihouffen*, even if successful, would not gain that cherished state for these tribes. They would merely delay the inevitable. If the far fires were indeed those of in-bound *Iroumin*, and if they captured or killed Akka, one of the few still capable of bold leadership, then the Imazighen might be dealt a final blow. And conquered.

He heard a medley of sound: bleating sheep; the breeze rustling the barley; the plash of river water over rocks; echoes of laughter; the chatter of voices; another burst of music and singing. In the last ambient light La Tour saw someone ignite a pile of brushwood. Nearby were the musicians and six or eight men: Akka, the council—and two other, conspicuous men. They were clad not in *tijjloubah*, but in European clothing. And one, at whom La Tour stared thunderstruck, wore what appeared to be a Légionnaire's uniform.

Several horses were led up beside that uniformed man and his companion. La Tour bounded to his feet, in waves of quiet panic, of uncertainty, of anger and sorrow. These two unusual fellows appeared to be guests, and if so they had been near him for two or more days! His potential rescue was almost within shouting distance. But the fragile illusion of his godhood was a great obstacle to crossing this divide.

La Tour was unaware that Addi Yacoub, the *amrabt,* had come up directly beside him, like a phantom. He was too startled to suppress his reflexive alarm.

"Where did you come from . . . ?" he hissed, before an immediate segue to serenity.

"Those two *Iroumin,*" Addi said in French, ignoring the question, "have been in the village. They leave. One, a holy man, was shot nearly dead by a brigand. His blood was a sign of a miracle to come. The wound quickly healed, and that too, a sign, praise Allah." "Tell me of this miracle," Jilani blurted, before thinking; through his powers of vision he should already know of the incident. That was why no one told him of the visitors.

The *amrabt* related in muddled French an unembellished tale of an event eight days ago. La Tour almost wept. *Two Iroumin traveled under Akka's protection. A soldier Aumont and one called Pierre were set upon by brigands. On this day was to be a crucial meeting of council and an Aroumi delegate. Instead we were called upon to save an innocent and righteous man from death. Aumont was to tell us more about our enemy. By the goodness of Allah he is recovered and leaves toni . . .*

La Tour stepped away to descend toward the stream. The blind wizard followed on the uneven ground beneath his sandals and the tip of his walking stick with eerie craft.

Jilani passed between the nighttime jade green squares of fields and ascended toward the *igherm* and the music. Seen from below, the lodge of Akka and some members of his council enclosed by the robust stone wall conveyed great strength to the world.

Behind him, Addi chanted in a resonant voice, a form of signal. The music, voices, laughter and clapping fell silent. Jilani halted. His last desire was to be conspicuous. Dismayed, he peered back to Addi, who just then raised his cane heavenward.

Akka pointed in Jilani's direction, as a command to all beside him, to behold the hooded figure in a ghostly white *tajjelabith.* Jilani stood at the center of the Ait Atta world, or what remained of it. Two hundred or more pairs of eyes fell upon him. He did not know what to do next, only that it must be subtle and symbolic and shrewd.

It was Aumont alright. Somewhat more world-weary, pale and almost haggard, but with a new relief on his Romanesque face, like having seen a wife through difficult childbirth. La Tour scanned him for a glimmer of recognition. He saw only curiosity. Clinical interest. Uncertainty. Nothing like comprehension or recognition or amazement. La Tour regarded photographer Pierre, too, who by his own boast was an expert observer. But upon neither face did the sight of the man in the white *tajjelabith* visit any shock.

Aumont took several steps forward, compelled by instinct, but was still too far away to perceive details. He paced slowly down the decline toward the white-clad figure in the black night, standing transfixed. Waiting. Fifty meters, forty, thirty . . .

"Blood-soaked lives lost. For what? Vive Mirvais!" whispered the specter. *"And let us drink Poireau with trader Graves. You still owe him money, I suspect!"* La Tour said, certain that the imagery of their drunken night in the garrison would clearly identify him.

Aumont was struck dumb. Paralyzed. This was unholy, grotesque, surreal. The village was fixed upon this encounter as surely as the world was hard beneath his boots. In this moment, an uncanny suspension between other moments past and future, Aumont sensed many intricacies at play, but knew he could not explain them. Nor was it wise to demonstrate any emotion or recognition. La Tour was somehow in a condition and in a place he should never be, defying every conceivable turn of logic and chance. Fate itself.

"Help me . . . ," the man in white rasped, helplessly.

So fortuitous, so singular was this scene that it could only be Providence at work. Aumont eye's welled with tears. He had been called to save another, and action was imperative.

"I will," Aumont heard himself say. Softly, so that the words would not carry.

Aumont watched as the man turned like a wraith and took a different path through the fields, avoiding Addi and proceeding to his aerie alone but for his thoughts.

THIRTEEN

MIRVAIS

"What do you mean, he escaped?"

"La Tour did not appear for daily roll call on April 20ᵗʰ—the day the plane departed from the valley. The superintendent's men conducted a wide search for him-suicide is not uncommon there—but soon realized he must have scaled the cliff and gotten away on the plane."

"La Tour isn't a pilot . . ."

"No, and the pilot is much alive. Three days ago he turned up, Jeaneaut was found in Marrakech. He is a drunkard and talks too much. They questioned him for suspicion of smuggling weapons and *kif.*"

"So then, La Tour . . ." Major Mirvais didn't finish-his words were suspended, as if ready to fly themselves but he held the thought and its incredible implication.

"Jeaneaut told the agent that halfway through his flight to Azilal, the plane was sluggish. He flew over a plateau southeast of Azourki—not far from one of Akka's villages. The plane barely cleared the ridge. The idiot could have drawn rifle fire. But right then, the plane more easily gained speed and altitude. As if it was suddenly lighter.

Mirvais stifled mirth. "Then he is surely dead. A Christian infidel. A Légionnaire. A leper. For which would they kill him first? Oh, but the fall itself would surely kill him."

"Yes, Major. Except that three days ago a Yafelmane scout was observing that plateau. With his good binoculars, he saw a man who looked more European than Ait Atta. He ambled about and avoided others. Like he did not belong there. He sat for hours on a cliff gazing west and north as if he were surveying the terrain. If he is not a Berber, then who is he?"

"Sergeant Saint-Avold," Mirvais stated in outwardly calm, deliberate phrasing, "the column is ready to depart Azilal. For now, tell this news only to the advance men."

"Yes, sir. But some officers believe the treacherous track of that route will retard their progress."

"That is what uninspired men say to excuse an illusion that they are doing all they can. Send word immediately to Rochet that we know where *Guardian* is hiding in those mountains. Those men who want to capture him as much as I should know he won't remain there for long."

"So why, sir, should we at all concern ourselves with La Tour if as you say he may already be dead?"

"I like to know the destiny of men who have served under me. If he is dead, I want it confirmed . . . Sergeant, why do you look at me so strangely?" Mirvais huffed.

Saint-Avold felt a blush of self-consciousness spread across his craggy features. He decided that a well-trimmed silence was better then a ragged reply. He briefly met the Major's eyes, but his reluctance to look into them spoke volumes.

"La Tour was a friend of yours," Mirvais observed without much tact. "Don't you care about his fate?"

Still, Saint-Avold bit his tongue.

"Speak up, Sergeant! You are not mute!"

"With respect, sir, Jean-Michel La Tour was my comrade in arms." He paused and drew himself up to a posture of discretion. "His fate was determined for him the moment he re-entered this fort by your decision, no longer a fit Légionnaire. Mirvais fumed. Glistening hazel eyes, tawny mustache, reddened cheeks, "Sergeant, see that the men of your squad are ready for inspection in one hour. We could find ourselves with the signal to move and we must be prepared."

"Yes, sir," Saint-Avold replied.

"The *spahis* will arrive shortly, Sergeant. See that they are given provisions."

Saint-Avold saluted with barely enough crisp courtesy to avoid a chastising.

During his first months here, Mirvais answered to Colonel Marcy, but when Marcy was killed in ambush, shot in the passenger seat of his lorry, With Rochet's consent, Mirvais took it upon himself to make assessments from the reports of scouts and informants. The Légion wanted a victory, and circumstances had proven Mirvais with the tools to gain one.

"We will send scouts tomorrow to the slopes of Adrar n-Ilito, past Ait Amour. They will then turn east by northeast," he said to 'Plau. "Arrange their relay. I intend to be supporting Rochet's right flank as he passes through Tizi n'Tirist into Ait Atta land."

"Yes, sir. I can have four mounted men ready before dawn."

"Good, Plau. Now send Rehou Khoussaila to me. He will take his three best men. All of them are familiar with that ground. They will ride their best horses for fast movement should they be pursued. I expect to follow their route on Thursday and link with Rochet on Friday."

"But, sir, that many kilometers for six men to cover in three days."

"Rochet will not wait. I have flexibility of action and should like to accompany him up Tizi n'Igrourane. I believe that the way is clear. Akka will not expect us to surprise him from there. Colonel Rochet will see what he and I can accomplish together."

"Yes, sir.".

"This is a crucial campaign. Small though it is, with only two companies that we can spare, if successful, we could end this miserable war in less than a week."

Plau noted the "we." Mirvais had received no orders for this action. His presence would border on intrusion, and his prickly methods and shameless self promotion did not fully inspire fellow officers. Mirvais would be reprimanded if General Lavernay learned of his imprudent decision to take more than half the garrison men in this effort. On the other hand, if with his assistance it turned out well, Mirvais knew he would be commended for taking the initiative. That was the gamble.

"Dallio goes with me. And Plau, refrain from discussing my plan with anyone. You command while I am gone. The experience, however brief, should do you well once I am returned to Marrakech. Same rules, a different face to enforce them."

In so many words, say nothing of this and I will promote you, Plau thought.

"Yes, sir. It has been quiet, so squads will build a water sluice and extend the road."

"Good. Because that is precisely what my diary already reads has occurred."

Rehou Khoussaila was a fine horsemen and a dogged scout who knew the terrain far and wide so well it was said he could travel it blindfolded. The Ait Yafelmane rogue exuded dark charm, unalloyed meanness and occult cunning. Those qualities together made him a good companion in battle. His gargoyle glare or scowl revealed hatred: for his Berber brethren, who were too easily conquered, and for most French, the agents of *shitan.* During bad weather or long saddle days, however, his scowl was not an expression of ill-will, but of pain in his right leg nearly blown off twenty years ago by Atta raiders. Besides taking revenge, Rehou sought their treasure there, the gold coins and bejeweled trinkets said to have been plundered from Saadian tombs in Adrar Sargho.

Rehou liked to be rewarded for his apparent loyalty with the trust he could parlay into bribes. And as much as taking or receiving loot, he enjoyed release from the need to satisfy and mediate his two wives. Still, the Berber with steel-coil nerves always felt it best not to upset Lallah; her language and nails turned vicious when she had been crossed. Berber women, especially in remote areas, enjoyed freedoms their Arab counterparts did not. They could argue with their husbands, even divorce them, laugh and walk in the market without the *haik* required of other Arab women. Rehou's wives respected him more when he returned with bulging pockets.

Lallah made a decent profit from making and selling *choukharas,* leather shoulder bags. His other wife R'kkiya was a fine cook; her artistry was every bit the equal of Lallah's leatherwork. Both of them were lovely, in their own way. Lallah was plump, with full breasts and a large rump. She never tried to evade her husband's abrupt advances. R'kkiya, on the other hand, made a specialty of being coy, but not so much that she offended him. She was younger, more girlish, and to Rehou, more delicate.

"Khoussaila, you're off again in the morning," Plau said through the flaps of the goatskin tent in which the Berber resided. "Major Mirvais awaits to give you the details."

The Berber was no more concerned than if he had been told that dinner was lamb over couscous and almonds. He had been back for a week after being foiled by Aziz's double-cross stupidity and he grew weary with this routine. The sooner he returned to the highlands near Abdi Du Kouser, the more quickly he could resolve the persistent rumor of the Saadian gold.

Still, the Major's tacit demand unsettled Rehou a bit. Mirvais was ever trying to conform him to Légionnaire ways, but he relished that prospect no more than a devout Frenchman's conversion to Islam. The tacit terms of his service was that he could take his horses and quit should he become unhappy. He had, in fact, already twice departed. But he agreed to returned to the fold after an increase in pay, the apology of an officer who had crudely impugned his skill and loyalty, and the right to take more booty from subdued men and tribes. *Mirvais, however, had recently tried to rescind this mutual arrangement.*

"Rehou, we will be near the area where you have performed several notorious deeds," said Mirvais. "For now your job is to interpret and guide. Please restrain your hatred and violence. It would be best if the Atta did not not know of your presence. The Pope's hat or the Sultan's umbrella are unmistakable. Likewise that red turban on which you wear a stolen Croix de Guerre and the dried finger of a recent foe. A sure sign of dark mischief."

"Will I be allowed to seize the gold myself, Mirvais?"

"Complete surprise is a major asset. That, I should think, will make it more possible to get at the treasure there. Our maneuver must remain secret until we strike."

Mirvais did not let on that there was still little or no support for the wild rumor of the Saadian gold. False but feasible hopes were good for the underlings. And if these shleuh needed such an incentive to fight, then so be it.

"I look forward to being a wealthy man, Major."

"Just not quite as wealthy as the sultan, Rehou."

"And anyway," Rehou snickered, as he was well-acquainted with his own thievery, "the Sultan is a thief."

Mirvais sneered within and remained stone-faced without. The Major's favorite humor was his own.

"Get an early start tomorrow," he said. "Draw three days' rations. And take your other horse. Your black beast is another sure sign of your presence. The gray mare I gave you is a fine and typical mount for the rugged country you will pass."

"I am sure that we will capture Akka so quickly that my horse will not have time to grow weary of the trail."

"That is as much up to you as me, Khoussaila. Please do as you always have. But there is to be no revenge for their ambush. It could have been much worse."

"Insh'Allah, Major."

"Yes. Thy will be done."

They bowed to each other, Rehou with somewhat more sincerity than the moment required.

FOURTEEN:

AUMONT

"What a miserable mess," the bourgeois fellow in the Mamounia café muttered to himself, rattling his newspaper in disgust. "An isolated mad mountain sheik is somehow influencing the policies of France."

"You refer to the irony that an Atlas chieftain is causing some in Quai d'Orsay to imbibe too much cognac devising explanations for their schemes," the fellow at the next table wryly replied. "Afraid they will be revealed in the scandal sheets?"

"I daresay sir, that when and where Frenchmen are dying it is more serious than an occasion for sipping cognac," came the somewhat rankled response. "What is more, I am a lawyer in Paris, and I assure you that *Revue des Deux Mondes* is not a scandal sheet."

The first man suppressed a titter his counterpart's defensiveness. He rejoined, "I am simply saying that their reach may exceed the grasp. Perhaps those hands should be content with what they hold. Even if they must admit to their brazen strokes. A strong desire to own exotic places is not mandate for brutalizing every native who expects *us* to have better manners about the division of *their* nation."

"Where did you get that idea? Reading those muddle heads at *Action Fran aises*?"

"I am an ex-soldier, sir. A medical man. And perhaps a future man of the cloth. Not long ago, I had experiences that could have and almost should have resulted in my death. But they ended with freedom and a great revelation alongside that mountain shiek. Here I am."

The lawyer stared at Alain Aumont, gauging his tone. Frowning skepticism turned to neutral acceptance and then to excited belief. "And who sir, are you?"

"A friend of brave men," Aumont replied, pointing to the newspaper photograph. "He is one of them. I assure you that Akka n-Ali is quite sane. And he wants nothing to do with French policies." He laid down several francs and stood. Pierre Duplessy would offer photos of the Ait Atta to the court of opinion. Now Alain Aumont would offer to find the pilot in Gueliz for a journey to void what was sure to be that court's judgment.

* * * * *

Alain and Pierre had descended the north side of the Atlas with three Iknifen guides. Aumont purchased safe passage-*tazttat*-through the lands of the other tribes, with proof that all traveled on behalf of Akka Ahêddây. In less than two days, the Frenchmen neared Azilal. The Légionnaire and the photographer entered the dusty town almost penniless and without one item of trade value except their clothing-and Pierre's camera.

"Anyone, including you, will have to gouge my eyes before I exchange my Rollei for bread or a bed," Pierre vowed. "You look very tired. Stay here by the fountain. I will look for a way out of this unpleasant place."

In that, he was not successful. They took turns sleeping on the street, fending off dogs and humans. But the next morning, the day of the weekly *souk*, Aumont was electrified to see a black, grit-coated Peugeot edge into the dusty *kissaria* among the braying mules and rickety carts. It stopped nearby at the potter's shop. Out of the automobile stepped a roguish European fellow in a rumpled linen suit, somehow resembling a doctor on his rounds, and with him, a plump, barefoot Berber woman bedizened in a Continental frock, a Soussi headdress and jingling jewelry. Alain recognized the man at once, as he was stepping forth to greet the potter, like caliph confrère come to call. He quickly devised a scheme and led Pierre to the shop where the potter was counting money into the man's upturned palm. Their polite but sudden appearance annoyed the tycoons.

"You're Christian Graves, a *soukier* from Gueliz," Aumont began. "A chum of Major Mirvais. Three months ago, you came to Bou Malem. I bought a blanket and a bottle of fair cognac. We got drunk, you, me, Saint-Avold and my friend, La Tour."

Graves coolly assessed this inquisitor, trying to recall this drinking companion and customer, at first recalling neither. At last, scanning up and down, he revealed recognition.

"Ahh, Aumont." He was almost blasé. "The Lieutenant with the phonograph. Hell of a place to find you! But Mirvais is no chum of mine. He's a thief and a coward and a lying bastard. Other than that, a fine fellow. Why are you dressed like a ragged *shleuh*?"

"The best uniform for a Frenchman in flight."

"You deserted?" Graves asked, baffled and almost shocked.

"Not strictly speaking. In good conscience, I ended my service a few days early after one too many brutal and senseless brushes with death. I have new worlds to conquer. Beginning in Marrakech, where I would like you to take us. You and I can plan to seize one of these worlds together. Perhaps we will make a few enemies. But you alone can make the money."

"How is that?" Graves asked, his tone signaling cautious, but rapturous interest.

"In a remote Berber village," Aumont responded, dangling the lure, "a brave Légionnaire, badly betrayed by Mirvais and Rochet, is in a strange confinement. I have the mission of freeing him. A terrible battle will soon come to that place and many men will die, he perhaps among them. God willing, we can stop it. But we must save him. Your reward might be some of the gold. What you need to do is listen to me and agree."

A charged silence descended upon them like a zone between two great storms. Moments passed. Graves measured the man, the proposal, and the credibility of both.

"Would this involve Akka n-Ali, Ahêddây, the *Guardian?* "

Again a veil of silence. Alain thought Graves a keen and crafty man. A fine ally.

"Yes, and a rumored cache of looted gold hidden in his village," Alain intoned.

Once more, silence as Graves peered at the source of these words. He was a self-proclaimed "black market artist." He took no good opportunity lightly. Graves rasped, "We leave for Marrakech in two hours. Explain during the drive. But if I think you lie about the gold or the risk, I'll throw you out. And you can deal with the *shleuh* or your Légion."

Aumont dared not look at Pierre, who should not allude to any misgivings. Here was the only safe and immediate means for Aumont, deserter and future man of the cloth, and Pierre, the maker of truthful images, to be effective. Alain could not abide failure.

The truck of the *kissaria* merchant, laden with pottery and tiles, trailed Grave's Peugeot all the way to Marrakech. Pierre slept in the truck bed while Aumont explained to Graves at length his final weeks in the Legion, the singular brush with death and salvation, Addi Yacoub and Akka Ahêddây—and what little he knew of the bizarre fate of La Tour. He said little about the "rumored gold." The less he said, the less he would lie.

"One of my pilots will fly you back. Soon. But landing fields are few. If you are committed to this course, prepare yourself. Day after tomorrow you return."

Vowing to remain mum about Aumont's "retirement," Pierre took his leave in the Red City with a wink about when they would see his photographs. Aumont, by now surely presumed dead, took refuge in Christian's warehouse in Gueliz.

But the next day, Alain risked being recognized in the Hotel Mamounia, believing that the beard and Fedora would disguise him in one of the few places in the old city to procure liquor-not Legion swill, but good cognac. He craved one hour, perhaps his last, among the garrulous Europeans here to explore or exploit Maroc. Aumont watched them with the eyes of one released from death's grip, reborn, feeling worthy of the salvation, but saddened they, with their worldly concerns, were ignorant. Yet, he himself had been confounded for days. One path to full redemption and revelation for all led back to Akka.

Flippancy, like that of the well-intentioned but misinformed lawyer at the adjacent table, raised his bristle. But how could he or anyone understand? A strange Berber foe had retrieved him, for no comprehensible reason, from the brink of death. And without any tools or tangible technique but a seemingly divine power manifested by his hands.

Akka, *"Le Guardien,"* stared out from an inner page of *Le Monde.* The nobility of expression and ardent, knowing eyes seemed to gaze from Olympus, or the Berber equivalent. He was a thorn in the side of those still exhorting the French venture in Maroc, seventeen years after the treaty of Fes had delivered much of it to their hands.

France coveted wide influence. Its policies sought to amend and enforce Moroccan law and to install a reliable tax collection system. The French had built auto roads, railroads, schools, ports, and cities, where previously there had been nothing of the kind.

France was born gradually and painfully over centuries. Alain had faith in the Lord's promise of peace and salvation. As St. Mathew said: *"For the gate is narrow and the way is hard, that leads to life, and those who find it are few."*

Alain recalled his early years as a poor young student, visiting the museums and galleries of Paris. He was swept by the joy of discovery, attending an exhibition of the master Delacroix, whose paintings *Arabs Skirmishing in the Mountains* and *The Sultan of Morocco* beckoned him to another dimension of life and living, one trapped in the amber of time.

He felt compelled to become an explorer. Six months later, he arrived in Tanger, and for two months, he retraced the painter's path through *souks* and alleys and the Middle Atlas. Nature was a great equalizer, a haven from the cruel artifice of the human world. When Alain returned to France, he felt himself evolve into a thinking man of adventure, suddenly willing to defer the safe, predictable serenity of medicine or seminary life, to live fully on the shore of chaos. He inquired of the Légion in Marseilles what duties he might perform. Alain had been seeking the narrow gate, but in the wrong place, he discovered halfway though his service.

Alain knew the French, and something of Akka, and certainly felt that the reports on this particular Berber were far from complete. He wondered if, in the frozen moment in Pierre's photo, Akka had revealed that the French knew the truth of his leadership, and that the *amghar* knew that they knew. The real purpose was to carve away his territory, using weapons, not words.

Alain fingered the silver amulet Akka had given him just before his departure. The talisman embodied a belief that their paths would merge again. He recalled with some uneasiness those Ait Atta eyes peering at him as he lay wounded, the same eyes now gazing upon his comrade, Jean-Michel La Tour. And he recalled leaving a helpless and terrified La Tour behind in Taboulmant. Akka and several villagers related the tale of Jilani. How bizarre that a human angel seeking only escape from captivity had been mistaken for a god come to save them! For Aumont, this was the way *that leads to life;* without La Tour, Addi and Akka, he would not be alive to enjoy his premature freedom.

He could not take up the banner of a man portrayed as a monster without taking a great risk. And he would shortly return to that far kingdom, this time to do the saving instead of being saved.

He ventured into the afternoon sun, gaze up but hat low, striding to Gueliz and the cable office where he hoped that by now Christian Graves would have sent a message about the plan he was helping to set into rapid motion. The *soukier* insisted that his contacts were not only native culprits and foreign charlatans, but a few people of good will.

FIFTEEN:

CRISIS

By late afternoon, the light was pellucid and perfect as the sun sank behind the summits. La Tour wanted this dusk to be as clear as that of yesterday, but he was anxious that the makers of the far fires would not recreate them—or that they would, but closer, and so confirm their advance and his fears. He watched and waited near the hut, out of sight.

From over the fields and villages behind La Tour, came the call to evening prayer. He fretted that his conspicuous abstention from *lmaghereb* and the three *rakaat* might be considered blasphemous. But he had a much more pressing task.

Strolling to the rim of the plateau, he beheld a crystalline view, seemingly to the ends of the earth. La Tour watched as night absorbed the glow, to be resurrected by dawn.

He saw something—glass or metal—glimmer in a last ray of sun, far to his left atop the mountain cul de sac, the base of which contained the complex of caves. It was a fine aerie for a spy. He edged from sight in rocks. For minutes, his intent eyes at the binoculars detected no movement. But it was almost certainly an advance surveillance party.

The mountains faded to silhouettes. The first stars peaked forth, the half-moon not yet risen. La Tour aimed his glasses leftward of Azourki, at the fires of yesterday, faintly hoping they had been only a mirage. Or a Berber horde. Or, if Armée or Légion, that they were moving north to Azilal or south past Ighil M'Goun. But within moments, bands of sparkles flickered against the crags, closer yet, taunting—and once again began to wink out. Those fellows, immobile by day, were night marchers in-bound from Bou Guemmez and the high pasturage. La Tour reckoned that by the morning, at least one force would be near. The hilltop spy was a beacon for the Légion, and few could march farther, faster than they. And perhaps this was not the only column. Tomorrow, too, would come bomb-laden planes, in the morning before warm air whipped by crosswinds rose to the coolness above.

The game was afoot. The Ait Atta could defend this formidable redoubt, if given ample warning. But the warriors were on the move as well—the village was now likely undermanned. La Tour wondered if they were simply letting the foe slice into their territory before executing a brutal counterstroke or blocking retreat. It was a fine tactic, well known to him. On the other hand, the Légion, long reliant upon firepower to thrash such maneuvers, were unlikely to be duped again. And they had ruses of their own: like campfires at the far horizon when a regiment might be in a near valley.

La Tour could not be an idle onlooker, for his own sake, and for those few comrades to whom he still felt some fidelity. And he knew that should Ait Atta warriors be lying in wait, this time no Légionnaire would be spared.

Suddenly, though, there were no signs of frenetic activity. No visible preparations. Just a blanket of tranquility. Except for a dog that barked harshly. Ominously. Together, he and the hound passed the threshold into crisis.

La Tour thought. *They need me. Without me, none of us will survive.* He passed several shepherds and their wives; they reacted as if an apparition or a demon was on the loose. Some scooted away in silence, others babbled that the god had gone mad—or that Jilani's dormant power had awoken. Allah had willed it so. They kneeled.

Kenza and Addi Yacoub were just then rising to the *agudal*. She held Jilani's evening meal in her basket. The *amrabt*, as ever, was placid, like a sleeping lion. Then Jilani loomed uphill. Kenza was startled by this queer, urgent behavior. Her smile faded.

"Kenza, I must speak to Akka Ahêddây at once. Where is he?"

Kenza and Addi were startled at the edge to the voice. They had expected the divine revelation to emerge with serenity, like a butterfly. Instead, it was a peal of thunder.

Addi translated, but Kenza got the gist. The hooded stranger's solitude was over. Jilani was not requesting an immediate audience with the chieftain, but demanding one. Jilani sought God's instructions beneath the moon and stars. His unease indicated the receipt of a fearsome reply.

"He meets in the *igherm* . . ." Kenza replied, "with the *taleb* to discuss . . ."

La Tour fought dual panic; his fate and that of the Ait Atta were simultaneously in the balance. But why was he filled with dread? Pushed out of the ranks and thrown to the wind, he no longer felt obliged to former orders, much less to join the Légion fight. Still, he was perplexed by the contradictions he felt.

La Tour promptly took hold of Addi's arm and led him across the stream to the *riad,* the equivalent of a town square. Addi almost balked at the brisk momentum and the grip on his thin forearm. Kenza trailed them, sputtering and dumbstruck.

As they neared Addi's *igherm*, La Tour's jangled emotions fought his rational mind. If truth were a double-edge sword, he might well be carved to ribbons. But in Ait Atta eyes, he remained an instrument or a vessel of the deity.

La Tour intended to be neither forceful nor irresolute. Simply fair. He would present the central facts. Akka must decide. He did not want to influence their response.

La Tour felt himself at another critical juncture as he stepped through the red gate of the stone wall and tapped upon the inner door. Opening it, Akka n-Ali was astonished to see his caller. Humility fought fear; honor grappled with confusion. Each of them was frozen and speechless. Amnay and the *taleb* hovered in the candlelit background. La Tour took every pain to hide his great disquiet.

"As-salám alákyum. Maytaanit idlabass ghourch?" *La Tour finally said in Tamazight. "I must speak with you at once," he continued in French. "It is very important."*

Akka, much more than taken aback, stepped aside for him. Never had La Tour seen a man of such fierce pride and authority become so modest. It was almost as if the *amghar n-ufella* expected to receive divine words or eternal commandments in ancient stone.

At last, Akka spoke. "*Áhlan wasáhlan. Berrkat.*" Welcome. "Please, *sherif*, please sit. I will get you *atai*."

"*Rebbi ad ekhlef, Akka n-Ali.*"

Akka retrieved four copper-bottomed glasses from a set stowed in a cedar cabinet. Though his right hand trembled, he deftly poured mint tea into each from a pot held customarily high. The hot brown-green liquid streamed straight downward to a froth. Akka bowed, gazed down, and with both hands passed the tea.

"*Rebbi ad ekhlef,*" La Tour repeated. He sipped. "*Izzil. Izzil.*" Very good. Addi sat in the shadow of a corner, to interact without being seen.

After an awkward silence, La Tour gathered himself. "Akka n-Ali, I saw your men today in the field," La Tour began, in French. "I watched as they prepared to strike your enemy."

Unbidden, Addi interjected with a translation. His tenor echoed from the nook.

"For this, I commend you. It is courageous. The Ait Atta fight bravely. Your men will attack and die with great strength in their hearts. This is a true sign of generous and strong leadership. You make all the people see what they protect. Your homes and women and children. Your land. Most of all, the noble heart of the Imazighen."

"O, my *sherif*, I thank you very much," Akka replied. "We remain humble, Insh' Alláh, so that we may be of worthy service to . . ."

Akka halted his speech. La Tour sensed he might have been about to say phrases like "Allah most Merciful" or "our destiny," or "you, our master." This last he did not want to hear. He took the moment to solemnly interject.

"But I must ask you, Akka, where have the men now gone?"

"My *sherif*," Akka replied with an edge of concern about Jilani's apparent error in ignorance, "they rode to Ait Mehammed. Yesterday. They and many other men. Upon enemy there. By now they will have joined forces and are soon to strike."

La Tour lamented this. Were Akka or anyone to clearly see his face below the hood and *achttan*, they would see anguish. Most weapons of great value—munitions, rifles, and a machine gun—had been carried away by the men best able to use them.

"Then listen all the more carefully," La Tour intoned. *"Much depends upon your understanding."* He paused to let Addi gauge the weight of this. *"So often your men perform brilliantly against the foe. Your tactics of taking war to them have been wise and effective, achieving much with little. But an* Iroumin *force is on its way to* you. *From Tizi n'Tirist. They would be formidable even if all your men were here. And they are not . . . "*

Akka's jaw tightened. He flashed rage and sorrow and alarm. La Tour saw that the chieftain clearly knew nothing of this foe. He may have diverted men from wide patrol to rally forces for this raid. And therein lay a potentially fatal mistake—leaving an invasion route untended. Now it would be Jilani's entirely bizarre position to attempt to mend this oversight. And worse, it was possible that the outbound raiders had already confronted the superior Légion ranks. Or been seen by them.

"Last night I saw an army in the pass near Azourki," La Tour said, deliberately vague about the source of his sight. "This night, they have moved through Tizi n'Tirist. The campfires are closer to Taboulmant. And they may not be the only enemy converging on here. Scout men must ride south toward Bou Malem."

Akka said, almost dejectedly, "Our warriors will return from *ihouffen* in four days."

La Tour eliminated the doom from his voice. He said matter-of-factly, "The enemy will strike tomorrow. As we speak, an advance party is watching us. At least one man was on the mountain back here," and he pointed yonder. "You have tonight to prepare. Perhaps only until the morning. When airplanes will come."

He formed his right hand into the shape of a plane and his voice into its engine. He punctuated with play-thunder, to imitate explosions.

"And so you must start at once. Now."

Akka was in a quiet frenzy. Berating himself. Looming catastrophe cast a long shadow. Long years of struggle could be undone in a brief day's lapse.

"And most importantly, Akka, the enemy does not come primarily to kill the people or destroy the village. The bombing planes can do that. Their main mission is you."

La Tour felt a hint of a prophet's power. He saw dismay and anguish etch upon Akka's features. And he felt an odd emotion. Sympathy. The *amghar* took the master's word, evidently without critical thought about the source of this information. Allah had simply sent it to Jilani. Akka n-Ali bowed and genuflected. La Tour grew terribly self-conscious; then almost lost composure as fear jolted him. If to now Akka had not regarded his worn black *brodekins* or their origins, this was the moment. His eyes just inches above them peered down for a long time. But when he looked up at Jilani, there was no trace of puzzlement at this oddity, no inkling that he and his village had been deceived or betrayed. Indeed, his eyes beseeched forgiveness for his failure of leadership and wisdom in the very hours it was most needed. The notorious chieftain, in a moment of truth, had revealed a flaw in character. A burden of guilt seemed to hobble his tactical logic. Faith and decisive action were disconnected. To La Tour, Akka seemed to have forgotten that Jilani, or his reincarnation, was the tool sent to repel this assault, the only one they were likely to need.

"We shall not panic, Akka. We have an advantage you do not see."

"*Ikh tinna rebbi.*" Akka did not ask what that advantage was. Perhaps he felt it need not or could not be explained. An unearthly force. Fire from on high. The wave of a hand. God's own multitudes. Jilani would not offer an explanation even if asked.

"We have two choices," La Tour said to Akka. "I must be honest. We can flee the village to gain time. You can leave now, with Kenza, Hada, Addi, and several others. Or we can fight." His tone emphasized the last sentence.

Addi translated in a robust voice. No sooner had the *amrabt* completed when La Tour was proud to hear Akka assert without any wavering: "Fight."

"Praise Allah, Akka, for being a true warrior. But you must let me help. I know best how to war against these devils."

"I put our lives in your hands."

"Ahh, not so fast, until truly all secrets are revealed." La Tour smiled and bid Akka to stand. He did also, and set his hands in motion as if conducting an orchestra. "This is what we will do. The dark is good for us. Send riders to nearby villages. Tarhia. Msemrir. Tilmi. Call to here every able-bodied man and woman. This will take several hours. Bring from all remaining munitions, as I must see the cache. And everyone is to remain quiet. Panic will alert the watchers. Send scouts and observers to high, hidden vantage points an hour in all directions. Find any spies and punish them. And if you have more of these . . ."

La Tour pulled the binoculars from within his *tajjelabith* . . .

"It would be most helpful."

La Tour did not know if it was for this blessing of mercy, from the reassuring tone of his voice, or for the hint of hope that triumph could somehow be snatched from the jaws of looming defeat. But he was certain that Akka would do exactly as asked. Or, more precisely, ordered.

La Tour calculated continuously; this endgame was a series of equations. He foresaw a successful defense; the spirits were willing and on his side. The vision was vivid; he knew it could be reality. His former brethren were the "other," a threat to him in every way. Saving the Ait Atta, for now, would justify their faith in Jilani the deity and earn a wealth of gratitude—a valuable dividend when he revealed his human form. With Akka's protection, La Tour could escape his compound disgrace—repaid with a bullet—and reach Azilal. There, using the back-pay money stuffed in his pants, he could flee to Casablanca, and by God's grace secure false papers and board a steamer for Marseilles or Toulon.

Akka Ahêddây dashed outside. La Tour watched him hail a villager and start a chain of instructions that would spread across the plateau, now preparing for night. A small, but dynamic machine surged into activity. Within half an hour, the atmosphere changed from day-to-day life to moment-by-moment crisis: fast chatter, muttered epithets, praises to God, hastened footsteps.

They convened at Akka's red door and bowed before Jilani, who held forth in French. Addi translated, immeasurably fulfilled that his prophesy was emerging as he spoke the very words to make it so. At the same time, he grew more puzzled at the odd details of these circumstances.

"None of you are to any more waste time or energy bowing to me. Tell this to all," Jilani pronounced. "I will later explain, but for now simply respect my wishes. There must be few lanterns. No loud talking. Tonight silence is as precious as air. By faith and by starlight will we work, and as your faith is strong so will be the work. I will labor beside you, as one with you.

"Akka n-Ali, when you have done all that I ask, please come to me near the terraced fields, and we will set new defenses against this beast."

BOOK THREE: BATTLE

FAITH

Lₐ *Tour stood by silently, waiting as they pondered his words. He saw Akka Ahêddây look at Addi Yacoub. Stare into the Sufi's blind eyes. Those unblinking eyes seemed to stare back, and the chief and the holy man were like eagles fixed in a mutual hypnotic gaze. La Tour hoped that their expressions were of wonderment, of kindred trust, of conviction and faith that at this moment they must step into the unknown.*

But why does this man suddenly sound much less like a deity come to enable peace and salvation than a soldier unleashing the beast of war? We accepted that our deliverance might unfold in mysterious ways. Perhaps we should take this gift as we found it. This pale man, of Iroumin flesh, bound up and hidden in Imazighen clothing, speaks in half-riddles, when he speaks at all, and at times has given us and his watchers the impression that he is lost, alone, and vaguely disconnected from Allah rather than one of his messengers. Jilani's conclusions about our situation are difficult to accept; yet that is exactly why we must do so. For our faith we will be rewarded with harmony, with freedom. With life. The alternative is clearly none of these, and Allah's wrath will be tenfold if we ignore this sure sign of His compassion for us.

"Perhaps you were expecting," Jilani intoned in French, "that with all-powerful sorcery I would turn the enemy away. I have no such power. Or you thought that by my presence they would not come at all. Clearly that is not the case. No one on Earth can hold back a river. But I tell you this. Some rivers at certain times flow backwards. They cancel their own progress to the sea. And in that way, I will give you a plan to help the enemy defeat himself."

SIXTEEN:

CITADEL

Alain Aumont began today, Thursday, with an uncomfortable risk by very publicly dashing after a taxi on Avenue du Haouz. Then he peered out the open window between Bab Taghzout and Souk el Khemis, looking for the man Christian Graves benignly described as "a tall, vulgar, sun-bronzed baboon pickled in alcohol."

Aumont feared that the official letter and cable in his pocket would at best be half-useful in any trek into Bled es Siba. Still, they would venture there today, after the belated arrival from Rabat of Graves in the new DeHavilland. But first Aumont must find Christian's black marketing cohort. The taxi squeezed across the maze of narrow streets in the upper quarter of the medina to Bab el Khemis. Beyond was the large, teeming site of the Thursday market's dither of buyers and sellers. He ordered the driver to stop.

"Arrêt."

He scanned for Europeans—men, women, soldiers, ramblers. He saw very few among the Berbers and Arabs, the mules, and swirls of colors in the merchants' stalls, and no tall Aroumi *baboon, suspicious and* conspicuous in worn overalls. After thirty futile minutes, he returned to the waiting taxi and commanded a pass to the Mamounia. If the pilot was not in the souk then he might be at the bar, buying rounds for the businessmen and offering them cargo service to and from Casablanca. "For the easy transfer of certain goods." Balafré used the phrase frequently, and had encouraged Graves to adopt it as a motto.

The silent driver continued past Route de Meknes around the western wall, and across Grande Avenue to Bab Jdid, skirting the lush gardens on the sprawling hotel grounds. The fragrances of roses, jasmine, and other essences of paradise wafted into the old auto. Aumont was petrified to enter the legal bar—frequented by men of his acquaintance—but reasoned that it would take but a few moments to find his quarry, slovenly as he often was.

"Arrêt."

Aumont walked briskly across the tasteful lobby, and lingered in a corner near several potted dwarf palms. A lovely, unaccompanied woman in royal blue at a table beside the door momentarily distracted him, but he swept the large room and its few late morning guests. Several Marrakshis were attired like Frenchmen, and two Français subtly emulated Arabs, but he saw no plane mechanic and pilot in the garb of his vocation. No Balafré.

It was 11:30. In six hours dusk, would fall upon Azilal; they had to leave this afternoon. Travel to the remote village would consume at least one long day. Aumont despaired that he would not arrive in time.

The last stop Graves had suggested was a tawdry tavern a gunshot distance from the new Velodrome off Avenue de France. "Arrêt," said Aumont at its intersection with Avenue du Haouz—almost exactly where he began two hours ago. The establishment covertly sold liquor to impious natives serving the French colonials and military, and openly to the Iroumin seeking wet spirits in a dry city. Aumont paid the pittance of fee and the tip.

As Aumont reached the tavern door, he somehow made a psychic link with the man inside, knew he would be here, felt his trek was complete. Only a few dissolute types occupied the smoky rooms; he was at a table in a corner. The unshaven and scarred pilot—perhaps an Escadrille veteran of the Great War—wore tattered black coveralls, a leather jacket and a dirty red beret. The swarthy captain of Christian's operation was born Luca Lamartine in Corsica in 1894, but renamed for his scars on face and soul. Balafré pensively nursed a blanc cassis that by early afternoon would become stronger libation. It was difficult to discern if the liquor was to revive his memories or to squelch them.

"Balafré, we will get Christian. At the station, by now I hope. We have a mission."

Balafré dutifully rose to standing, like one who, lost in the world, was awaiting a sign that would urge him to action, but determined when receiving it.

Two hours after arriving half a day late, Graves and Aumont rendezvoused.

"We are ready to go," Aumont said. "I trust your trip was profitable."

"Yes, but still not worth it," Graves grumbled. "Bribes are not made so easily as they once were, especially by telephone in this country. We do not know who might be listening on the line. The timing was not the best, but I could not delay. How can we otherwise arrange to get some of this out of the country. And you?"

"My man said only that Akka n-Ali will be in custody, or dead, within four days," Aumont replied unhappily. "And he said that on Tuesday."

The trio left Gueliz at 2:00 o'clock en route to the airfield. Graves would lie splendidly about their destination. Christian and Balafré were known there; the sentry merely glanced at the log and cargo. The De Havilland was shortly airborne. Balafré turned east by northeast, bound for Azilal. There, they would hire a truck to reach Ait Mehammed, where Alain would retain guides for the sixty kilometers to Akka's plateau. Fifty louze *would entice them, to be followed by gold coins when Aumont was more than halfway. Should trouble loom, he could trust only in God.*

* * * * *

Major Henri-Cybard Mirvais led his men to the valley of Asif Bou Guemmez, where they would join Colonel Rochet. The Colonel was pleased by his force: five Légionnaire companies, two Goums of one hundred men each, two fresh squadrons of *spahis*, sternly warned against flight, and two Schneider field guns. The solid, fast-strike detachment would surely be effective. Mirvais, however, was ambivalent. He had only one hundred and thirty men—his four best sections—and if the attack went as planned, they might not fight. Mirvais believed that his garrison and combat record spoke well of him, and that his clashes with the men of Akka Ahêddây, although flawed, counted for too little. Perhaps the Colonel felt him to be a bad omen. But he was Rochet's protégé, and would not be sent away, though that may be preferred. Perhaps it was to buy silence: this attack, planned and initiated on the sly, was a secret affair.

Many of the troops wore the medals and scars of other Maroc campaigns. A core of them had served in the Great War and were inured to hardship. With their brawn and their wily maneuvers since disembarking from the trucks, many considered this 70-kilometer trek to be a victory stroll. Furthermore, Rochet had slyly stolen a page from Akka n-Ali. For several previous days, deliberately misinformed Berber scouts and *amazan* were visiting villages from Azilal to Assemsouk, offering a reward for anyone who reported the whereabouts of a band of notorious Imazighen brigands.

"Fifty gold pieces to the first man who supplies information leading to the leaders Azou n-Drazi n-M'Gouna or Taher n-Mohammed n-Oultana. We want these monsters."

To conjure the trick of a large maneuver, to prove they meant business, *spahi* and Légion horse units made daylight dashes near Azilal. On cue, one night troop trucks and light armored vehicles roamed as if part of a larger force moving confidently but in haste. This implied poor planning, and might coax Ait Atta warriors to chase an easy victory, like pack dogs on a few lone sheep. Four hundred Berbers assembled in a valley near Talmest, to intercept the column thought to be moving south. That hunt was futile.

Légionnaires resumed the truck journey, and it crawled to road's end near Ait Mehammed; the horsemen took another route. By dawn the trucks had returned over the rugged tracks—as most of the troops marched toward Adrar n-Azourki and the Ait Atta bastion. By the time any *amghar* realized the ruse, the column would be ready to strike.

The unit camped for the day in a gorge awaiting the difficult all-night march eastward under clear skies and a half-moon. Pack mules bore ammunition, machine guns, and two disassembled 65mm field pieces. Tomorrow morning, as the assault reached its objective, several planes would bomb Akka n-Ali's plateau in a *coup de grace*.

The two officers met on a rise overlooking the daunting eastward terrain. Mirvais spoke in a tone calculated to put him on an equal plane with Rochet.

"I compliment you on this campaign, sir," he said. "Your keen discipline, the familiar, foolish Berber ways of war and this well-planned maneuver will all together do what few have done since our quest began."

He did not realize that with such false modesty he was including himself.

"That is why they pay us, Henry," Rochet replied with a hint of condescension.

Rochet cast a brief glance to signal he did not appreciate the indiscretion, even as bonhomie.

Mirvais was technically in violation of the directive to administer to his garrison. Two days before he departed, several messages warned of potential trouble near Bou Malem; they were most likely a ruse. But in long-distance pursuit of a real opportunity in one direction, Mirvais had left a flank exposed. He was confident, however, that there would be no Imazighen uprising in his absence; believed that he would not hinder Rochet; and expected that the men under his command would make certain their mutual success. He would share in the achievement of capturing Akka n-Ali. Standing in light reflected from a triumph could ease the way to a more suitable command. At last.

"Like you, I wish to see that this page is finally turned," Mirvais replied. "That the man who has so bedeviled us will be bagged or eliminated."

"It is not only him," Rochet asserted. "His people are not ragged, ignorant sheep herders. Part of the problem is that we underestimate the adversary, and then they elude us. Perhaps if that philosophy had been applied last year we would not be here now."

Mirvais winced. This was another rebuke, and Mirvais realized he had invited it. With that retort, Mirvais felt intimidated and understood that Rochet knew full well the game in motion on the table of these mountains.

"I must be candid, Mirvais," Rochet continued. "You and your men complicate my plans. We may or may not need you. Either way, I expect that my orders be followed."

"I will not be a hindrance," Mirvais replied. "But I have battled Akka's men. If you are not wise to their ways, you may be at a disadvantage despite best-laid plans."

"Scouts have been in position for several days," Rochet sighed. He was already weary of the *tête-à-tête*. "Undetected. A rider on the way to receive a message from one will soon report back to me. Then we will know our status. When so, I intend to decoy and win. If my tactics are undone, sir, I will assign blame where appropriate."

With that as a parting shot, Rochet spurred his horse forward to question a lieutenant. Mirvais stopped himself from appearing slack-jawed. No camaraderie would be forthcoming from Rochet for either the advice or the additional power of Mirvais's platoons. Worse, Rochet would deny them independent action. Mirvais had, in effect, traveled here to learn he would earn no official glory.

But his own significant decoy was moving parallel to them on another track some ten kilometers to the west.

A squad of *spahis* were diverting to a rearward ravine they and several Yafelmane scouts had reconnoitered. The terrain beyond it was fine for horsemen because there were few nooks where the foe could hide. A small mounted force could keep the cap on a bottle for some time, certainly long enough for the frontal assault to succeed. If any chose to flee out the back door they would find themselves trapped. What is more, Rehou Khoussaila had been trailing Rochet's force from Adrar n-Mezgounane, forty kilometers east of Demnate. Rehou and his invisible men followed them toward Tizi n'Tirist, on a rougher trail with less effort. Their combined forces would be formidable. But Rehou had a surprise maneuver, of his own design.

* * * * *

Alain Aumont despaired that he would be too late. Christian and Balafré had calculated that a potter's village near Azilal would be one of the very few places to find a lorry for rent. And so it was, but the only immediate option was a cafe owner's rickety junker, which began to burn oil and then failed just south of Azilal on the dirt-road to Ait Mehammed. Balafré set about dissecting its bowels, and shortly discovered the need for a critical gasket from any like truck.

"I can steal the piece in about thirty seconds."

"Ayy, Jesus," Graves imprecated, "for want of a ten-centimeter rubber hole the kingdom was lost. Where in the hell do I get that out here?"

Aumont was confounded by the ill-timed break in the chain. He could not sit idly by until a machine saved the hours and he arrived, a day later, too late, to save La Tour.

"Yes," said the toothless old shepherd outside his house in Ait Hag, "for an hour they passed. It was not our business, but we sent word. The couriers have not returned, and we do not know if the message reached beyond Tizi n'Igrourane. We care not greatly for Bou Iknifen and Oussikis, but they fight Iroumin." He was curt in his phrasing, almost contemptuous. "Are you not Afransawi?"

"Aumont," said Graves, "You must ride on. Tomorrow we fly after you."

"But where will you land?" Aumont asked, for he did not know.

"If there are three hundred flat, open meters," said Balafré, "I can land and fly."

Reassured but hardly at ease, Aumont hired eager young Marouche and his wizened uncle Assu. They did not grasp his urgency, and from the next dawn he wanted to dash ahead of them. Their long day's journey ended before dusk in the village of Ichkiss. He understood; the green fields of Orleannais he longed to see again were infinitely less wild. Paying his tazttat, Alain had Assu inquire of local men if Iroumin had passed by.

"Yes, many," was the reply, "night before last, and quickly. But late yesterday many hard-riding Ait Atta followed in their path." Alain, his guides, and the villagers, too, were uneasy. He feared that the hour may already be too late to save his French friend and Berber saviors. Aumont chose to ride on at once. Assu tried to dissuade him. Alain was sore and exhausted; a shove could send him keeling from the saddle. Yet he was bound by an unspoken oath, and asked the Lord to renew his strength, and so on the legs of horses, if not the wings of eagles, he continued the trek. Ahead to the east, in the light of the rising quarter-moon, loomed the wide mouth of a valley. His aim was to reach it by midnight.

* * * * *

Akka guided Addi away from Jilani to confer in private. Several sets of footsteps ran by them in the dark. A horse clattered across stones. People conferred in animated but natural tones about the rising crisis.

"The French are coming?" a man named Hiba inquired.

"Yes, my friend," Akka matter-of-factly replied. "This way."

"How do we know? A scout has returned?"

"No. Most scouts are on the raid." He paused, ready to confess his oversight. "Jilani has discovered this. Quickly he told me. We prepare to fight as quickly."

Hiba turned to Akka. "It is you they want. You can evade them. Please leave at once."

"I will not. The time has come. They are relentless. I must resist, not run."

"*We* will resist. *You* must go."

"No! Sidi Jilani will help arrange the defenses. This attack is no longer a surprise. They expect us to lose, to surrender. If we exert ourselves we can win."

"Many men are off fighting elsewhere," Addi reminded him. "We have but a few here. And a shortage of weapons. If the Légion brings a large force . . ."

"Holy man!" Akka rebuked, and immediately repented. He softened his tone. "I admit we have less than we need. But we also have more. Remember, there is a soul in the village wiser than all of us together. By the warning he saves us from annihilation. We have the courage, now we must trust him to give us the opportunity to win the day."

Addi Yacoub said nothing. This would not be the first time Akka Ahêddây was at the center of a marvelous deed.

"We have no time to discuss this. I give instructions. We work together."

"As you wish," Addi said softly. "I am your servant."

"No. You are my friend and my teacher," Akka replied.

Jilani stepped into the dim light cast by an oil lantern on a post. The image was as if the beloved one had stepped from another dimension at the very sound of their voices.

"Akka speaks truth, Addi Yacoub," Jilani intoned in French. "We three will help defy disaster. You know your people. How they respond. What they deserve. But I know your enemy more than you know me. More than

I know you. I read the *Afransawi* like storm clouds. We must not argue. I say and the people will do. Can we agree?"

Addi was both elated and puzzled by the authority in his voice. This was not the quiet, reclusive man of just yesterday. Addi translated. The *amghar* and the *amrabt* could not defy Jilani's suggestion. They pledged fidelity with short, simultaneous bows and hands on their hearts.

"Yes, shrif, we can do only this," Addi said.

"We three are too mighty for this enemy," Akka pronounced.

Jilani continued: "This is a very good position for defense. Wind timber. Planks. To build crude barricades, what the *Iroumin* call *chevaux-de-frise*. With them, horses or men cannot move up the *imi*. They will only be able to attack up the cliff. If we keep them off the plateau, they cannot kill all of us. But at dawn they will have airplanes with bombs. And field guns all day. With them they can destroy everything. So everyone must leave their homes. The feeble and the women and children must go into the caves and not venture out until we retrieve them. But first, take all guns and all explosives from there. I hope they will be useful after storage there."

Fierce warriors, Berber and Arab, knew how to outsmart their enemies, or cast a pall of fear upon them, perhaps winning the battle before it was joined. But they might also achieve noble justice without the extreme of war. Hearing Jilani's assertiveness, Akka grew certain that the demigod had both abilities—and that with them he could save the *amghar* from the disgrace of failing his people exactly when they needed him most.

"We will rip apart the houses to get the wood, shrif."

"Better that then the French blast them to splinters," Jilani replied.

Akka turned to a knot of men across the way.

"You there! Get wood tools at once! Then dismantle my house! And ten others!"

"Take your axes and saws," Akka repeated. "Choose the homes yourselves! I don't care how it is done! You have two hours!"

"But that is your home . . . ," Hmad implored. "I offer mine instead."

"Both of them then! Now get to work!" Akka said to echo Jilani's electrified tone.

After a moment's pause, Hmad dutifully said, "As you wish."

Jilani soberly said, "And I remind all that everyone must be quiet. Perhaps our voices and activity have not carried beyond the village. That is good. But anyone who does hear it will be suspicious. We are being watched."

"How do you know?" Akka asked.

"When you launch a sneak attack, do you not send men ahead to learn about enemy forces and to confirm that your target remains where desired?"

"Yes, as always."

"The *Iroumin* have done likewise. They do it with mercenaries. *Amazan* recruited from among rival tribes. There are many Berber assassins and spies. They move about freely and have no loyalty."

"Yes," was all Akka grimly said. Jilani sounded stranger every moment, as if he could read the situation through the eyes and minds of the devils in pursuit.

"Some are up there now." Jilani pointed to the ink-black hills. "Cursing the night, too far to hear us for fear of being captured, but during the day seeing several kilometers"—he curled his fingers and held them to his eyes like binoculars—"to read our behavior."

Something about his manner troubled Akka. It seemed too . . . natural. He wondered, again, if a transmigrated deity would be at ease with human behavior.

Jilani said nothing more and turned to the great task. Trailed by a throng, he walked along the promontory to the walled fields above the stony tract and below the crest, and gestured at the pathways bisecting them. Pile the wood at each, he said, in equal amounts.

Berber mountain homes were amenity-free, utilitarian shelters from the elements. Made of adobe mud, rocks and sometimes an artless wooden frame, many were not occupied year-round. But here in Taboulmant, civic improvements nearly thirty years old would be invaluable in deflecting the enemy advance tomorrow.

Men scurried to retrieve their tools and divide into teams. Soon there arose a strange, soft clamor of deconstruction, of muffled thuds as facades were bashed apart, as others hastily hauled furniture and pottery and the few valuables outside before the walls crumbled to expose the cedar skeleton and the adobe-and-reed roof crashed down and suitable wood lay in heaps. The heaviest timbers were hitched to horses or pulled by several men, who labored mightily to bear all that was usable from the ravaged homes to the precipice. On into the night they worked. Sweat, not sleep.

La Tour would have the quickly assembled spiked barriers anchored in rocks. Fortunately, two defiles were angled between high stone walls or recessed above a perimeter of boulders. Légion guns would not have a clear shot from their most likely positions on the ridge. And the third *imi* could possibly be held by the finest Ait Atta marksmen using the best of the stolen rifles.

The grave problem was at the opposite side of the plateau. If a force assaulted there, too, Taboulmant and Akka were doomed. Then there were the planes.

Mules conveyed the cave stores to the plateau. The supply was barely adequate only if small tactical miracles reduced the enemy before they breached the passes. La Tour saw a dozen familiar metal boxes of rifle ammunition, five cases of rifles, several useless bales of uniforms, and two crates stamped with a red word: "Explosive."

As a man with an oil lantern stood over him, and with villagers looking on, La Tour wrenched open the first lid. Squinting in the light he saw an array of tubes, most in good condition. The dynamite gave them an advantage—if he could figure how to best use it.

The key was the length of detonating cord in an accompanying case, for without a good amount a wagonload of dynamite would be half-useless. In that case, he would have to devise another method, like a catapult or arrow. But even in favorable conditions, either technique relied too much on luck to reach a small, dispersed or moving target. Battle was no time for trial and error.

Kenza squatted in the dim glow of a lantern and watched the last house being ripped apart. She did not understand this, even as she heard the men discussing where the wood was to be taken and how it would be cut and reassembled. She grew sleepy, but the odd excitement and great anticipation of war under the guidance of a god was a narcotic.

"I will now go to the first *imi* and begin to direct the carpenters," Jilani said to Addi. "Please tell them. One of them will watch me, and then relate it to the other teams."

Addi turned this too-fluid French into a stream of Tamazight. All of the workers indicated they wished to be Jilani's right-hand man. He pointed without favor to the nearest man and gestured that the others quickly resume hauling the wood. He hoped to have enough lumber for three sizable defense positions, and the time to construct them—and set up the other surprises he had in mind for these visitors as well.

I'm aiding enemy preparations to kill my countrymen. La Tour reeled from this bitter awareness, and that his actions would be a breach of every oath. But it did not darken his conscience nor evoke self-pity, and he had little fear of the consequences. Indeed, this crisis awakened his dormant desire for decisive action. If this was his only way to escape the dilemma and return home after this delay and dishonor, then he would willingly fight, and direct others to fight, and be a god-hero for the Ait Atta.

And it thundered into his mind: Were these Mirvais's men afar? Perhaps La Tour was about to engage his former mates in battle. Though the column approached from the opposite point, La Tour knew that if Mirvais had learned of the mission, chances were good he would have sought to join it to the end of Akka Ahêddây, perhaps one of the final episodes in the long conquest of Maroc.

As ten village men watched, Jilani paced off the distance between the rock walls of the first notch. It was twelve meters at its widest, eight at its narrowest. Knowing they would follow, he began to move rocks into piles on each side at the mid-point, nine meters from wall to wall. In minutes, the longest and broadest length of timber was wedged behind them, each end abutting tightly on its wall about one-half meter off the ground.

Then he demonstrated how shorter, thinner timbers were to be tightly spaced at alternating angles across the beam, the upper third lying atop it and the other end pressed into the earth. Lengths of rope lashed the transverse cross-pieces to the central spar. The result was an array of wooden teeth set in a jaw across the narrow span.

From behind boulders above and on both sides, riflemen could guard the approach and shoot down on assaulting squads whose numbers, limited by the passage, would make good targets even for poor marksmen. Of course, these snipers would themselves be easily shot when they ventured from behind the protective rocks, as would sometimes be necessary to get a clear shot at Légionnaire officers or grenade-throwers. Many Imazighen in these positions would be killed.

Jilani repeated this crude engineering in the other two positions. His mates now knew the technique, and eagerly performed most of the final tasks. Jilani made sure that the last barrier, the one most likely to be fired upon by any field pieces, was made doubly secure, though he had only half the hope it would survive for long. Most troubling was that this, the widest pass, could deliver the most enemy troops and horsemen into the village. Behind this position, in a boulder field adjacent to the gardens, he concentrated more than half of the best weapons and the riflemen with the most experience and spirit.

"You must fire in concentrated volleys. Two or three men firing at a time is not enough. When eight, ten, fifteen of you are firing at once; you are more likely to . . ."

"Kill them!" brashly interjected Mimoun. He was vigorous, hardy and eager to be unbridled. He boasted that this brother Brka, one of the men on the *ahouff*, was a fine marksman. Mimoun's blood lust was up, and ardent to follow Brka's example. La Tour was reluctant for a fine young man to taint his soul in warfare. Most of the other men had seen battle carnage, and were old enough to choose whether or how to step into its path.

"Yes, true," he soberly concurred with Mimoun. "But you will stay by me."

Mimoun was disconsolate. He was not content with a supporting role.

"Everyone will take positions here," La Tour continued. "Keep your heads down! Enemy counter fire is devastating! And if they bring a machine gun close by, run away!"

Mimoun demonstrated with rapid percussive sound effects and the mime of a soldier sweeping the gun barrel in an arc.

"But they are there, about twenty-five kilometers away, I think advancing on us at this moment, and there is nothing to do but prepare, wait, and fight. We will celebrate when they run from our courage. Until then, we build barricades. Roll more large stones to the edge of the cliffs. Speak to mothers, brothers, sisters, wives. Make peace with Allah, for I must say that if you do not know it already some of you will soon join him."

He walked away from the ensuing silence and was swallowed by the night.

* * * * *

"First light is six a.m.," Colonel Rochet informed Capitaine Arras. "All the men will move at three a.m., in five hours, and be in position at dawn. The village will have no time to organize a defense.

Mirvais departed the main column and met Rehou Khoussaila as pre-arranged at the mouth of Tizi n'Takchtant. Ten kilometers beyond the next ridge was the approach to Akka's lair.

"Rehou, I trust your men draw near the village?"

"Yes, Mirvais. But what if there are more of Akka's force there than you have been led to believe?"

"Return at once. I will try to delay Rochet's attack and await reinforcements."

"Oh, Rehou," Mirvais wryly beseeched. "And please reveal more of that mountain's secrets to me. For I will reward you tenfold."

Despite Rehou Khoussaila's decade-long business with the Légion, he still did not have a firm grasp of their language. The Yafelmane Berber often took Mirvais literally. He grabbed the leather case holding Mirvais's field glasses, deftly mounted his black horse and rode down the dim trail onto flat ground between broad ridges. The size of the promised reward would more than pay for a new home in the seacoast smuggler's town of Essaouira.

Danton Saint-Avold could not sleep. He had not fully rested in several nights. Mirvais wondered aloud about him and his reliability with the men.

"You are as close to a machine as I have known in my army years, Sergeant. How do you go without sleep?"

"By simply forgetting that I need any."

A biting chill entered the air after sunset. Men saw the wisps of their breath. They gnawed on dried meat and hard biscuits as they marched uphill and down. The majority refrained from their favorite habit of grumbling. The column outpaced its march schedule. On reaching a secluded ravine Rochet called for the men to bed down for four or five hours. Campfires for cooking or warmth were not allowed this near the objective. They had been told the fighting would be short, and not hard; only a small Berber force occupied the citadel. The dual surprise of direct pressure from the main body and a small encircling column of partisans and cavalry would likely send them fleeing. The cavalry would bag Akka if the Légion had not already done so, or killed him in the assault.

"Rehou Khoussaila nears his enemies again," Saint-Avold said to Mirvais as the Berber rode away. "He goes to find their heart. I doubt he can resist trying to carve it out."

"Not for long," Mirvais responded. "But his choice will be interesting. Either way, it will be good for this campaign."

Good for you, that is. You bribed him and his men to help your last attempt at self-promotion. The skin of that Yafelmane is wrapped around a beast with no conscience.

"Last winter he collected another Iknifen head," Saint-Avold uttered brusquely. "I don't know who that might be good for."

Mirvais loathed unsolicited advice of any kind. He cast the Sergeant a glare; it implied Saint-Avold should mind his own business, and keep his thoughts to himself.

"Don't worry, Saint-Avold. We will return you to Bou Malem in time to ride the next caravan to Marrakech and your rail car to Rabat. You were in last class entering the stinking bowels of the Légion, but first class going home."

"Shut up over there," a coarse voice muttered impertinently. "We need sleep."

At any other time that tone or choice of words from one below his rank would have set Mirvais off. But he said nothing and instead heeded the unseen trooper.

"Yes, sir," Saint-Avold wryly whispered. "From last to first, two weeks hence."

"You'll see the wife and leave these Moroccan BMC whores behind."

Saint-Avold flinched. Mirvais's idea of a worthy conversation was to encourage and insult at the same time. Danton didn't like the rough equation of "wife" and "whore."

"I'll see my family and leave it all behind, sir." He was polite, but almost curt.

Saint-Avold lay down upon the ground blanket and pulled the second heavier one over him. In the satchel beside him was the reassuring bulk of ammunition. Unlike his earlier, more eager days in the Légion, when he had cultivated a reputation as a ruthless marksman, he hoped to fire none of it in the coming hours. In the moments before sleep he prayed that this would be his last action.

* * * * *

La Tour felt like an animal in a cage. The night was protection from the assault; he wished it would remain dark until the danger had passed. But if day never arrived, the resolution would never unfold, and he would be trapped on this rugged hill while his life drifted away like hourglass grains. Best to bring the dawn and the decision.

There was much to do in the next few hours. His energy flagged. He sat for a cup of strong tea a team of women brewed in large batches so that all might remain invigorated in the chill. He was encouraged to hear laughter. Humor made a devil's medicine easier to swallow. And the children not yet gone to the caves with their guardians giggled as they scampered about, puzzled by the activity but still knowing little about the danger.

La Tour again inspected the dynamite, marveling at his calm. Only a few of the five dozen tubes appeared unreliable. The lot had been destined for the removal of railroad obstructions; with it he instead expected to remove soldiers who insisted on obstructing his progress. Escape. Liberation. These people trusted him. He felt responsible for their well-being. How cruelly ironic that if they were to have any hope of survival some of them would have to die. But the sacrifice of a few so that the greater unit could survive had been part of life here since Akka became *amghar n-ufella*.

La Tour's thoughts whisked to the chief's daughter. Kenza was no warrior woman. She summoned a joyful future in her hands, intimated an angel's pleasures with her eyes. La Tour could not know her emotions or sense her moods as he would those of a long-time friend—but he loved her anyway. This sensation was a mystery. But his feelings for Akka's daughter were achingly honest, he thought almost pure. The clarity of those thoughts startled him. It was as if Kenza was standing beside him in saffron sunlight, and with a bird-song laugh inviting him to . . . He shook off the distraction and pushed such reveries away.

La Tour took a step back from the dynamite. People were about to die. Their sacrifice would bust open this trap of circumstances. Oh, he rationally knew they had not been under his control, but in some way during these weeks he had helped to set them in motion toward this awful juncture. What move was next?

His eyes scanned a batch of various size clay jars arranged in rough rows before the house of the potter. He walked to there and inspected one.

At once La Tour knew how to use the dynamite. Villagers would tie a length of rope to each jar. Into it he would place a tube of dynamite, and a measure of detonating cord. When the troops assaulted, some would clamber over the talus and up the scowling precipice; the assigned defenders would light the fuses, and quickly lower several pots at once down the face from covered positions set back from the steep lip of the crag. The surprise explosions would blast men off the palisade or crush them with a tumble of rocks. This crude tactic would be as effective as modern artillery.

La Tour sneaked a glance at his pocket watch; first light was three hours away. The attack would commence before mid-morning. He half-expected that Berbers newly aware of the enemy column were racing here to alert them. Although the land was vast and wild, could any foe traverse it without alarming some of its inhabitants? Somewhere, a sheep herder or a night rider had seen the furtive Légion, and the alert was pulsing ahead of their march. By fate, the grace of Allah, the trick of the evening light and the ignorance of the enemy commander, they had been blessed with significant warning time.

"You there!" La Tour said in Tamazight to a fellow en route to the far *imi*. "Come here!" The old man, his beard streaked with gray, walked forward and fell to his knees.

"Stand up!" La Tour barked in French, supplementing the language strange to the Berber with clear gestures. "Go find the potter!" He held out the clay vessel and swept his arm across the jars and the house. "Tell him I need many water and oil jars!"

The old citizen could not fathom the need for these items, but certainly he would obey the command. The startled man bolted into the night on his task.

La Tour heard nearby the continuing, nearly complete construction of the wood and rock barriers. Voices chattered, large stones clattered, axes trimmed wood. He walked through the fields toward the barrier of boulders behind the escarpment. Beyond, forward to the lip, lay a strip of open, steep slope. No one below could get a clear view of the top behind the brink of rocks.

La Tour's problem was to quickly contrive a system to repeatedly lower pots toward ascending assault troops without exposing the Berbers to snipers far across the narrow valley, or to any unit which eluded the Berber rifles and breached the wooden barriers to threaten them from behind. And the village would be doomed if the number of riflemen fell below the minimum for effective defensive fire; he calculated that no more than a quarter of the men could fall or the cause would be lost. As the Légion would have nearly overwhelming volleys from the beginning, casualties would surely approach that ratio.

This episode of warfare would simply require more ingenuity than fighting skill.

For the first time, now that dawn drew near, he felt cold fear.

Akka and Addi approached; behind walked a third man, one who had helped rip apart Akka's house. La Tour stifled his distress lest Addi sense it. Jilani was a leader, a warrior and a prophet; less than full confidence might suggest that, at the least, he was surely not the latter, thus bringing his doom as escape beckoned.

"You must act immediately," he said in French, with hand signals. "The carpenters will build three V-shaped funnels a half-meter off the ground, from here at these rocks," he gestured, "over the edge of the cliff." He splayed three right fingers at downward angles.

Akka and Addi frowned in unison, mirrors of each other's puzzlement.

"It is over twenty meters," Jilani reckoned aloud. "We will need about forty-five meters of planks for each of three. You must find that amount. This is a fast solution, and we will have no better one before dawn. Without it or another, your men . . . our men . . . will die in desperation, and that could open the way to defeat."

Addi translated all the French to Tamazight.

"We have but two carpenters, *sherif*." Akka said. "Hani, go get them."

"When the wood is obtained Hani and I will do the work of a third man."

Akka turned to Hani, who at once dashed into the night. Within minutes he returned with Youcef and Aamar to consult the power trio.

All watched as Jilani bent to draw with his right hand the simple glyph of a "V" in a small patch of lantern-lit dirt. "The seams of wood," he told the two tired men, "must be closely aligned. So that the inner sides are smooth."

Akka did not ask the purpose for all this. Surely Jilani had perfect reasons. But Addi continued to frown with barely disguised concern.

Ten men set to the task of scrounging for more timber. Four long palm logs, hauled from the Dades last year, remained uncut. Without asking, wielding a makeshift handspike, Hani began to pry apart one of only two small carts in the village. The straight planks would yield nearly enough wood for one of the furrows. Haj the potter and Youcef the carpenter joined him in a frenzy of bare-handed yanking to dismantle the one cart and cleave the second. The wood torn from the ill-made metal pegs accumulated on the ground. Other fellows gathered several unclaimed planks from the houses, and then hauled the raw material to the ravines.

Hani carefully angled the boards and balanced them on improvised wood-scrap braces or propped them with suitable stones. The bottom interstice, where the adjacent board edges kissed, was to be as narrow as possible. So aligned, the planks were set in braces. This was the prototype.

Precious time would be consumed if error required it to be pulled apart and redone.

"Now bring cooking oil. *Zzit.*" Jilani said simply to everyone. "All that you have. Coat the inner face of the boards to make them slippery."

Again, on the face of it this command made little sense. The men and women looked at Akka, who nodded them homeward. Within minutes all returned. Jilani stood by anxiously as Hani, Haj and several others dashed two or more liters on the wood of the first sluice contraption and smeared its length with their hands. Akka and Addi saw that the divine guest was anxious to prove that his invention performed as planned.

Jilani roughly measured a dozen or more lengths of coarse rope between outstretched arms. A sizable throng watched in fascination. When done, he indicated that Akka cut the cord in mid-loop. He obliged with his *takummiyt*. Then Jilani tied one end to the handle of a jug. The other he wrapped around his right wrist and grasped in his palm.

With some ceremony he sat down several meters behind the large boulder, a leg on each side of the top of the sluice, a position someone else would soon take in grave peril. He lay the jug on its back smooth side in the opening. For a long, odd moment it remained motionless. Then gravity began to tug the urn down the sloping, lubricated ramp.

"Un, deux, trois, quatre, cinq . . ."

The jug gained momentum and plunged out at the far end, over the cliff edge. The rope in his right hand continued to play out as the jar fell. Then it snapped tight.

"Almost fifty meters," he said, to himself. "This incline is twenty meters long, so the jars will fall thirty meters down the cliff. That is too far . . ."

The group looked on as Jilani casually measured two arm-lengths of rope, and again gestured that Akka do the cutting. The *amghar* peered closely now; for a moment the Frenchman feared that Akka's blazing eyes displayed a new, troubling suspicion about the very human behavior of a reborn deity. But then La Tour detected signs of awe, of gratitude and grace similar to a child's love for a parent. He felt relief—quickly followed by guilt that his guise continued to impress and deceive these noble, generous people.

Youcef and Aamar worked on the second slide. Akka was quizzically smiling: Jilani seemed to be a divine genius effortlessly creating magic with raw material, an eccentric alchemist of war toys who contrived strange devices like a gleeful boy at play.

"Youcef, we will work these together when they come," Aamar said. "We tie the jar to the rope, shove the stick inside, light the fuse, shove the jar down the *auge*, it slides, drops over the edge, and falls to the end of the rope. If he is married, his wife is a widow."

The wry, macabre humor of this last line drew a round of uneasy laughter. The holy source of these lethal devices and their crucial importance stifled real mirth.

"Then pull the rope up and do it again," Akka continued. "Of course, the rope then may be a half-meter shorter. So we work our way up the cliff, just like the French will try. But the blasts will be close to them, and many who follow will be afraid. The fear we give them is our greatest weapon."

"Akka," La Tour interjected, "has all the ammunition been gathered? How much is compatible with the rifles?"

Akka paused before replying. La Tour sensed that the answer would not be good. His intuition bubbled that this, too, was a crisis he would be expected to resolve.

"My *sherif*, we count one hundred and twenty French guns and twelve nearly full cases of bullets. But one of them does not match the majority of rifles we possess."

Akka agonized. He had sent fifty of the best men on the raid. With them went sixty rifles and over one thousand rounds.

Mimoun edged away from the knot of men and ran uphill to his mare in sparse grass near several dismantled houses. The horse looked forlorn.

"Sidi, run fast."

Mimoun grabbed the reins, and the animal, keyed by the excitement, galloped toward the cave. Nearly all villagers but the warriors were in refuge there, though they were loathe to commune among the spirits. A few had fled down a treacherous secret ravine on the plateau's southern side, toward Zaouia Si Moha and safety. But everyone else knew that this day was inescapable, that the *Iroumin* would try to rout the Ait Atta wherever they went. They would not run. Akka Ahêddây, a princely messenger of Allah's will, would make his stand here. So would they.

La Tour performed quick arithmetic while the men stood beside him near the new chutes above the precipice. A full standard 8mm case held about one thousand rounds. One case of unsuitable caliber was eliminated, so that left less than ten thousand bullets or about eighty rounds for each man in this tiny army. Many of them would not be good shots, especially at a longer range. This was not reassuring.

The ensuing silence was long and strained. La Tour imagined he heard a Gorgon of annihilation pounding toward them. He could soon be shot dead, or captured to face trial as a traitor. If so, until he was in a coffin, and maybe not even then, he would never get any closer to Isère than a dungeon behind medieval walls in Maroc or France.

"Are you sure that is everything?" La Tour asked Akka, strongly suppressing the desperate tone his voice nearly revealed.

"Nothing remains in the caves," the *amghar* replied. "We have no other weapons."

"Very well," Jilani sighed. "We have made sure that many enemy will die. But I must say, Akka Ahêddây, without enough guns and bullets to fight the *Iroumin*, in the end only Allah himself can save your people. So I also suggest that you ask all to attend mosque, to pray for His strength that we may be the angels and the guardians of our fate."

Akka was exhilarated by these particular, dear words. But in a moment he also grasped the wider implication: after a point, one that would soon be reached, Jilani would be as helpless as any human, and could offer no divine miracle. The defenders must stop the foe with brute human force. If Akka n-Ali had any hope that Jilani would invoke some godly power to avert catastrophe, or to slay the Légion en masse, this was the end of it.

* * * * *

Keen eyesight and an intimacy with natural rhythms were required to measure the coming dawn. One by one, the fainter stars near the eastern horizon would fade and wink out. The charcoal black where land meets sky subtly turns to slate gray and that nebulous wedge of light would widen, but only with great reluctance.

Mirvais walked among silent men, leading his horse by the reins. The line ascended another ridge. Anyone observing from west or east against rising backlight might liken them to an undulating chain of teeth or mobile vertebrae on the spine of a rocky carcass. Within two hours they would be making a presumably surprise appearance. If the elusive devil Akka was asleep there, he would soon hear a shrill wake-up alarm. Nonetheless, Mirvais was cautious.

The column halted. A barely audible murmur swept down the rank. Rochet and several subordinate officers ran toward the rear. Mirvais fell out and followed discreetly.

A Yafelmane, one of several sentinels near area Ait Atta villages, had trailed the column around a mountain into a low valley to the east. Clearly there was a problem. The edgy Berber began to yammer. The annoyed interpreter demanded he begin again.

"Two Yafelmane detected activity during the night in main village Taboulmant. One crept close enough to see residents very alert. He relayed it to the man with a coded lamp signal," the interpreter said flatly. "The signal soon stopped."

More important, after midnight a scout trailing the rear of the column to the west had seen horsemen dashing east across the upper Bou Guemmez, where it narrows near the base of Azourki. This was near the point where the Légion would enter Tizi n'lgrourane on the approach to Akka's village. That was almost thirty kilometers back. Ait Atta on fresh mounts, even in rugged country and at night, could cover that in four or five hours.

SEVENTEEN:

HORIZON

By now most of the villagers were among the caves. Yet some remained at home, faithful that their presence would guard against the shells soon to be falling—and to avoid the *adjnun,* they were certain lurked in the recesses of the mountain. Most knew well, however, what field guns could do to people and buildings, and in the end would risk the cunning demons rather than the blind artillery. Most villagers stoically hauled away their most valuable belongings. A few went to shelter with nothing but the clothes upon them, seemingly indifferent, content to leave all to Allah.

Mimoun passed a small convention of villagers squatting outside the caves in the consuming dark, some silent with fear, others animated by anger.

"May God turn this pestilent French rabble into dwarves and vultures."

"We shall turn them into corpses *for* the vultures."

"Build a fire for the tea pots."

"We won't make tea until we are in the caves."

All seemed reluctant to withdraw to the dungeon just yet. And so they sat.

Mimoun took up a lantern and entered the main cave. He was familiar with the grotto, having dared to explore it several times since a boy. Mimoun always found the cavern grand and mysterious, more than any mosque of his imagining. From nearby it appeared to be only a broad gouge near the foot of the rocky slope. But an enemy man surveying carefully from the far ridge could see the caves, note their defensive value, and direct the placement of artillery upon them.

On his third quest into the cave Mimoun found it to be a deceptive formation, much larger inside than it appeared from without. Few ever ventured beyond the half-hidden portal to the second place, where one could explore for hours in enfolding darkness. The outer sanctum sloped downward beneath a rough, arched ceiling over an open area where two hundred villagers could cluster out of harm's way. Some thirty meters beyond, through a low, narrow threshold lay the large vault section.

Then and now, the human world ended at the dark void, where an arena for spirits began. Mimoun's cautious walk on the rocks produced ambient noise out of proportion to his sandal-footed steps. He imagined that the ghosts, or the cave itself, laughed at him, at his frailty, by amplifying his movement. But he was determined to not fear any *adjnun*.

Mimoun knew that his brother Brka and his friend Kessou had stashed several stolen weapons here. He held the lantern high and peered around. He was distressed to see that the trove was no longer where he had seen Brka set it down.

Mimoun rued that he would emerge empty-handed; but at that moment, his sight swept another niche of the cave and fell upon an oblong wooden crate and a black case tightly bound to it by two leather straps. Two tin ammo boxes bristled with steel-jacketed hellfire, but he would leave them there for now.

Mimoun held the lantern in one hand and arduously dragged the load with the other. At last he edged from blackness into the outer cave. Its tenants gazed at him in fright or wonder. Declining a few puzzled offers of help, he struggled down to the foot of the slope. The villagers eyed him and the peculiar cargo. Those nearest the crate could see a potent barrel poking from a breach in the wood. Excited murmurs made the rounds. Some inched away, others forward. Mimoun whistled for Sidi, and the mare loped forward. All watched the young man extract a coil of rope from a pouch, tying one end to the straps and the other to the saddle. Mimoun walked ahead and Sidi followed up the path through the field and toward the promontory, dragging the crate behind.

The Ait Atta world, still bathed in darkness, was entering its eleventh hour of activity. This night seemed an eerie and perpetual state, as if some spiteful force had stolen the sun. Mimoun believed somehow that the lack of light and sight muffled the sounds of activity. Several shadows moved past him on the path to the defenses still undergoing preparation. He hoped that Akka, Addi and most of all Jilani were still at the lip of the plateau to receive his dramatic delivery. Cresting the hill, he saw them motionless and silent, facing north, where in a few hours would be seen the gambit of enemy assault. They turned toward the sound of the crate rasping over earth and stone. Mimoun could not summon any words. His mute arrival made it seem like he was casually offering a strange artifact.

"What have you there?" Akka asked, peering at the case and the wooden lid underneath and knowing very well what it was. Ait Atta raiders had ignored his decree about captured enemy weapons and Brka must have been involved.

"A gift," was all Mimoun offered. "It may help." He loosened the straps and lifted away the rifles to reveal the nearly illegible Armée property markings.

La Tour, realizing the coup, struggled with the shock of another perverse miracle.

Akka was not satisfied. Mimoun glanced away, prideful and even a bit defiant.

Akka opened the crate lid. Within it, caged like some exotic animal, was the alluring metalwork of the machine gun. The 7.5mm Chatelleraut, and its cousin, the more numerous and more reliable Hotchkiss models, gave a few teams firepower equivalent to a rifle battalion.

La Tour doubted that any Berber here was capable of firing it. If not, this mighty tool would go to waste. He could not use it himself. One reason was the gun's reputation for explosive misfires in the face of its user. Far more pertinent was the image of a semi-divine messenger or enlightened man of peace pulling the trigger of a murder machine.

"Ammunition?" he asked. Mimoun pointed back toward the cave.

La Tour opened the case—and peered down at dark wood stocks, blue-steel breeches, receivers and bolt actions of twin, five-shot 8 mm Berthier rifles. The guns were originally military issue, but the receivers had been reconfigured, custom engraved, and a slightly longer barrel substituted. These rifles, clearly belonging to a privileged officer, were impressive pieces, and in the hands of marksmen could prove invaluable. And lethal.

La Tour briefly felt tension cut the sensory functions of his brain from its conscious mind. A pall of silence fell over everything. For a frightfully long moment his psyche deceived itself that he was falling into an abyss. Or was that just the pit of his empty stomach surging toward his pounding heart? So near to the solution, so far to the goal, too soon his demise. A void was closing around him, pressing down, suffocating his thoughts. Panic.

There was no time to properly plan, and yet he must quickly act.

"Mimoun, are there more?" La Tour heard himself ask. He felt so disassociated that the voice seemed to come from another person standing in the same space as himself.

"No your holiness. That is all Brka . . . ." He stopped his slip of the tongue too late.

Akka flashed anger. Mimoun did not want his brother to be punished, but out of honesty he forgot to respond about where he had found the guns without saying who put them there.

"I told everyone what was right and wrong in these matters," Akka barked. "That all weapons were to be accounted for. Did Brka plan to sell them?"

"My sheik, do not be angry with Mimoun or anyone else," La Tour interjected. "Brka has been helpful. In times of great challenge our strongest principles may weaken and fail to withstand the scrutiny of more knowing eyes." meaning, Akka should not look a gift horse in the mouth.

Addi translated. The amghar *did not fully understand the concept, but it sounded wise enough. He considered the ease with which Jilani spoke his wisdom.*

Taking a moment to calm himself, La Tour tried to calculate how to move the many pieces around this very limited game board. How could he hide his tactics several moves ahead? There must be a way to meet the three critical goals—remain to defend, escape to survive, and conceal the reasons for both—while doing so in plain sight under the watchful eyes of a thousand people in what would soon be broad daylight.

He purposely thumped the machine gun crate with his boot, got Mimoun's attention and pointed back at the cave. Mimoun mounted Sidi and rode away.

La Tour felt the pocket watch against his thigh. If only he could look at it, to know how long until the end of black sky. But gods didn't need a time piece. He estimated that an hour remained. Were there enough minutes to wander away, to leave the Ait Atta to their fate?

La Tour gazed at the Berthiers and the Chatellerault, the keys of his salvation.

La Tour knew one place in this circumscribed universe where he could help bring about the survival of these people-and then flee for himself.

* * * * *

Rochet relied also on his Berbers to inform him how to best reach the objective. The Yafelmane and Morghad were native to the region, intimate with every feature. Rochet, who had received this command largely because of his patrol experience in the Atlas east of the Demnate-Azilal axis, led them through this terrain by relying on their word and his memory.

He was proud to have troops that could help him gain the acclaim that would follow Akka's capture. He imagined himself in ten years an ambassador to an exotic nation after appointment through carefully cultivated contacts and, of course, his reputation as a man who had fought so nobly in Afrique.

Rochet was irked, then troubled by late-night reports from rearward scouts of trailing Berber horsemen who had not stopped or changed course. Worse was the growing possibility that somehow the target village knew of the column. The decoy of the roaming northbound troop trucks and the genuine long-distance motor transport moving in the darkness may not have been a full success. Desperate communications might have traveled more quickly between villages then anticipated. Still, Rochet's confidence was high. He expected a swift surrender. But if the Berbers were awaiting them, the attack could not afford finesse. And if Ait Atta were moving to outflank him or rush down the pass behind him, the force would be caught in a much less favorable position-than he could trap Akka.

* * * * *

As usual, Mirvais was less concerned with the stealth of Rochet or of the Berbers than with his own agenda.

"Do you think that soon we will get word from Rehou?" Mirvais sounded as anxious as a banker who asks his secretary to arrange a tryst with his lover.

"He knows that we expect a signal just before dawn. We must study that ridge," Saint-Avold said, pointing to the southeast, "and look for his light."

"Pardon me, sir, are you sure you can trust Rehou? A priest he is not," Saint-Avold said.

"No, certainly not. A fellow who wears a dead man's finger as a hat ornament is no scripture-quoter. Still, he is one of the smartest and most cunning men I know. In this country, ten of him is worth thirty Frenchmen."

"We will die by the hour if caught with our backs to this wall."

"Hmmm," was all Mirvais could say. Saint-Avold was right. He tried to imagine what Rehou Khoussaila, his last best trump card, was up to. Had the madman and his twenty cohorts already infiltrated the village? There were two men up there who Mirvais felt owed him plenty, everything, for his abundant frustration over the last few weeks and months. One was a Berber outsmarting too many French. The other may well be a Frenchman, apparently, somehow deceiving the Berbers. Either way, in the next several hours he hoped to bag them both so he could legitimately claim at least half the reward.

* * * * *

Mimoun toted the ammunition cases up the incline. He was weary of this service. And just simply weary. Soon, all would be decided, one way or the other and he wanted a view from the center of the action.

"Please leave this here," said Jilani, kicking the machine gun crate. He could not help but boldly command Akka's defense measures until he had time to think. "Mimoun, come with me. I will send him to the cave with the others before the battle."

Akka and Addi considered this a strange request. Akka said nothing for a moment, but finally nodded consent. He could hardly withhold it.

"I want to stay and fight!" Mimoun protested.

"You will do what you are told," Akka calmly uttered.

Jilani grasped the rifle case.

La Tour realized this might be the last he would see these people. Or they him. But he was reluctant to indulge sentiment; that would only raise his fear for both the villagers and for himself. And any sign of that in his eyes would be most ungodly. For lack of anything appropriate to say, he held his right palm toward Addi and to Akka, who bowed, and could not help but gently seize his hand. The one who was Jilani turned to Mimoun.

"Mimoun, back on Sidi. We shall cast our eyes afar like men at the top of the world."

The white-robe man took the reins and paced away toward the lip of the precipice. To the east, the veil of night began to part with a first faint glimmer of dawn.

EIGHTEEN:

BATTLE

Nearby objects took faint form in the murk. La Tour's internal reveille always tolled at dawn, as it had since childhood, in another life, when he enjoyed the summer mists or winter snows, the song birds and solitude. But this morning his solemn kingdom was without such splendor.

Cradling the rifles like beloved trophies, Jilani walked beside Sidi. Mimoun gazed from the saddle at the weary French boots, shufflers of countless kilometers, tied with thin laces to the agile feet of this patron saint, and at the frayed trouser cuffs below the *tajjelabith*. Mimoun had been chosen to aid the fulfillment of the prophesy, or the prophesier himself. The Ait Atta were not likely to survive without unconditional belief in Jilani's words and deeds. Theirs was a blind faith.

In the days since his fall to earth, no one had seen more than his pale hands and forehead, blue eyes, gallant nose, and contoured lips, around which sprouted a moustache. Who or what was beneath the shroud? As if, should sunshine fall upon his undraped head or body, he would crumble to dust or return to the sky.

Mimoun would never be so bold as to more than idly wonder about Sidi Jilani's form.

La Tour gazed eastward, to the horizon. Dark gray now; soon, dull blue, then the sun. They traversed a path familiar to Mimoun and Sidi, passing the spot of their first spoken encounter, and the gift of the precious binoculars. They reached the hut. Dismounting, with a glance at Jilani, Mimoun sensed his emotions amiss, a gnawing anxiety. Fear.

The prophet hastened past his humble abode ahead of his adjutant. His white cloak seemed to float over the earth, and then vanish as they passed a jumble of rocks down the dim curving path of the promontory.

La Tour reached the *tizi*. The redoubt had but one complete wall, the rest fallen to time and weather. And it would be closer to the field guns, be they Schneiders or 75s. From the unobstructed view the full northerly vista, now in rising light, was revealing itself.

To his far left, in the two o'clock direction and more than a kilometer off, were the caves, the terraced fields and the three apertures through them, now obstructed by makeshift snarls of wood and rocks. At the fire zones above them, on the precipice and within the upper ranks of defilade boulders, waited one hundred and twenty riflemen. Before him stretched over four hundred meters of rocky tract that the Légion men must cross. Behind that rose the ridge, the center of which, near the best troop assembly area, was a fine platform for field guns. Its boulder-strewn far end, well beyond maximum rifle range, though closer to the terraced fields and caves, was useless as a position for the guns. And below the ridge the gunners could not readily see if their shells had hit worthy targets. La Tour, however, assumed that spies had relayed all this to the commanders days ago.

He fully appreciated Akka Ahêddây's superb natural castle. Taboulmant fulfilled several ideal conditions: it held the high ground, forced a frontal assault to make a long approach over open ground toward ready-made funnels of fire, thus assuring that aggressors would pay a high price for conquest. Akka was truly a mountain king.

La Tour stepped behind the brittle wall of dried mud and stone. Four narrow, unevenly spaced holes remained in the crumbling facade: two shoulder-high rectangles, and two beside and below them, near the ground. Defenders could shoot standing or lying prone, with a commanding view. His angle would be slightly offset from the ridge guns.

He envisioned how the clash would unfold. The men would descend to the field and march toward the precipice, in the last moments of belief that their approach remained a surprise. To maximize confusion and limit the attackers' casualties, the field guns would fire soon after the assigned units shoved off. It was crucial that by then the artillery officer be disabled or dead.

Halfway across the field, the units would clearly see the barricades— just as they came under fire. The men would rush forward, but be able to move into them only five or six abreast. They would quickly counter fire, then take cover near each draw at the bottom of the incline. By then other troops would have begun to ascend the escarpment.

Some of these men would be perilously near the *tizi*. La Tour could be seen by those scaling high enough to peer upon it. And by stepping out into plain view, he himself would be a target from several directions. If men reached the top, he and Mimoun would be outflanked and cut off. He hoped to briefly silence the field guns, but in turn the dynamite droppers must protect him by decimating the first wave and deterring others. Most ominous were the guns. All that would be required to blast him to bits was a quarter-turn in position and a recalculation of elevation. His best hope was that the gunners fixate on the barricades and the plateau.

The squads assaulting the precipice would need support from sharpshooters. But few targets would be seen. No Ait Atta rifleman would stand near the lip of the precipice for a few shots at easy targets while their brethren crouched behind the huge boulders, sliding dynamite-laden jars down the troughs and over the abrupt lip. Nor would the riflemen at the passes, also atop a steep angle, be readily visible. The only points from

ALBERT O'HAYON

which the assault could safely return fire would be the far end of the ridge, near the limit for their own rifles. Much depended on the two field guns to punch holes in the defense.

And planes. With bombs. Certain to arrive during the battle.

It was crucial that those firing the guns be put down. He prayed for the absence of a breeze. A mere whiff could divert a bullet trajectory.

"Mimoun, look that way," La Tour said in French, presenting the binoculars and pointing at the far ridge. "Tell me the moment you see movement. Then you will return up the hill and ride Sidi to the cave. Do you understand?"

No, Mimoun did not understand. La Tour gave the young man the glasses and again pointed to the western end of the ridge. That immediate desire was plain enough.

"*Eh sherif, righ admouathegh d'Iroumin nekindik.*" Your holiness, I want to fight the Frenchmen with you.

La Tour did not grasp every word, but he sensed the meaning. "No," he said firmly with words and hands. "Two guns, two shooters. You will not be the second."

Bloodlust was rising in him. Mercury climbing the thermometer. Tree sap rising to the leaves. He had killed only three men: for Maroc, for himself, and for the Légion. And here he was, because of the Légion. Or was it just Mirvais? The circle was turning again. La Tour would push until the rotation was complete and he was back in Isère.

Standing at the junction of walls, Mimoun aimed the glasses. He resembled an olden sailor scrutinizing waves for whales or enemy sails or the first sign of land.

Iron-gray light washed the ridge. Stark details—textures of rocks, striations of ravines—were about to appear. So, too, would many targets. He could feel them, gathering like wasps. Sudden, searing flame was the best way to destroy a colony. He searched the bottom of the case and found a clutch of gun-care items: tools, cloth, brushes. These rifles belonged to someone who valued maintenance, a marksman with Swiss watchmaker principles. He quickly wiped all surfaces on each Berthier with a soft cloth to remove dust or gun oil. He noted "MAC"—Manufacture d'Armes Chattelerault—and "1926" stamped on the barrel, indicating place and year of origin. He whisked the breechbolt and receiver block mechanisms with the camel hair brush. Inserted a fleece-lined rod into a barrel. Removed a compact black iron scope wrapped in chamois as if it were a black jewel.

He carefully assembled one of the rifles. Praising Providence for the tools, he mounted the scope with a small screwdriver. In pieces, the rifle and scope spoke to high handicraft; together they were a tool for the black art of long-range killing. But he would get no practice with it. This would be like free-climbing a cliff: senses heighten reflexes, but both must relax to clear the mind. He flipped up the eyepiece cover. Placing warm flesh against cold metal, he poked the barrel through the upper right porthole, placed the butt into his right shoulder, nestled his right cheek along the stock, balanced the barrel in his left hand as if he were cradling delicate glass, and eased his right forefinger through the trigger guard. With that curved five-centimeter steel strip he would express unspeakable frustration.

* * * * *

For the last two hours Rehou Khoussaila and twenty-five men had ascended a nearly obliterated trail on the steep, crumbling southern side of the plateau, creeping up lest they noisily dislodge the scree. Even the hardiest cohorts labored to breathe, but Rehou pressed them on to a ravine at the crest into which the thin Asif Oussikis flowed from above. The plan was to follow the stream about four hundred meters into the rear of the unsuspecting capital. Much of that length was barely deep enough to hide them, but any defenders on the naked, gradual slopes would also have little concealment.

Rehou's companions were veterans of past and recent raids against the Ait Atta; amazan *all. They trailed in twos and threes toward the junction of ravine, plateau and stream. Beyond it was an irrigation channel, a* tarugwa, *into which the Ait Atta had diverted some of the Oussikis into terraced fields. Maleem was scouting ahead, nearing the old granary. The treasure house. There, perhaps, the old* amrabt *was contemplating Allah beneath the sinking quarter-moon. Rehou felt con*fident with the Beretta in the holster and the Lebel in his hands. Next *would be gold in his satchel. He could start anew in Essaouria, secure in riches.*

La Tour peered through the lens that in this dim light barely captured distant objects. But through the vanishing veil of darkness slowly rose large rocks on the ridge—like one who fancies forms in the clouds, he thought that from his angle they resembled an elephant herd he had seen in a safari photograph—and the umber hue of the downslope dirt. He would shortly see anyone standing there.

La Tour would have to shoot the second rifle without any optical aid. He adjusted the gun sight elevation to provide maximum range. He loaded bullets, five each, into four respective clips. He felt strange; this ritual was likely to be performed only once. *I will not fire all of these before the deed is done, or before I am dead.* He stared hard at the rifles and projectiles—and for the first time fully felt the horror that he was about to kill his own countrymen. Perhaps men he had known. Befriend.

Mimoun hissed in response to what he was seeing in the glasses. He suppressed the sound, as if afraid enemy ears might hear an echo.

La Tour leaned the rifle against the wall and stepped forward to grasp the proffered glasses. He directed the lenses at his eyes toward the far end of the ridge.

He saw the tricolor pendant, a symbol of unit identity, hanging limp in the dead air above the ravine. La Tour had twice paraded with elements of this unit, but mercifully he saw no acquaintances below. Its officers were beyond the Berthier's range. While he did not want to make widows of their wives, one killed a snake by chopping off its head.

Teams of pack mules bore components of two field guns on to the ridge. Crews promptly unloaded them and began to assemble the dead steel—wheels, carriage, barrel, breech—into lathes of thunderbolts. The guns were compact but formidable, although impersonal, when the target was elsewhere, when the shooters were safe from return fire; but at this moment, looking upon the drab, ugly snouts of them, the pieces were diabolical.

La Tour heard the thumping footsteps of an approaching runner. He hastened for his rifle, and reached it, as Hani the carpenter burst into the *tizi.* He was wearing an old, shabby *zouave* uniform, the red pant and beige shirt ensemble of colonial conscript soldiers who had fought along the Algérie-Maroc frontier before the Great War. Hani had binoculars of his own. And he spoke in French, through gasping breaths.

"Shrif. I beg you listen. Akka saw you here. With these," holding his glasses, "and asked for a volunteer. A rifle shooter. That is me."

"We need a *good* shot, Hani."

"I am. Men in the *hammada* at four hundred meters. Or more." Hani's face took on a feral cast, one of a predator's disdain for his quarry. "Down upon them, like from here. The vultures did well by me. I worked for the *Iroumin* then."

La Tour was impressed by his confidence. And by that expression.

"I think that I will choose the targets, Hani," La Tour asserted grimly.

"Don't you wish to join Akka Ahêddây to direct the battle?"

"Here will be a critical part of this war. We fight, you and I. Make Akka proud."

"Oh, yes, shrif. Much proud." He smiled. Half his teeth were gone. Broken off, in some terrible impact. Much pain. But somehow Hani looked younger than his years, elemental, with a biting gaze and demeanor that suggested his mettle was born in a crucible.

La Tour turned to Mimoun.

"Mimoun, *bonjour,*" La Tour said suavely. *"Al cha wwas inshaâllah,"* in passable Tamazight. Goodbye. See you later, God willing. He gestured for the young man to return to the village; a firm hand on the shoulder and his emphatic eyes suggested haste. His body language said Mimoun should remain out of sight behind the rocks.

Mimoun was reluctant. La Tour suspected it was either some boy-man craving to see hard killing first-hand, or a bond of loyalty. He affectionately patted his young friend, smiled confidently, then turned the lad about and shoved him off.

"Ak iâawen rebbi. Afflan n-familanch." Goodbye. Say hello to your family.

The head of a four-abreast troop column crested the ridge, stopped briefly near the field guns atop it, and then began to flow down the incline like a centipede. Faster than a stroll, slower than a run; not the pace of men expecting to be fired upon. At the bottom, like a cell dividing, the soldiers separated into four equal sections. La Tour watched with the binoculars; some of the men seemed to believe all they had to do was show up to claim the glory.

Mimoun departed like a dog being cast off. He passed the edge of wall into the rocks and looked down upon the notched squares of moving men in the meadow. He accelerated uphill, away from the terror, bewildered how he could best help to hold it back.

The men below numbered more than eight hundred. In one mass they would occupy only a small area of the tract. But spread across it they were more imposing. In illusion and reality, they outnumbered the defenders by a factor of nearly five. La Tour peered at them with and without the glasses. *What folly and bravery. To die way up here for a prize that, Allah willing, will remain beyond them.*

Hani the carpenter took the scoped rifle with the assurance of someone who knew his tools as if they were but extensions of his hands. He understood the game they were to play, and its stakes. He seemed fearless. This was a transaction of strong spirit between him and Jilani, one they would use to direct bullets to the enemy.

La Tour lay prone upon the ground at a lower window, as did Hani, each peering through their binoculars. La Tour was anxious to identify the gunnery officer. The defenders would fire as the Légionnaires neared the barricades, and their ranks would shudder in shock at the immediate casualties and the abrupt prospect of a fierce fight. For a precious minute or two the Ait Atta would have the initiative—until the field guns fixed upon them.

Hani poked the barrel of his rifle through the aperture. He would have more control from a prone position, and also remain unseen by any troops scaling to their left or behind them. Hani swung his view along the ridge. He sighted on four men around the two gun tubes. At each, a man opened the breech and his mate inserted a shell.

The separate blocks of advancing men diverged at mid-field. They resembled a precision marching team, so deliberate and practiced were the moves.

Hani's finger remained off the trigger as he tried to ensure that the crosshairs would link his barrel's angle to the target. Right now, that was the chest of a gunnery Sergeant whose smug expression hinted that he expected to enjoy his function.

Mimoun reached Jilani's hut and Sidi beside it. Jilani had instructed him to ride the horse to the cave. But as he trod down the incline behind the long pale of boulders he saw Akka, in brisk parley with a group of thirty or so men, pointing urgently to the far rear side of the plateau. He handed sacks to two designates who hastily led away half the assemblage. Akka gestured to those remaining that they take position behind the boulders. These men would send the dynamite-jars of punishment onto the foolish climbing enemy. Spotters in the caves would signal that moment.

"Nothing else stands between you and our homes," Akka said firmly. "Work well and quickly." The nodding men turned to their duty.

Mimoun passed by. Akka asked, "Mimoun, Hani is with Jilani in the tizi?"

"Yes. Against the enemy. With the rifles. To silence the big guns."

Akka Ahêddây reflected for a moment. "Find your father," he said. "Make sure he has taken Addi to the granary with my family."

Mimoun brightened at this; he preferred to remain near his father for the fight rather than follow Jilani's directive. He would not see enough from the cave.

The dull amber sun was just below the far horizon. Rehou Khoussaila wanted the attack to be underway when his men could see but still not be easily seen in the fast action to come. He saw the lead man stop in stride, as if in seeking the source of a muffled sound or an apparition. The fellow remained inert for several seconds before resuming his slow advance. Rehou glanced at the brutish band of shadow men behind him. These Yafelmane and Morghad rogues and pillagers were not fighters for freedom or any other ideal. Still, they were fierce, intending to search and destroy for the treasures Rehou had insisted were stored here.

Two ancient and imposing boulders stood where the ravine met the plateau. The five-meter rocks were like portals to a city, a bab; even without the horizontal rampart it resembled a proscenium arch. The passage of Rehou's men through it would be traumatic, their assault ruthless. Taking captives was not in the plan; Ait Atta would survive through gallant resistance or lucky flight. Rehou studied the pocket watch Mirvais had provided him; the short wide pointer was set at the bottom and the long thinner one was nearly a quarter-circle past the top. They would attack in two sweeps of the third, ticking hand.

Rehou's price for the stealth and hazard of his maneuver was to open the assault, even without the permission—or the knowledge—of Colonel Rochet. Mirvais had reasoned that Rehou would cause much scurrying to the rear, making the main assault that much easier, and in the confusion Rehou could find the treasure in the old igherm. *They would both get want they desired, and it would cost them very little. Fortune favored the bold.*

The lead man stopped between the gateway rocks, and Rehou two long steps behind. The others halted in turn, waiting to charge downslope to the old granary and spread chaos, perhaps rousing the amghar *prey to flight. Rehou had been gleeful to see the Ait Atta horse caravan head northwest with guns and munitions. Somewhere out there the Légion would catch hell from these fighters. But Rehou never told Mirvais or Rochet of this departure, as it might alter their strategy and interfere with his own business.*

The reports of overnight activity on the plateau had not improved his confidence. There must be good reason for these hamlets to be awake at such hours. But the explanation could be mundane: men returning from a mission, perhaps with wounded. It may even have been a mutiny—a thought that pleased Rehou. No matter; he and his men were committed, and because few Ait Atta remained here to pose serious opposition, they could do whatever they pleased. Some killing, much more looting. His heart beat a little faster.

Rochet was proud that his men had reached this remote zone and quickly deployed, as eager or anxious as he to complete the mission. Thus far his strategy had worked perfectly. The plateau was dormant. He expected few casualties when the Ait Atta beheld the force rushing its few ill-armed and barely awake defenders. He watched the sections diverge with machine formality, more like on parade than in prelude to battle. Two hundred men approached each of the three lanes rising through the terraced fields, and one hundred more arced toward the boulder-strewn bottom of the promontory—a force nearly equal to the known enemy men. Two squadrons of spahis *stood by should the Ait Atta mount riders. Rochet expected that ten field gun shells lobbed into the hamlets would deter the few stubborn or suicidal resisters. As most of the Berbers chose life, the*

Légion would finally have Akka Ahêddây, and for a brief time Rochet would be renowned from Marrakech to Metz.

He found it curious that, after a preliminary show, Mirvais had opted to shrink from the battle's first scene. Rochet had never planned to send any of the Major's troops into the fray—but it was puzzling that Mirvais had not made a stronger request. Perhaps his opportunistic protégé at last realized that the mission was not his, and properly felt chagrin at the several failed attempts of his troops to rout the Ait Atta or kill Akka Ahêddây. That record appeared even worse when, several times during that span, his men had raided far and wide, killed more than fifty soldiers, and vanished like smoke.

Three-abreast, the soldiers began toward the ravines. The escarpment climbers chose easy paths through the talus, to where the earth met the steep incline up to the plateau.

Sergeant Maurice Baud readied the guns. He wore a face not unlike an adolescent who is craftily truant from school in order to leer at lovers through a keyhole. He awaited the order to fire.

Colonel Rochet and Capitaine Marcel Dallio peered through binoculars. The gloom was almost dawn. The only son of a deceased Alsace miner was near to making good on a promise to his war veteran Father. If Rochet held out a mirror he would like the reflected image as it smiled with self-satisfied pride.

Rehou heard an odd sound. A faint but increasing hiss. A flying cobra. He could not associate it with anything else he had ever seen or heard. The hiss, its source not yet visible, fell like an ungainly bird, wobbling down into the ravine.

Twenty meters behind him the object thumped against rocks. Rehou turned. A length of cord, its tip in a consuming frenzy of sparks, protruded from a tube. For half a second, its form or purpose did not register, other than a clear signal that their presence was no secret. All turned gazes upward among the rocks on the left slope, in the direction of the village. From behind one, another tube lofted among them. Then a third . . . The throwing man was seen by all. Several raiders raised their guns.

"No!" Rehou yelled—just as harsh light flashed the ravine and exposed every detail of the place more quickly than his brain could register them. It was followed rapidly by a second flash, and a third, which together yielded a maelstrom of concussion and whirling stones, a hard unfurling echo and the shrill cries of men.

Rochet's spirit plunged. The detonations became one thunderclap that embraced every rock and ear. But the advancing men met no fire. The blast was occurring near enough to be clearly heard, at least in rebound, but not so close that he could see it.

None of the units under either his command or Mirvais's could have made a flank attack. He had not known where to make it, had deployed no other men, and in any case would not have done so. Then who . . . ? Rochet reeled at the only option: other Berbers were making the assault. There must be more to this game than the rules allow, some other prize so worth having that others risked catastrophe just as triumph was in hand.

Bitterly bidding adieu *to his grand* coup de main, *Rochet greeted his rude awakening.* Mirvais. He sent men up another route that only he and the Berber scouts knew of.

The realization was sickening and inconsolable. Rochet had been disobeyed—betrayed—by one of his officers, with the consequence of casualties, and perhaps failure and disgrace. If Mirvais had been standing beside him now, Rochet would relieve him of his duty and his life. That was one reason the deceiver was lurking behind the ridge.

Rehou Khoussaila had been hammered by the first blast and a fist-sized rock flush to his back. He was lucky; six comrades were ghastly corpses. Those not near the blasts shot uphill at swift forms that seemed more ghost than human. Rehou rose unsteadily near the pulp of Maleem. Their years of outlaw raiding and leading packs of dog men for rogue caïds were over. As Rehou briefly lamented him, a man in a black turban dashed from the rocks and advanced with a glinting knife. Rehou yielded ground, raised his rifle and shot point blank at the same moment the attacker hurled the knife. The bullet hit dead center and punched the man flat. But the flying blade glanced off the barrel and as if guided by a hidden hand, careened up the stock to carve a chunk out of Rehou's splayed right thumb.

Rochet peered through his field glasses at the plateau. The rightmost ravine was barricaded at a choke point. Three front ranks came upon it at a slight curve in a path worn by countless feet and hooves. They stopped, and the trailing fellows did, too. Rochet had no time to ponder this: one section of the rocks just above the far right pass pulsed with the sudden blooms of discharging guns. The air rippled with their reports. He could almost hear his men groan. Out of what: frustration, fear, the primal surge before terror?

The other two ravines would also offer such a welcome. He panned his glasses to the central one, to an identical scene, and then to the leftmost notch as well. Too many men would soon be casualties. He turned toward Sergeant Baud down the ridge. Baud beheld the cheveux de frise *with his own glasses as the defenders' rifles opened up. The gunnery sergeant knew he could not reset the guns and discharge them at the blockades without endangering the troops for his first trial shots. But he also foresaw that the men there would prudently retreat and devise alternate tactics. Many would attempt to climb instead.*

"Baud! Fire at once on those passes!" Rochet bellowed, almost out of earshot. "Take out the rifles and destroy those blocking contraptions! For God's sake, lay it on!"

Jean-Michel saw Baud in his lenses. He felt it would be easier to kill a countryman he didn't like.

"Hani, do you see that big man down there beyond to the far gun? Talking much?"

"Yes, shrif, I see him. You want him to die?"

"No. I just want him not to fire his gun."

"You want him to die . . ."

Hani edged the barrel downward, adjusting his eye against the scope to fasten Baud in its center. La Tour watched as Porc-épic, with an expression of twisted glee as that of a gremlin boy about to destroy a bird's nest, bent over to quickly check the gun alignment. His battery mate grasped the firing lanyard. Hani squeezed the trigger.

The field gun discharged. The bullet sailed undetected to the left. La Tour saw a squib of dust rise up as the metal caromed away.

The first shell detonated above the center barricade. The peal was an ugly thunder.

Hani seethed with distant memories and fresh anger, but maintained a tight, almost severe control. The fingers and palm of his right hand deftly worked the bolt—out with the spent cartridge, chamber the new. Hani had the intense but almost casual proficiency of someone whose months in the Tafilalt were enlivened by his hunting skill. Now reflected in his dark eyes, too, were days of the Marne, outside Cogny. He was among the few survivors of the assaulting Moroccan Blondlat Brigade. From his château, General Humbert observed their slaughter by German machine guns; still, he sent them on. Good enough to die on French soil then; but so poorly thought of now that conquest was better.

Baud and his gunnery mate would take two seconds to reload—enough time for Hani. He placed the crosshairs on the pale, young, blank-faced creature at the nearer gun. The mate was set to pull the gun lanyard. Hani squeezed his trigger first.

The bullet glanced off the barrel. This did not go unheeded; the young fellow looked about anxiously, as one might react in seeking the source of an invisible flame that had kissed the cheek. The gun shell was away, soaring to the precipice.

La Tour watched Hani from the corner of his right eye. The carpenter mumbled an incoherent curse, chambered a new round and drew a second bead on the fellow. Baud's weapon discharged again. The shell hammered a section of rocks above the furthest pass, almost out of sight. La Tour was unable to observe the damage that Hani—or the rifle scope—had failed to prevent, but as he had foreseen, this position and the section of plateau behind him could not be easily bombarded by the present angle of the field guns.

The ravines erupted in a din as more than five hundred opposing guns discharged within a moment of each other. The volley of the defenders could slash the Légion ranks, but that of the attackers might well deplete the Ait Atta below a crucial threshold.

La Tour trembled. Battle was fully joined.

Now the young gunner again poised to pull the lanyard. La Tour studied him. Pale Face appeared to heed a shouted order from Baud. He leaned to check the barrel elevation, then stood upright, about to pull the lanyard. Pale Face crumpled at the entry of the hard bolt moving on a flat downward angle. The young man's sternum burst. La Tour shut his eyes; surely the fellow's death was immediate. La Tour could only consider him an impediment to his own survival and journey, not as a human being with a past and a future. Pale Face would be listed as killed in action and his family would receive a posthumous Croix du Combattant and perhaps his name would be mentioned in the local newspapers and the Légion would send a letter thanking them for the gift of their son in defense of honor and the national interest.

La Tour did not resist the macabre desire to peer upon the unfolding scene. As the young gunner hit the ground the teeth of confusion were sure to be bared. But La Tour was afraid: inevitably and soon, someone would deduce that the tizi *was the sniper roost.*

Very methodically, as if about to solve a minor but vexing problem, Hani raised the rifle slightly to fix the scope on Baud. La Tour watched through the glasses; Porc-épic had seen the casualty fall twenty meters away. He recalled the Sergeant's boasts about his prowess in combat with the "shleuh *barbarian." At the garrison, Porc-épic seemed to believe he was another Hector. If the Sergeant were such a bruin, the animal would be preparing to discharge his gun despite the bloody evidence of lethal danger crumpled beside the other gun.*

Instead, Porc-épic scrambled behind a rock. His kepi *fell off. Only his balding pate was visible. La Tour prayed that Hani would not take or make the gruesome head shot. And he might miss, and with every bullet fired their position was more likely to be discovered. Each shot before that moment must strike true. There were far more soldiers than both of them could dispatch in the half-minute needed to reposition those pieces.*

La Tour swung his view to a corporal who rushed to fill Pale-Face's post. He nudged Hani and pointed. The corporal was much more stoic than Baud, and thus more impressive. His demeanor implied he understood that casualties were a natural consequence of war, like rain from storm clouds, and one could only endure. The corporal decisively pulled the lanyard at the same instant Hani fired. The shell slammed into the far rocks. The bullet blew a hole in his thigh. Through his lenses La Tour saw the man topple in agony, and others around him scream. That was a crippling wound, or a lethal one.

Rehou Khoussaila could rally his men and fight on for the loot. Or he could retreat and possibly live to hunt another day. Rehou was enraged that long-held plans, compelled by prophesy, had been so thwarted. Over these past days he had recalled the feeble, half-crazed caretaker of a koubba *near Tinejdad. It was just before* Tafaska, *a week before* almouggar. *Several times a year Rehou indulged in beer and puffs of* kif. *This was such a night for the sins Allah would have to forgive. Rehou expected only entertainment for his small donation. But the mystic enthralled him with a vision that he would lead men to victory on a mountain—and electrified him with the prediction that he would seize an* amrabt *whose "eyes had gone dark," and who guarded great treasure in an* igherm. *Rehou and the oracle were complete strangers, so he was convinced of the accuracy. Of course, Rehou had been baffled by the further, ambiguous augury of an ill, pale* wali *not speaking Tamazight who would fly from afar to the tribe of the* amrabt *and distress their enemies.*

He ignored that harbinger then—and soon forgot it. Now it rattled to life.

Rehou Khoussaila howled.

The flat ridgeback position of the field guns was in turmoil. Three artillery men scurried for cover. One bearded olive-skin man arose from the rocks to herd them back to duty, wielding the authority Baud did not and had not. He was more alert than his fellows—and by educated chance or blind instinct gazed up to the tizi. *Directly at the binoculars. And the scope. Into the eyes of La Tour and Hani. Down the barrel. The bullet lifted him an inch from the ground as it tore through, knocking the limp body back among the large stones.*

Echoes of gunfire bellowed, then lapsed, and the interval was filled by the loud, gravelly voices of two officers shouting orders to shift the troops. One man was steely, the other furious and revealing a streak of fear. Rifles crashed again. The Berber guns in the narrow passes, fewer now, still roared with enough defiance to dissuade a direct assault. Some troops would partly withdraw so that the field guns could pound the vexing positions. Others would shift along the base of the promontory to follow those ascending. Now they would realize that the guns had been oddly sporadic in the last few moments, and the officers and men were wondering why.

La Tour's binoculars took in the wider view. Four men gazed up at the tizi. *Two pointed frantically. Hani had shot three of their gunnery comrades, killing two. Without the steady and crucial output of the guns, the attack would lose impetus until the officers revised their plan. And the snipers were eliminated.*

The action was not even ten minutes old. Rochet was revolted to calculate ten percent casualties among his men, at the conquest of nothing. He lowered his field glasses and turned to Corporal Remo standing prudently nearby behind the rocks one hundred meters to the right of the field guns. He thrust his entire hand at Baud.

"Remo!" he bellowed. "Tell Baud to get those guns firing more quickly! If he does not, please convey that I will shoot him myself, one limb at a time!"

Remo ratcheted his stiff legs forward. He felt a resemblance to that crude rigid metal automaton he had seen on the cinema screen.

Akka Ahêddây was pleased that the bulwarks were defying the enemy tide. He did not fear for himself, but for his people, his family and Addi Yacoub should they be breached. Anyway, the amrabt *had long ago predicted this scene. Addi, however, had omitted several key details—some of which, in the rapid events since last evening, seemed odd in the light of Jilani's new day.*

Akka crouched among the three roughly equidistant flumes behind the screen of boulders. Two men sat near the mouth of each, beside them a small fire. One had inserted an unlit tube of dynamite into a motley of pottery jars. He would pass them to his partner, who would tie the cord, light the fuse with a flaming reed and shove the jar down the slick, inclined channel. The first such vessel was already tied to the long rope. If merciful Allah agreed that His children must be saved from the wicked, the plunging jar would fall onto the enemy and educate them about their cruelties. Akka could only hope that the lessons exceeded the costs the Légion was prepared to pay. Unless reinforcements or bomb planes arrived first. He would then walk down and surrender on the sole condition that his people not be annihilated.

Akka raised the pole bearing the mushiddad—*a green palm frond crossed with a red* takummiyt *on a field of white—and waved the battle flag from the center of the promontory.*

Addi Yacoub heard the explosions and then the rifle fire at the rear, western edge of the fields. Soon came the commotion of frightened women and children running past the old igherm *toward the school, surging downslope away from the predator against whom there was no defense. Most available men and guns were far across the plateau. A woman screamed.*

"Damn your father, you miserable scum!" yelled old Mouhou. "You foul . . ." Two rifle cracks ended his harangue.

Addi heard the guttural voice of an intruder. "Where is your treasure?"

Someone grabbed Addi's hand and guided him away from the voice.

Praise God and the men Akka had sent with the few spare blasting sticks. Were these raiders the only men to survive? Or just those angry enough to rampage on? Was not Akka their intended target?

Addi concentrated on his hearing. Like the desert foxes seen along the Asif Ziz, he could heed details of movement beyond normal human range. He could identify the type of bird taking flight by the signal poem of its wings, or greet some villagers by name before they uttered a word because he knew the subtle rhythm of their gaits. For this Addi Yacoub was said to have baraka, *though he knew it was only the great enhancement of a natural sense. If that was holy, so be it. He even knew the hands of his chaperone.*

"Who are they, Haj?"

"Yafelmane and Morghad I think," Haj the potter replied with a gentle voice and insistent grip on Addi's left hand. "Last year coming from Agoudim I think I saw one of them robbing someone. I do not forget bad men."

"Yafelmane id bu-inighan. *May God curse them all . . . "*

Images of events from another lifetime bubbled in his memory. When he had another name. And good vision. To see the madness of men. The trophy heads of warriors hanging from Yafelmane igherman, *each of them a warning. His long-dead* aami, *the patriarch of their dwindling clan, praised the killers' prowess, but lamented feuds and blood oaths sowed seeds to lay dormant for years, then in mystery sprout when almost forgotten and least expected.*

The school where Sidi Baha and sometimes Addi taught the male children was behind the old igherm. *Its entrance was marked by simple* kufic *script. Beside it was a garden that from April to August was daily bathed in sun through the afternoon. Kenza and her mother grew pineapple broom and other flowers there. The plot was just a short span up from the Oussikis. To Addi's ears the burbling current wrote the music of a waterfall. He reveled in the trickery of sound; in the right conditions a mere whisper could be mighty. To that end, Allah and the spirits implied, so could men.*

Past the school was a span of rock, then a wide courtyard, and beyond it the large old igherm, *nearly a fort in itself, in which the council had convened for decades. Last year Akka had directed that all surplus grain—the people's true treasure—be stored here for siege, poor crops or supply interruption. The great bins were presently half-full of barley, maize, and other staples harvested here or hauled by mule last autumn to prepare for these days of wrath.*

Two round barred windows were in each long wall. The northerly view overlooked the barricades; to the southwest was the ravine and the impeded but not thwarted attack.

Kenza stood atop two burlap sacks of grain, peering toward the new battle at the rim.

Haj bounded onto a stool and gazed out from the western window.

"Four enemy men are coming this way!" he hissed.

Kenza, Hada and Hejjou flinched. Immediately, they came together in a huddle.

"Describe them," directed Addi Yacoub.

"The first one is a stocky-legged fellow with an Aroumi *rifle. He wears a red turban. He looks like crazy man-beast. Three men follow him, at extra paces.*

"This crazy one, does he walk oddly?"

Haj paused. "Yes, holiness, with a limp."

Addi sighed. "Truly, both . . . . I have expected him." A pause followed. "Haj," he said solemnly, "take Kenza and her mother and leave me to these men."

Haj replied assertively: "No. They will have to kill me first."

"And so accomplish nothing except to buy me two more seconds of life."

Haj saw four defenders dash into the yard between the school and the igherm, *unseen by the cul-de-sac intruders. They fired their Lebels, and two of Rehou Khoussaila's laggard henchmen were cut down, dead or dying. The third man hastily retreated. But Rehou whirled Beretta in hand and expertly gained identical results: two shots, two dead men and a third in flight. The fourth fellow attempted to eject a spent cartridge, but it had jammed in the jaws of the breech. Rehou approached him, pistol raised execution-style.*

"What say you, Yafelmane?" a young voice snarled behind him. "Pig!"

It was Mimoun. Rehou still aimed his pistol at the angrily fumbling rifleman before him, but with sulfurous eyes glanced over his shoulder toward the voice.

Haj could hear but not see his son. Leaping from the stool, he dashed to the door ajar and pulled it open. Mimoun stood three arm-lengths away, facing down an armed murderous Berber with only a smooth round stone in each hand.

Haj did not see or hear Addi Yacoub walk up cat-like behind him. The father exited into the new sunbeams piercing high clouds to dance along the ground where Mimoun stood not twenty meters from Rehou. Then Addi followed him.

Rehou Khoussaila eyed the hapless man with the jammed rifle. The Ait Atta warrior stood defiantly, prepared to die, but also clearly determined to kill this Yafelmane devil should a half-second opportunity arise. Rehou glanced over his shoulder again.

His gaze fell into the unsettling glare of Addi Yacoub.

Addi edged perilously behind Haj and Mimoun. The amrabt *was aware they would block him from immediate harm, but only for a brief moment.*

Guns erupted in a full-on clash at the fields six hundred meters away. A greater volley came from the stalwart defenders than the attackers, whose salvo indicated they were still in some disarray. Over the thunder arose a throaty war whoop of women to belittle their foe. This was a signal that for now the enemy was checked.

After these few minutes of action less than half of Rehou's cohorts remained—a situation he once considered inconceivable. Four more Ait Atta, including the one who had fled, converged on the igherm. *Rehou remained steely, cobra-like. The man with the malfunctioning weapon was before him, staring woefully at the pistol. Giving that warrior due mercy, and wary of the rocks in Mimoun's hand, Rehou turned from the rifleman to face the* amrabt, *and took one, then a second step forward.*

So spared, and given that one instant, the brave man clenched the barrel of his impotent weapon, sprang forward and swung it as a club. With merely a glance, Khoussaila aimed behind and fired. The Berber died with a bullet to the chest, but his momentum carried the rifle butt to Rehou's head, knocking off the garish turban, exposing cranial scars and a top knot. Rehou could not avoid the rock Mimoun hurled. The hard, roughly spherical granite bashed the sternum and drove the air from his lungs. Pain blurred Khoussaila's mind and eyes and briefly neutralized his rage with a flare of self-pity. Still, he raised the Beretta and for a moment held unseeing Addi a prisoner.

La Tour saw the adjutant corporal scamper toward the gun from his nook among the elephant herd rocks. La Tour then studied Rochet as he turned his binoculars to peer at the foot of the promontory. The Colonel's lenses inched upward—and stopped on the incongruous wooden gutters hanging in strange purpose over the lip of the precipice.

La Tour partly withdrew his eyes from the glasses. Peripherally, to his far left, he glimpsed the first wave of climbing troops, perhaps thirty in all. He truly pitied them; the humiliation and pain about to befall them had few equals in the annals of this war. It was a waste of fine men, a testament to the folly of poor planning, a command blunder writ large.

The adjutant scolded kneeling Baud, who was gathering himself to rise and be counted among the effective soldiers of the day.

Hani worked the bolt and inserted a fresh shell into the chamber.

Baud would be chastised to his death.

La Tour watched as once-boastful Baud strode to the gun, barked an order to his second as if his temporary flight from duty was a brief and nearly harmless anomaly. The second man, who had remained standing during the minute of Baud's defection, obediently placed a shell into the breech and prepared to yank the lanyard.

Mirvais had no way to know the result of Rehou's attack. He could not read the lower volume of gunfire as a good or a bad sign. But clearly the village had been well prepared by someone with more tactical sense than even these cunning Berbers could enlist. This was not yet a disaster for him, but it would be no victory. His best men were here to show the garrison flag, and to validate his presence. They might be needed, but in his uncertainty whether Rehou had helped or harmed the assault he would be reluctant to commit them. Rather than assure a triumph, they might die for his folly. He felt his grasp of events slipping away like snow on a warm rock. The lustrous image of participating in the capture of *Gardian* faded into the muddy hues of a man turned from fame and cast out.

Saint-Avold surveyed all from the western end of the ridge: a far hill and a warren of caves, to the top of the promontory and the main Berber positions, to the barricades and terraced fields. He saw a shell blast a union of a stone wall and a cheval-de-frise, *obliterating both. Troops moved laterally along the base of the precipice, where others waited and two more units moved up for assault. He swung his view along the precipice, to a jib of cliff jutting from the plateau. Atop it was the weatherworn shell of a fort. The ruins offered a fine position from which Mirvais could launch a flanking maneuver or a diversion.*

Saint-Avold gazed down the back of the ridge to Mirvais, who was shrinking—almost hiding—from the battle, unable to conceal his dismay. Saint-Avold raised the glasses toward him, a gesture inviting his view. Mirvais nodded glumly, and labored uphill.

"Sir, that fort to the left is an excellent position," he said as Mirvais reached the top. "Rochet should have ordered it taken right off. We can advance unseen behind this ridge. Once there, a section can hold it while the rest move on the village."

Mirvais did not register everything Saint-Avold said. But he sensed a chance to save military face, his personal honor, even his life. The gamble on Rehou had been justified. Yet all was in vain. Mirvais had not seen or heard any of the pre-arranged signals, nor did any villagers appear to be fleeing a rampage. And the capture or death of Akka Ahêddây would have triggered a collapse of Ait Atta defense: seize the king and his warriors lose spirit. But the gunfire at the boulder defilade was akin to the laughter of devils. Akka was almost surely still alive. And Rehou likely was not.

Sergeant Pierre Dutroix viewed the steep, jagged side of the cliffs over sixty meters high. The rubble at the bottom of the scarp rose to a tilt-back top none of them could see. Two waves of thirty men climbed eagerly, to get to the top alive, and wreak vengeance for the drubbing their comrades below had been taking. And they were confident; a section of marksmen waited in mid-field, ready and able to murder any shleuh *foolish enough to show his head.*

Dutroix climbed around the large boulders but remained near them should the enemy loose a fusillade. After this first line of men had gone halfway the second would follow. One methodical way or another, they would reach the top, plant markers as targets for the field guns, and the best shooters among them would take up sniping positions.

After one year in the army, ten months in Maroc, and about twenty engagements, Dutroix could not recall a day when so many of his mates had become casualties before they fired a shot. This hill was a death trap.

His boots gripped scree and hard dirt. Each man was a unit, constantly moving forward to the best position with initiative and agility. Almost halfway; he looked up to carefully pick his route. No shleuh *heads poked over the edge; he wondered if any were above observing the approach. Perhaps the small force would indeed meet its objectives.*

Dutroix climbed. He looked up again. To the odd wooden gutters overhanging the edge above. What was their purpose? They protruded just enough so that an object emerging from what appeared to be a funnel . . .

At that moment a brown cylinder clay jug rattled out the end and dropped, fat bottom first, into a guided free-fall at the end of a rope. Inserted in the mouth was a sparkling candle, bigger than those held by smiling youngsters in Bastille Day crowds . . . .

Dutroix reflexively stopped, grabbed a loose palm-size stone, turned his back to the slope, gained a perilous foothold, and batted the jar as it passed near him. The pottery shattered. Out fell a tube of dynamite with about two inches of naked, sizzling fuse. The horrifying baton spun beyond his reach, into a well of gravity, taking a wide, rapid arc down toward the base and the second line of climbers.

"My God!" he bellowed. "Dynamite! Look out below!"

Puzzled faces upturned to him, with no firm grasp of his panic.

Then from each gutter to the left and right all of them saw objects that looked like small buckets attached somewhere above to rapid spools. Falling toward them.

"Everybody fall down!"

Most of them tumbled to a face-down fetal position. At that instant, the loose stick detonated, propelling dirt, sharp shards, and fist-sized chunks with the blast wave. Struck by a wild swirl of rubble, men howled in anger or alarm.

The two additional vessels hit the ends of the ropes some twenty meters above them. The opaque lanterns jolted to a jiggling halt. They, too, exploded. A cascade of rock debris, sweeping large stones among the pebbles, filled the air with the rattle and rumble of its descent. Some men dared to glance upward. Many saw a small avalanche studded with deadly hammers and dashed away from the incline.

The falling mass began to swell bounding outward upon the rushing men. The wave of shards and rocks inflicted bruises and concussions. But two large stones were kinetic brutes. One crashed upon a Frenchman as he fell under this hail. It crushed a lower leg. His hideous shriek was well heard at a timely lull in the gunfire.

* * * * *

Alain Aumont awoke with a start and blinked in the daylight. That whit of action alone summoned up his great fatigue. Disoriented and fearful, for several moments Aumont doubted he should be here. From his berth among the rocks he scanned for bandits, Ait Isha Berbers and their sheep, men with guns. He saw nothing but brown-green earth scattered with grass and flowers, and a vaulted dawn sky of lavender-blue. The garden and mountain needed only a great painter to capture their spirit.

Hamou and Assu threaded Aumont's route below the northern peaks. They passed Adrar n-Mezgounane on a trail along the borders of the Ait

Mehammed, Ait Ounir and Ait Isha, to the igherman *of Lhassane and Tamda, in the track trod by the Légion on consecutive nights before last. The cost of Aumont's* tazttat *offerings rose each day. They bought food, hospitality, and safety from harm, but were only as good as the willingness of the clans to honor them. His small donation at a* zawiya *earned him priceless good will, but his francs and* goursh *would soon be gone, leaving only the gold pieces in his vest beneath the* tajjelabith. *The objective was Tizi n'Tirist, almost thirty kilometers west of Akka's plateau.*

"We go no more from there, no matter how much you pay," Hamou said.

*Many times Aumont had uttered Akka Ahêddây and the Berber word for good—*ifulki—*in the same sentence. They all knew that Akka's baraka was strong. Nonetheless, the two would proceed only to that landmark. Then Aumont would be on his own.*

The tethered horse waited patiently. Alain struggled to rise. Hamou and Assu were watching their horses graze. In ten minutes they would be southbound toward an uncertain result. He prayed that the first men he met were Berber, that they did not think him mad, and that the Légion had not removed his friend from the earth.

* * * * *

The Légion was impatient, and their attack reeked of the assumption that Akka would quickly surrender. The reality was less certain: that is, until the airplanes arrived. La Tour peeked up to the sky. No sign of them yet. They preferred to take Akka alive. Indiscriminate bombing might ruin that chance.

La Tour glanced again at the broad incline three hundred meters leftward to gauge the results of the dynamite deliveries. He would have to stand to view the entire panorama, but from here he could see that the cliff was naked of ascending troops, brushed off like flies.

He turned to peer back onto the artillery ridge, to Sergeant Baud.

La Tour carefully watched him. When Baud stood upright, La Tour saw his confidence that he had set the field guns properly to eliminate the threat.

"Hani, that man there. He is about to do something terrible."

"Yes, shrif, I see him. I think he is a strange man. Up. Down. Running away. Angry returning. Time to die . . ."

At that instant Baud turned sideways to command his second. A slug tore through his rib cage and flung him down. La Tour felt a surge of guilt. The shock and despair that beclouded Baud's swarthy features resembled nothing he wanted to cause in a human soul. Baud would likely linger for some horrible moments before succumbing to the dark grip.

The gunners, moments before very concerned about the sniper, now fled to the elephant rocks. They pointed frantically at the tizi, *as if identifying a cheating gambler who had taken all of their money and fled to a far riverside. La Tour watched them discuss how to eliminate the problem. Who would leave safety to move, align and fire the guns?*

La Tour waited to see if anyone went to Baud's aid. He read his lips. Sergeant Baud was whispering to himself the last rites.

La Tour blinked away his black sorrow and pity.

Rochet was aghast to see Baud shot down. The attack could be blunted if those guns were not accurately and immediately fired. Other options were in chains or tatters. He would have no choice but to send another wave against those ravines. But which one was more likely to yield? Like a mad bettor at a bloody dogfight, he roared into the morning. Major Dallio stood beside him, marveling at this onrush of fury.

"Marcel, forget the plateau top! Turn both guns on that center pass! Bury those goddamn people in rocks! And send four new sections to assist those men! I want those positions! Accept no surrender! Do you hear me?!"

"Yes, sir. What about Mirvais's men?"

Rochet paused to contemplate that dilemma.

Mirvais, Saint-Avold and a nearly full section scurried along the backside of the ridge on a precarious field of scree. It was the best option; the easier route on the crest was exposed, and the rock-choked base was fifty meters below. They went unseen by Rochet and the others above. They would emerge from behind the spine at a large rock outcropping less than three hundred meters from the foot of the escarpment under the fort, then dash across a narrow neck of the stone valley. The sniper, looking at the ridge through the leftward embrasures, would not see the force approaching from the obscured right. Not until it was too late.

As they neared the end of the sheltering slope, Mirvais hastened to the head of the formation. Thirty men would be enough to rush the bluff and overwhelm the few inside the fort. There was safety in numbers, and until a few minutes ago, Mirvais had felt as helpless as a sacrificial sheep. But he could erase the certainty of disgrace with a decisive stroke. This low-risk, high-gain chance was the perfect chance to salve Rochet's hauteur and lead men to victory. It was providence that he was here to do both.

The four village men dashing toward Addi Yacoub and the gnome-like Berber brandishing a pistol were suddenly harried by a squall of bullets, source unknown. None of them were hit, but they were forced to dive behind a low wall made of stones long ago dug from the fields. This denied them view of the scene and any power to affect its outcome.

Khoussaila linked his keen eyes and ears to pinpoint the gunfire, most likely on the rocky knoll toward the ravine behind the igherm. *The view from there was unobstructed; anyone looking this way would easily see the cast of characters in this drama.*

But at the split second Rehou looked away, Mimoun slipped between the mercenary madman and his merciful father, and shoved Addi back toward the granary, nearly bowling him over. Haj saw them edge that way and followed in tandem, but also moved closer to the gunmen, thereby offering himself as the first to be shot. The three scurried together. But they had moved only several steps before Rehou redirected his cobra gaze.

The bullet drilled through Haj's ribs and into a lung. He did not utter a sound. A glimmer of peacefulness entered his eyes. Mimoun was horrified. It was almost certain that one of them become a casualty. His father's sacrifice was noble. He would not let it be futile.

Immediately at the pistol shot, two of the four village men behind the wall rose and, aiming haphazardly, discharged their Lebels. Mimoun and Addi were as likely to be shot as the fiend. Then rifle fire came from the knoll; one villager fell with a grotesque grimace and a gaping wound in the right shoulder. They were in a suicidal crossfire; in rising to kill the villain, some of them would die, too. But if they remained hidden and the amrabt *was shot instead, the shame of not having risked all for one so beloved would be unbearable.*

Mimoun kept running, gripping Addi's arm, pulling the amrabt *along, awaiting the bullet that would slay him. But by that fatal instant he could move Addi the next two meters, two steps closer to the granary door. Time seemed to protract into elastic strings, as if every molecule in this tiny corner of the world was vibrating less frantically than all others.*

"Youcef and Aamar, rise and shoot behind us," said Zin Mennou, one of the three unscathed men, to his fellows. "They may get only get one or two of us. I will hit that monster in front." He awaited their consent. Receiving it, all three rose in unison.

Zin Mennou sighted on this devil assassin, who ran at Addi but, curiously, not with his gun raised, as if the man was not solely intent on killing the old amrabt. *Now, an instant too late, he skillfully aimed the pistol. But at Mimoun the rock thrower.*

Mimoun reached the open door between them and the gunman. He must throw Addi within, yank the door shut and latch it from the inside.

Zin Mennou aimed carefully. One sure chance was worth the extra half-second.

Youcef and Aamar fired to the rear. Three staccato shots returned. Two missed, but the third drilled Aamar in the chest. He pitched backwards.

The falling body of Aamar jostled Zin just as he fired his rifle. The bullet clipped through the flesh of Rehou's upper right shoulder. It would prevent further right-hand shooting. He staggered, but lurched on like a mindless beast.

Mimoun stepped behind the open door. A bullet burst through a chink in the planks, shattering the parallel edges of wood into darts of shrapnel. A thick, sharp spike pierced Mimoun's cheek at the most harmful point, pinning the flesh to his upper jawbone. A bell of agony rang through his head that seemed equal to the sum of all injuries he had ever suffered. The young man gasped, whimpered and nearly fainted. He could not open his mouth to breathe. Blood flowed in too much volume for him to swallow.

He summoned the strength to shove mightily at Addi. The impetus carried the old man into the tetragonal granary, into the waiting arms of Kenza and Hada. Mimoun grasped a length of fat rope fastened to the inside of the door and yanked it behind him. The door slammed; the tremors set off a blinding quake in his head; he would scream from the pit of hell could he open his jaws. He vainly sought a rope hitch that for a moment would prevent the door being pulled open.

Veering at the angled wall, Rehou passed from the sight of the riflemen and stood at the door. His shoulder burned as if under a jet of flame, but it was a mere annoyance to his fury. Beneath his woolen shirt blood poured down his back and arm and dripped to earth. He dispassionately eyed the random, abstract pattern of crimson droplets there.

Akka could not see the old tizi or anyone within it from his position on the promontory. But he could feel the savior still living; his spirit was like a wave of energy, like sunlight cutting through shadow.

He saw a short file of enemy, several abreast, emerge from behind the ridge. They descended a broken slope toward the buttressing incline of the tizi that slanted to the blind-side right of the sniper's roost. Now the column gathered speed. They were almost within rifle range, but his fighters had no spare weapons, and no men close enough to do so even if they did. The mass of Iroumin would shortly disappear from view below the lip of the escarpment, and then be blocked by the tizi itself. Unless Akka were to reveal himself to the marksmen in the field, there was no way to witness this maneuver or the fate of Jilani.

La Tour watched Hani squint. The movement and angle of his rifle indicated that the Berber was eyeing Rochet through the cross-hairs. Mercifully, the Colonel remained beyond a bullet's reach. La Tour was already sickened by this debacle.

La Tour grew alert when an adjutant among the rocks approached Rochet and emphatically pointed down the ridge, across from the tizi. The Colonel flew into a rage. La Tour could sense doom approaching.

Dutroix was irate. He resumed the climb, with ten other men who as a matter of personal and unit pride would not squander two days of hard march in thirty seconds of flight. He was fatalistic; if Death intended to open its arms before his old age, it could as well do so in this tempest, in the couloirs of Pelvoux or on the streets of Marseilles. By allowing himself any doubts about his duty, he may as well have stayed home in Belfort.

Dutroix was twenty meters from the top, far closer than the fellow with the crushed leg, and another with a stone in his skull. The rest that could have fled to safety, and now of no help. Out of sixty men here, eleven remain. *A third set of dynamite vessels on ropes had fallen well past them before detonating near the bottom, where no unharmed Légionnaire remained. The explosions were exclamation points, hearty laughs, insults to injury.*

He looked forward to pumping bullets into these dastardly cowards. He had come to do battle in the classic brawn-and-bravery tradition, but the shleuh *waged war from rocks to avoid clashes with superior men. He expected to go over the lip into enfilade, and prayed that marksmen below would provide fierce protection. He glanced back for reas-surance—and to his left saw Légion men maneuvering toward the rise beneath the* tizi. *Dutroix could have told the officers it was valuable high ground.*

Mirvais ran ahead of Saint-Avold, leading two of his four sections toward the base of the escarpment. Closing in, the task grew arduous; the slope was one hundred meters of scree and stones. Mirvais decided that the rear section would remain below to cover the ascent. He expected minimal casualties if the position was occupied by only a few shleuh, *who would be neutralized by fire from below. Mirvais intended to maximize the glory.*

Frothing so near to his prey, Rochet seemed indifferent to the observation he was under. La Tour eyed the exchange of the furious Colonel and his dutiful Major; then both peered toward the fort, and him, with amazement. If he looked below, to the foot of this scarp, he would see Légionnaires.

Looking to the promontory, La Tour saw men edging closer to the top. Only by freezing could he and Hani remain unseen. The main attack had been blunted, but these brave, stubborn few could prove troublesome. He hesitated at the quandary: shoot to the rear at the climbers, or forward to troops who were about to storm his battlement frontally.

His fighter's blood was riled. Mirvais felt in his element: an arena where the crusader is tested by crisis, where valor defeats damnation. He was propelled up the hill by the frustration of every futile march and the casualties charged to his command, by the authority invested in him that had yielded nothing but despicable submission to a wily chieftain he had never even seen. The decrepit fort walls scowled at him. Beyond them lay his salvation.

Mimoun feared that a crack had formed in his skull and his brain now oozed out the fissure to ease unbearable pressure. The broad splinter—it felt like a metal spike—had pierced the left side of his face where the jaws were joined. Tendons and muscles were pinned to bone, immobilized, locking him in a ghastly visage. He wrapped a section of rope around his hands and prepared to hold the door against the adjnun on the other side.

Kenza took position behind Mimoun. Grasping the excess rope in her hands, she made ready with him.

Rehou tugged at the door; not surprisingly, it was latched from the inside. He had no time to waste. Riflemen approached; he would be dead in seconds whether he entered the granary or not. Not caring that he would be defenseless and that his right shoulder was useless, he slid the Beretta into his waistband and wrenched at the wicket with both arms.

The double tension pulling in and yanking out snapped the rope off the ring holding it to the inside of the stout door. The portal gave way.

Rehou collapsed to the ground at the sudden release.

Propelled by their own abrupt release from effort, as if driven by the kick of an invisible mule, Mimoun and Kenza staggered backwards, toppling over grain sacks. Screaming through clenched jaws, Mimoun steeled himself as the door swung open.

Addi moved along beneath the window of the eastern wall. He well heard the grunting beast outside the door five meters away. His mind formed an image. Coexisting within his acute sense was a strange, terrible anger, and a calm, reassuring voice that he could face this fiend without fear. Addi tried to fully recall Rehou—the madman of Aoufouss. What did he want here?

"Come here, old man, and tell me where the treasure is . . ."

Groping against the wall, Addi found a rough-hewn sheep-skinning staff . . .

Rehou Khoussaila bounded to standing. Very quickly and wholly irate he took two strides to the threshold where the new sunlight met a dark interior, pausing to scan the shadows. No less directly than a man who could see, blind Addi Yacoub ran forward with the flaying blade affixed to the cedar staff. They met at the border of light and dark.

Demon Rehou screamed again. Shocked and utterly dismayed, the sound exploded from him in a harsh wave that was amplified by the stones of the high-ceilinged *igherm*. One in which grain, not gold, was stored. The murderous Berber had been skewered through his belly by a *tassarite*-an implement used to skin sacrificial sheep.

Jean-Michel La Tour rose up like a fiery ghost. He grasped the second, unscoped rifle and hastened to the far wall in bold, dynamic strides. He stole a glimpse over the broken rampart down the incline. Twenty or more men were scrabbling to this roost.

Dare he linger long enough in view to choose his target, or just fire at random? At best he would get off two shots before the reply.

Behind him Hani also rose, now to put rounds in the men on the precipice. Firing in one direction or the other would reveal them, and he had to protect Jilani, whose back would be exposed. From the tizi *wall he could see the targets, but did not have a good angle from cover to shoot them. His rise to plain sight placed him in peril.*

La Tour leaned his torso atop the eroded pisé, *left elbow upon the rough surface, right hand cradling the weapon. In half a second he swung the sight onto the lead man.*

Onto Mirvais.

"Merde. Mon Dieu. Maintenant tu t'aneméne batard."

Dutroix injected a shell into the rifle breech. He saw two Berbers, one in a brown tajjelabith, *the other in white, in his sight line. They were too distant for good facial views, but too close, at fifty meters, to miss. He commended their bravery as the sole occupants of the fort. And he noted oddities about the man in white. French boots. An* achttan *about the head. Pale hands. And the deft combat manner with which he held his rifle. Dutroix braced against rocks and turned his Berthier toward him. Now a second fellow, in a turban, raised a rifle. At him. The others may retreat if they wished. Death was death.*

Everyone heard the planes before they saw them. Above the next hill or a dozen kilometers away, the trickery of mountain acoustics resounded across every stone the drum of several engines and the promise of destruction.

La Tour could now only break for the promontory and there organize squads of riflemen to shoot them down, and man the machine gun himself.

He waged a greatly accelerated battle with his conscience. Mind and soul clashed. Duty vis-à-vis justice. Pity and anger. Peace versus hatred. Now or maybe never.

He recalled the sneer with which Mirvais had bid him goodbye.

But he could not bring himself to pull the trigger. Not yet.

"Hani!"

La Tour ducked hastily, turned to his comrade, and was fascinated to witness two tiny jars pop in unison from the ends of the distant gutters, trailed by rope umbilicals, subtly effected by random nudges of air and gravity and momentum upon their mass.

They fell, fell, down toward a man in particular, aiming his rifle.

"Hani!"

He gestured for his comrade to fall forward. As he complied, the rifle cracked, the bullet grazed the top of the wall with which Hani's head had a split second before been aligned—and the fuse of one jar bomb abruptly detonated and displaced a tide of debris.

The two hundred Légionnaires between the ridges saw no sign of the Ait Atta before they unleashed their flanking counterattack. Two volleys sent ten or more Iroumin *down. Forty mounted men wielding* tikemmiyin *thundered upon the astonished* spahis *waiting idly in reserve, and sent them reeling in a grotesque ballet. Berber losses were heavy, too, but they seemed to care not in this wicked attrition.*

Major Dallio's men wheeled and with fine discipline shot down the front rank of the foe. But the Légionnaires were bewildered; the number of enemy was unknown, and without that knowledge the remaining men could not be deployed for optimum effect. Dallio ordered a section to concentrate on the Beber horsemen; the mounted flank attack was decimated. But the Ait Atta had the initiative. They loosed irregular fire on the increasingly disjointed reserve ranks in the ravine.

The Légion men at the foot of the plateau heard this new battle erupt. In twos and tens they abandoned their assault and rushed rearward to consolidate. The attack had begun twenty minutes ago with full confidence it would last only long enough to pluck the prey from his lair or kill him. Now the force was trying to save itself from annihilation.

The planes appeared. Three drones grew ominous in scale and purpose. Laden with bombs, they soared over the hard, ageless terrain several kilometers away.

Boldly, almost recklessly, Akka n-Ali dashed to the edge of the precipice, unaware that five meters below him crouched six soldiers, and they equally unaware of him and wholly uncertain whether to clamber upward to suicidal valor or to flee in disgrace.

The planes roared above the far ridge and flew dead-on for the plateau. Intent on a punishment more deadly than any field guns could inflict, they bore straight for the cluster of buildings at the far center of the plateau.

Jean-Michel Sidi Jilani La Tour raced up the incline to rocks five meters from the top, toward the near side of his hut at the precipice. Far to his right two of the three planes—late-war Brequets—were about to pass near the makeshift bomb runnels and the hut on a line to the far village. A shot rang out, and a bullet whisked through the billowing front of his tajjelabith. *He felt the turbulence of its passing and heard the rifle echo as a crack in hard, close space. He dashed behind the hut, past it on the path along the promontory, in full view of shooters. The menacing planes flew onward. Gasping, he ran, ran on for the machine gun, with Hani close on his heels.*

Afar, he saw Akka, stripped of his tajjelabith, *down to trousers and a* gandourah, *peering from the edge of the precipice with little thought to his danger, uncertain about his most proper place, fearful of the planes but also almost ignoring them on this cusp of victory. Guardian was boiling for a fight to the finish.*

Looking down upon the still-embattled main ravine leading into the terraced fields, Akka n-Ali frantically waved his arms—so that he could be seen by someone there.

La Tour bellowed, in French the amghar *found incomprehensible: "Ahêddây! Sit behind those rocks!" Taken aback, Akka turned hastily about to locate the voice.*

La Tour saw Brka spur his intrepid, sure-footed animal into full gallop up the slope. Bullets now peppered the earth near horse and rider. Akka had been furiously signaling the machine thief, and Brka was responding. The rattle of the Brequets' Darne guns began as the sound of hasty concussions, but moving in came to imitate a mighty engine grinding a great chain against cogs. Lines of bullets churned across the promontory. Following Brka. Where the ground became soft, where the animal gained speed, both crashed to earth in a frenzy of dust and limbs. Still, the bullets came on, pursuing Akka n-Ali.

Akka took protection behind boulders. Ten meters away, a stream of shells burst into two village men and turned them to red pulp.

Jilani ran on, alternately eyeing the planes and the course of their ravenous bullets. The machines passed. He, reaching his goal, ceased running, an oddly breathless god.

Brka was upon the ground, unmoving, his noble horse bleeding out. Jilani gazed to the farthest village where the planes were bound, and wondered: did Kenza get to the caves?

Kenza, mother Hada, grandmother Hejjou and now several other women huddled, like geese in a storm, in the old igherm, *and listened to the fitful, hideous but oddly ebbing battle.*

The rumble of approaching engines pulled them to the southern windows, to a vista of the near-empty village and their home. Three machines, a miniature but mighty flock, glided low and slow over the plateau. Airplanes. Similar to the one that had dropped Jilani among them. That had attacked in Tarhzout. Now, for a purpose that was too-briefly a mystery, one, two, four objects, like eggs, fell from them. There was unequal distance between them. For one second or two the things wobbled on descent, and then hit in broken sequence. Blasts of dirt and rubble was a shocking spectacle, as if the surface of earth was vomiting skyward.

The third and fourth bomb soared onward and down. The third device impacted in the courtyard between the school and the old igherm *where lay the bleeding bodies of several villagers and rogues. The fourth detonated atop the wall of Akka's* igherm, *shattering the red door.*

Akka n-Ali saw many of the riflemen still alive from their defense dash down to the perimeter of the stony field and peer at the foe. What they lacked in good sense they made up in resolve. Gathering themselves, bodies and souls, like a breeze becomes a gale the long line of frenzied ragmen sent up a taunting clamor of triumphant yowls. In near-unison, of the same mind, fifty or more of them began to walk, then run toward the seesaw battle. The predator was now the prey. Two shells from the field guns, fired in haste and inaccurately, opened small holes in the line but too far behind for great effect. Most implacably advanced toward the sound of battle. Akka could do nothing to dissuade them.

Kessou pulled the machine gun from the crate. He demonstrated a moderate knowledge of the weapon by preparing it for action: bolt back, breech open, ammunition strip in, chamber loaded. La Tour could not use the gun without revealing himself.

He heard the three Brequets turn about and begin a reverse sweep of the village, strafing as they came. Soon La Tour would have no choice about the form of his action.

"Kessou, all Ait Atta men. Quickly!"

Akka cupped his hands at his mouth and emitted a shrill, demonic rallying cry.

Kessou lifted the gun, Jilani the ammunition, and both sprinted toward the boulders. Moments later, a dozen, fifteen, twenty men arrived in response to Akka's bellow.

Jilani smiled at one fellow, patted his back, and gently took the rifle from his grip. All watched him step behind a boulder, into a slight declivity, to demonstrate. But these men knew exactly what to do as the birds monsters flew over. They took cover among the boulders, to use as a brief shield from the strafing guns, and aimed their rifles skyward.

Kessou stepped forward proudly with the Chatellerault, eager to fight fire with fire.

Akka Ahêddây carried the battle flag pole to them. Several bullets had precisely pierced the axis of the palm frond and the sword.

The thirty-man army clustered at the hut and paused briefly in their advance. They aligned in imperfect triple file behind Mirvais, and tramped down the promontory pathway. The fields, the far cave hill, the village clusters all loomed into view. This was the heart, the capital of enemy country. Now many of them grew anxious that the sounds of battle were ebbing. That it was a tactical mistake to be so far from their lines in blind obedience to their commander.

"Sir," Corporal Schondorff brazenly offered in the belief that their actions were now well above the call of duty, "I believe we are entirely on our own here."

"Perhaps we will get no rescue, but we claim all the glory."

The same men emitted murmurs of disenchantment. "That glory may come by slow death and an unmarked grave," Schondorff replied.

Mirvais did not respond.

The three marauding planes were far to the left. An outbound breeze bore most of their machine growl away. One turned over the village near the old igherm, *unleashing its last ordnance, enveloping a tract in fire and blast. The rear gunner employed his Darne. The second plane trailed close behind, unleashing destruction. The third banked right, seeking a target.*

Mirvais and the troops emerged into full view. Below them, between green fields and a line of boulders near the edge of the plateau, they saw a flock of Ait Atta men about equal to their own number. The Berbers gazed toward the ominous timbre of the Brequet—just standing there. Winged death was approaching, and they seemed unconcerned. Then a fellow in a white tajjelabith *paced rearward to a cordon of boulders, and every one followed in a quick but orderly manner. A planted battle flag spread on the southerly breeze.*

Suddenly, two men among them, first the white tajjelabith, *and then a second in brown, clambered upon adjacent rocks and waved their arms. Making of themselves a conspicuous target, surely trying to lure the pilot down to a height for most effective strafing.*

With each new minute the Légionnaires in the ravine at the far ridge were less capable of continuing this operation as planned; they were barely averting a rout.

"Squares! Squares!" Rochet shouted frantically. They directed ferocious volleys on the foe. Imazighen shot spahis *from their mounts. They eliminated the field gunners; the once-daunting pieces were now little more than encumbrances, but more than half of them were casualties. Many Légion troops were wounded, too. Their care, and the extrication of the battered force as a whole from Berber capture, now took priority over the primary mission.*

"Gather the wounded!" Rochet ordered. "Cover them with Hotchkiss teams. When complete, we will withdraw and stage an orderly regroup."

The planes might hammer Taboulmant from the air, but he must sadly admit that his ground troops were no longer capable of breaking through the gates.

"Sir," said Dallio, "Mirvais and his men . . . They . . ."

"What the Berbers have done to them perhaps I would have done myself."

Larbi's badly tattered men could not dare to stem the Légion's retreat. This victory had been excruciating. Still, even the wounded, including Larbi himself, were in a froth and with their unscathed comrades wanted to press on, if only out of sheer spite.

The Brequet soared closer to the boulders. The Darne gunner directed his fusillade forward, on the area where the two foolish men had drawn the attention of the pilot and himself. The magazine he fully discharged among the rocks in these few seconds should be wielding awful damage to flesh. The gunner paused.

"Now!" Akka and Jilani exclaimed together.

Twenty men stepped out from the screen of rocks. Kessou and the Chatelleraut, and the rifles volleyed at the noses and bellies of two machines. The engine and skin of the nearest one were riven and mutilated. Through bullet holes spewed oil, petrol, and blood.

The Chatellerault fell from Kessou's hands and clattered to the ground. Kessou pitched forward with a pulverized torso, against Jilani. The sacred white tajjelabith *was thickly splashed with crimson.*

The far Brequet flew on, but the other, guided by what remained of the dying pilot's consciousness, cleared the promontory, and reared up over the stony field as if it had been shoved skyward, then plunged into a shallow-angle dive, skidded across the rough surface with a drumming, rattling grind, and careened to a halt just beyond midway of the expanse.

Every witnessing Berber, man and woman, sent up a rousing cheer so that the plateau and adjacent hills resounded with jubilation for themselves, and scorn for their enemy.

Mirvais was aghast at the success of the Ait Atta ruse.

"Sir, we . . ." Schondorff reiterated.

"Shut up, Corporal!" Mirvais hissed.

Schondorff saw Mirvais quickly weigh his options. There were only two—and Mirvais's bitter mood did not bode a retreat. But with the dire collapse of the main attack, the band was indeed on their own, in the last moments of a futile and likely suicidal foray.

He glanced around at the men, most of whom were clearly thinking: if our comrades were only with us, we would and could make a good fight of it. Most of the men on this ad hoc assault peered backward, of half a mind to turn and retreat whence they came.

Now that option, too, was taken away: two dozen or more silent, bristling Ait Atta assembled behind them in a semi-circular noose, around the small symmetrical square.

Women drifted in pairs and groups to the tableau and broke into taghwrirt, *an ancient technique of jubilant, trilling exhortation, here slightly sinister, like an oratorio of ghosts. The current of sound washed across the breeze-swept fields and up to the sky.*

"Légionnaires, you are a volunteer serving France faithfully and with honor!" the Major proclaimed in a steady tone. "Sing! Sing La Boudin! First stanza!"

The men struck up a chorus, at first raggedly, then with some harmony.

Au Tonkin, la Légion immortelle Légion	At Tonkin the immortal
A Tuyen-Quang illustra notre drapeau, described our flags	At Tuyen-Quang
Héros de Camerone et frères modeles and his brothers	Heroes of Casmerone
Dormez en paix dans vos tombeaux! graves	Sleep peaceful in your

"Remember who you are! Keep forward!" Mirvais ordered. "Forward and sing!"

The planes on high swooped in a lazy circle, as if the rapt-witness pilots were uncertain whether to continue their action or fly home. They did neither, but knew well that soldier comrades below were hostage, and that continued air attack could incite their death.

Au cours de nos campagnes lointaines, homeland facing	Being so far from our
Affrontant la fièvre et le feu,	the fever and the fire
Oublions avec nos peines, pain	Forgetting with the
La mort qui nous oublie si peu, forget us	the dead which never
Nous, la Légion	We, the Légion

Front and rear, more Ait Atta warriors, and women nearby, closed in on them. Ahead, a dozen Berbers stepped from behind the rocks. The enemy bodies converged.

"Three sides!" Mirvais ordered. The well trained Légionnaires formed a triangle phalanx and prepared to shoot right, left and front.

The unflinching Berbers responded with a like readiness.

La Tour was horrified to see so many comrades, Légion and Ait Atta alike, about to be shot down.

First, Akka n-Ali and then Jean-Michel La Tour stepped forward, into the span between the facing lines.

From Mirvais's jittery point of view, the man before him could well be Akka Ahêddây. He began to raise his pistol and opened his mouth to proclaim: "Fire!" But it froze on his lips. He stood statue-still and his mouth fell open in sudden apprehension of the abyss into which he stared.

A number of Ait Atta men moved yet closer. Perhaps the better to see enemy eyes while they die. Or scare them so that many collapse of fright before they can shoot.

"You bring death . . . " La Tour said in French, "for your . . . "

Mirvais, Saint-Avold, Schondorff, the entire section, were agape . . .

A bullet ripped and seared through La Tour's left thigh, slugging him off-balance, backward. He could not fight his body, which pitched to rocky earth shoulders first. He felt an intense burning sensation, as if pierced by a fiery rod. He felt the outrush of blood but the true agony was the view from his mind's eye: the utter foreclosure of escape, the revelation of his ruse, and the terrible secrets under his robe. He fell helpless among the boulders where just brief hours ago he had taught the Ait Atta how they could help themselves.

Corporal Pierre Dutroix was glad to triumph in his moment of death. By taunting the plane, Akka Ahêddây had given himself away.

Dutroix then turned barely in time to meet an Ait Atta warrior and his takummiyt. *The curved blade slashed deeply into his ribs. The rifle clattered to the earth and he drew his own knife and whirled with the man in rags. They grappled for seconds on the promontory edge, beside the hut, before Dutroix buried his twisting blade to the hilt, carving into vitals. Falling wide-eyed and silent, the warrior grabbed his opponent and pushed backwards, and the both of them reeled in a lethal plunge onto the rocks below.*

Mirvais was stupefied.

"Sir . . ." Saint-Avold whispered, "We are thirty guns against one hundred. We will surrender and live to fight another day."

"I will not!" shouted Schondorff.

"Nor I," said Pressiat.

A number of other men concurred.

"All of us must do so it, or no one will get the chance," said Saint-Avold.

Mirvais was faced with the choice of suicide or submission. And it was all his fault.

The Ait Atta men before them near the rocks parted. Out stepped a young warrior, wielding the light French machine gun. No Légionnaire saw mercy in that fellow's heart.

Struggling to sit upright, Jilani fumbled at the upper thigh. Pain and fear gripped him in equal measure, and blackness closed in. The in-and-through wound had ruptured the artery and gouged out flesh. He could not say if it had hit the bone. He saw Akka peering down.

Akka n-Ali found it inconceivable that a true deity would allow himself to suffer and bleed. The near-panic, the actions, the angry passion of this now evidently European creature were all too-human. The man looked up at him. With pleading eyes. Like those of a man-child caught by someone he loves in an act both know to be terribly, irreparably wrong.

"Don't kill them," he gasped in French.

Akka was non-committal. If he unleashed his darkest side, all of them would die immediately. But he would keep the monster in check. For now.

He stepped away and moved into the front rank of Ait Atta men to face the Légionnaires. Mirvais recognized him immediately: Ahêddây, as if straight from the photograph, but sorrowful now, even in the glow of greatest victory.

The amghar n-ufella *took a step forward, and eyed each Légionnaire and the rifle barrels before him in turn, implicitly inviting them to shoot him and then die.*

Then Akka gently, charitably pushed his right palm toward the ground—signifying that all the men should place their weapons there. In the eloquent gesture was a hint of fairness—but in the stern, steely set of his jaw was also the implication that the refusal of one would be fatal for all. And this was a one-time, non-negotiable offer.

Akka's eyes shifted left, right to Kessou and the barrel of his machine gun, and forward to the Légionnaires. One word from him, and . . .

Saint-Avold was the first to lower his weapon. Others shortly followed.

Mirvais, like some Viking determined to die armed and standing, raised his pistol. In defiance. In a last spasm of honor. In folly. In refusal to die a meaningless death. In fear of the future, so rife with disgrace, he dared not think its name. The action was not complete before a dozen or more rounds pierced him and his dreams of final glory. Blood pooled rapidly in a wide blot around the body. The silence was such that the Légionnaires could almost hear it ooze forth. And the earth drank it hungrily.

Akka addressed his warriors:

"Now bind their hands and take them to the cave."

The ritual of taking enemy men into captivity was witnessed by all. Silence reigned. The humiliated foe, eyes cast down, less in fear than with regret and chagrin for the reach that had just barely exceeded their grasp, were led off through the barley fields.

Lahcen dashed up to Akka Ahêddây. He was distressed and ashen, in a dither such that Akka had never seen.

"Addi Yacoub and your family are safe. But Mimoun was badly hurt protecting them. And Haj is near death. Can you come?"

"Yes. In a moment," Akka replied.

To Amnay he said, "Keep men at the barricades. Guard the women as they gather our wounded and dead. Soon the enemy will send a Goumier to request that we permit the collection of their casualties. Consent to this. The bearers must be unarmed. Observe but do not interfere. This time the *Iroumin* will not be able to claim that we have been inhumane."

With various degrees of skepticism or disbelief, like witnesses to a strange miracle or water running uphill, Akka, Amnay and Lahcen turned to regard the false demigod. The man once called Jilani and deemed their savior looked up at them with a pale, pitiful face. Naked recognition of the truth passed between everyone in hard silence.

Then the Frenchman fell back against the tawny earth, unconscious.

NINETEEN:

UNVEILED

Akka Ahêddây achieved victory, at pitiable cost. With so many dead or wounded, he could not afford another such triumph. The irate Légion had counter-fired with a fierce accuracy not greatly impeded by the men lost in the first volley. But with that salvo, the Berbers may have won, for it proclaimed that the cost to the Légion would be very high, and if they were willing to pay it they would all die together. And with too few unwounded Légionnaires to take and hold the plateau, it would soon return to the Berbers the way rising water spills over an undersized or untended dam.

Berber blood trickled into pockets and furrows from the upper tiers of the ravines where the field guns had inflicted the most carnage. Men moaned. Women came running. A broken chorus of cries and wails and prayers were offered to and for the dead or dying. Nearly half of the defenders were casualties. But all had persevered; upon and before the barricades lay the grisly harvest of enemy bodies.

Akka attended to his men, attempting to summon baraka. *But he could not clear his mind of Jilani, the fallen, wounded god. He watched Amnay and Brka ease the helpless man onto a transport blanket. Shock from the loss of blood, and shame, were obvious in the misery etched on his face.*

"Bring him to the igherm."

Along the way, every detail that no one had questioned—or had pretended not to notice—confirmed suspicions: the boots and pants of a Légionnaire, fair skin and hair, the lack of observed miracles, the alternating tongues of perfect French and spare Tamazight, his keen knowledge of enemy plans and tactics. Akka mulled the new truth—the reincarnated god was a mortal impostor.

Addi marveled at the extreme contrast between the din of the morning battle and this placid afternoon. Sitting in the garden's sunshine, he struggled to accommodate the carnage, and his contribution to it, with the view that all such acts were ultimately senseless, even if it was kill or die. Addi knew his actions to have been guided by a higher power, of vision beyond sight, and that the revelation from that terrible trek in the Tafilalt was one reason he still breathed. And he knew that the village would desperately need his compassion and guidance in the days ahead. He passed from the garden, down the bomb-shattered pathway, and knelt outside the granary. One by one, people joined him in prayer.

Lahcen cut off the blood-soaked pants leg and wrapped the ugly thigh in hot compresses, but no one else touched the visitor. Every villager was of two minds about him. No suspicions could be confirmed or conclusions drawn until he awoke. If he ever did.

The dead and wounded Ait Atta were gathered quickly. Every few minutes another casualty on the back of a comrade or a wife or a mule was carried to the *igherm* and assessed. Some were already dead, or had died in transit, and others would soon join them.

Under a fragile, unspoken truce, an unarmed Légion detail under the wary gaze of Ait Atta men approached the barricades and bore away the bodies of their own fellows.

A yema a yema! Ah yema nou a yema! Oh, Mother! Mother! Came the cries of the men. Still, loud weeping was infrequent. Suffering and loss was a largely private matter, between the living and the dead and the determination of Allah. In this land of turmoil the all but inevitable death in battle was simply a function of His will.

More than fifty men and several women were laid out on the earthen floor of the granary. It was the largest building in the village, and the only one suitable as a hospital. Outside, fires boiled water in large kettles.

Women tossed in fragments of *tijjloubah* and other thick, soft fabrics fit for dressings. Kenza and Hada lifted steaming strips from the pots with sticks and placed them in baskets. The wads cooled, were squeezed of excess water, then taken within and applied. The used, bloody compresses were boiled in fresh water from the river. The scene was sanguine, somber, tragic, and heroic. Anxious councils, electrified by common pity and urgent duty, talked softly.

" . . . I don't know if he will live out the day . . ."

" . . . he is strong . . ."

" . . . they will amputate the leg . . ."

" . . . says he will be up and about soon, maybe helping us. God be . . ."

" . . . Where is Fadma with the *tahrirte*? A sick man needs . . ."

"Larbi n-Haddou has died."

Pained silence. A most respected member of the council had passed. At great cost did the dead inspire the living.

"Kenza, we need more bandages."

Akka cursed the available methods of treatment, which were almost no methods at all. The wounded would get little relief; archaic techniques of herbal healing were futile against abundant mayhem. The villagers had scant knowledge of how to use the batch of looted medical supplies. Oh, to have pharmacies and field hospitals like the *Iroumin*. Several women, including Kenza, were preparing poultices. Most such remedies for infections were of limited or no value on perforated flesh. But with the exception of Addi's powers, it was all the village had.

By mid-afternoon, Akka passed into exhaustion. He was in awe of Addi's stamina and kept pace, but he was drained in the long night by seeing and hearing the agony. Of the fifty-two men here, perhaps twenty would not survive. Many non-fatal injuries were crippling or disfiguring: a shattered knee, a lost eye, a blasted jaw. These casualties were in addition to forty already dead. All told, a third of the defenders, villagers and returning raiders together, had been killed or wounded. And it could have been much worse, a near-catastrophe, had the noncombatants of the *tamazirt* not gone to the caves.

Addi tried to summon the light in his hands, but the prospect of so much need was daunting, and his strength was finite. Some of his struggle might have been a whisper of guilt; he could be in the place of any casualty here. Instead, he was merely heartsick. Numb.

Akka guided Addi among the rows; they stopped over Mimoun and Haj. Father and son lay side by side. Mamoun reached over to hold his father's hand, as if to pull him from death's grasp. The young man would survive the torment of his injury with a moderate scar to his handsome face and a damaged jaw beneath it, and this qualified as a small miracle. But his father's condition was grave. It was well that the bullet had passed through him and ruptured only the lung, but the blood loss was dire. It all depended on Haj's will to live, and on Allah's grace.

Addi knelt between them and put a hand on each. He could feel their strong bond. He passed some of himself into Mimoun, where it was enhanced and flowed into the man, for whom Addi was inexpressibly grateful.

Akka studied the key figure. No one mentioned the paradox of him. But it was the crux of every thought, revealed in every eye. Everyone glanced repeatedly at his form, as if expecting him to rise and heal himself like a demigod—or wake up screaming like an ordinary man. No one disputed that the organizing and actions of the visitor had saved them from disaster, or had given them the means to save themselves. But how would it affect their sanctity if he was not who they had thought him to be? And when not eyeing the mystery man, they glanced at Akka and Addi, whose steadfast faith had inspired their belief. It would be almost profane to question their official or holy pronouncements. Because trust and faith were the *tamazirt's* greatest treasure, to this moment no one had done so.

Akka searched his heart for the borders of the contradictions. The key to resolving them was to fix where they began and ended. The spectrum was nothing less complicated than Christian and Muslim, French and Berber, subservience and freedom, the choice between ancient tradition and modern extinction.

Addi gestured for Akka to confer with him outside.

"You must not let him die," Akka began.

"I have no intention. But much of it is up to him. If he is a god, if the spirit rules the flesh, then he will heal himself."

"I no longer believe he is."

They stood at a great, hushed chasm. This last observation, if true, would demand much reappraisal. At last Addi asked the central question: "What will you do?"

"Justice must be served," Akka firmly replied.

"Perhaps it already has been. He saved us, you, from disaster."

"Did you not once say that we are but a few words of God's infinite expressions? If He chooses that by death we be silent, than so we must. Our experience today proves Allah has chosen our survival, that we are to act for ourselves and speak for Him."

"We cannot judge His providence," Addi responded, "any more that until now we sought to judge the saint claiming to be His representative."

Akka thought intently before replying. "If he is not the one, and we help him live, how do we know he will not trick others? Hurt others? Inspire others to trust in the light, only to be eventually cursed by darkness because they believed the lie?"

"I do not know the answers. Only does he, if anyone at all."

"Then make him live so that we may learn what he does know."

"Yes. Simply as a matter of compassion. But who shall decide his ultimate fate? That is a more difficult issue."

"Lies are a great sin. They must be punished," Akka reiterated.

"His bravery, even for reasons we may not know or approve, may be its own truth."

"Perhaps he was brave was for reasons that do not entirely concern us," Akka reasoned. "Looking back, his behavior seemed too human. He was worried. Anxious. Mimoun reported such on the first day. And I don't know that he has performed any miracles when so many friends are dead or wounded."

Kenza had lingered nearby during this exchange. She was concerned that a strange mixture of piety and pride would set a course toward an action that once taken could not be revoked. After a long moment she heard Addi speak again.

"I will try to heal him," he said, almost mournfully. "He will repay us with words."

Both men fell into another prolonged silence.

Kenza entered the granary. She knelt beside him, and with a steaming bandage pressed a poultice to the ugly wound. The mildly burning paste would check infection for several hours, but the shock from blood loss was another matter. It was a hopeful sign that he remained alive nearly two hours after the battle. If Father's suspicions proved true, Jilani, or whoever he was, would survive only to die. Kenza tried to not feel sorrow, but she feared his fate. She did not know why, except that it was linked to his strangely luminous smile, which could not be that of a deceiver or a devil nor, it would seem, of the divine. That smile, in human form, would no longer convey ethereal wisdom, but rather uncertainty and a lovely, lonely desire. Of course, blinded by his presumed light, she had not seen this, nor had any reason to do so. When Allah wants his children to see, He reveals. And Jilani's arrival and deeds were a harvest of all the revelation they needed. Until now.

Across the granary, two sisters wailed at the death of their brother. Shot twice, he had never regained consciousness. They exposed a deep, inconsolable grief. In this village today, no death would fail to affect anyone. The lament, so shared, was all the greater.

The strong emotions apparently stirred the man to consciousness the way a sudden breeze would the inert leaves of a tree. He moaned and blinked his eyes open. For long moments they fixed blankly on the granary ceiling, and the image seemed to confuse him. Then he looked about, first across bodies to his left, and at Kenza leaning over him.

"Are they gone?" he weakly rasped.

"Who? The *Iroumin*? Yes, they march back the way they came. Less of them."

Kenza glanced up at a man awaiting her signal near the doorway. She nodded, and the fellow was off to deliver a message.

"Why are you so sad?" La Tour asked her in wonderment.

"We have many dead and wounded men for our heartache."

He was silent before saying, "I am very sorry. It could not be avoided."

"Yes, we know," Kenza replied, softly and crestfallen. Others observed her conversation with him. "But that does not make it any easier." A curtain of silence fell between they and their secrets. She said, "I must go and help the others." She rose. He watched the young woman tenderly remove gory compresses and replace them with fresh, hot ones.

The nature of his predicament hit him anew, more distress or dread than shock. With some relief he saw that his *tajellabith* had not been removed. Very possibly, the second of his two great secrets was as yet undiscovered. But these Berbers, though accepting that gods could wear the same clothing or speak the same language as their mortal enemies, would not also abide that one of their deities suffered human wounds.

The granary door opened. Akka stepped through, and his thoughts were instantly clear to La Tour. The *amghar* no longer appeared reverent or compassionate, but angry for the peculiar shame he seemed certain was his alone to bear. Still, there was a hint of reprieve in his demeanor; he was more disappointed then enraged.

Addi followed Akka. The attendants fell silent and moved aside. On unspoken cue, all but those caring for the critically wounded made an exit. Akka and the *amrabt* walked slowly to La Tour and stood a body length away, gazing across the charged, intimate space between them, not judging but clearly wary.

"Everyone in the village extends their gratitude for your courage in the defense of our homes and people," Addi said in passable French. "We shall be eternally grateful."

La Tour could think of nothing to say. Neither French nor Tamazight. He willed his mind to offer a reply, but to no avail. Akka, too, waited, but only silence filled the void.

"This action of today answers some questions about what is to become of us, but also raises others," Akka continued. "Please stand up."

"You know I cannot," La Tour replied dejectedly

"And that raises still other questions. The greatest quality of man is mercy. Second, is the desire for truth. The truth can be merciful. The truth can also destroy if it hides itself behind a lie."

"I became the truth you wanted me to be," said La Tour

Akka considered this. This man spoke the truth. And thus revealed the lie.

"I have been *amghar n-ufella* for ten years," Akka intoned sharply, with Addi translating. "The *Iroumin* were moving from several corners of Siba when I was elected. They killed, conquered, bribed, marched or crawled over every obstacle. Setting tribe on tribe. They want me gone, like the last large rock in a fine garden. But I will not go. Nor be humiliated. I will die first."

"I understand. I do not take that away from you, nor want you disgraced. And as you have surely seen, I do not want you dead either," La Tour replied submissively.

"Stand up."

"You know I cannot."

"If you were Sidi Jilani, you would."

"I have done much that he would have, just in a different way." LaTour's words grew softer. "Your people have been saved," he beseeched.

"We do not know that."

"That is the truth of this moment. You said it yourself."

"The other truth—La Tour—is that this is a grave breach of faith,"Akka replied.

He felt his other, less tolerant self rise to challenge this sophistry and emerge in his tone.

"I do not know how you have come to be here. But your actions seem to be perjury before

Allah. We are the victims. I would not tolerate this from any of my people. Worse yet, I . . ."

Akka gazed about as he formulated the words for a severe pronouncement and a conclusion. Kenza held him in a stricken stare with wide, glistening eyes, overwhelmed by what her father was about to imply, not wanting it to be true. A sound escaped from her, a brief whimper not unlike that of an animal suddenly caught in a snare.

La Tour eyed father and daughter in turn. He saw something pass between them that he could not understand, that he faintly believed even they could not fully grasp. Then intolerable pain, fatigue and fear washed over him. He fell back into unconsciousness.

Akka was astounded. Kenza was beguiled by him. Lured by what she could never possess, by a world beyond this one. With this wordless scene he realized that one of the hearts closest to him had come to desire this other, a stranger and a fraud.

Kenza ran out the door, in the grip of impulses she could neither name nor describe. She was a wise young woman, but she had lived her entire life among these people only. This man offered a first glimpse beyond, to mysteries and possibilities far different than this hardscrabble world. Through him she felt vaguely connected to a mysterious light, hoping or believing it would illuminate her own dark and dangerous world. And she wondered if he would describe his core feelings in a similar way. Why else look at her as he had in these past days—as an object of interest, a mirror of desire?

Kenza's distress flew like a signal to Addi. He sorted all possible causes and effects. Acquaintances could withhold few secrets from him; his soul mates, none at all. He was stunned. In turn, Akka noted Addi's unmasked, reflexive reaction. Addi had accurately read Kenza in one complex instant, but in the daily, sometimes lingering visits to Jilani he had failed to see the hoax. Addi would surely have expressed any doubts. Apparently, until yesterday, the keen, devout *amrabt* had been unable or unwilling to be more heedful.

"Addi," Akka said, indicating the man at his feet, " . . . help him."

"But you can, too," the *amrabt* replied. "In your own way."

"I cannot. Yet. Perhaps I never will. Please tell me what you have not before."

Akka strode from the granary into the late afternoon. Russet light bathed the desert horizons and golden hues the peaks. Clouds cast vast shadows upon the terrain. He ascended to the rock near which Jilani had first fallen from the sky, gazing past houses destroyed by *Iroumin* bombs and Ait Atta hands, toward the promontory. He could see the farthest half of the stone field, the ridge and the distant cliffs. He could not quite view the patch of earth where his father had died, or where Aumont almost had. The land, deserted of animals and people, seemed forlorn and almost forbidding in its silence.

* * * * *

Alain Aumont easily followed the tell-tale tracks: a spoor of marching men and horses, overlaid by the hoof prints of more furious horses, all moving east to the Ait Atta stronghold. He and Assu well knew the implications. Aumont imagined a scenario from the patterns in the dirt. Not far ahead a battle raged. Perhaps if he stopped to listen, its horrible signals would tell him he was too late in his feeble rescue attempt. But he did not.

He heard the men before he saw them. Their dispirited march echoed dully downhill toward the mouth of this shallow pass. Alain and Hamou slipped off the track, up a buckled hillock two hundred meters to their left, and dismounted. Aumont could see men, several at a time, crest a small ridge. Minutes later a section of hollow-eyed soldiers appeared, ahead of the main body, alertly scanning the rocks above the trail. The silent snake of a column came into view. Some were walking wounded; others angry; all exhausted and perplexed and clearly without the prize of victory.

The last point men and the first of the regiment passed before Aumont and Hamou. Alain strained to see unit designations upon the uniforms but was too far away. The unit flags emerged into view, seeming to float above the rocks unattached, airborne.

A Sergeant helped another bear a corpse upon a litter. They were followed by a dreadful line of other fellows struggling with such wreckage, and still more with bloody men in shock or pain, and all, whether upright or near-dead, in dejection.

The scene was baroque, a somber parade of bloody wraiths. *Who are they?* As he silently posed the question, he saw Colonel Rochet riding beside a color-bearer, head pitched low, jaws clenched like furrowed rocks, eyes unblinking, and looking like a man who at that moment would gladly trade the life he had for any other.

* * * * *

"There is nothing that I have not told you," Addi said to the men. Amnay and Ousaïd looked on. "If now he is different than what you would like—that he be one of us, who belongs among us—we cannot forget that until just hours ago, he acted as what he had appeared to be. Do you understand?"

"Yes, certainly," Akka replied. "Jilani by another name."

"And because we did not foresee *this* man also does not make him a lie or a liar. There are reasons behind reasons. We can question the man, but what he has wrought in these days and hours is very plain. The prophesy said he would save us, and so he has."

"But at what cost to our dignity?" Akka retorted. "A murdering thief who randomly gives his loot to the poor is still a murdering thief. He is not absolved. And the poor are tainted by what they receive from him."

Addi replied. "Soon, or eventually, you must consider abandoning the village. We are too vulnerable here. What the enemy did not accomplish, their flying machines very well might."

"Where would we go? We cannot move higher. And lower means towards them."

"Perhaps we can revisit the Glaouis."

"Thalmi is a ward of the French, who grant him guns and power. I will never add my strength to that of a coward and a prostitute."

"Perhaps you have only one possible solution," Addi said sagely, pointing out of the house toward the granary. The gesture was clear: the man who was not Jilani must live. "No saint, but perhaps an emissary," the *amrabt* responded like a born diplomat.

"Bring him here and make him well," Akka said after an interval. "I promise nothing. But now that perhaps we can understand each other without a veil of mystery and deceit, we can learn better how to use his fighting spirit."

Dark water boiled in a pot at a hearth. Addi dropped herbs into it from a selection upon the table. The unconscious Frenchman was carried on a blanket held at each corner into the intact section of Akka's *igherm* and placed on a straw mat atop a pallet of reeds. From the corner, Akka noted the resemblance of the scene—the position of the players, the colors of the room—to the arrival of his father's corpse, and to the ministrations of Aumont.

"Remove his clothing," Addi directed Hada and Hejjou. Kenza knelt beside the mat with a supply of hot wet poultices in a bowl.

They peeled from him the white *tajjelabith*, the symbol and the armor of Jilani. Beneath, a small pouch was slung over one shoulder. They removed his boots and slipped off the bloody, tattered pants. Out tumbled a watch and chain. It fell to the earthen floor with a plinking murmur that seized everyone's attention. Grasping the golden object, Kenza peered at the burnished case, brushed it with her fingertips, and turned it over to regard the alien markings engraved on the rear plate. She inverted the item again and depressed a tiny clasp. The front cover sprung elegantly open and the watch emitted a faint, brief mechanical melody. After a moment, Addi held out his hand for the heirloom.

They peered at the ugly jagged holes through the left mid-thigh. The blood around it was again brown and crusty, and within it the tissue had coagulated into a moist, pulpy mass. The bullet had bypassed bone but nicked the main artery; blood had gushed from the entry and exit. The lower leg had a gray-blue tinge, a sure sign of low circulation. Addi did not seem concerned. Perhaps it appeared worse than it actually was.

Kenza removed the Frenchman's pouch, Hada and Hejjou his shirt. All five of them were puzzled to see a wide band of cloth about his left chest, under the arm, over the shoulder and around his neck, firmly tied so as to cover and cushion the skin. Hada unwrapped him. The women gasped at the sudden sight of sickly, speckled patches of flesh.

Akka did not panic; rather, he assessed this new development in an almost clinical manner. He glanced at Addi. Here lay a man, nearly naked and utterly at their mercy. Did he have any more secrets to reveal?

"*Taddoute*," Hejjou said the Tamazight word for leprosy in a tone of revulsion and compassion.

"First we must cleanse the bullet wound," Addi pointedly reminded them. Mother and daughter proceeded to do so with the poultices.

"Now, Kenza and Hada, lift the sheet from the pot," Akka instructed.

With two long sticks the women removed a swath of sodden muslin from the steaming vat. Addi and Hada rolled La Tour onto his side. With the ease of a ritual performed many times for those among them, the sheet bearers opened the cloth and lay it lengthwise alongside the mat. Addi rolled the limp form onto it. He sprinkled powders evenly onto the body and thickly applied a yellow granular mélange to the wound. He rested his fingers near it for a long moment, then pulled the excess of heavy cloth over the patient and covered him with a blanket. It looked vaguely like the death bed of a king.

Kenza and Hada ladled steaming water into a large second pot and placed there swatches of clean fabric. In a while they would cool to a therapeutic temperature.

Addi began to chant, as a summon to a sacred light visible only to him. Soon he seemed in ecstasy, a state in which to him all life was the same, where the barriers of humanity had no relevance. The anthem went on for nearly an hour, most often in a faint whisper, at times rising quickly to a deep-toned solo before falling again.

He stopped, emerged from his trance, and nodded at Kenza and Hada. He and Akka drew the blanket from La Tour's form as Kenza lifted more fabric from the vat as they squeezed steaming water across the body. The *amrabt* flipped the blanket over him again.

This continued for two hours, until dark: Addi chanted, and then peeled away the blanket. Hada replaced the bandage, Kenza poured hot water over the body, and the *amrabt* replaced the blanket. The herbs and the heat together were to spur internal reactions. The warmth elevated La Tour's circulation, the sweat opened his skin, and both processes would carry the remedies into his system. The chanting invoked laws higher than the mechanisms of human biology.

Weeping cut through the night. Akka exited the *igherm* to comfort grieving kin. Men recited prayers for the dead while women keened in a broken chorus.

Kenza tuned out this pitiful music. Addi removed the blanket once more, in a manner that suggested this would be the last for now. In the lamplight she saw that the leg flesh below the wound had restored itself from blood-starved blue. Addi prepared a thick bandage of clean cloth. He set the leg above it, piled the fabric under the exit wound with a wet clump of herbs, capped the entry with more, and loosely wrapped the thigh.

Akka returned and knelt beside the *amrabt*. In several minutes, the *amghar* put a hand over the thigh and Addi reached out to the area of blanket under which was the leprosy. They sat there, unmoving and nearly expressionless, for many minutes. The three women, kneeling about the tableau, were equally rapt. Shortly, Hejjou closed her eyes and dozed, but Kenza and Hada remained awake.

Except for the few caregivers in the granary, most of the exhausted village was long since asleep. Silence reigned. The hearth fire began to wane again. Hada refueled it with the kindling beside the flames. Oddly, though the night temperature had fallen to a chill, within the hut it seemed to rise. There was a strange, almost palpable energy, bringing pervasive warmth not entirely attributable to the fire, hot water vats and six bodies.

Addi and Akka had entered a trance, and most likely were unaware of Kenza. She leaned forward, tilting closer to her father, the holy man and the patient. She was amazed to feel her face enter a zone of warmth, as if into a ray of sun. She withdrew so as not to disturb the spiritual or supernatural forces at work. She gazed at her father and the *amrabt*. Their visages suggested minds locked in a waking dream, close and yet far away, in tandem channeling a vigorous, invisible current. Kenza held her arm out, across a margin of warm energy that she imagined was a sweet liquid she could taste if properly guided.

She removed her hand; as she did the sensation, and the image that came with it, vanished. In moments she became drowsy and lay down on the floor beside the Frenchman, on the threshold of the strange warmth. Thoughts faded and time dissolved.

Kenza awoke several hours later beside La Tour's undamaged leg. It was still dark. She saw no others in the flickering lamplight. She was alone with him. Startled, Kenza quickly resumed the watchful kneeling position she had been in before falling asleep. It seemed as if no time had passed. Perhaps so, but it was enough for the spell to be broken, for her father and Addi, Hada and Hejjou to leave. Wondering if the last few hours had been nothing but a dream, Kenza rose and passed from the *igherm* toward the granary.

Kenza stood in the doorway, cast in deep shadows by two lamps, watching Addi and her father comfort and heal the wounded. Everyone had known hardship all their lives, and by equal measure were inured to suffering. Some of them even saw the discomfort as a sign of God's compassion. They were in pain because God so respected their bravery, that He let them live. They were happy to know that the righteous defense of their homes had been awarded with God's approval through anguish that would remind them to be good.

Far to the side were two of Rehou's rogues. One was unconscious and near death, the other bound, awake, wounded but alive, and in apparent dismay; perhaps realizing that the structure in which he lay, so tantalizing to the gold-lust attackers from afar that dawn, was but a granary, and depleted at that, and no vault of plundered Saadian treasure.

Kenza could see that her father and Addi were waning. The candles of their vigor had been burning intensely for hours, and by now were nearly extinguished. Addi ground to a halt and rested among the men, within several paces of where he had impaled Rehou Khoussaila. That fight to the death in this very place seemed not to trouble the *amrabt* in the least. Not bothering to find a blanket, he was asleep in seconds. And Akka, deep within himself, did not notice Kenza's presence. He sat down to rest on the barley sacks. This pause had slowed his momentum. He fell back on the coarse sacks of grain and closed his eyes. As Kenza covered Father with a blanket, so did an attending woman place one over Addi.

Kenza returned to wait upon La Tour, as she knew Father would want her to do.

At dawn the Frenchman was in fever. He twitched with small convulsions. Beads of sweat erupted on his face. He mumbled incoherently through clenched teeth in a fitful sleep, as if in dreams he was speaking syllables to himself without a tongue.

Kenza watched with alarm. She removed the wet, lukewarm body wrap and recovered his shivering form with several blankets. She had hoped that the intensive ministrations through early this morning would have borne the man from danger. Every so often, the Frenchman uttered a comprehensible fragment in a disjointed stream of language, Tamazight to French to Arabic.

Addi entered to monitor the patient. He did not seem alarmed.

An hour later, still alone with La Tour, Kenza awoke from a light sleep. She inadvertently brushed the Frenchman's leg. She gazed about the hut room, and then looked at him. He was awake and staring back at her with wide eyes that blinked just once. She was taken aback at this abrupt change in status, as if she had seen a *djen*.

"Am I that frightening?" he said in French.

Kenza did not respond, except to hasten to the water jar and pour a cup.

"*Aman*," she said. Water.

His lips were dry from dehydration, but his skin was no longer clammy from shock. He grasped her wrist with a self-assured firmness as she placed the cup to his lips. It was not just for the sake of guiding the water, but for touching her without pretension.

"*Comment vous appelez-vous?*" Kenza asked softly.

He looked at her like a child would gaze up to a beloved mother who had caught him in a minor lie: contrite but confident he would not be punished, that he would share the secret in exchange for her understanding. It took a moment to form his name, as he had not identified himself by voice in some time. Even then, he was reluctant to utter it, for this was one of the last barriers and thresholds before officially rejoining the human race.

"Jean-Michel La Tour." He lightly squeezed her hand to raise the water again.

"*Tres bien*," she said and complied.

"I am sorry you have not heard it before now," he said after a cool mouthful.

Kenza did not respond. Because she did not comprehend. But she smiled like the first rays of sunshine after a storm. "How do you feel?"

"I am much better. Remarkably better." And he thought about why as he sensed his body for a long moment. "Strangely so. How many days have I been unconscious?"

Kenza intuited his question, and waved a forefinger which she hoped would indicate yesterday. She knew what he was thinking.

"Last *night*?" he marveled. "The battle was just yesterday?"

"Yes."

"But I was badly wounded. I feel too well to have been shot down just yesterday."

Kenza was again silent, but seeming to sense the gist. Her typically winsome expression offered no clue.

"Where is Akka Ahêddây? Or the *amrabt*?"

Kenza pointed out the door, toward the granary.

"Do not heal too quickly," Kenza said in poor French with some worrisome gravity.

"Why? Akka would only kill a well man?" La Tour replied in a half-joking tone.

Kenza turned her sober face away. He realized his words had revealed an unpleasant fact. And that she was dismayed at his misperception.

"Good Lord," he muttered softly. She seemed to care that he may be about to die. La Tour felt fear, but little resentment. He could hardly blame them for their outrage.

La Tour gazed at Kenza, and she at him. He tried to cast a spell, borne of memories of his beloved *grand-père et ami* who would elicit this prayer from him:

"Rejoice, young man," he slowly recited, "and let your heart cheer you in the days of your youth; walk in the ways of your heart and the sight of your eyes. But know that for all these things God will bring you into judgment."

Kenza understood almost none of these words, but was rapt at every one of them.

"Remove vexation from your . . ."

Akka Ahêddây appeared in the doorway like a ghost unwilling to haunt but unable to leave. La Tour stopped the rote Ecclesiastes. From behind Akka another man emerged.

Alain Aumont. He wore riding boots and a long gray woolen coat. La Tour was sure he must be hallucinating; having seen no such likeness in many days, in recent hours and minutes he had concluded that he never would again.

Alain stood over him. His countenance evolved from a furrowed brow of brotherly concern, to calm and neutral reflection, to a generous smile. *A most fabulous fellow, La Tour thought in a daze. He has come all this way and seems so sincere about my welfare.*

"Good morning, Jean-Michel La Tour," Aumont began with startling directness. "I hear that you have quite a story to tell. You are one of two reasons they did not bomb this village to pieces. Truth be told, I am the second. In this regard, under the watchful eyes of Akka Ahêddây, perhaps we can help each other a great deal."

TWENTY

COUNSEL

L̲a Tour blinked in disbelief. Another ladder of deliverance had fallen from the sky.

"Hello, old friend," said the familiar face and voice.

La Tour could only stare and nod, but he felt suffused with equal parts joy, gratitude, and confusion.

"A month ago we were soldier comrades of the same nation," said Aumont. "Now we are expatriates, and I, a kind of secular priest. I find that my first good work is you. Several days ago I told an acquaintance of ours the part of this strange tale that I knew. He is a profiteer, but a good man, and he accepted every word as true."

"As you are a righteous man, sir, I would expect so," La Tour retorted.

"Here you are, fresh from the Légion, in a most unusual predicament . . ."

"That is certain," La Tour replied. "These people are very angry with me. I don't know that I will get out of this village or Maroc. Almost no matter. I would not live one hour among our own people."

"Akka and I have discussed this," Aumont replied. "On balance, the fellow agrees that it is better you should survive as a fool than die a wise man."

"My plight in short form," La Tour said. "I fell from a plane and these people proclaimed me holy. So I accepted their love to live. Reject it and die. Rather simple, yes?"

"Yes. But deception for any reason always muddies the equation, don't you think?"

La Tour skirted the question to ask his own. "How did *you* come to be here?"

"I have returned to repay a favor, to help save Ahêddây and you from the dogs of war. A bit late, it seems, as you have already done much of the saving. I will share my story, and you yours. Now, tell me, *u*s, are you a Berber saint or an infidel demon?"

"Perhaps both. Without me the Ait Atta would be dead. And the reverse is equally true. I dropped in at the exact moment they were hoping, praying, for someone who matched my description. They so eager, and me so desperate. We were the perfect match."

"In his fierce way, Akka is grateful. If he could, he would shoot you dead and then resurrect you."

"I suppose that is a reluctant compliment."

"But most sincere. Since you have saved his people and his daughter and wife, all is almost forgiven."

"*Almost?* Have you explained all this to him?"

"Oh, yes. He waits so that you can explain it again. Please do so now."

Jean-Michel turned his head to the doorway where still stood Akka n-Ali in a fresh *burnoos* with an expression of stern but softening concern.

"I have been lying here for some time and I should like to sit up properly."

Alain folded a thick blanket against the wall and helped Jean-Michel ease into a sitting position. La Tour was astonished at the relative comfort of his movement so soon after sustaining the wound.

"I feel . . . almost wonderful. How is it so?"

"That is something only the men with the power may tell you," Aumont replied. "And they will not. Cannot. It is an inexpressible pact between them and their God."

In a jolt of remembrance, Jean-Michel reached to his neck and arm. His fingers discovered newly restored flesh.

"Good Lord . . ."

"Yes indeed. Your affliction is almost gone."

"How did you know?"

"I rode in before dawn. Akka has related everything he knows. Remember that we infidels want to kill and conquer these people because of their so-called barbaric customs. But they know more. Much more."

"My leg was damn near shot off."

"Wait a few more days. You'll be walking." Alain gestured for Akka. The chief stepped forward in a gracious but guarded manner, towering over both of them.

Lightly grasping Addi by the arm, Akka n-Ali escorted Addi Yacoub into the *igherm*, more as a respectful formality than a guide. Hada followed with a kettle of tea. She set four cups upon a tray set on the hard dirt floor near La Tour, and into them deftly and ceremoniously poured sweet green-amber *atai benaanaa*. Sensing that words were unnecessary, the *amrabt* was silent. But he glowed like a wise, blithe spirit beside Akka. Addi knelt to La Tour's left, Akka at the end of the pallet, near the tray, and Alain to his right. The quartet formed an equidistant square. Now they were complete.

Kenza took up the tray and gracefully offered the tea to her father, then to Addi with a whisper, walked it to Alain, and lastly, with blushing deference, held out the last cup to Jean-Michel. Then Akka n-Ali and Hada departed.

For an expansive moment no one spoke. La Tour was awash in emotion.

"What do I say?" he asked Aumont. "What *can* I say?"

"They are as astonished as you," Alain replied. "Sidi Jilani you are not, but you have performed that role. Allah has willed it. Having discussed it among themselves and with me as best we can, they desire to give you your life. And whatever else they can."

"I should like answers. How do they heal this way?" He pushed away the blanket to inspect his leg. The wound appeared more grievous than it felt.

"Addi Yacoub is from an ancient race of mystics, fewer any more in this world. They focus your natural energy and God's love. Not many ailments or injuries can resist that combination. I experienced it myself. Look . . ." He pulled up his *gandourah* to display a large red welt in his side. "Otherwise likely fatal."

Addi interjected, in French. "What Allah does not want He does not take. And He did not want you yet. We had the power to heal your body. The heart is up to you."

Alain continued. "The Lord speaks in mysterious ways, and he has chosen them as His voice. I shall tell you that story now . . ."

Aumont recounted his own experience here three weeks ago, spinning a rapt narrative of war and religion, a bandit's bullet, Graves the black market runner, and himself.

"When I left," Alain recounted, "Akka gave me this." He held up the silver piece. "It was this token, and seeing you here that day, and Akka's photograph in a newspaper, that compelled me back here. I have spoken to them about your leaving."

"I should like that as soon as possible. I am desperate for a return to home. My mother is very ill."

The *amrabt* displayed great sympathy. Addi and Akka bowed their heads in a brief prayer, which neither Alain nor Jean-Michel understood.

"I have read the letter from your brother. I did not mean to pry, but it seemed . . ."

"Quite alright, sir. I am weary of secrets. I have no more to keep."

Aumont poured more tea. He gestured for Akka and the *amrabt* to settle into La Tour's tale. "Then tell us of your life to the point you fell here. That is the greatest secret."

La Tour began with the episodes in Marrakech: Rochet and Mirvais and the abductions. He segued past the combat. To his captivity and discovering the leprosy. His scene with Mirvais in the infirmary. Vallée de l'Enfer. His crazed escape. To the village, Akka n-Ali, and everything to the moment of his wound.

Akka spoke a stream of Tamazight to Addi, who translated it to French.

La Tour was elated. "Akka Ahêddây will grant me freedom, two guides and a letter of passage. What may I give him in return?"

"*We* must act to protect the sovereignty of these people," Alain asserted. "I have told Akka n-Ali that he must make no more attacks. Then we can do what Ait Atta resistance has not. Force the Administration to offer a truce and a treaty to end this struggle."

"And he agrees to this?" La Tour asked Aumont.

"I am tired of war," Akka said in Tamazight. "*We* are tired of it. The cost is too high when we go so close to the abyss and the loss of all. If not for you, Insh'Allah, we would have fallen. We will have peace, at a bargain if we keep our land and our dignity."

These incisive, candid words ushered in more silence.

"I should like to offer another bargain," La Tour finally. Ahêddây's words presented an opening too good to let pass. He could scarcely believe the leap he was about to take. He prayed it would not be perceived as an insult, but rather a form of praise and respect. "One that may bring the kind of peace you never saw in your dreams."

Addi smiled like the sole possessor of a knowing, cheerful intuition who arrives at the key to a puzzle of words before anyone else. Akka peered curiously at his friend, as if wondering why he had been omitted from this small circle of knowledge. Or, maybe he remained fully within it. Noting the subtle change in La Tour's tenor, and recalling his previous conversations with Akka n-Ali about the mystery guest, he re-established with Addi the connection of secret language and soul. Akka reflected, and then he knew.

La Tour waited a moment before launching the key words.

"I am enchanted by your daughter," he declared. "I feel that I could love her. That I already do. I should like you to think on that."

Alain was startled. Addi translated. Akka's cast was a compound of bliss, wistfulness, and irritation.

"That is most bold," Alain whispered. "Are you not somewhat premature?"

"Have I done wrong? Broken some taboo?"

"But you are from two completely different worlds."

"I will be the same person they have known. They will just *think* of me differently. As a man, not a savior. I certainly prefer that."

"I should hope so. But perhaps *they* prefer that you just go away."

La Tour was addled by this prospect, the way one would be by a dust mote in the eye or sudden exposure to a frigid wind. And he saw that his hours here, as god or guest, visitor or soldier, were about to end. He no longer had a place, and they no longer needed him. La Tour would almost feel homesick; the meaning of the word *France* seemed distant in his emotional frame, rather than a world he was eager to re-embrace.

Addi and Akka retreated to a corner, near the doorway.

"I must go," La Tour continued. "Home. But when I return, as I intend . . ."

"Listen carefully," said Aumont. "A Berber daughter, and a Berber sheik's daughter, is a soul bond. She is not only blood, but property. This is asking Akka to give *you* a piece of himself. Do you realize that you suggest progression from an enemy to a profound liar to a blasphemer to his son-in-law? Think clearly."

"Akka n-Ali made my life bright when I may well have gone mad, shed my *tajjelabith* and gotten shot dead. Kenza's smile and kindness were sent to me by heaven. May God strike me down if I lie."

La Tour gazed at Addi and Akka. He listened quietly to their soft exchange in packets of syllables, observing verbal and facial shorthand peculiar to a long partnership in grave situations. War and looming annihilation were familiar to them. But, by their reactions, this was a very strange animal, a singing camel or an *adjnun* from the caves. An *Aroumi* infidel asking to wed a Berber princess suggested a cloud of change, of loss; the mere possibility of parting with his daughter in this way caused Akka's facade to crack. La Tour had a brief glimpse of a man whose armor of faith was weakened by fear.

"Even if Akka wanted to, he may not be able to meet your request," Alain soberly said. "Akka n-Ali has pledged Kenza to Brka. These people grasp their traditions with an iron hand."

"I admire that," La Tour responded. "But he should ask Kenza if . . ."

"He does not have to ask her anything," Alain asserted. "Kenza must listen. But you have made a strong impression on her. In these extraordinary circumstances you expressed wisdom, in spite of yourself, I imagine. They are hosts and we are guests, at their discretion. It is best that we offer something of substance before we ask an intimate question."

"I already have asked it."

"Not formally. The bride must have a dowry. The groom must bring the father a gift. To assure happy union."

"I have nothing. Nothing but several thousand francs."

"We already have what Akka wants. The ability to help his people live in peace."

"We are not diplomats!"

"The wheel for saving this place and the Ait Atta is in motion," he said to La Tour as Akka listened. "You can help plan strategy by telling me all that happened here.

"Before leaving Marrakech," Aumont continued, "I sent an anonymous dispatch to an attaché that an unidentified envoy—me—known to Akka Ahêddây was on an unauthorized mission of peace. The note stressed that bombing or renewed attacks would add to the fiasco. In a true leap of faith, perhaps a moment of my very own prophesy, I declared that the Ait Atta were holding many Légion prisoners. Imagine my surprise to learn that

Taboulmant had even survived, much less that Akka had indeed captured thirty Légionnaires. For credibility, I brazenly invoked an uncle, who is a comte and an old acquaintance of Foreign Ministry counselor Briand. All of them must surely be mystified . . . brilliant timing, all this. A rider followed me here with a reply," Aumont said, holding out a message.

"Command received the letter just after the assault began. An immediate inquiry confirmed that Rochet and Mirvais were off on an unsanctioned march. As for our war, command welcomes this emissary to the Ait Atta—they want to know who he is, ha!—and state that for now actions against Akka will be suspended. I guess old Uncle Gaston has some respect. Furthermore, they do not know you are here. Your name has not been spoken. That must remain so."

Aumont sent the courier back to Azilal with a somewhat cryptic note. *"15 May. We are delayed. Expect us soon. Need plane. Human cargo. High confidentiality. As of this date, ready in five days. Please send immediate response. Will contact upon receipt."*

The message prompted anxiously waiting Christian Graves to make several discreet inquiries. A day later he returned an affirmative message with a rough plan for rendezvous.

TWENTY-ONE:

HOME

T he sun arced across a cobalt sky. Jean-Michel noted the patch of flowers beyond the doorway, a hint of the May bounty abloom in Maroc. He fancied the plateau, a mystical island of harmony whose dwellers had been predestined for some divine scenario. Eager to pace in the sunlight and at last depart, he progressed from a half-dead cripple to a lively man and tried to reconcile his wound to a process that surpassed common healing arts.

La Tour watched over several days as the houses torn apart during the battle were rebuilt. The use of the Légion prisoners was an ironic and ingenious solution. Akka, however, postponed repairs to his own humble and ruptured palace so that La Tour would not be disturbed. That is, seen by the Légionnaires.

The *aggrawe*—Akka, Addi, Lahcen and others—conferred with Alain for hours, explaining events since the arrival of "Jilani," and gaining more understanding of them. La Tour knew they would, and when they had; he could feel and almost see the distance between himself and they, like intimate strangers who knew mutual secrets but dared not speak of them. Aumont and the Ait Atta bridged gaps of culture and comprehension. He strongly advised Akka to accept a reasonable peace. And as a practical matter of virtue and decency, they agreed this would have to include resolving the issue of La Tour, who could not simply be cast away. How and where to set him free? Lastly, the Légionnaires held in the cave feared for their lives

"Akka n-Ali," Alain said, "I can prepare letters of reason to the authorities. They may agree to your independence if you abide by the Pasha and the French. You will not attack them any more. In return, they will not attack you."

The convoluted politics of Maroc were subject to sudden, radical shifts. Guarantees were few, but Alain hoped his hasty and tenuous efforts could lead to a treaty.

"We will not make war again," Akka replied firmly. "But we will defend. And we will not surrender our weapons. And we want no *Iroumin* here. Except you."

"And La Tour?"

Akka was silent but he smiled. That was sufficient. Then he offered: "I would like you to make sure he gets safely to his next destination. I will help. Never have I known a man who one day so deserved to die but, four dawns later, is so completely forgiven. For a good reason Allah desires him to live. And we will abide that desire."

"We both thank you. I am making plans for La Tour," Aumont replied. "All that remains is for him to be well enough for travel. And that must be soon, within days."

Alain received the response from Graves the next morning. But the first phase of smuggling La Tour homeward would rely upon Akka Ahêddây.

Addi appeared once or twice a day, usually with Hada, to monitor La Tour's healing. The more satisfied he was, the briefer the visit. Akka was seldom seen, and the Frenchmen were idle. Alain read from a Bible, silently, and aloud to La Tour. In turn, La Tour more fully recounted his travels.

On the morning of the fourth day, Kenza she peeked in at them. La Tour beheld the true smile in her cream-and-cinnamon skin beneath luxuriant raven hair, and her heart's hard-won but irrepressible joy.

A moment later Kenza was gone.

On this day, too, Jean-Michel proclaimed himself ready to walk.

"I did not almost die to lay here without living!"

The wobbly marionette upon makeshift crutches trailed his comrade outside to the sunny terrace, in the same spot where that night last week he had been so shocked to see Alain from afar. A curious crowd gathered, quite different than the reverent throng watching after his plunge from the metal sky bird. Now they were interested in greeting him and in marveling at the holy healing work of their leaders. Despite his pain, La Tour fixed a humble grin, nodding affably to fellow warriors among them.

Later in private, Aumont related his plan to La Tour. "We leave tomorrow night for Azilal. My friend will truck us to the plane, on to Marrakech, and by some means to Marseille. All the way home, no one must identify you. Hide your injury as you can. If anyone asks, say that an Arab Sebbah shot you in Erfoud. I will accompany you and convince the officials. I can arrange to have your family waiting in Provence."

"I prefer to arrive home unannounced," said Jean-Michel, flushed with excitement that this was finally coming to pass. "But thank you, sir," he offered wholeheartedly. "Without you, I would be doomed. For a man of medicine and of the cloth you have a fine talent for intrigue."

Toward sunset, four fine horses were saddled and fitted with regalia, and two mules laden with supplies. Word spread that the guests would be leaving. The populace departed work in the fields or rebuilding homes or repairing an irrigation ditch and began to gather at the heart of the *timizar*. It was to be a departure fit for a conquering king.

Akka Ahêddây entered his home-turned-hospice with quiet, ceremonious dignity. La Tour and Aumont gave the amghar *their earnest attention as he knelt before them. And then Akka uttered in slow but passable French:*

"But they who wait for the Lord . . . shall renew their strength, they shall mount with wings like eagles . . ."

La Tour gaped at Aumont, who was alight at these heartfelt words from the Word.

"Isaiah, 40:31," Aumont said to enlighten La Tour. "That is what I quoted when Akka's men hauled into this village for trial two of the three outlaws who shot me."

Akka continued, now from the Qur'an: "Biss me Allah. 'Be not weary and faint-hearted, crying for peace, when you should be uppermost: for

Allah is with you, and will never put you in loss for your good deeds.'
Surah 47, Muhammad the Prophet."

Akka rose, then bowed, and having delivered his gift, he smiled and
departed.

Moments later, the Frenchmen emerged from the *igherm*. A raw but
lively *nouba*—a band of strings, woodwinds and percussion—struck up
and shortly joined by four female singers. The lyrics were durable stanzas
of praise and farewell and honor.

Two escorts—Brka and Hani—led them to the horses. Everyone
beamed with joy. Knowing that nothing would ever again be as it was,
that there would be no untainted return to a simple life, no one cheered
or waved, but all smiled.

Mimoun, his cruel facial wound quickly healing, offered the reins
of Sidi to his brother Brka. The spirited horse bobbed and pranced and
tossed its mane. Still enfeebled by his bullet-torn lung, Haj observed from
a chair beside his mostly rebuilt house. The happiness and honor he felt
for his courageous sons more than eased any discomfort. Addi Yacoub had
generously provided great care for him body and soul. Haj was grateful
for a faster recovery because the villagers had suddenly placed many
orders for pottery.

Akka n-Ali and Alain Aumont embraced, kissing the other's cheeks
in brotherly gratitude for recent days, and of hope for the future. Lahcen
and Addi stood by to translate.

"Many men of my country will become honorable," Alain said,
"when they learn to swallow their pride and proclaim it delicious. I think
we can convince them you are an enemy they would better convert than
conquer."

La Tour stood next to his horse, a well-appointed and handsome roan,
and savored the delight of the scene. These might be his last moments
here. Akka had not responded to his declaration of interest in Kenza. But
he agreed with Alain that the chief must believe peace was at hand before
consenting to such a great departure from tradition. If Kenza's blithe
expression was any guide, the *amghar* had discussed the prospect with
her. La Tour took the absence of an explicit "no" from either of them to
be a tacit "maybe."

He scanned the crowd, bowing his head in humble respect, all but beseeching forgiveness for his days of falsehood. In some, La Tour saw uncertainty or lingering resentment at his theft of a holy mantle and the affront of Addi and their chief. On impulse, to demonstrate contrition he limped to a vaguely sullen, stooped elderly man in a worn turban; his sad eyes seemed to retain some offense at the masquerade. La Tour was not given to dramatic displays, but with effort, he knelt down, a gesture that invited either pardon or contempt. The musicians stopped playing; a hush fell over all. How the man responded would likely determine the tenor of his leave-taking, and if he should ever be truly welcome here again. The old fellow was surprised—but he could not embarrass anyone, including himself, by expressing disdain. Both men were frozen. Seconds passed, and then the graybeard grasped the Frenchman's shoulders and exclaimed: *"Vive Jilani!"*

A rhapsody rose from all. La Tour embraced him cheek to cheek, in the Berber way, shook his hand in the French manner, and clapped him on the back for good measure.

"You should be an ambassador!" Alain shouted. "You certainly have the knack!"

Addi Yacoub seemed to float to La Tour, as always amazed and unnerved that the blind man could thread a route with his inner, third eye. Akka walked behind him, bearing two flat packages of plain cloth loosely tied with cord. Akka offered the parcels to La Tour and bid him to open them. The top one held a clean Légion uniform, that of a Sergeant. La Tour wondered morbidly if it had belonged to one of the few fatalities not carried off the field. But it was bloodless, and he realized it was for him to wear, a thoughtful, or sly, provision of a viable disguise for wherever he should go in Maroc, as his own uniform was a rag.

In the second parcel, standing out against the drab wrapping fabric was a new, white, light woolen *tajjelabith*. La Tour rejoiced. He unfurled the garment and indicated that Alain should hold it while he peeled off the old one. La Tour eagerly donned the gleaming, custom-made robe. The villagers thrilled to the symbolic rite.

Hani reached into the leather pouch slung on his shoulder. *"Haj le potier,"* he said, and grasped an exquisitely painted jar, capped with a wooden stopper and wax. Inside was water.

La Tour glanced at Kenza, who stepped forward from the singers. She opened a hand; in it was a freshly carved cedar top depicting a water jar, an airplane, binoculars, and a falcon equally spaced around the body. She passed it to his fingers.

"So you don't fall out of sight and into trouble," she said warmly.

Addi Yacoub stepped into the middle of the crowd to speak. The buzzing crowd fell into silence. He spoke in Berber, then in French.

"Biss me Allah. 'Whoever works righteousness, man or woman, and has Faith. Verily, to him, we will give a new Life, a life that is good and pure, and We will bestow on such their reward according to the best of their actions.' Surah 16:97, Nahl."

Addi finished, and Akka beside him said,

"Return to your world. When you have completed your tasks there, to your needs and to ours which you agree to represent, you are welcome to return. You will enter here in peace and security."

Hani helped La Tour to mount his horse, which he did with small discomfort and a large smile. So as not to prolong the scene, Akka waved for Brka and Hani to lead the *Irmounin* off. Villagers held torches to illuminate their twilight passage along the stream, across the fields toward the battle ravines. The red-purple sunset sky and the golden glows of the dancing fires bathed all in a heavenly light. The horses and riders paraded through a half-kilometer concourse of murmuring people, vocal well-wishers, tightly smiling men holding out five fingers, curious bobbing children, women with hands over their hearts.

The journey began from the simple pis homes, on a northwesterly course toward Azilal, and another waiting airplane.

The steady pilgrimage into the night and the next day was uneventful. Brka and Hani were in safe territory through Tizi n 'Tharramt, between Azourki and Aloui, to the edge of Ait Isha land at Tizi n 'Balek. There, they paid a toll for tazttat *and entered the protection of a chief who respected them for their raids on French posts to the west. Anyone attempting to harm them would be due no mercy. The Ait Isha clans were intrigued by the proud Bou Iknifen guiding two* Iroumin *as if they were royalty. But under Allah's sky, nothing was impossible.*

They traversed the arid heights of the Atlas to the western slopes, where moisture raised fields and flowers. The procession wound past Arhbalous, Ait Mazirt, the old kasbah at Oukerda, into the land of Ait Messat. Another toll was paid and another amghar befriended. Adrar n-Mezgounane loomed ahead. Early in the afternoon of the second day, Hani and Brka stopped to beseech Allah in a vista of brilliant flowers. La Tour removed the garments under his tajjelabith and donned the slightly undersize Légionnaire uniform. In a small rite he buried the cast-offs, then packed the new tajjelabith carefully in the takrabte.

Alain closely watched the ritual, observing Jean-Michel.

"I keep changing uniforms, clothes, horses, houses, directions. Identities. I've yet to get where I want to be, though in each place I become more than who I was and for a while I call it home."

La Tour wondered if his odd fondness for exile was almost strong enough to regret its ending. He was also aflutter at what would be his abrupt, secretive return to Fontaine, in Isère, anticipating the shock of the new or old, the unknown or tragic. Was Mother alive? If so, what had she been told of her son's fate? That her youngest son was missing, or a cowardly deserter in the throes of disease, or dead? His joy to be none of them was best shared in person. Still, his escape remained far from certain.

The Berbers completed their prayers. La Tour refocused on Brka's mood. The typically voluble fellow had so far remained taciturn. Kenza's suitor glanced at him in a manner neither baleful nor benevolent, but always penetrating.

They slept that night under the stars in a ravine cul-de-sac, surrounded by all-enfolding silence. La Tour dreamed intensely, but all he could recall on waking at dawn was a surrealistic bird's view of the village as he plunged from the plane. He heard voices in Tamazight.

"When we take leave of him, no sentiment," Hani said to his comrade. "This is only our duty. He is a friend, but not a brother. And we will see him again, Insh'Allah."

Ambivalent Brka said nothing.

La Tour reached deeply into his new trousers. He extracted the misshapen wad of francs still in his possession. Both Berbers stared in amazement. The amount appeared like more than it was, but it was still a fortune to people accustomed to small exchanges.

"Brka, I respect and honor you. As a fighting man, a defender of your people."

Hani made the translation; Brka bowed in humility.

If you permit me, I should like to make you the present of a fine new saddle, and a second horse, too."

Brka struggled with his pride. The resources for a new mount and the accoutrements he greatly desired would enhance his status. With his desire for Kenza, which in recent days he suspected may not be requited, and with or without the rivalry of La Tour.

Brka looked to Hani for advice. In a moment the carpenter rifleman offered a gentle, smiling nod of assurance. Brka did likewise. Both Berbers nodded in happy tandem.

La Tour reached forward to grasp Brka's hand. First he clasped it in a shake and then turned the palm up and spread it flat. From the collection of money he split off roughly a third of the inch-thick stack of notes, and laid them gently into the callused brown hand.

"When I see you again, I will expect you to own a fine new saddle and steed."

Brka's expression was of sublime wonder, as if a rare bird had flown to him. They remounted for the last few dusty kilometers to Azilal.

They came upon a battered but road-worthy lorry in Azilal. The dust-coated open-bed beast looked peculiar among a medieval tableau of horses, mules, and a camel in the plaza near the hostel and disintegrating *kasbah*. The warm air of early afternoon was pleasant but it also carried a preview of the sweltering heat that a month hence would settle here in the Atlas. Several dogs wandered aimlessly. One woman trekked under a load of barley stalks, and beside her another wore two babies cocooned in a blanket tied over chest and shoulders. Ahead, an ancient bandy-legged water seller clamored for customers by clanking two brass cups. Alain paid several *idrimen* for two helpings. The white-bearded old man poured from a bulging goatskin into copper goblets he detached from a bandoleer. He curiously peered at each of them in turn. Aumont nervously shooed the man away.

At their final gulp, a lone burly Frenchman emerged from the *fondakk*.

"Hello, Christian!"

The Frenchmen embraced with hearty claps on the backs.

"Thank you for coming to the rescue," said Alain with sincere relief.

"You still owe me for a bottle of cognac! Unless you've sworn off drinking," said Christian in a voice made of gravel and cheap booze.

"I have no choice. I can buy from no one but you and the Légion!"

"The pilot is at the plane. Balafré wanted adventure, but he saw troops and grew nervous. By now he will be frantic. I have come to ferry you past the gauntlet. If I can," Christian added uneasily. "These are your Berber friends?" he asked of Hani and Brka.

"Yes. Loyal, intrepid souls. And fine fighting men, God have mercy upon them."

"Hmm. There is fire in their eyes. Many French widows." Christian gazed at La Tour. "And this is the cargo?" he stated in a tone simultaneously proud and cynical. "Bonjour, La Tour. You are the one who helped Alain drink the cognac he owes me for."

"Where is the Army?" Alain inquired, to speed their passage through the town.

"We will see them again to the west. I have a letter from the regional Governor. His credentials and my false itinerary on official letterhead. Waving this paper has helped thus far. However, it mentions only two men. Myself and my pilot."

The water seller re-entered the orbit of the three French and two Berbers, peering in like a curious goat. La Tour more closely regarded his withered features and dog-like eyes.

"Soldiers back soon," the *porteur d'eau* mumbled in inelegant French.

With that, Hani nudged Jean-Michel's arm. Mission accomplished, obligations met, the Berbers were eager to be off. They did not want to waste time here, far from home, prey for angry *Iroumin*.

Jean-Michel and Alain turned to their faithful guides. The pairs of Frenchmen and Ait Atta only bowed, but more deeply than usual. There was no display of emotion. La Tour lifted from the saddle horn the *takrabte* holding his gifts and the remnants of his old uniform. With reins of the now spare horses and pack mules in hand, the Berbers re-mounted their animals and offered broad smiles.

"*Ak iâawen rebbi*," said Hani. Goodbye.

"*Sellem aflan familanch*," said Brka. Say hello to your family.

"*Ak iniaawen rebbi!*" proclaimed Jean-Michel.

"*Ighoudagh rebbi leyagh tougguite*," said Alain. We're blessed that you came to see us off.

Brka and Hani smartly wheeled their horses and the trailing mules toward the majestic Atlas peaks.

"Your guides have the easy way out. Perhaps we have no way out at all." Christian said, heading toward the truck. "We shall see, Mr. La Tour. Or is it Sergeant?"

"Neither. Just Jean-Michel. They want me for that fiasco up there," he said, pointing to the peaks. "Before that, I was in hell. A hole in the ground where I was sent to rot. But I have done nothing wicked or against my conscience. I just want to return home. My family has needed me for over a month. Take me away. I will pay you all I have."

"Alain vouches for you," Christian replied. "But it does not solve the immediate problem. Unable to use the nearby airstrip, Balafré found a suitable alternative. A field near Ait Taguella. But soldiers pass by it to and from the mountains and Beni-Mellal."

Christian yanked back a tarpaulin laid over heavy wooden crates—two of them empty and large enough to hold a man—and beckoned La Tour to clamber up. He did so, and peered back at his Ait Atta comrades far down the road, who turned in their saddles to peer at the receding plaza, at La Tour, and any pursuing enemies.

"Sit under the canvas," Christian commanded. "Alain, you will be atop one of the crates. You look back, and me ahead."

The truck strained over the wretched serpentine road, groaning uphill, jolting down, as comfortable for the passengers as riding a bull.

Christian slowed only to avoid crippling damage. He howled in perverse amusement, probably as he had on his way to Azilal yesterday before the French appeared. He was a true friend to have trekked here in the first place. La Tour glanced to the sky from an aperture in the musty canvas. A bloated, hazy sun floated above a far southwestern ridge. Gray clouds clustered close by to the north.

Christian crawled to a stop on a broad rise; the road was visible far ahead and well behind. Only a brisk breeze broke the utter silence. Several fat raindrops fell from a passing cloud to splatter staccato on the windshield and the canvas. Christian stepped out.

"That is Ait Taguella. The Army is there. I don't know if we can pass them. La Tour, I think you would do well to tramp to the plane. It's only about ten kilometers away. You'll be there in a few hours. Head south around the village, then . . ."

"Good Lord, Christian!" Alain protested. "He can't walk through this country! He's recovering from a bad leg wound! And how will he find his way? Have you put up signs? . . . No, we go to the plane! If it has not already been found! It's not exactly invisible, you know! An Ait Messat tells a French troop or spahi riders, oh, there is a flying machine in my olive grove. What will your man do then?"

La Tour's voice emerged ringing and resolute from beneath the tarpaulin.

"For four . . . long . . . bizarre . . . frightening weeks I have been hanging by a weak thread over a very deep pit. I go homeward to see my mother on her deathbed. Now get to the wheel and drive as if it was your mother, or so help me I will wring your neck."

"Alright. Alright," Christian conceded. "Alain, here are Balafré Guillaume's papers. Forged, of course. Give me yours to hide. And take this bottle of wine. Act like you've been drinking. When we come to the soldiers, we'll banter like characters from Voltaire."

"You have a good friend here, Alain," La Tour observed.

"Say *we* or I turn you over to them," Alain wryly hissed.

"We. We. We."

As Christian was about to resume the driver's seat, faint, rapid hoof beats resounded from back around the bend they had just traversed. Horses were approaching at a gallop. Christian and Alain turned intently toward the clatter.

"La Tour, draw that canvas down around you!"

Then the source revealed itself: Hani and Brka, leading the horses that had been ridden by their charges. The Berbers sharply reined in the mounts, then cut across the view of Christian and Alain into a low field of rocks and grass to juniper trees near a gully. They dismounted and pointed wildly up the road.

Alain again peered in that direction, and chilled to the sight. A short, slow convoy of several vehicles entered a sweeping curve around a crag several kilometers behind. Cantering along on either side were short lines of grandiose spahis, very visible in red.

"Christian . . . !" Alain said, and gesticulated toward the oncoming threat.

Christian trained his binoculars on the cortege, at the brightly-hued pendants bristling on the hood batons. "Shit!" he snarled. "An Agence cretin!"

La Tour peered from beneath the canvas at the approaching column to the rear, and at Alain's indication of the Berber duo on their left.

"They are trying to warn us," La Tour said. "They want me to come to them . . ."

"We can't stay here!" Christian barked. "And we will be stopped ahead!"

The rearward unit was nearing them.

"If you're going, La Tour, go now!" Christian commanded.

The oncoming procession briefly passed from sight. La Tour could not know if the truck was visible from the village below, if he would be seen scooting away. But their sojourn was now caught between the rock of the approaching column and the hard place of any checkpoint or sentries below. It would be far too risky in Ait Taguella; escape from two suspicious groups was unlikely. La Tour struggled from beneath the tarpaulin. Disappointment was heavy, but this was no time to be dejected at the near-miss of liberation.

"Jean-Michel," Alain said with false cheer and a rending sigh, "We can do nothing here. It is best to return to the village. I will guide the pilot."

The prospect of an arduous return, of retreating in order to progress, utterly dismayed him. La Tour commended the former Lieutenant's tactical thinking. However:

"Alain, you don't intend to land a plane on that field? It is scattered with rocks . . ."

"Believe in miracles, Jean-Michel!" Alain shouted. "We are made of them!"

Surprisingly nimble, La Tour dashed over the road to the rocks, toward the trees and his friends who had horses and cunning and complete knowledge of the land. He was a naked infant in the storm.

Neither Alain nor Christian nor Jean-Michel himself saw the lovingly handcrafted top given him by Kenza fall from his takrabte *on the edge of the road.*

Alain sat atop the crates in the truck bed and gripped the rickety side panel as Christian hurtled down the incline. The road ran straight along a rightward colonnade of thick thatches of ash, and past the first mud facades clustered on a low plateau. They needed to be through the guard checkpoint before the column closed behind them.

From the blind, La Tour watched the truck move apace to the village more than a kilometer beyond. He absently prayed aloud: " . . . walk in the ways of your heart and the sight of your eyes. But know that for all these things God will bring you into judgment . . ."

Christian lit a cigarette. The truck ground to a halt before an Armée car, six wary soldiers and a skeptical Lieutenant. The officer slothfully held up his palm—rather like the traditional Berber and Muslim greeting—and walked to the driver's door.

Hani guided his comrades ahead, farther into safe cover from the approaching escort. Gazing back in the other direction, La Tour saw the truck stop at the road guards.

"Sir, where do you come from?" said the officer to Christian.

"Why, Nemours, thank you. And yourself?"

"I mean," the officer sneered, "with this truck."

"We have crawled from a master potter's shop in Ait Mehammed with jars and vases for sale at home and with tiles for Marrakech. And other items of interest."

"You are?"

"Christian le Faure. Working with the Governor's consent. Here are my papers."

"Are you crazy to be crawling out here on this road with all that is going on?"

Christian played dumb. "All of what? I have seen nothing."

"And you there," the officer muttered to seemingly indifferent Alain before opening Christian's proffered identification. "Come here and present yourself."

"Balafré!" Christian bellowed. "Let go of that goddamned wine in a Muslim country and come here to speak with the Sergeant!"

"I am a Lieutenant."

"Excuse me. The Lieutenant wants a word with you!"

Alain rose with feigned annoyance and leaned over the side of the cargo bay.

"It is by your own admission, Christian, that we will not make Marrakech tonight. And so should it rain and we have nowhere to sleep, I will blame my discomfort on you."

"Balafré, you blame everything on me," Christian replied. "I have consorted with many women, any six of whom together complain less than you!"

Several of the Frenchmen laughed. The Lieutenant chuckled.

"Why are you stopping vehicles on this nowhere road, Lieutenant? Is there a fugitive sheik about? Or has the *khalifa* run away with more French gold?"

"We want two Frenchmen for questioning."

"Well, we are two Frenchmen. What would you like to ask us?"

Again the soldiers laughed. But two of them stepped to the rear of the truck and poked at the canvas edge with the barrels of their rifles. Alain pretended not to care.

The Lieutenant turned his attention there.

"Vases and what?" one of them asked Alain.

"Jars," Alain replied with artful poise. "From a master craftsman. In Ait Mehammaed. An ugly place. It belongs to the brother of Christian's wife, a Berber who lives in Marrakech. I do not mean that the town belongs to him, just the goods he makes. He is said to be a *marabout* who puts spells on all his work."

"We would like to see this work."

Alain nonchalantly peeled a near corner of canvas to reveal two crates of pottery lined and stuffed with dirty sheepskin packing.

"We sell some of these to traders in Marrakech, and in Casablanca to French and Moroccan merchants. And take some to Marseille for sale there. Many Moroccan and Algerian immigrants, you know."

La Tour felt a whip of premonition the moment the first spahis *came into view. Three cars edged past him on the decline toward the valley. But a lead horseman slowed and halted. He stared at the ground to an unknown item of interest, then dismounted and nudged a rock with his boot . . .*

La Tour was mortified. He could not see the object, but sensed it was . . . Hani and Brka edged him back toward a stretch of ground that they believed was not in the line of sight of the spahis.

The Lieutenant strolled to the rear of the truck, Christian at his side.

"It is most unusual and unwise and maybe illegal for a lone truck to be crawling through this area without escort," he said brusquely. "Not if you want to see France again."

"We are known among the locals," Christian replied.

"*Shleuh* bandits don't give a damn. You could be robbed, shot and left for dead."

Alain would certainly agree with that.

"We are not carrying contraband," Christian asserted. "No hashish or guns or wanted Berber bastards. We are businessmen. I am sort of an enterprising anthropologist. There. Please look at my papers."

The Lieutenant glanced cursorily at the documents. "How nice. But these are much less effective than a good weapon. Are you armed?"

"Yes. I have a rifle."

"Let me see the cargo."

"Very well, sir," said Christian with world-weary charm.

He and Alain pulled the tarpaulin. Alain opened a crate and removed a specimen. The smooth clay was painted in simple figures. All eyes fell on the open, empty crate.

"You haven't much freight here," said the Lieutenant. "He must be a lazy potter."

"Oh, no, sir. My brother-in-law is always too busy fighting with his wife. That is one reason why I left my first wife home, in Le Havre, drinking cassis . . ."

The soldiers laughed. The Lieutenant grinned but remained noncommittal, until the approach of the three-vehicle convoy and its mounted escort resounded off the pis *walls.*

"Very well," the Lieutenant consented. "Proceed. But you will not get anywhere near Marrakech. Tanant by dark, no more. Tell any units ahead that Lieutenant Lamotte said to give you passage. We will talk later in Tanant."

"Yes, Lieutenant," Christian replied in a cooperative tone. "By then I think anyway it may rain, and the mud on this road will do my tires no good."

He swung into the cab and shifted into gear. Alain prayed that he not hurtle away. Wisely, Christian tarried past the troops, but accelerated uphill to a humpback crest where the rise behind Ait Taguella remained in full view. Alain rapped the top of the cab, hailing for a stop so that he might discreetly locate La Tour with binoculars.

Hani and Brka were not readily visible, but neither could they see the road. Mounting up would surely draw attention. Hani crawled a few meters to the top of the rise for a peek . . . and immediately scrambled back down, in a panic. At this signal Brka leapt onto his horse and with no words convinced La Tour to do the same. The three men pulling an extra horse rode headlong up the hill behind them. Pursued by ten spahis.

La Tour was only a modest horseman. Three years ago the cartographer had likened "horses" to "adventure" and "military"—all terms now useless. He was clinging to the back of a powerful beast in full stride across a ridge of scrub trees and stone debris below the grand Atlas looming to the south. In front, two loyal men were risking their lives to lead him on. Behind were the gaggle of horsemen. La Tour wondered what Hani and Brka would do should they be run down. On that right now he would give even odds.

Christian and Alain both peered back to the distant crest. When the spahis *began their pursuit of the quarry, Christian ground the truck gears to drive on. He was out of sight by the time the troops in Ait Taguella could have realized something was amiss.*

The proxy landing field was ten kilometers ahead, south of the track and hidden by trees. To gain time over the oncoming vehicles, Christian careened around curves, cutting off-road at the landmark kasbah, *through a large* agudal, *passing stone sheep pens and the agitated animals within them. Wide-eyed shepherd girls watched the roaring* adjnun *veer around a water hole, thrash up a* tagmunt, *and disappear through a far barrier of junipers.*

La Tour glimpsed the valley from the ridge, and the distant village vanished as the animated figurines of three men and four horses accelerated up a sloping ravine against a vast canvas of mountains and sky, pursued by a line of other men who seemed somewhat less inclined to the full exertion of themselves or their animals. Still, they were dogged.

"Can't we circle around to the airplane?" La Tour plaintively asked.

"Where? We do not know!" Hani replied. "Live first! Fly later!"

La Tour was wedged between Hani ahead, leading the spare horse, and Brka behind. They guarded and guided, pull-push, plunging headlong into the wilderness. He wondered if or how they knew where to go . . . He felt himself connect to the profound strength of the horse, becoming one beast. They pounded downward, into trees. Several hundred meters on flowed a wide, swift stream. The stretch directly before them was the best ford, and without pause they spurred into the water. The iron-hard but supple horses maintained great momentum despite the demands upon them. As loyal as their masters.

La Tour was stunned by the cold and fast meter-deep water. The animals drove through it in brawny bounds, churning up high, chilling douses. He dared not look behind him lest he be unnerved by sight of the pursuing spahis. *He instead concentrated on each consecutive second, determined to match the efforts of his cohorts, and keep his wits.*

They emerged on to the far bank and faced a broad, flat stretch of scrub land. One decent rifleman could bring them down before they crossed half of it . . .

So realizing, La Tour saw Brka and Hani trade glances. In some unspoken way, through the yield of fighting years and the power of brotherhood, Brka consented to the measure of devotion. He slowed his horse and slipped the Lebel off his shoulder.

"Brka!" La Tour bellowed at the loss of contact. "No!"

In fluid motion, like a raptor or an acrobat, Brka vaulted from the saddle and raised his rifle at the Moroccans just then entering the stream. He fired twice at the nearest man, two hundred meters distant, striking with a more carefully aimed second bullet. In the pause, he slapped his own horse away, lest it be shot in return fire leaving him stranded.

La Tour glanced behind to see Brka taking the meager cover of a niche in the earth. Nine cavalrymen raggedly responded and the bullets drew a pattern around him.

Hani, too, peered to Brka, and in response to what he saw dropped the reins of the spare horse and urged that La Tour keep a slower but still brisk pace.

"We go on two hours, then rest until nightfall. Village tomorrow. Hard ride."

"We will make it?" La Tour uneasily asked.

The rifleman carpenter smiled, like he had in the tizi. *Not to worry.*

"Why did the two of you come back?"

"When you jumped from the truck, something fell from your bag. The Arab spahis *discovered it and is why they chase us."*

La Tour rummaged in his takrabte; *while it could have been lost on this wild ride, the handcrafted top was indeed missing.*

"We are bound to each other," Hani said soberly, then grinned. "You may be a Frenchman. Called La Tour. But you are almost Sidi Jilani. And Ait Atta at heart."

The truck rumbled to a halt. Christian nervously noted that the blue De Havilland was not as inconspicuous near the trees beyond the field as twelve hours ago in the murk of dawn. Yet it apparently remained undiscovered. But Balafré was absent; he did not greet the shuttle as it arrived. In fact, no one, French or Berber, was to be seen here.

"Balafré!" shouted Christian.

Alain dashed off among the trees in an attempt to locate him. Precious minutes passed. What energy he and Christian did not consume in anger they burned in anxiety.

"Balafré!" shouted Alain.

Christian alternately fumed and fretted. It was his plane, but only Balafré could fly it. Its loss would be a catastrophe in these days of less opportunity and more competition.

"Christian!" rang a familiar gruff voice. "Christian!"

Christian sprang from the cab. There was Balafré, clutching a spyglass and loping like an old dog down the field toward him.

"Not one hour ago a shleuh *go by with sheep," he gasped, "see plane and ran away like I was a* djen*! Said this was his field and he would go for French!" Balafré spoke in a peculiar cadence, dropping words and compressing the statements he spewed into chipper exclamations. "So I watch for them!"*

He peered quizzically from Alain to Christian. "I thought you say two men?"

Christian climbed on to the truck cab roof and scanned the terrain with binoculars.

"Change in plans," he said. "This is Alain! Alain, meet Luca Lamartine. Alias Balafré! Winner of a Croix de Guerre. Wind up the girl! You two have another stop to make!"

"I think we not go to Marrakech now!" Balafré replied.

"Not today. You go opposite way. Alain will guide you. I drive away fast."

"Then this is more money, Mr. Christian! We settle now!"

"Double what I've paid! But you go now! We settle in Marrakech!"

"Mr. Christian, big trouble here! I have bad feeling!"

"Go now, Balafré! You've known me for two years. I won't be squeezed!"

"What if the French get me? Who pays for my family?"

Alain interceded. His calm demeanor eased Balafré's jitters. "I will see that no harm comes to you. And that Christian pays you more. We are all friends. But we must fly away now. You can be a big hero."

"A hero? I can be a hero. So long as the money is not zero . . ." He paused to think. "Okay, I will start plane. But you watch out for that sheep man . . ."

Balafré dashed to the DH80 and climbed through the pilot's door. In a few moments the two-hundred horsepower engine coughed into a resonant squall. Christian and Alain were concerned; the din would carry some distance. Alain gave a thumbs-up and a smile.

"We'll meet soon and share many cognacs!" Alain said. "I've become a teetotaler, but there are exceptions and this will be one of them! Bon voyage, brave friend!"

Alain was Christian's polar opposite and alter ego, both of them skeptical, each struggling to understand what may be unknowable. Concluding this strange scene in a hostile outland, Alain took to a plane beside a complete stranger simply on the strength of a faithful promise to another. Christian was certain that at any moment a French or Marocaine patrol would appear. But he would not leave before seeing them airborne.

The plane lumbered ahead, accelerating in a crescendo of pistons and propeller, reaching minimum lift-off speed a quarter of a kilometer down the hard, dimpled field. Balafré pulled back the wheel and the plane ascended steeply like Apollo's chariot.

"Balafré, will you need a field this long to land in?"

Alain was concerned. He did not know how much of the area below the plateau could be prepared. And the wreckage of the Brequet might be in the very middle of the field and impossible to maneuver around.

Hani and La Tour faintly heard the engine. Gazing eastward, they saw the tiny insect of an airplane bank across their view. The two men exulted. Everyone was going home. Again. All that remained for the horse-bound fellows was to cross sixty kilometers of rugged landscape, on mounts already weary.

Christian immediately reversed his route. The plane roaring from this field would likely draw suspicion, but he was also reluctant to go, as that convoy could now be just above or below this point in the road. On reaching that strip of dirt and gravel, however, he was pleasantly surprised to see nary a soul. He turned left. It was a long way, almost two hundred kilometers, to Marrakech. He would drive hell-bent through until black night, then ride with headlamps on low beam before stopping beyond Tamlalet. With luck, Christian would outpace French suspicions moving down the line, and he could return to the city as righteous and reputable a character as when he left.

Alain was amazed that he could navigate the plane by following the contours of the terrain he had covered by horse and foot. Using the hazy Azourki massif as a guide he instructed Balafré to maintain a heading directly away from the low sun.

"We will land in forty minutes."

"Land where? You take me right into the mountains."

They sat in tense silence for long moments. Azourki loomed closer.

"Swing gently right. And lower, Balafré. Go lower."

"I clip flowers for you, boss, you get me to the right place." He grew alarmed. "No one shoot at me flying, eh? Shleuh love to kill planes like that. I had enough in the war."

"No, Balafré. Nothing bad. The worst will be a tight place to land."

"Tight?"

"Small." Alain gestured with his hands. Balafré was not happy.

"Must do?"

"Only thing to do."

"Oh. Then no problem. Insh'Allah, they say, and I believe them."

The plane reached the last juniper forest and high scrubland, and passed over the arid heights, a zone of demarcation from frequent green to mostly brown.

"Ahead, Balafré, see there? Follow that prominent notch. It is a long ravine."

The plane skimmed about one hundred meters above tableland. To the right loomed Azourki, to the left the wilderness around Zaouia Ahansal and the Falaise du Brack beyond. In twenty kilometers, five to six minutes of flight time, the plateau and the village would be in sight below them or ahead. What they had flown in thirty minutes would take La Tour and his escorts nearly a full day to cross.

Alain removed a writing pad, a pencil, a white shirt and a gun from his satchel. He scratched on the paper several French and Arabic words and a diagram, wrapped the paper around the gun and tied the shirt tightly around the paper. This would be his primitive low altitude message delivery system. Akka and the amrabt *would know what to do.*

The plane ran low and slow over the village, north to south. "Circle back, Balafré." As the De Havilland neared the rearward section of the village, Alain opened the passenger door and prepared to drop the communiqué where it could be readily retrieved.

La Tour abandoned most hope of ever seeing Brka again. He stayed in the saddle; Hani walked to rest his horse lest the plodding animal pass into complete exhaustion. Daylight was waning, but they must find water before bedding down until the full moon after midnight. But the sky was not clear, and rain would be a threat.

The white-bound message arced from the plane. Faces turned upward in fear. The engine thunder rattled the mud walls and sent sheep in terror and again the villagers thought the sound to be a harbinger of calamity.

"I want to see field better! Rocks in field?"

"Some."

"Not good!"

The hard, white object thumped down near Akka's igherm. Five, fifteen, thirty people gathered while Akka opened the fabric and poked the lower layer. The crinkle of paper imparted a clue. He unfolded the message and tried to decipher the scribble beside a crude diagram of the plateau and the stone field marked with an X.

Plane sleeps here. Take rocks. Need torches and fires to light it. Do now. Alain

Akka issued a frenzy of instructions, and the villagers scattered, half to the meadow to begin clearing large rocks, others to prepare the flames.

The plane circled high overhead in fading light. The sun disappeared. Soon the options for glide path approach would go from difficult to almost suicidal.

"Light not good for eyes! Not good for eyes!" Balafré repeated like a mad mantra. At the same time, he seemed subtly thrilled by the challenge. He gleamed.

A thin line of torches moved to the lower part of the plateau and the terraced fields. A fire was well-stoked and from this more torches were ignited. Their proliferation created a lovely spectacle, a choreography of candles. A series of larger fires soon flickered around the perimeter, a shape and scale by which Balafré could gauge his approach.

Five more minutes transpired. More than ten since their first pass overhead. The field was almost ready. The enclosing torches were not thick and uniform, but the light from them would suffice. In any event, a safe landing was entirely up to Balafré's skill.

"Balafré, we eat well when you set us down."

"Yes, monsieur *boss. A side of sheep would be very good."*

Balafré banked the plane and squinted out the window. Not good. He eased the wheel forward. The nose, engine and airframe canted down, down, perilously steep and parallel to the angled slopes on the western edge. Then he cut the engine and struggled with the wheel and foot pedals. The beast glided forward, leveled out and Alain heard a hard whoosh of soft air pass over the rattling wings and saw the line of glowing torch flames dimly illuminating white tijjloubah *and upturned faces.*

The wheels bumped the earth, skimmed it, and then punched a small, unyielding mound that slammed the undercarriage and fuselage. A partial tilt to the port side sent the creaking machine careening to the left. The torches there hastily scattered, but as the unpowered propeller stopped spinning the beast decelerated. Growing silence and faces in focus signaled the flagging momentum of the plane. Still, it carried to the far end of the field, nearly out of room, finally to stop ten meters from where the ground rose toward of the first imi.

"Oh, that was good!" Balafré exclaimed happily.

Muffled cheers went up from the crowd. They did not know the reason for their display, nor for whom, but it was quite a show at this hour of magical light.

Alain pushed open his door, hopped onto the meadow and knelt to pray. Survival was an art in itself. With sober concern Balafré emerged to walk a length of the makeshift runway down which he would have to fly on the morrow. He was not pleased.

The two men, one a new guest, were welcomed. The amghar *and* amrabt *related their fascination with Balafré, whose complexion resembled their own. The pilot was the bastard son of a Riffian mother and a deceased Corsican railman working for Spain.*

"Your highness," Balafré began, spreading his arms like a bird, "I ask that many more stones be removed from the field for safe flight." Addi translated. But the hosts were puzzled by the request and the concept that the plane required space to attain lift. Balafré simply asked that crews remove from mid-field any protruding stone much larger than an orb of "horse manure." *Laghbar*, he said, and mimed, and everyone laughed heartily.

Akka assigned a nighttime crew.

"Alain, what about La Tour?"

Aumont's answer was but half spoken when the amghar *issued orders. Three groups of four men would set out for the soldier and his guides, and were not to return without them.*

La Tour and Hani, by now linked in the psyche, snapped awake at the same instant to the clack and patter of stones. Near enough to fracture the silence. Muffled footfalls resounded among the barren rocks, over which sound carried twice the distance.

A horse emerged in the dim light of a setting full moon screened by clouds.

Hani ran forward before the image was clear to La Tour. Brka slumped in the saddle of his exhausted, tottering Sidi.

La Tour and Hani gently pulled their half-conscious comrade from the saddle. A wound in his right thigh was heavily encrusted but still moist. They carried Brka to their hidden furrow. But, still far from home, the consequences might well be worse. Blood loss was considerable. La Tour inspected him for other wounds and found none. Hani tilted the goatskin for Brka, and only after several seconds did he respond to the cool liquid. His dry lips parted and he gulped hungrily. Finishing, he sighed, now conscious and twice as alert.

"They follow me. French, too," Brka said, Hani translated. "Eight or ten. Not far. I took a hard route to lose them. They very stubborn. Still coming."

La Tour knew what must be done. "Hani, take the freshest horse. Ride ahead. Bring help."

"No, I stay, you go."

"It's my turn now," La Tour insisted. "Do as I ask."

"No to both of you," Brka firmly interjected. "We all go. Now."

With a clumsy but remarkably spirited effort, he jerked himself to sitting and feebly to standing. Brka pointed to the tethered horses of Hani and La Tour, to indicate that, like him, they had no choice but to ride again.

"It's not far. Three hours." Hani made it sound so simple. "We there by dawn."

La Tour could scarcely believe this vicious roundabout. His energy was minimally restored through their several hours of rest. He was famished, but the supply mule was by now someone's trophy.

"They not chase much more," Hani continued. "They come too far in, we chase back. They die. They know that and turn around. Come now. Hurry."

The three men—Hani walking lead, Brka limply riding, La Tour last and limping—crept uphill in deepening blackness as the moon disappeared behind the western ridges.

One hour later La Tour could not walk another step. He would either mount a horse or fall down. But his animal, having traveled so far in a full day, was capable of bearing him. Their faithfulness was extraordinary. Brka's horse staggered uphill, but it was within minutes of refusal.

La Tour imagined this climax to his life to be something like a fatal birth struggle. His Légion life was conceived in years of happiness, endured to term in months of frustration, born into these few weeks of pain, and now about to end abruptly in the next minutes of agony. He sat down, or rather collapsed. His physical relief exceeded his humiliation for this surrender. Death would almost be pleasant. Hani understood. The horses sighed wearily. Brka eased from the saddle. All three looked behind them, downslope to the pursuers they expected to hear but would not see until it was too late. Silence.

"So near and yet so far," La Tour muttered.

"Akka will send men for us."

"If he even knows where we are."

"He knows. I can feel it. Ahêddây is strong."

They heard scuffling hooves below. Not two hundred meters off. Five minutes.

"Come," Brka said. He, badly damaged, was the most determined.

Praise God, in a few steps they reached a welcome descent through scrub grass.

Ahead were heard approaching horses. Surely the end, La Tour thought. Hani hobbled on, then shortly bird-whistled. He was acknowledged by four staccato taps. On his very last energy La Tour lunged to a quartet of mounted Ait Atta men. Friends. Joy.

Hani spoke to them softly. The rescuers exhorted them onward, then dismounted and like specters dashed to the takummiyt *ambush of the pursuers. While Brka and his companions rode fresh horses over the last kilometers to village safety, Frenchmen and their Moroccan retinue were dying quietly and gruesomely in the dark.*

Dawn broke in moody hues identical to the morning of battle. Emerging from the ravine, La Tour saw the blessed plane. To his eyes at this moment it was the most beautiful sight in creation. At last, his deliverance, neither encumbered nor denied.

They rode the kilometer to the rebuilt wall and new door of Akka's abode, which just yesterday had been painted in red. The amghar *met his two brave men and La Tour.*

"Aumont and the flying man are at the school," he said to Hani, who translated for La Tour.

"Better to go this morning, this hour, now, when they are still unaware I have escaped," he declared. "And send planes. We fly soon, please. Hani, my brother, would you please bring Alain and the pilot so that we may at last depart?"

Gazing about him, La Tour felt compelled by memory, by déjà vu—it was nearly the same morning hour, the light was identical, and he again wore a white tajjelabith—*to revisit the site of his near-death fall to earth. Though exhausted, he strolled past the barley field to the rocky knoll upon which he in his billowing garment had crashed.*

Kenza knelt over the diverted, unaware of him. He approached silently, near where she first offered him water, observing as she washed her hands and splashed her face in a delicate way. Diamond-bright water drops glistened on her skin. She adeptly lifted a large container into her arms, then turned back at the juncture of path and field. Their eyes met.

La Tour offered, by hand gestures and words, to help her with the burden.

"La!" she said, girlishly and almost blushing. "Vous êtes fatiguè."

"Not so much that it was not truly worthwhile to come all the way back and see you once more," he burbled in French, she hardly comprehending.

Kenza said nothing, but the words delighted her.

Now it was La Tour's turn to smile and remain silent.

Kenza slipped down the path. La Tour followed. Near the door of her igherm *Brka lay on the mat of reeds and straw. His pallor and position, and the nature of the wound, reminded La Tour entirely of himself a mere eight days ago. Next to him sat Hada, and Addi Yacoub. Brka would survive.*

La Tour joined the amrabt, *the chieftain's daughter and her mother Hada in vigil. Addi looked at him with luminous eyes charged by that ethereal power.*

In a few moments La Tour said to Kenza, in French, knowing that the amrabt *would translate: "Brka is very brave. I know that he will love you as much as you want him to. I think your father wisely suggests your marriage. I look forward to the celebration of it. You will, please, when I am gone, relate what I have said to your father."*

Kenza gleamed. How like an angel. He rose, touched his heart, held out his hand with fingers spread, then bowed humbly in his European way.

"You will return very soon," said Addi, seeing nothing but gazing deep within. "Before the sheep are sheared. When we erect tents for ceremonies. After you reach your far valley. I have the dream."

La Tour had all the faith in the amrabt. *But he could summon no response as the aging but sprightly man returned to his mystical medicine, tapping his stick in the peculiar rhythm that con*jured visions and connection to the power of his saints.

La Tour slipped out into soft morning light. He shuffled down to the plateau, past the cemetery with its new graves, toward the terraced fields. Amnay and Lahcen met him, with a light gray bareback horse, and urged him to mount. From his elevated perch, La Tour gazed around, again with new eyes and growing perspective and transformed status, at this extraordinary place he called home. He slipped from his revelry on realizing that most villagers were again gathering for his departure, this time at the foot of the battle plateau. Many there rejoiced in Allah's will that he would travel to his land of birth in the same manner that he had arrived in theirs.

La Tour and Aumont met near the plane.

"We should finally leave Maroc," Jean-Michel said wryly to his friend. "This circuit of returns and reunions has grown somewhat tiresome."

Alain opened the passenger door for his companion. At the same moment, Balafré stumbled from the fuselage, to meet him face to face, wearing the wild, ashen visage of a man in sudden thrall to an apparition. La Tour was reunited with his Vallèe-bound nemesis, the pilot with the stained overalls, scarred face, and pistol in his waistband. Eyes locked, in disbelief. At the unfathomable, tantalizing, tortuous joke of fate or random choice or God.

"You!"

"You!?"

Silence. The silence of the stunned and uncomprehending.

"Where are we going?" La Tour asked finally.

"To Fes. I have just enough fuel," Balafré said, retreating back into the plane. "I deliver you safe and sound."

"I should hope so, this time around."

The two Frenchmen followed him into the cramped four-passenger cabin. La Tour observed Balafré pump the engine primer and depress the starter button. The blue beast rumbled to life, and the villagers beyond the glass stepped hastily from the sound and the fury of the metal demon. The plane wheeled nose-away from the slope as if shrugging off a slumber, seeming to spit anger at the far rise from which the Légion had crossed. Balafré aligned the revving snout with the narrow, newly graded lane across the expanse.

Like important visitors leaving the Ministry, Alain and Jean-Michel waved good-bye to the line of enthusiastic supporters out the rightward window.

Kenza, Akka, Hada and Hejjou observed the scene from atop the palisade. The machine taxied across the field. Halfway down it futilely reached for the air, returned to earth, but at once onward gained sharp lift, altitude and magical harmony with the sky. Heading west, the Fes-bound bird banked high and returned to sweep low over the field and plateau where several hundred villagers bid Godspeed.

RETOUR

T he sun above the far Chaine de Belledonne, to the southeast across the Drac and Isère, was swept away for long spells by dense, billowing clouds. The raw air threatened rain, but erratic spears of sunlight escaped from the gray vault to chase the gloom with a promise of renewal.

En route to Tanger the day before yesterday, Balafré's plane had bucked violent crosswinds over the Rif; for several minutes La Tour again envisioned his demise. He laughed at the gods for yet another display of trickery. Balafré cursed, Aumont prayed. The turbulence abated shortly, and they quipped to landing at an airfield near the city about who was most responsible for their safety, about whose righteous convictions or good deeds or aerial skills had the greatest influence upon the Almighty.

The two-day voyage by cargo steamer, under the auspices of a grand Algerian steward retained by Christian, had been uneventful except for the heavy seas glimpsed from the porthole of their stifling berth. La Tour thought he was a mere shadow of Ulysses; returning home after great and bizarre travails, not to boldly reclaim hearth and spouse, but simply completing his escape. He was hopeful but uncertain that on arrival in Marseilles his forged papers, civilian clothes and full beard would dissuade prying official eyes. Any concern was moot; with hardly a word or a pause, Amin the mischievous steward escorted them from ship to dock to a waiting taxi. Christian chose his intrigues well. At the train station, Jean-Michel asked a dozy operator to connect him to François in Sainte-Foy, but after a minute of waiting he hung up at the first ring in a flash of caution bordering on paranoia. What would he say? Might anyone be eavesdropping? Even had François been at home, Jean-Michel felt reluctant to speak for fear of causing great shock. It would be a better gift to appear in person.

He and Aumont made a stealthy, deliberately last-minute boarding of the overnight Marseilles-to-Paris train. They ducked into their compartment and locked the door.

"The front page of this newspaper, Alain, announces that construction has begun on a long series of 'impenetrable' border fortifications in Alsace. The Foreign Ministry and the Senate apparently do not have high confidence in the future relationship of France and Germany. And an economic crisis in America may be coming to our shores. The article mentions the harbinger of social and Socialist unrest . . . Oh, hell; I have just arrived and don't want to read any pessimism."

He tossed the edition aside. Disregarding the stress of a furtive return and the worry of what would greet him in family home or garden, he floated into fitful slumber.

The train was scheduled to make a post-midnight stop in Lyon. There he parted, fraught but free, with Alain, who was ultimately bound for his hamlet near Metz.

"We will meet again, good friend, and very soon," said Jean-Michel, firmly clasping Alain's hand.

"No matter what," Alain beamed sincerely.

"Even should all-seeing Rochet command us to join another Atlas patrol."

"Then we will flee to Devil's Island!" Alain retorted. "At least we can choose the time and place of our misery!" They chortled heartily.

After walking for more than an hour with his simple luggage through deserted streets, Jean-Michel arrived to the home of his brother François, which was just beyond the western bank of the Saône. Shivering more with apprehension than fatigue in the pre-dawn darkness, he pulled the chord to the house bell.

He received no greeting and waited at the unoccupied stone house, not daring to beseech a neighbor at that hour. If François was not here, then almost certainly he would be in Sainte-Foy. Jean-Michel thought through his priorities and few options. He cautiously walked north, expecting to reach Rue Pizay in the 1ˢᵗ Arrondisement. He would discreetly inquire at the boulangerie and cafés near the family business. But halfway there, he realized that this may be futile and even foolish.

At the river bridge on Quai Fulchiron, he saw a taxi discharge a fare. After the final offer of his last francs, he hired the driver for another two-hour journey. After a detour to fill the tank with essence, the sedan carried him down the green lane, finally arriving at Mother's door.

In a dream-like state, he conjured familiar images. Bounding horses and rising earth, falling bodies and Kenza, Légionnaires and lepers and Ait Atta, all slashed through his psyche. Bloody action was offset by blessed relief, filtered through bittersweet nostalgia, all distorted by his senses, as if he was stirring from ten years of sleep.

Jean-Michel heard François within, mumbling a morning annoyance. He willed himself from the surreal waking dream, pushed open the oaken portal and stepped across the threshold into the familiar but faded aromas of polished wood and dried flowers.

Stunned, speechless and disbelieving, François beheld his bearded sibling raptly.

"I received your letter, François, but was very unable to reply," said Jean-Michel.

For nearly half a minute neither moved, but stared wearily, and François warily. From his vantage, this return, with little baggage and no prior announcement, was more than peculiar. Then they exchanged hearty embraces and enormous sighs of bittersweet joy that spanned a void of lost, unknowing weeks.

"Where is Grandfather?" Jean-Michel asked as he stepped from the vestibule, almost dreading the answer.

"Still sleeping. He does that a lot. But he is well, considering."

And his dreaded next question, pushing the weight of the world: "And Mother?"

Tight silence. François's averted eyes. La Tour's ship of hope sank like stone in the sea of regret.

"Three weeks ago," François whispered. The sound of silence returned.

"How on earth did you get here?" he asked Jean-Michel.

"Took my every last franc. Money well spent. My circle is complete, however sadly. I will tell you of it, at length . . ."

The nuthatches and other songbirds near the feeder stopped dining and chirping, and some flew away, when Jean-Michel stepped through the gate in the Spanish broom which divided the garden and the family cemetery. The crumbling outer stone wall and inner trellis laden with untended vines sequestered the property from Bois du Vouillants which rose gradually beyond the grass across a dirt-and-gravel path. He clutched a bouquet of gladioulus, iris and primrose picked along the forest lane, and set them upon the low oblong brown mound that in the last weeks had slowly settled of its weight or been compressed by rain. All was silent in the breeze but for the whispering of new leaves and the occasional flutter of the winged creatures perhaps curious about these beings below.

The outer branches of the lone châtaignier—the sweet chestnut—hung over the small burial yard. In the autumns of his youth Jean-Michel would pick the fallen hard fruit from and around the three graves to roast them on a brazier or in a kitchen pot. Now the tree, likely two centuries old—perhaps sprouted in the last years of Louis the Sun King—only reminded him of all that was no longer in his life.

Helene Celestine La Tour, nee Arnoux, was dead at the age of 58. Pleurisy and pneumonia acted together, after a mild stroke. She battled for a month, into a sullen late April much like this morning—the days of her son's trek from the garrison in pursuit of Akka Ahêddây and the Ait Atta—and finally succumbed.

The garden was indeed in a state of neglect. Weeds were vying with the budding peonies, and the two pathways were encroached by exuberant grass leaning in from the new cypress spurge and the ancient, dark green yews. It was only mid-May; the half-acre would be overrun by June.

The fourth gravesite still retained haunting proof of a recently interred body. There was no headstone; as yet, the only markers were a white cross and the bell-shaped brass bird feeder atop a six-foot pole to the left that Mother, perhaps in premonition or resignation, had in early March requested François to place there.

François and Émile stood behind Jean-Michel, near the gate. The old man was enthralled, horrified and enraged at his grandson's tale. But proud and pleased, too, at his triumph, however bloody and belated. It was, perhaps, also temporary; Jean-Michel had been disloyal, despite the cruel tangles. Punishable by a fate worse than expulsion. But Émile restrained his tears; there was no sense adding more woe to what could not be undone. He would think of the good in these events, hopefully those to be told when Jean-Michel related his tales of escape.

The story Jean-Michel related during hours at the table was too incredible for their immediate belief. Brother and grandfather gaped and squirmed with his recounting. Over the balance of the day—lubricated by several bottles of exquisite Burgundy—Jean-Michel told them of vicious combat. Of leprosy. Betrayal. Falling from an airplane. Of noble tribes. Their leader. Of false godhood. The battle against his own kind. But still he refrained from describing nubile, vivacious Kenza, daughter of the Ait Atta chieftain.

"A fortnight ago," Grandfather finally interjected, "we inquired for the third time if they knew of your status. "No," they said, "we do not know if he is dead or alive." Those are strange words to hear. And my several private inquiries led nowhere. But I think you will be pursued if they discover your trail. Then what will you do?"

"I have disappeared," La Tour brazenly offered. "With luck, in time the fools will think me dead. But in any event I've decided to shortly return to Maroc and with the help of friends complete a task. Perhaps something wonderful can come from all this."

"That would be foolish!" Émile protested. "You cannot travel there incognito!"

Grandfather, now nearly 79 years of age, had outlived his son, his daughter-in-law, and nearly his grandson. Though still hale, the toll of time was evident. But in impassioned moments such as these he seemed fit to outlast the sun itself.

"I have already done it once, by getting out," La Tour asserted. "Gaining re-entry will be more difficult than moving about in the country. If you know the natives."

"You sound like a daredevil. Stay with us a while. Then hide."

"Only for a week or two. I've done more than enough hiding. It is exile and punishment by another name. I will not announce myself, but I must return to Taboulmant."

"What could be so important as to risk your life again?" François beseeched.

Here was another moment of truth. "Not what," Jean-Michel said with an intriguing tone, then continued after a weighty pause. "Who. She is Kenza. The daughter of Akka n-Ali Ahêddây. Another pause. "I think beauty is her other name."

Grandfather and François exchanged glances laden with silent thunder. With awe. Alarm. Terror that their tiny family was almost certain to lose another.

"Surely," Grandfather appealed, "you do not expect to gain her hand? To overcome centuries of custom—and religion—merely by expressing a sincere desire?"

But Jean-Michel swayed them, despite their questions and the improbability of the very idea. "They are trusting people, and they can be confident I will not break my word."

"What is more, I wish for intervention for the people in Vallèe de l'Enfer. Their lives are appalling. Doctors would surely go if they were told of it and sent there."

Grandfather was mum for several hours as he nursed cognac in his chair at the window overlooking the garden where his son, wife, and daughter-in-law were resting.

"Well, then," he casually broached as dusk fell. He had a familiar gleam in his eye. "I propose an adventure. Let us meet what may be . . . the new family. If François and I can see your new world through our own eyes perhaps we will be wiser for the experience."

"You will actually plan a trip there?" François asked incredulously.

"Yes, quite. You and I will go to Lyon in a few days to withdraw a portion of my remaining funds. I will contact an old friend in Toulon that next month, he should confidentially expect to sail a party of three to Tanger. Together we can make a good plan."

* * * * *

As a precaution to foil any official inquiries, La Tour took his leave the next day, renting a room under an alias in a village a few kilometers from Grenoble.

Two weeks hence, he and Aumont reunited in a bistro there. Alain digested their conversation, and then cabled several veiled greetings to Graves in Marrakech. The last culminated in: Would like return to hamlet for visit. Four in party. Will you arrange? Need rapid transport. The man who flies seeks nuptial permission. Please make clear to host.

The merchant received their fantastic communiqué. That same day Graves enlisted an Imazighen scribe in Souk el Khemis to craft a Tamazight note and a diagram. Then by one of the usual ruses he sent Balafré over Taboulmant for its delivery. The intrepid pilot would return the next day for one of three replies: a display of captured Légion banners near Akka's igherm *would signal agreement to the proposed date; alternatively, the number of horses tethered there would declare another day; and the absence of banners or animals would indicate the chieftain's decline for another form of relationship to La Tour.*

The next day Balafré laughed madly as he glided low over the plateau: a dozen village men were bearing Légion artillery pennons and running about like adjnun.

Christian had fine alibis for all this air activity—he served the right clients—and he had few worries of raising suspicions. He learned that ten days ago the Protectorate, and thus the Légion and the Armée, had agreed to a truce with the Ait Atta that enabled the clans to maintain their lands in exchange for nominal submission to Glaoui rule and the end of all hostilities against any Iroumin. *That and the immediate return of all Légion prisoners. Christian was trying to learn the fates and whereabouts of Colonel Rochet. The Légion being such a proud and insular body, he knew this might take time. Certainly, however, his rogue action had riled his superiors. Perhaps more important was the Légion's position on Jean-Michel La Tour. Declared killed in action? Or Missing? Was he wanted? Or persona non grata?*

The date was so fixed—the third Hamid in Yunyu, or Thursday, June 20—for the arrival of the former, false god and his small cortege. The battlefield below the plateau was further cleared of rocky impediments so that their two winged beasts may come to rest there. That Akka n-Ali or the village would consent was yet to be determined—but La Tour's declaration to again brave danger proved that his passion was true.

$$* * * * *$$

They flew straight from Tanger, where they had docked in the middle of the night after a windy three-day voyage from Marseilles aboard the nondescript sloop of Grandfather's old friend Marco. True to form, Christian recruited a Riffian official who redirected several artful bribes and cleared their entry with imperfectly forged papers. Christian and Issef—who claimed to be an uncle to a confederate of Abd'el Krim—came to the harbor in welcome of the three "renowned Berber archaeologists from Toulon."

It was early afternoon; the high bold sun cast the metal birds in a flux of sharp, solid shadows against deeply wrinkled dun-colored ridges and a great swath of green cedar forest. On this first day of summer, Christian Graves's two De Havillands passed south over the spines of the Middle Atlas, to Kasba Tadla. Jean-Michel and Balafré were new friends in the old yellow open-cockpit ferry. Émile, François and Alain were crammed in the blue craft flown by Graves. The tallest spires, true and ancient giants, seemed to wave in a brisk westerly breeze as if beckoning at the passing planes. Level with them, to the left and toward the rising High Atlas, two eagles soared tranquilly on stretched, fixed wings in a bracing updraft.

In another hour, the familiar profile of Adrar n-Azourki and Ighil M'Gouna rose to the west. Closer to them, and waiting, was the Ait Atta capital. The blazing June sun was slipping from its high perch as Balafré's lead plane descended over Ait Yafelmane territory, the western border of which was marked by the village of Tilmi and the Asif Imedrhas.

The sentinel plateau of Akka n-Ali stretched before them, then its adjacent battlefield valley, and then the new runway in it, presumably cleared of stones and bunch grass. Closer now, they saw people forming a corridor to mark it, perhaps the whole of Taboulmant and more Ait Atta as well. Women in their colorful garb were distinctive even from afar, like bright random tiles or flecks of rainbow. Or flowers. Along the Dades, the Drôme, or the rivers of the Gardens. La Tour took the reception to be a grand welcoming and a prelude to a celebration of peace and liberation the *timizar had not held before his departure, or a visible public statement of Akka's decision about Kenza. Or perhaps both.*

The plane dipped below the ghostly sentinel tizi. *On the promontory above it the stone hut of La Tour's exile and salvation once again belonged to the* amrabt. *From the cockpit he could just now hear the first quavers of a jubilant welcoming choir of female voices, of* taghwrirt, *echoing across terrain where death had made its bloody claims.*

Balafré cut the engine, glided downward and set the wheels onto the coarse earth. The plane decelerated and La Tour saw familiar faces ahead on the left, near the end of the queue. Haj. Hani. Mimoun. Ousaïd. Amnay. And Addi Yacoub, away from the gathering but seeing all. He extended his hand from his heart.

At that, the planes came to smooth halts.

La Tour stood in the rear bucket and scanned the shoal of faces upturned to him. He did not see a defiant or contemptuous or indifferent one among them.

"May taanam aye im doukal!" said the crowd.

"Inghaye oumary noun!" Hello my friends. I missed all of you!

"Wa âalaykum as-salám. Labas al-hámdu li-llá. Tesherreftagh!"

Men and women burst into laughter, cheers, and shouts. La Tour alighted from the wing and tried to reconcile his self-image as a returning visitor with that of a conquering hero.

Brka looked on, in stoic acceptance but wistful at what might have been. There would be nothing to gain in rivalry. His old world could not completely deter this new one, only accommodate itself to co-exist. He would not be a spoiler. Akka n-Ali had been quite clear that his honor, already well-served, would only be enhanced.

Now passing down from the central ravine and through the concourse came a superb gray horse. Upon it was a rider beneath brightly-hued robes, a vermilion headdress and a blue veil. Walking ahead and holding the reins was Akka n-Ali, garbed in a fine, delicately embroidered white tajjelabith. He extended his right hand graciously to his compatriots, and then to Jean-Michel. Hada walked beside him, beaming but shy.

The rider lifted the finery. Almost at once, Kenza's regal nonchalance dissolved in a radiant, blushing smile. The young woman was more like a goddess: eyelids and brows had been wispily limned with kohl, cheeks rouged to a sheen, and three blue ahejjam *on her chin declared her raised status. The headdress was adorned with chains strung with trinkets and amulets, and from her neck hung gold and silver necklaces suspending ornate medallions embedded with green, amber, red and onyx stones. The ensemble seemed to embody every shade to be found in Maroc, and Kenza glittered in the afternoon sun.*

"*Marhbanch gher sagham nech,*" she said. Welcome home.

"*Ighouda,*" was all he could mumble. Beautiful. The crowd tittered like children.

Jean-Michel stepped before Akka n-Ali. They beheld each other—new friends, intimate strangers and kindred spirits exchanging precious gifts. Jean-Michel placed his right hand over his heart then held it out toward Akka, bowed deeply before him, knelt, rose and turned about, smiling brightly for all to see.

The crowd again tittered happily, in near-unison, although many among them had not yet fully accepted the purpose of this pageantry. Their consent would be complete when La Tour had made a pledge aloud, for all to hear.

The prodigal Frenchman, self-decreed Berber son, turned to Kenza. As Akka held the reins, Jean-Michel held out a hand for her, and grasping it she eased gracefully from the saddle. The rustle of brocaded cloth. The cheery jingle of jewelry. Eyes cast downward, but as a trait of elegance rather than as a sign of hesitation, and therefore beautiful to him.

Émile saw, more importantly, he felt the respect and fascination with which Ahêddây beheld Jean-Michel. Kenza as well. And the people.

Ever the envoy, Grandfather approached Akka and bowed, and then genially extended his hand. And François did the same. Gazing at the proud beaming father, at a staunch chieftain who had routed his countrymen's Légion, and at a once-deceived host of a false god, Émile knew that whatever these coming days had in store would surely be vivid.

"Great amghar, *mighty warrior, honorable man and friend to my grandson, I am Émile Duprés, former envoy of French trade to Tangiers, traveler of beautiful Maroc, and your honored guest* . . . . *And François La Tour, my other grandson, and Jean-Michel's fine brother, gracious and at your service."* Mimoun stepped from the crowd to La Tour's side. The young man's facial wound had long healed; his cheek was now embossed by a pinkish scar that for all his days would attest to courage. Mimoun grinned with easy warmth, held his saddle satchel and reached in as he had for the binoculars. To La Tour's amazement he instead pulled out a camera. *Mimoun asked:* "Et comment ça marche?" *How does it work?*

"Magiquement capturer," *said La Tour.*

Winking at them, Émile took the camera—one probably appropriated from a Frenchman—and gestured for the group to converge. He carefully framed Akka, Jean-Michel, Kenza, Hada and the horse against the old yellow plane.

Addi Yacoub and Akka n-Ali led the *aggrawe* to Jean-Michel. Si Baha the *taleb,* elderly Lahcen n-Assu and Ousaïd n-Hmad and several other, newer members of the council formed a loose circle around him in a courtly but almost informal manner. They seemed ready to hail their bonhomie despite the great divide of words, culture and God. The villagers ebbed to silence, like an opera audience as the performance is about to begin. Only the breeze whispered, perhaps conveying caution or approval from the spirits of the dead.

"Beginning this moment," said Akka n-Ali, "there is no hiding from our truth or from yours." Addi Yacoub peered at and it seemed, *into,* La Tour with a vision that would not again fail to see any spark of untruth. "We know you now. We grant an opportunity to know more about us. You will live here. Learning our ways. Then, perhaps, marriage."

Jean-Michel was at another boundary from which there would not be a simple return. He gazed across these many Imazighen witnesses; and they at a free and common man. He peered in turn at François, Grandfather, Alain, Christian, Balafré, and to the far, bright russet mountains. The gathering was poised, like the interval between movements of a symphony, or a shift of stars in their nighttime sea.

Akka Ahêddây and Addi exchanged subdued words with the council. Once again, La Tour heard: *"baraka."* Akka ceremoniously removed from the saddle of the horse a red woolen cord. He turned to daughter Kenza and held out one end of the prized, symbolic tether, and to the former Légionnaire foe and new resident and future family member he offered the other. Their brief ties would be bound for years, and by something much more than war, if La Tour took that woven braid in his hand and its commitment in his heart.

Jean-Michel reached for the cord with the faith that at last he was home.

GLOSSARY

A—Arabic
B—Berber (Tamazight dialect)
F—French

aami (B)—uncle

aasam (B)—belt that wraps a dress called *dfinth*

a'azib (B)—guardian, usually of a child by an adult

achttan (B)—colorful scarves that men and women wear around their heads and faces. See *chech*

adrar (B)—mountain (in Arabic, called a *jebel*)

Affairs Indigène (A.I.) (F)—French soldiers and civilians, engineers and planners of many specialties monitoring Berber tribes and acting as liaisons, mediators, informers, and so on.

agadir (B)—fortified communal granary. See *igherm* and *ksar*

aghrum (B)—bread

aggrawe (B)—tribal council, comprised of elders and notables who govern in civil and military matters

agurram (B)—saint; analogous to a*mrabt* (pl. *igguramen)*

aguryan (B)—one year-old ram

ahaidous (B)—Berber dance

ahejjam (B)—facial tattoos on women. The more, and the more elaborate, the designs, the higher a woman's status. Girls get their first tatoos at the age of 14 or 15, to first announce their marriageability.

ahouff (B)—raid; attack (pl. *ihouffen)*

ait (B)—people (or children) of

Ait Arba'in (B)—"People of the Forty". The traditional name given to a council of elders who guide tribal life. Even when the council numbers much fewer than forty, the term remains. See *aggrawe*

Ait Atta—a confederation of migratory Berber clans and tribes in the
   central Atlas and adjacent lands to the south and east. In the 1930s they
   offered the last effective, organized resistance to French advances.

ait ashra (B)—lineage mates. The direct male family relatives, by custom
   usually numbering ten men, of a murder victim or a murderer

ait l-'ar (B)—the people who want vengeance

Al-hámdu li-lláh (B)—If God orders it.

akkrabe (B)—small leather bag

allemou (B)—collective communal pasture with fixed dates of usage

alloune (B)—skin drum

almouggar (B)—alternative Tamazight term to *moussem*

amazan (B)—Berber messengers sent by French Affairs Indigène officers
   (or other Berbers) to the villages of rebellious tribes to warn or
   negotiate, to recruit agents or gather information

aman (B)—water

amghar (B)—chief pl. *imgharin*

amghar n-iggran (B)—chief of the fields

amghar n-ufilla (B)—top chief

mrabtin (B)—alternative Berber spelling and pronunciation of a saint
   (*marabout)* or spiritual leader

amrabt (B)—(pl. *imerabtin*) (B)—A spiritual leader or holy man. Though
   not perceived to descend from the Prophet, the *amrabt* nevertheless
   possesses *baraka*. Often an ascetic and knowledgeable of the Qu'ran,
   the *amrabt* may represent the mystical side of life. Alternative spelling
   is *mrabti* or *marabout*. Also see *agurram*

amuqqrann (pl. *imuqqarann*) (B)—notable men. Leading members of
   council (*aggrawe*) most responsible for governance. See *ikhatar*

amzttid (B)—paid tribal protector of a traveler

anafalman (B)—peace

anahcham (B)—lay judge, oath administrator

Aroumi (pl. *Iroumin)*—Generally speaking, a European Christian. It is
   derived from the word for citizens of the Roman Empire. From the
   1st to 3rd centuries, Rome traded goods along the Mediterranean coast
   of Morocco and Algeria. Client kings of the Empire ruled the Berber
   kingdom of Mauretania from the city of Volubilis, near present-day

Moulay Idriss and Meknes. Volubilis was one of the most remote outposts in the Empire. Roman troops never penetrated the wild tribal territories to establish a strong presence. Sometimes used interchangeably with Nazarenes, or Nazranis, to identify Christians

aqbil (B)—confederacy, tribal coalition

aqrabe (B)—leather bag

Assif (A, B)—river, stream. Also, *Oued*

askiff (B)—thick soup

aspirant (F)—in the Foreign Legion, a rank equivalent to Second Lieutenant

asserdoun (B)—mule, donkey

azzmoul—(B) branding scars or tattoos meant to identify the member of a sect

bab (A)—large gateway or portal into a city or a section of it

baraka (A, B)—blessing, divine grace, a talent for miracles. Berber and Arab holy men have *baraka*

Bled es Siba (A)—or simply, *siba*; the "land of insolence," the areas outside the control of the Sultan government (and after the 1912 Treaty of Fes, by extension, the French Protectorate). Many tribes and federations resisted both the French Protectorate and the Sultan, who was under French influence.

Bled es Makhzen (A)—or simply *makhzen*; "land of government," those regions under the control of the Sultan (and therefore, in the days of the Protectorate, of the French). As opposed to Bled es Siba

BMC (F)—Bordel militaire de campaigne.

bouynaghan (B)—paid killer; murderer; assassin (pl. *bu inighi)*

burnoos (A)—long hooded woolen robe or cloak worn by Arabs and Berbers (see *tajjelabith, djellabah)*

bu ruh (B)—murderer

caid (A)—the governor or chief of a city, town, tribe or group of tribes in the service of the *Makhzen*

Chaouia—Region between the Atlantic and the Middle Atlas. An area of great unrest early in the Protectorate, and the site of several major battles between the Legion and Armée and large Berber tribes

ched (A)—head and facial scarf. See *achttan*

cheikh (B); *sheik* (A)—chief of the tribe; *amghar*

choukara (B)—leather bag or satchel

Chtouber (B)—October

ddiya (pl. *diyat*) (B, A)—bloodwealth: the customary payment in some acceptable form by an offending Berber to the clan of another for a murder

dfinth (B)—long dress, usually colorful

diffa (B)—great feast

Djen (pl. adjnun) (B)—demon, ghost or spirit, usually evil

djich (B)—looting raid or tactical foray

djellabah (A)—long, hooded woolen cloak; also *jelaba; burnoos; tajjelabith* (B)

Doukalla—Region northwest of Marrakech, bounded by Oued Tensiff and Oum er Rbia and the coastal city of Safi

elmoussouer (B)—photographer

essrouel (B)—linen trousers or pants

fondouk (A); *fondakk* (B)—part of a *zaouia* or a separate hostel where visitors and traders sleep and their animals are stabled

igembri (B)—stringed musical instrument, similar to a lute

imi (B)—mouth of a ravine

gharess (B)—cutting the throat of a sheep in sacrifice

Glaoua/Glaoui—Name of the tribe, and by extension their leaders, based in Telouet in the Atlas Mountains east of Marrakech. In the late 19th century they rose to extensive power throughout much of central and southern Maroc, which they maintained through the end of the Protectorate

Goumier/Goum (A)—colorful native Moroccan or Algerian Arab and Berber troops, usually horsemen, recruited by the French to fight Berber and Arab insurgents

goursh (B)—coin of small denomination

habelmlouk (B)—cherries

hammada (A)—great stony-desert plateau along the border with Algeria; the western edge of the Sahara

haram (A, B)—forbidden (by God)

Ibekhanne (A)—Descendants of black slaves taken north along ancient trade routes from Niger and Mali. They have no tribal allegiances, and attach themselves as share-croppers in villages, often in the south.

Ibrir (B)—April

id bu-inighan (B)—professional killers (sing. *biynaghan)*

igherm (pl. *igherman*) (B)—fortified family homes, village, or granary. See *agadir* and *ksar*

ighazwa (B)—raid

Ihansalen (B)—High Atlas caretakers of Zaouia Ahansal, founded by a patron saint of the Ait Atta

ihêsan (B)—good works

ikhatar (pl. *ikhataren*)—notables. Leading members of council (*jmaâa* or *aggrawe*) most responsible for governance. See *amuqqrann*

IkhTinna Rebbi (B)—God willing; if God orders (wills) it. See *Insh'Allah*

Imazighen (B)—A general term with which the Berbers describe themselves. Translated as "free people"

imi (B)—ravine

imishki (B)—tribeless individual; persona non grata

imzwagen (B)—descendants of someone who has been murdered

Insh'Allah (A)—God willing; if God orders (wills) it

iqettaân (sing. aqattaân) (B)—highwaymen, bandits

Khalifa (B)—A deputy to a tribal governor in Arabic lands, in this case, Bled es Makhzen

koubba (A)—the shrine of a saint, sometimes part of a *zawiya* (religious school) the saint had founded

koummia (A)—Berber curved dagger. See *takummiyt*

ksar (pl. *ksour)* (A)—fortified village or tribal stronghold. See *igherm* and *agadir*

l'ada (B)—donations of food, money, and animals made to a saint, or *mrabtin*

laafit (B)—fire

Lalimane (B)—Germany

Lebel—standard issue French rifle used by the Legion and Armée; a line of models was produced from the 19th into the 20th centuries

leff (B)—Alliances between tribes or districts, usually to fight wars

leguembri (B)—stringed musical instrument, similar to a lute

lhêrka (B)—tribal war party. The Sultan or a *sheik* directs a raid or an attack upon upstart tribes to forcibly collect taxes or to impose authority

lhûrm (A, B)—the sacrosanct zone around the tomb of a saint affording protection to all who enter it

llouze (B)—almonds

louise (B)—jewelry, derived in name from gold coins bearing the likeness of French kings

lucham (B)—Tamazight female facial tatoos. See *ahejjam*

Maghreb—Northwest Africa, geographically Morocco, Algeria, Tunisia, Mauritania and Libya.

Makhzen (A)—The Sultanic government of Morocco; the land under his control

mederasa (A)—religious university. The most famous ones were built during the Sultanic dynasties, of the best materials, architecture and craftsmanship that wealth could buy

mehallah (A)—An unruly and rag-tag army, sometimes led or accompanied by the Sultan, that marauds and ravages the countryside to "collect taxes" and loot uncooperative Bled es Siba cities and regions.

Moghreb (A)—evening prayers

mokhazni (A)—a (paramilitary) agent in the service of the Sultan (Makhzen) and the French. *Mokhaznias* often worked with and protected French Intelligence officers whose duty it was to learn about, and to some degree subvert, the tribal customs of Maroc, usually in Bled es Siba

moukhla (A, B) (pl. *mokahle*)—old-fashioned, large caliber Berber flintlock. Also called a *bu shfar*

moussem (B)—regional festival in honor of a local saint, drawing pilgrims as well as traders, merchants and buyers

mushiddad (B)—battle flag

murrette (F)—1-2 meter protective, defensive stone wall Legionnaires would erect around campsites

oudad (B)—mouflons; wild sheep

pisé—packed wet clay, dried in the sun, mixed with straw and/or gravel, to make bricks or building blocks. A widely-used construction method in Morocco

Protectorate—official and general term used for the period of French administration in Morocco, 1912-56

quart (F)—the tin cup of a Legionnaire's mess kit

rezzeth (B)—turban

Rharb/Gharb (A)—fertile coastal plains between Larache and Kenitra

ridha (B)—divine contentment

sadaka (B)—small feast, banquet

sasbu (A, B)—1874 French Gras single shot rifle, the "chassepot"

shitan (A)—Satan

shleuh, chleuh (B)—General designation for Berbers of the Atlas and southern Morocco. Used somewhat pejoratively by the French to describe Berbers as cunning, primitive, untrustworthy. It once specifically meant the people of the South, the *Soussi*

shrif (B)—saint, a descendant from the Prophet Muhammed. In Arabic, *sharif, sherif, shorfa*

siba (A, B)—insolence. See *Bled es Siba.*

siyaha (B)—Roving life undertaken by an ascetic in order to achieve complete detachment

spiro (F)—paving machine used to construct roads. Machine enabled roads across desert and mountains.

tachekart (B)—leather satchel (see *choukara, aqrabe)*

Tafaska (B)—Aid-el-Kebir, the sacrifice of the ram, a major Muslim feast holiday. In Arabic, *fard.*

Tafilalet, Tafilalt (B)—a region of palmeries and oases along Oued Ziz and Oued Rheris in eastern Maroc, where many uprisings and new dynasties have been born

tagalft (B)—sheep rustling

taghwrirt (B)—ululation

tagmunt (B)—mount of earth dividing fields or property

tagununt (B)—sole male child, heir

tahrirte (B)—soup, stew or barley, maize and other ingredients

tajine (A)—Traditional Moroccan stew containing lamb, chicken or beef

tajjelabith (B) *tijjloubah* (pl.)—long, hooded woolen cloak; also *djellabah*; *jelaba; burnoos*

takat (A)—fire

takrabte (B)—large leather satchel

takummiyt—Berber curved dagger (pl. *tikemmiyin)* (see *koummia)*

taleb (B)—a Quranic scholar. In towns and cities, he acts with the *moudden* in affairs of the mosque and Koran. In villages, often the *taleb* alone instructs in religious matters, summons the people to prayer, reads and interprets the Qur'an, and so on.

tamazirt (B)—local land; group of clan settlements or villages

tambour (A)—hand-held drum

tamaghroust (B)—sheep

taoudite (B)—a musical instrument similar to a lute (pl. *tiouadine)*

tarbat (B)—girl; daughter

tarugwa (B)—irrigation ditch

tatsa'it (B)—French Lebel rifle

tazttat (B)—a pact of protection for a temporary traveller in hostile territory. Bought with cash, usually from an *amghar*, and was good for a one-way, one-time journey. Related to term and concept of *amzttid*

thini (B)—dates of the palm tree

tiknariyin (B)—prickly pear

tizi (B)—fortification; defensive position in or overlooking a mountain pass

taleb (A, B)—religious leader educated in Koran, reading and writing. He calls the faithful to prayers.

ushshn (A,B)—jackal

Yunyu (B)—June

zawiya (zaouia) (A)—a religious school or center of a Muslim order, founded by an *amrabt/marabout* and maintained by his descendants and/or adherents. Similar to a monastery. *Zaouiat* is a member of that order, somewhat like a monk or an abbot

ziyara (A)—donation at saint's tomb

zzit (B)—cooking oil

And We have set on the earth mountains standing firm,
lest it should shake with them, and We
have made therein broad highways between mountains
for them to pass through;
that they may receive guidance.

The Qur'an, Surah 21:31